The
Angel Room

I0694608

This book is a work of fiction. References to real people, events, establishments, organizations, or locales are intended only to provide a sense of authenticity, and are used to advance the fictional narrative. All other characters, and all incidents and dialogue, are drawn from the author's imagination and are not to be construed as real.

The Angel Room
Copyright © 2022 Lee Call

Cover Art © 2022 Lee Call

ISBN: 979-8-9861535-2-0 (Paperback)
ISBN: 979-8-9861535-4-4 (Hardback)
Library of Congress Control Number: 2022908429
First printing edition 2022.

J Emrys Press
San Tan Valley, AZ

WWW.JEMRYSPRESS.COM

Lee Call

J Emrys Press
San Tan Valley, AZ

For Jon

ONE

"**E**llie…"

I blink, focusing on the far corner of my bed, where Creep is hunched in the dawn gray. He could be just a paper cutout, he's so flat and still. But I see his head swivel as he turns to look at me, the black globes of his eyes catching the dim light from the window. He unfolds one skinny arm.

"Morning, Ellie." He's gravel-voiced, swiping at one spiky ear with the back of his hand like a dog. "What are you thinking about?"

I've been lying completely still for a while, the way I do, in that strange floating place before sleep comes. Thinking about tomorrow. How everything changes tomorrow. I didn't realize that my thoughts had started to sink until I heard Creep's voice.

Breath in my ear. His arms.

"None of your business," I tell him. I turn my back on him and curl up. I tuck my hands under my cheek and close my eyes. Maybe if I pretend to sleep, he'll leave me alone.

I feel him move. Over my ankles. Padding slowly up the bed on all fours until he's crouched by my elbow. I open my eyes again to see him hanging over me. Flaky skin the color of coal, his skeletal fingers kneading the blanket.

If I look too closely, his eyes look backlit. Like there's a lamp somewhere behind them, shining through smoky glass. I don't look too closely anymore. "I'm sleeping," I tell him.

"No, you're not," he says. He flashes that glistening, fish-boned smile, laced with strings of saliva. "You didn't sleep all night. Tell me what you were thinking about. Daydreams? Plans? Memories?"

So he's not going to leave me alone.

"No," I say.

He snaps his teeth together the way he does when I say something he doesn't like. I sit up away from him, cross-legged, and run my fingers through my hair. He watches me pull it into a high ponytail. I secure it with the elastic I keep on my wrist.

"Aw, please?" he says. "You have the best memories of anyone I know."

I roll my eyes. "I'm the *only* one you know."

"Correction," he says. He pulls a scab from his shoulder and then examines it. "I know everyone. You're the only one I *love.*"

I'm watching him touch the scab to his oily tongue when the bedroom door opens and Mom bustles in with an armful of cardboard boxes. She has her hair tied back too.

"Oh good," she says. "You're up." She drops the boxes and pulls a Sharpie from her pocket. Creep hops down from the bed to sniff around her feet. He sticks his head into one of the boxes. "How did you sleep?" She looks at me.

"Fine," I lie, my head swimming as I watch Creep. It was another night fuzzy with insomnia, but I don't tell her that.

She nods. "Great. Dad's arranged for a truck tomorrow morning, so you need to finish getting your room packed." It's hard to concentrate on what she's saying when Creep starts hacking like a cat about to vomit. I stare at Mom. She looks around and then puts her hands on her hips. "Honestly, Eleanor. You haven't started yet?" She doesn't notice Creep at all. She never does.

I look around too. Odds and ends, books, piles of drawings. Everything clutters together on my shelves, seeming dingier under the Mom-gaze.

"You've known about this move for weeks," she goes on. "You're fifteen years old now. It's time to start acting like it."

Creep's voice comes, echoing from inside a box. "Fifteen. Only three more years 'til the age of consent."

My neck is tight. I pull my legs up and I wrap my arms around my knees.

When I don't answer, she sighs. "I'm sorry, Eleanor," she says. "I just want this to be a new start. For all of us. Let's make a goal, okay? See if you can get everything you want to bring to the new house, that isn't clothes or books, to fit in one box."

I look at her, doubtful. "I don't know about that."

Creep laughs, something about fitting a body into a box.

"It will be easy," she says, "if you don't bring any of this junk." She sweeps a hand around, indicating things on the shelves that I used to pick up as a kid: rocks, twigs, shells, feathers. She ends at the horse wall, my collection of pictures cut from books and magazines. My own private herd of horses. *Junk.*

"Look," says Mom. Creep scrambles out of her way as she leans down to pick up two boxes. One says *Things To Keep,* and the other says *Things To Throw Away,* both labeled with Sharpie in Mom's tight lettering. "See?" she says. "Easy."

Things To Keep. Things To Throw Away. Fit Ellie in a box. Easy.

Mom goals are my *favorite.*

"Okay," I tell her.

"Great," she says again. She tosses the Sharpie onto my bed. "And when you're done, come help me in the kitchen."

Then she's gone, her buzzing energy gone with her, tension left behind like a haze.

I fall back onto my pillow. She didn't close the door, so I can hear her waking up Joshua. Dad is thumping around in the living room. Creep's head appears at the foot of my bed. He rests his chin on his folded forearms. I glance at him.

"Easy," he says. "Easy Ellie." When I don't answer, he goes on. "Why did you ever stop talking to Mom about me?"

"You know why," I tell the ceiling. "I got tired of being told that you weren't real."

He tilts his head. "Who cares if she thought I wasn't real? *You* know I am. That's what counts."

I sit up. The opaque marbles of his eyes roll in their sockets. He grins.

"I got *whipped* for talking about you."

"I know," says Creep, like it's his favorite memory. "It's been almost ten years since you stopped talking about me. And I found it very hurtful." A chuckle jitters in his throat.

"Can we change the subject?" I get out of bed and wrench open a drawer. "Anyway, it worked. They forgot all about you." I throw jeans and a t-shirt onto the bedspread.

"A new start," he says, changing the subject for once. "How do you feel about that?"

I don't tell him that I'm okay with starting over. A new start sounds like a dream. A good one. I just don't know where to begin.

Creep says, like he knows what I'm thinking, "You should start under the bed. There's all sorts of great stuff under there." He ducks his head and crawls underneath. He's still talking, his voice muffled, saying something about mushrooms and dental records and human remains. I try not to pay attention as I get dressed.

A new start. A new school at the end of the summer. A new Eleanor. What would that look like? I decide Creep is right. A new start can start *there*, with what has been moldering away in the dark. I tighten my ponytail.

The room gradually lightens as I pull things out from under the bed: an old clarinet mouthpiece from elementary-school band, a scuffed pair of roller skates I got for my ninth birthday, a torn grocery sack full of fabric scraps. Creep is crawling around out of sight, droning on about how people go missing and all they find are perfectly preserved shoes.

I pull out a box marked *Ellie's Things*. When I open it, there's a white church dress folded, ribbons and ruffles. I rub the fabric between my thumb and forefinger, remembering how hot I felt wearing it. Hot and bored and anxious. I lift a handful of skirt to see what's underneath. It's a green baby blanket. I close the box and put it into *Things To Keep*. I find an old school folder full of "100%!" math tests. A latch-hook rug I abandoned. A copy of Ray Bradbury's *The Martian Chronicles* with a broken spine.

Then I find the shirt box.

I turn slow and quiet as I pull it out. My fingers make tracks in the dust when I lift the lid and find it filled with crinkled papers. I stare at the top sheet. Two stick figures grin out at me, one with a sharp wide mouth. Scribbly clouds over the top of the page, the rest filled in with fat raindrops. I shuffle down through the stack and it's all black line sketches of me and Creep, most of them drawn in crayon. No drawings of Mom and Dad. No drawings of Joshua. Just me. Over and over, just me and Creep.

I think about little-kid me, drawing these. I see my thin arms stretched across the paper. Fingers gripping the crayon. My blue eyes concentrating, dark hair tucked behind my ears.

I trace the outline of me on the page now, the triangle dress, the scrawled hair. I don't feel like I've changed at all. My eyes prickle. Blinking fast, I look up at the sun coming in through the gauzy curtains. The light hits a teardrop of crystal I have hanging from the curtain rod. Every morning, the walls are thrown with rainbows. I've always loved it. Creep says it gives him a headache.

He sticks his head out from under the bed.

"What are you thinking about?" he asks, wrinkled eyebrows raised.

"Nothing." Quick, I put the cover back on the box of drawings.

I can hear Dad talking loud about things he's not going to get rid of. Mom calls him a packrat. His voice barrels down the hall and I get up to shut my door.

Sometimes my brain feels like an episode of *Hoarders*.

Creep pulls his head back and disappears under the bed.

"Look at this mess." His sandpaper voice is muted. "You are such a dirty girl."

My shoulders tense. "I wish you wouldn't call me that."

Creep says, "What…dirty?"

I want to say, *No… girl.* But I don't say it. I never say anything like that out loud anymore.

Words for things like that froze inside me a long time ago. Cold and dark. They'll always be there in my throat, like an ice cube getting stuck halfway down and never melting.

Creep's voice makes a grocery list of lost underbed objects: two apple cores, five library books, three missing socks, one headless Barbie. He tells me he'll keep the Barbie and pretend it's me. I imagine him sticking it with pins in the middle of the night.

I turn around to see that Mom wrote *Ellie's Room* on all of the boxes. I uncap the Sharpie. I scribble over my nickname, thinking about the night we went box hunting, when Dad boosted us into a recycling dumpster behind the grocery store. I write *Eleanor's.*

A new start. I say it to myself, over and over, like a mantra.

Creep's drone has fallen silent. He crawls out from under the bed. "More secrets?" He points a clawed finger at the shirt box full of drawings.

"It's nothing," I say.

"C'mon, Ellie, you should know better," he says. "You can't hide anything from me."

"Whatever," I tell him. But his words scoop out my chest and I shiver. *A new start,* I think. While I don't want a hundred pictures of Creep, I do want to show six-year-old Eleanor that someone remembers her. So I turn and put the box of drawings in *Things To Keep.*

Creep watches while I toss lots into *Things To Throw Away:* papers from school, old sketches, tattered stuffed animals.

I take down the horse pictures. Careful. One by one. There are fifty-seven altogether. I spend most nights staring at the wall of horses until I fall asleep: all long legs and graceful necks, manes streaming out in the wind. Horses rearing, leaping, running. I stare at the wall and imagine myself in the golden pastures, on the salt water beaches, lost under green leaves.

"You can't keep those," Creep says. "This is a new start, remember? No *junk*."

"I'm not going to do something just because you tell me to." I press the stack of pictures in a copy of *Where The Wild Things Are* and put it all in *Things To Keep*.

"Wanna bet?" It's a snap of his teeth.

"Whatever." I almost say, *You're not the boss of me*, like I used to. Our patterns are so ingrained. Instead I say, "Besides, they're not junk." I start stacking novels from my bookcase.

"Horses don't really fit you anyway," he says. "You've never seen one up close before." He scratches behind his ear, looking at the ceiling. "What would be a more fitting mascot for Ellie?" He ticks them off on his fingers. "Alley cats. Cockroaches. Horny toads. Oh, I know. Those anatomically-correct dolls they show kids at the police station." He laughs, rolling onto his back, hands clutched around his stomach.

Creep laughs like someone choking.

"Would you shut up?" I tell him. "And don't call me that."

He digs in his ear. "I can't help it," he says. "That's what *everyone* calls you." He puts his big flat feet all over my bedspread.

"Not everyone," I say. "Just Joshua, and you, and –" I stop.

Creep lowers his head. He looks at me from under his eyebrows. "And who, Ellie?"

Just almost *saying* his name makes goosebumps come out on both arms. I rub them away and unclench my jaw.

"Get off my bed." I swat at Creep with a copy of *The Last Unicorn*. He scurries backward and ends up sitting on my pillow. He is hairless-cat skin and bones, crouching on my pillow.

"Always pushing me out." He folds his arms in a sulk. "I remember when you used to invite me in."

"Things change."

A knock at the door and I say, loud, "What!"

Joshua pokes his head in. "Can I show you something?"

I nod, sorry I yelled. He comes in, carrying a shoe box. "Remember that baby bird I found last year?"

"I forgot about that," I say, remembering the rescued hatchling, limp in a nest of fabric.

His eyes glisten, lower lip trembles. "So did I." And he lifts the cover off the box.

Inside is a folded hand towel and a plastic food container lid turned upside down. The bird's head is twisted back, beak gaping – with its toothpick skeleton and paper-dry skin, crooked wings spread like it's going to fly, wire legs curled.

Joshua gulps. "It's dead."

"Yeah." I nod. He sniffles, head bent. We kneel over the box. I put my hand on his shoulder. He reminds me of the bird, with his too-big head and hunched-over back. He's only eight, but probably my favorite person in the world. I hate to see him sad.

"I killed it," Joshua says.

Creep cranes his neck to see from where he sits.

"I meant to keep it alive," says Joshua. Words come out of him, fast and falling over each other. "I was going to feed it and I left water for it and I was going to let it go when it was stronger but I put it under the bed and I forgot one day and then I forgot again and now it's dead and it's all my fault."

Swallowing hard, I squeeze his shoulder. "It's not your fault. Baby birds who fall out of the nest always die. The mama bird is so worried about taking care of everything else, getting food and keeping things safe up in the tree that she forgets one is missing."

Joshua looks up at me with moist cheeks.

"It would have died anyway," I tell him.

He wipes his nose on the back of his hand. "What am I going to do?" Animals in his room mean Mom's grounding and Dad's belt. I grew out of spanking, but Joshua is still fair game. Both of us listen for footsteps, the rustle of Dad's camouflage cargo pants, any hint that his brown hand might turn the doorknob.

I cover the bird up. "I'll take care of it. Just go finish packing."

Joshua puts his arms around my neck. "Thanks, Ellie," he says. I decide not to mention the nickname. I pat his back.

After he closes my door, I pull out my sketchbook. I study the tiny carcass. As I draw, I wonder what it was like, to be put in a dark, dry place and forgotten. Just silence – just close my eyes and fade away into dust.

Creep is quiet for a while and then climbs down to get a closer look. He says, "It's like your room -- a casket for little lost souls," and then giggles.

I snap my sketchbook closed, turn away from Creep and put the bird coffin in *Things To Throw Away*. I dig in *Things To Keep* and pull out the box of Creep drawings.

Junk, I think as I toss them, and then I spend the next three hours splitting my life into two boxes: the part of my life I want to keep and the part I want to throw away. This is the only place I've ever lived. When we move, Creep will stay here. If I leave the crayon drawings behind too, it will be like he never existed.

<u>Things To Keep:</u>

Horse wall
Sketchbooks
Pictures of Joshua
Books

<u>Things to Throw Away:</u>

Ellie

TWO

I don't like the place all empty. Creep sings and the walls bounce his rattling voice into the hollow spaces.

The shelves are all dismantled. The peeling kitchen cabinets stand open, empty. Beds are all upright, leaning crooked against walls, moved so we could vacuum under them. Boxes are stacked in the living room: a whole life. Four whole lives, packed away. As my eyes sweep across them, I pause for a moment on the boxes that hold my parents' room. Part of me is surprised that the boxes don't say *Angel Room*, instead of *Master Bed*. But I shouldn't be surprised. My parents never knew I called it that. It was only in my head, and whispered to Creep.

I can't imagine the room dismantled like mine was, taken apart in pieces. Rattling in a box like a jigsaw that doesn't make sense when it's not assembled. I can only imagine it as a room: complete, airy, filled with light. The only place in the house I wasn't allowed to go unless specifically invited, and decorated with things I wasn't allowed to touch. I imagine the Angel Room whole and furnished inside the cardboard box, like a genie's bottle or The Doctor's TARDIS. I want to open the top box and see the room there, complete, inside. My mother's sanctuary.

I wonder why my room doesn't feel like a sanctuary and then I see Creep skulking around the corners, sniffing at the frayed carpet. No place is a sanctuary with Creep inside it.

The rest of the boxes say: *Kitchen, Master Bed, Josh's Room, Bathroom, ~~Ellie's~~ Eleanor's Room, Storage, Books.*

Dad's friend Ray comes early and starts helping Dad carry furniture out to the truck. They hitched a trailer on the back, so we can fit all our furniture too. Joshua bounces. He can't stop smiling. I think he's just as happy as me to leave here.

It takes us five hours to get all the boxes in the truck and all the furniture stacked in the trailer. I keep waiting for Dad to yell at us for getting in the way, but we just carry boxes and keep our heads down and he seems fine with how we are helping. Maybe he's glad to leave this place behind too. I told Creep to stay in the closet, but he follows me everywhere. Down the hall and out across the burning sidewalk to the parking lot with tar-filled cracks that bubble in the heat, and then back into the apartment for more to carry.

The men tie everything down with a complex spiderweb of rope. The sun is directly overhead when we finish. We stand on the brown carpet in the living room and Dad's friend puts his arm around my shoulders.

"Whaddya think, kiddo?" he says. "Move up in the world?" His hand is heavy. The back of my neck prickles.

Casual, I slide out from under Ray's arm and tell Joshua, "Let's go take one last look." My brother runs around the corner and down the hall. I follow, the heavy hand print sticking to my shoulder. I want to brush it off. Joshua can touch me, but anyone else and there are worms burrowing under my skin.

I step inside my bedroom door and stand with my hands in my pockets. Joshua whoops. He circles, arms out airplane-straight. His fingertips trail along the wall all the way around. Creep stoops in the doorway behind me.

I thought my room would feel different – just a room without all my things in it. We scrubbed everything, but it's like my secrets coat the walls and drip from the ceiling corners. Phantom voices almost seem to echo: Dad yelling that I'd better pick a belt and take my whipping without a sound, Mom telling me she'd confiscate my books if I stayed up reading after bedtime, my name whispered between deep breaths. By the time Joshua stops, my head is spinning. He falls on the floor.

"It's big enough to do cartwheels." He smiles.

I nod.

"Eleanor?" he says. Brown strands of hair cling to his sweaty forehead.

"Yeah?"

"Are you excited to move into a real house? With stairs inside?"

"Yeah," I say. "I am."

We're lying where my bed used to be. I imagine myself as the headless Barbie, sightless in the dark under the bed skirt. Bodies tangle on the mattress above me. I close my eyes.

Mom's voice comes down the hall. "Hey, time to go."

We look at each other. Joshua shows me his dimples. "Race ya," he says and jumps up.

Creep ducks out of the way as my brother runs past. I close my eyes again and pretend I'm asleep. When I wake up tomorrow morning, I will open them in a new room. My room. And no one will come in unless I want them to. I smile.

I open my eyes and there is Creep. He leans over me, upside down. His eyes bulge.

I sit up quick. "Don't do that," I tell him.

"What were you thinking about?"

"I'm thinking about how nice it will be to leave you here." I finger the hole in the knee of my jeans.

"What makes you think I'm staying here?" Creep smirks.

"You live here." I say.

"Eleanor!" Mom's voice again.

I get up before Dad has a chance to join in. Creep follows me down the hall. Three other people stand in the living room with Ray and my parents. I stop at the end of the hall.

"The Taylors came over to say goodbye," says Mom. "Isn't that nice?"

I look from Mr. and Mrs. Taylor to their son, Ian. He smiles at me. I automatically smile back.

"Yeah," I say, but I'm not sure anyone can hear it.

Mom says, "Where are your manners?"

The Taylors have lived two doors down for as long as I can remember. Ian is twenty-four, but he was thirteen when he became my babysitter, long before Joshua was born. My feet feel like rocks as I move across the room.

"Goodbye, Mr. Taylor," I mumble. "Goodbye, Mrs. Taylor." They take turns shaking my hand. Electricity jolts up my arm each time. When I get to Ian, my palms are moist. I stand in front of him. With our parents watching, my arms hang numb by my sides. He leans down to hug me. He pats my back.

"Bye, Ellie," he says into my ear.

Ian's shirt smells like laundry detergent and sweat. It fills my nostrils, thick. I close my eyes. My head spins. I've only been with Ian a handful times since he got back from his humanitarian mission trip. But he smells the same as he always did, clean and musky. Mom and Dad are talking to the Taylors. The words in the room swirl together. Mashed up words fall into my ears all jumbled with Ian's arms still around me.

- - - Mrs. Taylor says I know he's really going to miss your kids and Mom says He's been helping us out for a long time now and Mr. Taylor says He's basically an older brother and Mrs. Taylor says Since we never had any more kids, I'm glad Josh and Eleanor could be like family for him and Mom says We can't express how blessed we are - - -

Even though I can't see, I know they are shaking hands and hugging each other. Ian smell inside my nose. Thinking about the last time, his smell all around me. Fists curl inside my chest.

"Call me," he whispers, and lets me go. His fingers slide down my arm and he squeezes my hand for one second. No one sees. Our eyes meet. Then he's turning to my parents and Dad shakes his hand and Mom gives him a hug. I look at the floor. Sounds in the air come out of my parents. Words like they're in a blender.

- - - Good luck with your fall semester says Dad and Mom says Thanks for everything I don't know what we would have done if you hadn't volunteered to watch Eleanor all those years ago - - -

Mom doesn't get home from work until six or later every night, and Dad's not around much. But three years ago they decided I was old enough to be in charge when they weren't around. Ian left on his mission trip not long after that. When he got back, things were different, and the same. He's managed to find ways for us to be together. But now we're moving.

No more Creep.

No more Ian two doors down.

And it will be up to me, I think, *if I want to see him again. Never again, unless I call. Unless I want to.*

I think about this and move my feet toward the door. The Ian smell hangs around me like a cloud.

I walk outside. Joshua sits in the marigold garden. Bees hum around him. The flowers are up to his chin.

I tell him, "Let's go."

He stands up, walks on the stepping stones to the sidewalk. Orange and yellow marigolds dust the legs of his shorts. He has a long stick in his hand. Joshua always finds a stick, no matter where he is.

"I saw the Taylors come in," he says. "I hid in the flowers and they didn't see me."

I used to hide in the flowers.

"They wanted to say goodbye," I say.

He makes a face. "Mr. and Mrs. Taylor are okay, I guess. But I don't like *him*."

I tell him, "I know you don't."

I tighten my ponytail. My chest feels looser when I imagine the new house. New room. New house. New neighborhood.

New me.

"I'm going to miss this place," says Creep, distant. "So many memories."

I wish Joshua would beat Creep with that stick.

We go around the corner from our front door so the Taylors won't see us when they leave. As they walk away from us back to their apartment, Joshua gestures with the stick. He pokes each one with an imaginary sword.

When Joshua opens the car door, he stops to wave at our building.

"Bye!" he shouts. While he's turned away, I watch Creep slink past his legs to boost himself into the car. Creep looks back at me while he does it, smile ever-widening. I want to scream. He curls up on my *Things To Keep* box.

We drive with all the windows down. The air conditioning has never worked. We cook in the car, but the oven-door air dries our sweat instantly. I want to cry when I look back at Creep. I feel sick. I thought he was part of the apartment, like a ghost. I guess it wasn't the apartment that was haunted. I guess it was always just me. My old room, where I was afraid of the dark. My old neighbors, whose son was *such a good kid, such a great guy*. My old school, where I had *behavioral issues*. A new start, Mom said.

But I don't cry.

Things will be different, I think. *They have to be.*

<u>Things I Will Miss:</u>

Mom's marigold garden...
I can't think of anything else.

THREE

It takes over an hour driving through traffic to get to the new neighborhood. A neighborhood with actual houses, one for each family, instead of hundreds of people packed into tall, crumbling apartment boxes.

I wonder what it's like in other cities. I read about them all the time, but it's hard to imagine anything else. Phoenix is hot, dry like a mouth full of concrete dust. The broiler sun cooks everything bone-pale.

We drive down Baseline Road behind the truck trailer. I guess people don't really look at their own stuff from the outside very often, but with everything stacked up and tied down like this, it's hard not to notice how trashy everything looks.

The kitchen table bounces, with the broken metal legs Dad screwed back in tight so they'll never come off again. The black plastic chairs from Mom's office. The bricks and boards for bookshelves, dressers that Mom says will last 'til doomsday, flat worn mattresses.

I watch my mattress strain against the ropes. I try not to think about Creep sitting on the box behind me.

When we pushed my bed up against the wall to get ready to move it, I noticed an Eleanor-sized trough in the center of the mattress. That's because I always sleep right in the middle curled in a ball, or with my arms crossed over my chest. Joshua says I sleep like a mummy.

The trailer jounces up and down so hard, I expect everything to fly out of it. I put my elbow on the edge of the car door and then move it immediately, rubbing the burned spot with my other hand. Heat presses in. The hair-dryer wind blows across my eyes. Joshua talks about everything he sees. Mom says he talks too much, but I like it. It covers up the sound of Creep's humming – that guttural drone that gets in behind my eyes.

We drive past flower fields, marching stretches of orange and red and white. I wonder what they smell like, but the heat bleaches away the scent. I imagine horses standing knee deep in flowers. Lowered noses snuffle. Curled eyelashes flutter among poppies.

Joshua goes on, "Matthew said if his dog ever has puppies, he'll let me have one. Oo, a firetruck! When I grow up, I'm going to be a fire-fighter. Can I have a gerbil, Mom? I promise I'll give it baths and everything."

I see the horses in the fields. When they run, flower petals will scatter like colored raindrops falling upward; tissue paper ovals caught in manes that smell carnation-sweet. I imagine hooves churning dirt in a gallop to the foot of sandy buttes in the distance.

Rows of flowers turn into rows of trailers. Then the trailer parks phase into a housing development. Squat boxy houses with black roofs. We follow the truck into the neighborhood down a main residential street. A lot of the yards are gravel with upward-reaching cacti gathered along driveways.

"Hey, Mom." Joshua's hands are on the ledge of the rolled down window. "Which one's ours?"

"It's coming up," says Mom.

At the next corner, a leaning street sign says *Lynn Lane*. The truck turns there and stops in front of the second house on the right. Mom pulls into the driveway.

Joshua piles out of the car as Mom opens the driver-side door. He runs across the lawn. A real lawn with grass not gravel, even if it is flattened and anemic. It looks like the picture of a house that little kids draw. A box with a cornflower-blue door right in the center. Four windows, two on either side of the door. The bottom windows sit right at ground level. The house is weathered, wood siding with fake blue shutters attached. There's even a massive tree with widespread limbs out front. The branches hang down low, creating an umbrella of leaves.

Joshua turns two cartwheels before his arms collapse under him and he rolls from his head and shoulders onto his back. He blinks up into the tree shade.

"Look, Ellie," he calls. "Our own front yard. All to ourselves."

I slide across the seat and get out on the same side Joshua did. Crabgrass pokes up through cracks in the driveway. Mom stands on the concrete block porch and clinks the keys on her key ring, looking for the right one.

"Mom!" Joshua is at her side. "Let me do it. Can I do it?"

I turn up the front walk and stand behind them. Dad and Ray untie the ropes and begin to pull them off the load.

"Sure," says Mom. She shuffles, jingling. "It's this one."

Joshua takes it. He tries to push it into the deadbolt lock, but it won't fit.

"Turn it upside down," says Mom.

Joshua reverses his hand and the door opens inward. A rush of cool air hits our faces.

"Oh, that was nice of them to put the cooler on for us," says Mom.

Once we step through the front door, we stand on a staircase landing. One set leads up, the other down.

"Our own house," Joshua crows. He bounds downward into the basement. "C'mon, Ellie."

I follow down seven steps carpeted in beige. A hallway runs perpendicular, so that there's a wall directly in front of me when I reach the bottom; bedrooms to the left, family room to the right. Joshua's voice drifts down the hall.

"Ellie," he cries. "My room is huge!"

I turn toward his voice and follow the hallway to where it ends in two doorways. These are our new rooms. Joshua has claimed the door on the left. He runs a race around the perimeter, running his hand along the wall like he did in my old room. The closet has mirrored sliding doors. The ceiling fan thumps out a quiet rhythm.

"Look, look," he points at the window. "We're under the ground. Like squirrels. I mean chipmunks."

"You mean groundhogs," I tell him. Through the opening, the grass is at eye level. I put my forearms on the windowsill, rest my chin in my hands. A ladybug crawls through the weeds that sprout outside the glass, and beyond that, the truck and trailer are parked at the curb. I watch Ray and Dad put furniture on the sidewalk.

"Hey," Joshua calls from outside the doorway, already down the hall. I follow his voice back past the stairway and into a sprawling family room so deep that the corners are shadowy. I walk toward the back of the room, away from the window.

"It's like a cave," says Joshua. When I turn back to look at him, he is lying on the floor, arms spread. He closes his eyes and sighs big.

He's right, down here under the rest of the house these rooms are cool, twilight grottoes. Light from the window filters through the leaves of the tree outside, blue-green instead of blinding summer white. I have no idea what we will use to fill this room. Our whole apartment could fit in here. Joshua sits up.

"What do you think Mom will put down here?" he wonders.

"She said the family room is downstairs." We've never had a family room before.

"Maybe the TV. I'm gonna go ask her," says Joshua and he is gone.

Footsteps tromp through the upper level as the front door opens and closes. I don't want to go back out under the sun yet, so I wander toward the second bedroom at the other end of the hall. My new room.

The door stands open. It's twice as big as my old room. The window looks out the back of the house at the walled yard. Weedy grass, knee-high and yellow, stretches from wall to wall. Outside a ceiling of beams crisscrosses over the window and stretches out, held up by wooden posts set into the ground. My room has the same fan and closet as Joshua's, but the best surprise is a door to the right of the window. Pushing it wider, I find a long narrow bathroom.

My own bathroom.

Creep hunkers in one end of the bathtub. I can see his knife-sharp angles, black against the porcelain. Disappointment rises in my throat.

"Where have *you* been?" I ask.

He tilts his head to one side. "Just looking around. Same as you," he says.

A large mirror runs the entire length of the counter. I turn to look at myself in the mirror. I don't want to look at Creep anymore. I splash water on my face but with no towel, my eyes are streaming. I look at a reflected Eleanor blur. The dark shape floats, cut in half by the counter at my waist. I wonder what it would be like to be just a top half. Head, shoulders, torso, nothing below the navel. Numb.

"So what do you think, Ellie?" Creep is on the toilet lid. He says *Ellie* like it's candy in his mouth. "How do you like your new room?" He clambers onto the counter.

I swipe at my eyes and Creep swims into focus. Watching myself in the mirror, I tighten my ponytail and tell him, "Don't call me Ellie."

"Why not?" he asks. "Josh has been doing it all day."

I look into my own eyes. They're blue chips of glacial ice. *If my reflection was the real Eleanor,* I think, *what would that make me?* Flattened paper-thin behind glass, I imagine the reflection to be cold, calm. Capable only of corners, like an Egyptian figure in profile. Just an outline colored in.

"Why do you do that?" Creep asks. His oil-slick eyes watch me.

"Do what?" I say.

"Look at yourself like you expect something to change." He stands on the counter, as tall as me. I can see myself curved to one side and repeated on the surface of his eyes. "You'll always be Ellie. Forever."

"Don't call me Ellie," I tell him.

"Ellie," he sings. "Ellie, Ellie, Ellie."

"Stop." I want to put my hands over my ears.

Creep laughs. He jumps down from the counter. He's not saying it anymore, but I can still hear it. Ellie, Ellie, *Ellie* – a thrusting rhythm, jagged. I rub my temples.

"Stop," I say again. A touch at my elbow and I drop my hands, surprised.

"Who are you talking to, Ellie?" Joshua asks.

I turn on him, fierce. "Don't. Call. Me. Ellie!"

He steps back. His face crumples. "I'm sorry," he says. "I forgot." Tears gather.

Creep crouches behind Joshua and grins.

"I'm sorry," I say. Head pounds, but I hold my hand out. "I'm sorry."

I don't like it when Creep stands so close to him. Joshua wipes his eyes. He leans into me for a hug.

"I'll try to remember, Ellie," he promises. "I'll only call you Eleanor." His forehead rests against me.

Creep watches from the corner.

Like always.

<u>Things I Won't Miss:</u>

My old school
My old room
Ian?
~~Creep~~

FOUR

Dad is gone for dinner again. Mom and Joshua and I sit around the table and eat spaghetti. Creep sits in Dad's chair, across from me.

There's homemade sauce and a green salad that I made after we found the knives in a box. I told Mom that I would help after I heard Dad leaving. Mom frowns when Dad misses dinner.

I watch Joshua eat noodles one at a time. He puts the end in his mouth and then SLUUURP, sucks it up in one breath. Mom pushes food around on her plate, her jaw hard.

Mom says. "Don't play with your food. Just eat it."

Joshua slurps. "I *am* eating it," he says.

Creep watches the exchange and then chokes on a laugh.

Mom looks mad. Eyes glint. She says, quiet. "Don't argue with me."

Joshua stops. He puts his head down. His bottom lip starts to tremble.

Mom gets up to take her plate to the sink. She starts banging around in the cabinet doors. The corner and walls are stacked with boxes.

I touch Joshua's leg with my foot. He turns to look at me as I put the end of a noodle in my mouth. My face is close to the plate. Grainy clods of meat sauce spread through the pile of spaghetti.

I suck hard and the noodle zips up into my mouth. Joshua laughs. I smile at him and wipe the sauce off of my face.

"Eleanor," says Mom. "I want you to do the dishes while I set up Joshua's bed. Then we'll do yours."

I want to say, *Have Joshua do dishes for once.* "Okay," I say.

After she leaves, Joshua starts slurping again. "I like our new house," he says to me while he chews down a mouthful. "Don't you?"

"It's okay," I say.

"Just okay?" he protests. "What about our awesome backyard? And the deck? And the family room is big enough for a whole bowling alley."

I feel Creep's eyes on me. They're heavy like Ian's arms circling my shoulders. His lips part over his gleaming teeth.

"It's not our house," I tell Joshua. "We're just renting it."

I look out the sliding glass door while Joshua keeps talking about how great the new house is. A platform of peeling planks stretches away from the door outside, with a chest high banister that wraps all the way around. Stairs lead from the deck down to the grass.

"Eleanor," Joshua says. He has eaten all of his food. "Eleanor." His plate is smeared red.

"What?" I say.

"Don't you like all those things? Isn't this new house great?"

Creep climbs down from Dad's chair. His head disappears as he slinks under the table. Cold breath. I stand up and grab my plate. "Yeah," I say. "It's great."

Sudsy mountains pile in the sink. I slip the plates into the lemon-scented water, move the plastic scrubber in circles.

I can hear Creep's breathing behind me.

I try not to think about it. I take each dish from the rinse water and stack them in the drainer. Creep sings to himself.

Joshua comes into the kitchen. He has a toy airplane in his hands, big enough for action figures. I pause and lean my elbows on the edge of the counter. My fingers curl through the hot water. Joshua mimics crashing his airplane into the counter.

Creep asks, "Why does he always get to play and you have to work?"

"Joshua," I say. "Why don't you go find something to do?"

He turns in a circle. Airplane satellite orbits, held up by Joshua's tanned arm. He purses his lips to make jet engine sounds.

"I *am* doing something," he says.

"I mean something productive." I drop a piece of silverware into the rinse water.

"I don't wanna be productive," Joshua says. "I wanna play. Play with me Eleanor."

I unstack cups and submerge them one by one. "I can't play," I tell him. "I have to finish this and then unpack."

"Okay," says Joshua. "But Mom says she wants you in your new room. She's done with my bed and she wants to do yours."

I'd rather sleep on the floor.

Joshua brings the airplane down for a landing on the kitchen table.

"What's a V.A?" he asks. He sits in his chair, opens the cockpit door on the plane.

Creep climbs up into the chair next to Joshua. He bares his teeth at my brother. A silent snarl. I want to knock the chair over so that Creep falls on the floor.

"It's a hospital for veterans," I tell Joshua.

Cups float crooked in the rinse water like sinking ships.

"Do the veterans work there?"

"No," I tell him. I stick the cups on the drainer basket hooks. Rivulets of water slide along the counter.

"Why does Dad go there?" he asks. He pulls out two army action figures and walks them across the table. "Are animals there too?"

Creep giggles. His laugh cuts the air. A headache begins to burn inside my right temple.

I turn to look at Joshua. "What do you mean?"

Joshua looks up at me, one of the little men falls from the table. "I thought veterans were animal doctors."

Creep laughs out loud again.

"*Veterinarians* are animal doctors."

Joshua scrunches up one side of his face. "What did *I* say?"

"Veterans."

He pushes his lips out. "What did *you* say?"

I turn to unplug the sink. Water begins to suck its way down. Suds lower. I pull a kitchen towel out of a box on the counter. Turning back to face Joshua, I wrap my hands in the towel and then hang it on the oven door handle.

"Veterinarians," I sigh. I press my fingers to the side of my head.

Joshua retrieves the fallen soldier. "Veterans," he tries.

A smile sneaks onto my mouth.

"Veterinarians," I tell him.

He smiles too. "Veterans."

I smile bigger. "Okay, say it after me. Veterin–"

"Veterin," says Joshua.

"Arian," I finish.

"Arian," he repeats.

"Veterinarian," I say.

"Veter–inian," says Joshua.

We look at each other for a moment and then laugh. Nobody tells us to be quiet. The headache lessens.

"What kind of airplane is that?" I ask him.

"It's not an airplane, Eleanor." He sits back down in his chair, settles the miniature men in the cockpit. "It's an F-14 Tomcat fighter jet." Joshua lifts the plane from the tabletop, simulating the sound of a takeoff. He flies the toy out into the living room. His footsteps hop down the stairs.

I turn to follow. I see Creep, where he crouches on the chair, ready to join me.

"Why don't you stay here?" I ask him. "You don't have to follow me everywhere, you know."

He looks up at me like a starving dog. Gargoyle-ugly features twist into a smile. "I love you, Eleanor," he says. "You know nobody loves you the way I do."

<u>Things I Like About The New House:</u>

My own bathroom
Backyard
~~My room to myself~~

It's dark here, and cold. Just a featureless corridor. Doors on either side and I can't see the end, it extends so far, disappearing into a pinprick of black. I've been in this hallway before. I remember the sterile, freezing air. The unadorned doors. The dim light bulbs hanging from a high and invisible ceiling. Pools of light dot the gray carpet in yellow circles wide enough to stand in. I look behind me. The hallway stretches away into forever in that direction too.

I can't see Creep anywhere.

I turn back and take a step forward. The carpet is silent underneath my feet. And I think, if I were to speak, it would make no sound. The air is like a giant dampener, muting even the noise of my breath.

I pass a door. It's black, just like all the others, with no discerning marks. The doorknob is dull silver. I walk past several doors. Walking faster, doors pass on either side. I don't know which one to choose.

I've been here before.

I start to run. Doors flash by. I run until my legs and arms burn, until my lungs heave, until I have to lean over with my hands on my knees, my breath condensing on the air into clouds. I look down the *hallway and then back the way I came. Nothing has changed. Every door, every bulb, every foot of carpet looks the same.*

I've been here before.

I don't know which door to choose, so I step to the closest one and put my hand on the knob – ice-cold and slippery. I have to lean into the doorknob to turn it. The latch clicks and the door swings open.

"Just in time," says my mother. She smiles at me. "We need you for the finishing touches."

She sits on the corner of the bed in my childhood bedroom. My big flat teddy bear is on the pillow. The room is shadowed, fingers of darkness reaching out of the corners. I feel for the light switch, but the wall is bare. My hand slides across the wall. Nothing.

"Come here," she says.

I step into the room. My mother gestures at the closet. I can't see what she's referring to, because the open closet doors obscure my view.

"What do you think?" she says.

I step around the door and look into the closet. A small girl, with black hair and blue eyes, settled on a pile of pillows. She sits against the back of the closet with her head among hems of flowered dresses hanging from the rack above. She is tied hand and foot with thin, white coils of rope. The rope circles around her shoulders and torso as well. Her hands, bound at the wrist, hang between her knees. She leans forward.

"Please," she says.

"Uh-oh," says my mother. She hands me a toddler-sized t-shirt and a pink sash. "Can't have her talking. You better take care of that."

I take the fabric and look down at the girl.

"Please," she says again, her voice like the chirping of a bird.

I push her back against the wall again and shove the shirt into her mouth. She whimpers. The air from her nostrils tickles the back of my hand. I tie the sash around the back of her neck, holding the fabric in place. She makes a gagging sound. Blue eyes water. She blinks up at me.

"Why are we doing this?" I ask.

"It's for the best," my mother says. She stands up to close the closet doors. They creak, metal on metal, as they flatten shut. She hands me a stack of wrinkled papers. "Now go on, and take these with you."

I take them, but it's too dark in the room now to see what they are. I step back into the hallway. The door closes behind me. In the dim light of the bulb overhead, I look down at the papers in my hand. They're drawings. Black crayon drawings of me and Creep. I shuffle through them. Me and Creep, over and over.

FIVE

I open my eyes. The room is dark. I can feel Creep sitting on my chest. He leans forward, his face close. *Sniff sniff.* Like he wants to breathe me in. I blink into the outline of his black round eyes. He cocks his head to one side and puts his face closer.

"What were you dreaming about?" he asks.

"Get off me," I tell him and roll to one side.

He scoots on all fours to the edge of the bed. "Tell me," he says.

I turn away from him, toward the window.

"Nothing," I tell him.

He clicks his teeth together. "Nothing?" he asks. "Or nothing you'll tell me about?"

I stare at the window. I don't have my curtains up yet. The deck above makes the constant city-night light much darker than I'm used to. I lean across to click on the bedside lamp. Creep shakes his head, like an animal walking into sudden sunlight.

"Tell me about your dream," he persists.

"I don't want to talk about it," I say.

"I don't know why you're being so sensitive," he says in a hurt tone. "You used to tell me everything."

I think about the little-girl me, hiding in the pillow fort with Creep, tea parties with Creep and stuffies gathered around, the drowsy retelling of dreams and nightmares, Creep hanging on every detail. Before Joshua learned to walk and talk. Before I realized not everyone had a best friend like Creep.

"Not anymore," I say.

I fold the blanket down and hang my feet over the side of the bed. Boxes pile in corners. That musty smell of old cardboard. I kneel on the floor, open the flaps of the first box marked ~~Ellie's~~ *Eleanor's Books*.

"You're going to unpack?" says Creep. He hops down from the bed and kneels next to me. "In the middle of the night?"

My bookcase is skeleton empty.

"What else am I going to do?"

He shrugs again. "Sleep?" His eyes are wide, hopeful.

I shake my head. I'm tired of dreams.

I begin in the middle, third shelf from the bottom. Novels line up, paperback spines straight with the edge. I group them alphabetically by genre. Science-fiction. Fantasy. Picture books. I touch every book, run my hands over the covers, fan the pages briefly. I fill one whole space and then open the next box. *Where The Wild Things Are*, hiding my fifty-seven horse pictures. I decide to put up the horse wall instead.

I know there will be tape upstairs, so I click open my door. Joshua's door stands wide across from mine. I poke my head into his room. He sprawls, mouth open. Small snores. I like to watch him sleep. Makes me feel calm.

Creep follows me down the hall and up the dark stairs. The fourth from the top squeaks. I turn right toward the kitchen, walk through shadows and the stretching black. I prop open the fridge door with a box and find another box marked *Kitchen: Junk Drawer*. In the fridge light, I dig through the contents, until a noise makes me sit up. The front door creaks open, brushing carpet. Dad sniffs loud in the dark. I push the doorstop box with my foot. The light closes in on itself as the fridge door drifts shut. I listen to Dad close the front door, hard like he leans with his shoulder. I stay still in the kitchen. Hiding.

Heavy footfalls on the stairs.

"Where have you been?" Mom's voice.

Dad clears his throat. "The V.A. I told you."

They are talking around the corner, at the top of the stairs. Voices loud in the dark, but Mom's is quieter than Dad's. It always is.

They argue quietly about how long he was gone. I feel frozen, like a deer caught halfway across a midnight highway. I realize I've been holding my breath when Dad says loudly, "Well, I'm here now!" and I jump.

Mom shushes him. Then the voices move down the hall, their door clicks shut and they become just a tense murmur.

Creep hisses a laugh through his teeth. "You ever wonder why they're so unhappy together?"

I don't answer. There are invisible hands at my throat. When my fingers finally find a roll of tape in the *Junk Drawer* box, I stand and hurry back through the living room and down the stairs. I keep a firm hold on the railing so I don't trip.

It doesn't matter how fast I move though. Creep always makes it into the room with me – I close the door and he's there. Somehow he always slips through.

He sits in the corner, elbows on knees, humming *Pop Goes the Weasel*.

The picture book opens easily to the pressed pictures. I lay them one-by-one, face down on my quilt top, careful, so they don't rip. Loops of tape are pressed to each corner.

Creep stops humming. "You should put them on the closet doors," he says. "Then you can cover up the mirrors so you don't have to see yourself."

I narrow my eyes at him. The mirrored doors reflect a ghost-version of Eleanor. I stare into my own shadowed eyes, tuck my tangled black hair behind my ears. I attempt a smile, but the reflection only looks scared.

"See?" says Creep.

I dig my sketchbook out of a box and draw a self portrait, pale on white. But I end up crossing out the eyes. When I'm done, I close the sketchbook. I look back into the mirror and put the first horse picture over my own reflection, smoothing it onto the glass.

A bay leaps through a spray of water. Sunlight glances between strands of mane.

Another picture: a white mare and two foals graze in a meadow dotted with lavender flowers. Snow peaked mountains rise in the distance.

Another: rainbow spreading over an ivory beach. A black Arabian gallops across the sand.

A palomino picks its way around desert-red rocks, golden sun falls through pink shreds of cloud.

A multicolored herd thunders across an open plain.

A roan stallion rears on a mountaintop before scattered stars, pinpricks of light in an indigo sky.

A red and white paint trots through bright green grass fetlock high.

Hairy-footed Clydesdales draw an open carriage.

Show horses, mustangs, hunters, even a few unicorns.

Creep's voice comes back to me. It's been a deep buzz in the background while I've wallpapered the mirrored doors with my collection.

He says, "You should ask your mother to have them over for dinner."

I sit back to admire my horse wall. The two sides are interchangeable as I slide the closet doors back and forth.

"Who?" I ask.

"The Taylors," he says. "You need to pay attention."

I make a face. "Why would we want to invite *them* over?"

Creep watches me. "You could see each other."

New start. New me. "No," I tell him.

"You're no fun, Eleanor." He turns in a circle, sniffing the floor. Then he looks up. Creep's eyes shine in his craggy face. "It's Sunday." He points at the window.

My eyes follow his finger and I see that it's lighter outside. Dawn gray colors the dark. I yawn. I climb up onto my bed.

"Are you going to sleep?" he asks.

I curl up on top of the blanket. I turn toward the horse wall, blinking heavy eyelids at the pictures.

Creep crawls underneath the bed. He hums *Amazing Grace.* His voice drifts up through the mattress, like he's trapped under my pillow. In my family, church is compulsory, and since I turned twelve, Sunday is Creep's favorite day. He loves to follow me to Youth Ministry, where they talk about dating, and relationships, and appropriate interactions with the opposite sex. Creep thinks it's hilarious.

I stare at a photo of two snow-white horses walking through a dappled forest glade. Manes are long, falling in foamy waves about their shoulders. Forelocks drift into their eyes. Beds of soft foliage crackle underneath careful hooves. Ferns bend and spring. Dust motes suspend in shafts of sunlight. Birds twitter high above, invisible among twisted branches. Horses whicker. The air smells green.

I close my eyes.

<u>Places</u>

(from the horse wall)
I Would Rather Be:
The Redwood Forest, California
Isle of Skye, Scotland
Venice, Italy
Mount Aspiring, New Zealand
Machu Picchu, Peru
Santorini, Greece

SIX

“**E**leanor.”

I sit up. I rub my eyes. The forest glade is gone. Mom stands next to my bed, wearing a lavender skirt and white top, her brown hair pulled back, her makeup already on. She looks hard at the horse wall. Creep sits next to her.

“Eleanor,” she says again. “What’s this?”

“My collection,” I say.

Mom puts her hands on her hips. “I asked you not to bring any junk.”

“It’s not junk,” I tell her.

Creep looks up at her while she talks. Teeth showing.

“Eleanor, I didn’t want you to bring all these ratty things to our new house. This is supposed to be a new start.” I’m afraid she’ll start pulling the pictures down. “You’re not a little girl anymore. You can’t just slap everything up wherever you want. There has to be some order.”

"It's *my* room," I tell her.

"Cleanliness is next to godliness. You'd rather live in clutter?" she asks. Then she heaves a big sigh, not waiting for me to answer. "I don't have time to argue with you," she says. "Get up and get ready for church."

Creep rocks back and forth on his heels. His face splits into a grin.

"Can't we skip it today?" I ask.

She moves back into the hallway. "Worship every Sunday, Eleanor," she says cheerfully. "You know that."

I fall back onto my pillow. Stare up at the ceiling. A nice smooth ceiling with no popcorn spackle. The fan sits quiet.

Mom wakes up Joshua. She calls him sunshine. She tells him we're going to our new church today.

Joshua groans sleepily. "Aw, Mom. Just this once? It's our new house."

"You know better, Joshua. Sunday is God's day, not ours. Even if we're in a new house."

"Maybe God could let us borrow his day every once in a while?" says Joshua and I smile. I pull my knees up to my chest and listen to his closet doors open. Hangers clink. Mom tells him what to wear.

"Can I bring my Tomcat?" asks Joshua.

"No, you may not."

A muffled thumping. "Can I bring my Blackhawk?"

"No. Don't jump on your bed."

A final thump and then silence. "Aw man, I'm not allowed to do anything!"

"Yes," says Mom. I can tell she's smiling. "Your life is so hard. Now get dressed. We only have an hour and you still have to eat breakfast."

Mom leans into my doorway. "Eleanor. Now."

"Alright, alright," I answer. But she is already halfway up the stairs.

JOSHUA BUILDS A FORT OF CEREAL BOXES AROUND HIS BOWL. HE pushes one aside and peers at me through the crack. "Mom has a goal for us today," he says around a mouthful. Milk dribbles down his chin.

Creep hunkers between our chairs.

Great. "What kind of goal?"

He stirs with his spoon. Four green army men cluster on one side of his bowl. One lifts a gun over his head. Another points his weapon at an unseen enemy.

"She says we should each decide to make one new friend."

I roll my eyes. *Like it's that easy.* I reach out and push the cereal box to close the gap.

"ELEANOR," MOM CALLS. "IT'S TIME TO GO."

I stand in front of my bathroom mirror. I run a brush through my hair.

"Why do you even bother?" asks Creep.

I regard my reflection. A curtain of dark hair around my face. Dark circles under my eyes. Long black skirt and a rumpled black v-neck. Is this the kind of person that makes one new friend?

"Eleanor, we're leaving!"

Creep follows me up the stairs. He sings *Jesus Loves Me* with his own words in place of the lyrics. His voice grates.

"Jesus hates me, this is true
When God made me, He said, 'Ew.'"

Mom waits at the door.

"Oh, Eleanor," she says. "Do you always have to wear black?"

I shrug.

Creep stands behind me. He sings.

"In heaven I do not belong

Jesus says I'm sick and wrong"

I force down a laugh.

Mom frowns. "I don't know how you expect to make any friends when you're not presentable."

I don't expect to make friends.

"Sorry," I say.

She looks down at my feet. "At least the black flats are… tasteful."

I look down at my tasteful feet.

She sighs. "Just get in the car."

I follow her to the driveway. Creep scrambles into the back when I hold the door open for Joshua.

"Come on," I call. "Time to go."

Joshua runs over. "Is Dad coming?" he asks.

Mom lowers her brow. "No."

"Why not?"

"He has a migraine."

"Oh," says Joshua.

We both know what that means. Dark room. Cool washcloth. Absolutely no noise.

Creep sings again as we drive out to the main road.

"I am weak and I am poor

but Jesus hates me all the more

Doesn't care what I go through

I'm just gum upon his shoe"

<u>My goals:</u>

Don't get in trouble
Don't draw attention
Be normal
~~One new friend~~ (-------Mom's goal

SEVEN

It takes twenty minutes to get to Shepherd's Fold, another chapter of the church we went to in our old neighborhood. Mom tells us that it's going to be just the same as our old church, so we shouldn't worry. I'm worried.

It's already over 100 degrees. Creep does somersaults in the back of the station wagon. Then he leans his forearms over the seat back, pointed fingers dangling next to my shoulder, and hisses in my ear.

We pull into a parking lot with family vehicles arrayed in lines. It's mostly glittering minivans. As Mom gathers her purse and books, Joshua and I get out and stand on the blacktop. Heat rises. I lift my hair to fan the back of my neck.

Shepherd's Fold is a red brick rectangle with a roof that slopes long on one side. There is a sign that says: *Visitors Welcome*. Growing out of the ground in front of the church, significantly taller than the roof, a pointed metallic cross stabs into the air.

I stand in between Creep and Joshua. We all stare at the cross. I imagine Creep's body impaled on it, dangling like a bony flag.

Creep squints up, clicks his teeth together. "Nice," he says.

"Yeah," I agree, watching the Creep flag shudder in the breeze.

Mom comes up alongside. She straightens her skirt. "Alright," she says in a sing-song. "Sunday faces." She turns to look at us.

We both smile at her. Creep puts his fingers in his cheeks to stretch his lips out in an ugly grimace.

"Eleanor," she says. "Don't slouch."

She turns and we follow her across the parking lot. Joshua sticks out his tongue at me. I stick out my tongue back. He grins.

An icebox breeze greets us at the open door. Gray carpet, wood paneling, blue flowered armchairs under a large painting of Jesus sitting on a rock with multiracial children gathered. Creep jumps into one of the chairs and does a headstand. His scrawny legs beat the air.

Mom greets a few adults standing just inside. I watch Creep wipe something from his nose on the arm of the chair.

Mom waves us forward. "I'm Jill Moreno. This is my son Joshua and my daughter Eleanor."

"Oh, you're the new family!" says the man Mom is talking to. I wonder what he knows about us. He holds out his hand to Joshua and me. "Nice to meet you."

Joshua puts his hand out and they shake. I put my hands behind my back and show the man my Sunday face.

Mom ignores me. "We better find a seat," she says. The man gestures us into the sanctuary. Joshua waves at him as we walk past.

The sanctuary is a long room with a tall ceiling. Rows of benches. The low rumble of a waiting crowd to the soundtrack of church music. The wall at the far end is stacked with vertical organ pipes. The room is all flowers and streaming light from long windows and globe lamps glowing near the ceiling.

Mom chooses a bench near the back on the right. I wonder if *she* has a goal for today.

I sit by the wall, Joshua sits closer to Mom, and Creep emerges from under the bench to pull himself up next to me.

"What do you think the sermon will be?" he asks me.

I don't answer.

The front wall above the pipe alcove has a painting of Jesus falling across a tree limb. Languishing in the Garden of Gethsemane. A white-robed angel with great drooping wings kneels beside Jesus, a look of sympathy on his face. The angel glows. His hands rest on Jesus' contorted face, as if to comfort him. When I was little I used to wonder why Jesus got an angel and I got Creep.

I don't wonder anymore.

The pastor stands up at the podium. He wears a charcoal gray jacket and wire-rimmed glasses. He taps the microphone. He looks too young to be a pastor. More like he's going to start singing a Beatles cover at an open-mic night than talk to us about God. I imagine him breaking into a rendition of *Yellow Submarine*. I laugh under my breath.

Mom flicks her eyes toward me and then back up to the pastor.

"Before we begin," he is saying, "I want to welcome a new family to our flock."

He says our names, including Dad's, and gestures for us to stand up and all the heads in the room turn. Mom stands and pulls Joshua up with her. She smiles out at the room.

I would rather sink down than stand up.

My legs straighten as I rise, scanning the blur of faces and then dropping my eyes to the floor. Whispers, people wondering where Dad is. A million pairs of eyes bore into me and suddenly I am transparent, like they're looking in through my bedroom window.

The pastor says into the microphone, "Now, we understand that Brother Mike is ill today. We will keep him in our prayers, won't we?"

A murmur from the congregation. I sit down.

"Those of us in the congregation who wish to welcome the Morenos, please share," says the pastor.

As one, the reply shoves toward us through the air, spoken from the congregation like a giant door drifting shut: "Welcome."

"Thanks," says Joshua back. His small voice echoes. Ripples of laughter among the crowd. The pastor smiles.

Then the pastor says, "We will begin with *Come Thou Fount*, after which an invocation will be offered."

The organ begins to thrum.

"I love hymns," Creep says. "They all sound like dirges."

He sits on his haunches between me and Joshua.

Mom passes a hymnal down to me. I turn to the right page and mouth the words. Creep sings in his loudest voice, a nails-on-chalkboard screech. The words are his own again.

"Come thou source of every sadness
Crush my heart between Thy hands"

I smile. Creep's twisted church songs always make me laugh.

"Streams of cruelty, sowing madness
Never ceasing Thy demands"

I straighten my face when I feel Mom's eyes on me.

Creep continues.

"Teach me some new way to hate myself
Some new way I'm incomplete
Now I know, no matter how I try
I will never be redeemed"

Creep stands on the bench. He holds out the last note along with the organ, putting one hand on his chest and lifting the other above his head, like an opera singer.

I try to suppress it, but I can't help myself. A laugh escapes just as the music ends, echoing in the quick silence after the organ notes fall back down to earth.

As Creep bows, heads turn toward our bench again. Mom sighs. We are bathed in stares. Creep snickers and then climbs over me to sit on my other side, near the wall. A head four benches in front turns to look. My cheeks are hot.

I meet brown eyes and long eyelashes through a feathering of black bangs. Eyebrows rise. I can't see the eyebrows, but I know because the eyes get taller. The girl, maybe my age, is wearing red lipstick. She smiles a little.

Joshua elbows me. He sees her. He waves. Mom reaches over and puts his hand down. The head turns back around.

The pastor stands up at the microphone again. "We invite members of the congregation to testify at this time. Let it be known that we encourage new members and visitors to testify as well. We like to hear from those we haven't before."

A groan gets caught inside my throat.

Creep claps his hand bones. "I love witness meeting."

My fingers pluck at the weave of my skirt while person after person gets up to testify. Tears. Wobbly voices. The word *Jesus* said over and over until it stops sounding like a word.

Creep keeps up a running commentary. I imagine that I'm circling the yellow light-fixture globe above me, and I'm tiny, like a planetary satellite, but the microphone voices swirl together on the ceiling, pushing me out of the way. A headache blooms above my eyebrows.

Jesus lives. Jesus saved me. Praise Jesus. I close my eyes. *Praise Jesus praise JesuspraiseJesus.*

"Good morning." Mom's voice, magnified into the microphone.

I open my eyes to see Mom standing at the podium. She squares her shoulders, smiling. From this far away, I can see how pretty she is when her eyes aren't colored with disapproval. I like it.

She introduces herself while Joshua puts one hand in his pocket and pulls out an action figure. He walks the action figure along the bench.

The girl four rows in front turns around again to look at me. We share a glance.

Mom is talking about us. "...Eleanor turned fifteen this spring and Joshua is eight. We look forward to making friends here at Shepherd's Fold."

I steal a look at the girl. Still watching. Mom is talking about Jesus.

The action figure considers the barrier that is my leg. He raises one hand to shield his plastic eyes. I wonder how tall it looks to him. Mom continues. "Jesus loves us," she says. "He will take our yoke upon Him if we ask. If we give Him everything. If we pray, He will take our burdens. He will make our problems disappear."

"Hallelujah. Praise Jesus," says Creep. His onyx black eyes roll in their sockets. He turns to me. "Have you tried that?" His voice itches in my ear.

The action figure disappears into Joshua's pocket as Mom walks back down the aisle toward us.

Dear Jesus,
Please make my problems disappear.
Take my yoke upon you or whatever.
Amen.

EIGHT

We stand as people exit the sanctuary. Mom moves into the aisle, talking to two other women about Bible study.

Joshua kneels on the upholstery, walks his action figure along the top of the bench back. A boy with red hair about Joshua's size comes out of the crowd.

"Hey," says the boy. He grabs the bench near the action figure and leans back, extending his arms. "I'm Sam. I have that guy, but his legs came off."

Joshua puts the action figure in his pocket again and sticks out his hand to the new boy, grown-up like.

"I'm Joshua," he says.

Sam shakes hands. "You're in my class. I'll show you where it is."

Joshua reaches to pull on Mom's sleeve. "Hey Mom, I'm gonna go with this kid Sam to Sunday School, 'kay?"

Mom looks over, distracted. "Okay. Find Eleanor when it's over and meet me out at the car at noon."

Joshua and Sam skip through the crowd and out the sanctuary doors.

One new friend.

"See how easy it is?" asks Creep.

I watch as he balances on the back of the bench. He leapfrogs from bench to bench that way. All the way to the front of the sanctuary. Then he climbs up to the podium and pantomimes giving a speech. He raises both arms, clasps black fingers, wipes his eyes.

The headache presses like a bag of rocks. I rub my right temple. My mouth is dry, watching him, wondering what he might say with the microphone on. Would he talk about me?

He is balancing his way back when I hear: "Hi."

I turn to see the girl from before, short and thick with a mass of wavy black hair. Her mouth is a sculpture in red, carved out of clear brown skin. She wears a black, scoop-neck dress that barely reaches her dimpled knees and ties in the back, a choker with a silver cross, like a girl in a vampire movie. Boots, lace up, shiny black. She's wearing fishnet stockings.

I remind myself that I'm supposed to be a new me. "Hi," I say.

She holds out her hand to shake. "I'm Mia."

I leave my hands at my sides. Creep drops onto the bench next to me. Wide grin.

Mia raises her eyebrows and then lets her hand fall back. "You're right," she says. "Shaking hands is so Gen-X." My eyes trace the way her dress clings to rounded lines. Her hair spills over her chest.

"I'm Eleanor," I say.

She smiles straight white teeth. "Yeah, I caught that."

I don't know what to say, so I don't say anything.

She shoves a thumb in the direction of the doors. "I'm fifteen too. You're in my class. Wanna walk together?"

"Okay."

"Cool," she says.

I move past Mom. Creep hops to the floor behind me.

"Going to Sunday School," I tell her. I catch Mia watching me roll my eyes as I turn away from Mom.

I follow her out the doors and into the foyer. She leads me down another hallway bustling with members of Shepherd's Fold. Creep follows us on all fours.

Walls with pictures of Jesus. Open doorways. Kids settle into chairs.

"So what were you laughing about?" asks Mia. I look sideways at her. "In church," she says.

"Better not tell her," says Creep from the floor. "You know what will happen." He lopes next to us.

I've lied for so long that it's easy. "My little brother."

She shakes her hair out of her eyes. "I always wanted a sibling," she says. "It's just me. It would be nice to have them concentrate on someone else for a change."

"I like it," I say. "I mean, I like having a little brother."

"Our class is up here." She points. She stops before a door on the right.

I stand behind her. Creep continues down the hall, sniffing at the carpet. Mia waves me forward. There are six other kids in the room: two girls, four boys, with their chairs forming a semicircle facing a chalkboard. There is a chair at the front near a table, and another at the end of the row by us.

Mia begins a whispered orientation and I realize we aren't going in just yet.

"Those two are sisters. Obviously." Honey-blonde identical girls with their heads together, leather-bound Bibles on their laps. "Hope and Grace. They go to private school."

"Those three are The A-Team." Two boys lean in to hear what the other is saying. Then they all laugh and look at the twins. Mia continues. "There's no point learning their names. They operate as a single unit of assholery, hence their title."

"And that's Virgil."

The last boy occupies the chair at the other end of the row, looking out the window. The copper of his hair is shot through with dusty highlights.

"He's cool. We're friends," says Mia. "He's mostly quiet around new people. But he's really smart." She shrugs. "Mostly he just talks about his horses."

I swallow. "He has horses?"

"Yeah," she says. "Four. He's obsessed."

"Girls," says a voice behind us.

I jump and bump into Mia's back. We both turn around.

"Hi, Brother Chad," says Mia.

Brother Chad is a blond pinstripe suit on stilts. His eyes squint as he smiles, like a really happy anime character. He has a stack of books under one arm.

"Who's this?" asks Brother Chad, like he wasn't in the sanctuary ten minutes ago.

Mia gestures to me. "This is Eleanor."

"Welcome, Eleanor," he says. "Where's your Bible, Mia?"

Mia takes on a forlorn expression. "Oh, Brother Chad, I forgot it. I left it next to my pillow. You know I read myself to sleep every night."

"It's alright," says Brother Chad. "We are only perfect in the Lord."

He steps around us to the door. Mia rolls her eyes at me.

"Coming?" he says.

We follow Brother Chad into the room.

"Hey," says one of The A-Team. "It's the dwarf."

"Bruh," says another, elbowing the first. "You can't say 'dwarf.' It's—," he does air quotes, "— little person." They all snicker.

"Who's your girlfriend, Mia?" another one says.

"Settle down boys," says Brother Chad. He puts his stack of books on the table. "This is Eleanor."

I stand next to Mia by the doorway. Everyone looks at me.

"Why don't you girls sit down?" asks Brother Chad. Then he says, "Oh silly me. There's only one chair left. Here, use mine. I'll stand."

He picks up his chair and puts it at the other end of the row, so that there's an empty one on both ends. So I'll either have to sit next to The A-Team, or Virgil. Mia lets me pick.

I choose the chair by the window, with Virgil on my right. I slink through everyone's stares to be able to sit. Mia plonks down at the opposite end. We share a glance before I see Creep edge his way into the room.

He crosses to my side of the semicircle and crouches next to my chair. I ignore him as Brother Chad writes *CHASTITY* on the chalkboard.

"Whew," sighs Creep. "Glad I didn't miss *this*."

Brother Chad turns back to the class. "Can anyone tell me what this word means?"

"Prude," says one of The A-Team. They all laugh along with Creep.

Brother Chad tells us to open our Bibles. Everyone begins shuffling. The headache pierces toward the back of my head. Brother Chad is saying something about where to find First Thessalonians. The shuffling quiets. Outside the window a green lawn lies wide under a high pinprick of white sun.

"I'll read," says Brother Chad. "Starting in verse three: For this is the will of God..."

I imagine a horse cropping grass outside the window. Forelock falls into liquid eyes. The soft crunch of plants being pulled up by their roots.

"...even your sanctification, that ye should abstain from fornication...."

A finger taps my arm. Goosebumps thrum. I pull away from Virgil who holds his open Bible out for me to look at.

"Don't," I whisper.

Surprise shows in his green eyes. "What?" he says.

"Please, don't touch me." It comes out loud. Louder than I meant it to.

Brother Chad stops reading. "Eleanor?" he says. "Everything okay?"

I nod. I can feel myself turning red. I fold my arms and cave into my chair. "Fine."

New me. I sigh. Sweat trickles between my shoulder blades.

"Okay," says Brother Chad.

While Brother Chad is writing the words *sanctification*, *abstain*, and *fornication* on the board, one of The A-Team whispers something about the *"new girl."*

Virgil scoots back. His stomach creases where his Bible presses in. "Sorry," he whispers, almost too quiet to hear.

Brother Chad is drawing the group into a discussion. The voices are all jumbling together. I can't pick out anything specific except for the words *sex* and *purity*, over and over. My face is getting hotter and hotter until it feels like it's going to slide off my skull and puddle in my lap.

Then Virgil says next to me, "God wants us to remain pure by not having sex outside of marriage."

I'm sure everyone is looking at me. I want to run. I look out the window instead, trying not to cry. Far off across the parking lot, beyond the lawn, I think I can see heat rising in waves from the blacktop. I imagine pressing Creep down onto the ground. His skin cooks – bubbles against the stove of asphalt. Screams rip from his scrawny throat. He melts under my hands.

Brother Chad is saying, ". . . and for our purposes, sex means any intimate or sexual contact. That's chastity: abstinence from sexual behaviors outside of the bonds of marriage. Another word for purity is clean. So why does God want us to remain chaste or clean?"

No one answers.

"Who knows where we can find the answer?"

Mia says, her voice flat, her face expressionless: "The Bible."

Brother Chad squints in her direction. "Very good, Mia. It says in Ephesians that no unclean person deserves the kingdom of God."

No unclean thing.

"Too bad for you," says Creep.

In my head he is still screaming. But now the screams sound kind of like me.

<u>Places I Would Rather Be Than Youth Ministry:</u>

Algebra class
The dentist
The Mariana Trench
The mouth of an active volcano
The Spanish Inquisition

NINE

"What a waste of time," says Mia.

We walk to Youth Ministry. Mia said it's everyone ages twelve to eighteen. Same as Lamb of God.

"You don't believe in chastity?"

"No. I'm sex positive," says Mia. "But that's beside the point. Boys are disgusting."

I want to ask her what she means by sex positive.

She lifts her chin at a group of older boys sauntering ahead of us in the hall. The way she curls her lip makes me laugh, like she smells something bad.

They hold Youth Ministry in a room about half the size of the sanctuary. We sit second row from the back in chairs facing a giant sign with a heart and the words *Chastity = Love*.

"This day just gets better and better," says Creep. He climbs up into an empty chair beside me. I want to fold the chair up with him in it, like a mouse trap snapping shut.

I see Virgil sitting on the other side of the room next to the wall. I wonder why we aren't sitting with him if he and Mia are friends. Mia sees me looking at him.

"We *would* sit with him," Mia explains, like she knows what I was thinking, "but I've been banned." The rest is accompanied by ten kinds of eye rolls. "Brother Chad says Virgil needs *space* on Sunday to concentrate on his *spiritual growth*. Apparently my habit for religious commentary is disruptive?"

I watch the back of Virgil's head. Mom talks about *my* need for spiritual growth too. I wonder what else we have in common. I wonder what kinds of horses he has.

The noise is more like lunch in the school cafeteria than a meeting at church. A woman announces her excitement in sharing the message: Chastity equals love. She tells us how much it means to her that we're all saving ourselves for Jesus. She asks if everyone has gotten a purity promise ring. Murmurs rise.

"Are you going to get a ring?" Mia asks me.

I shake my head. I never got one at Lamb of God. They offered them, but as Creep said then, *What's the point?*

The woman is talking again. About choosing to wait until you find *the one*. About how happy she is that she saved herself for her *dear* husband. About all the diseases we *will* get if we have sex before marriage. About how *proud* Jesus is of us, his army of chaste youth.

Praise Jesus.

"Hey." Whispered from the row behind us. "Hey, Eleanor."

"Someone wants you," says Creep.

I don't turn around. I put my head down, trying to sink into the collar of my shirt.

"Don't listen to them," whispers Mia.

My headache starts to throb. I sit on my hands.

"Hey," Something pokes me in the lower back, through the space between the seat of the chair and the backrest. I stiffen.

Mia turns. Her whisper scathes. "Cut it out, assholes. She doesn't like to be touched."

Snickers. "Freak."

The A-Team.

I want to get up and walk out, but I can't move. My legs are frozen. Heart hammers. The woman's voice fades. The room disappears.

Two hands on either side of the back of my chair and a voice in my ear as The A-Team boy leans forward.

"Hey, Eleanor," he says, low. I can feel the air from his mouth. It moves my hair. "I'm so glad you moved to Shepherd's Fold. I'm really looking forward to getting to know you… biblically."

I squeeze my eyes shut. My back tightens.

"Levi, you're such a primate," Mia begins, not in a whisper, her voice echoing.

But we don't hear the rest because I stand up suddenly and whirl around. The A-Team boy is so surprised that his chair falls back with a clatter. He looks up at me from the floor. Instead of The A-Team, I see Ian. My fists are clenched.

No unclean thing.

His face blurs and I don't want to cry in front of everyone, so I walk away. Out the doors. Down the hall. Face burns. The hallway becomes a dark tunnel closing in.

"Eleanor."

It's Mia.

"Eleanor!" she whisper-shouts. She tries to grab one arm.

I turn fast. "Don't."

She stops. "Sorry."

It seems like she's going to say something. Instead she says, "Come on."

She pushes open a door that swings into the women's restroom. Creep slips in behind me. We go in through a tiled room – stalls and sinks. Then Mia pushes open a second door at the end of the bathroom and we pass into a smaller darker room. Three rocking armchairs huddle. A long counter with a sink.

Mia sits in one of the chairs. She gestures that I should too. Light fades upward from a utility nightlight in the corner. I knit my fingers. I glance at Mia. Looks like it's time for the talk, but I didn't think it would happen this soon.

Mia says. "It's a room for breastfeeding mothers. So the pure eyes of men won't be offended by evil boobs. But people with babies usually go home before this time."

I sit down in one of the chairs. Cushioned blue upholstery that rocks a little.

Creep takes the third one. He looks back and forth between us.

Silence widens.

Mia's voice starts the long walk to my chair. "So, what happened? I mean, I know The A-Team is, well, you know... I call them The A-Team for a reason."

I look at my hands.

She tries again. "I know they're Neanderthals. No one ever stops them either. This church is such a circle jerk." She pauses. "They're old-school bullies. Like, name calling and pulling hair and adults telling you 'He's doing it because he *likes* you.' But they're actually harmless."

"Yeah, Eleanor. What's the big deal?" Creep sneers.

My hands look tiny, far away.

"Are you okay?" asks Mia.

Creep picks at his teeth with a slatey fingernail. "You better answer her. She's going to start thinking you're crazy."

I want to scream at Creep to shut up. Instead I swallow the rock in my throat and say: "I'm fine. I mean, why wouldn't I be fine? I'm at church. Praise Jesus."

Mia shrugs. Then she leans forward, elbows on knees. Her brown eyes look black in the dim light. "You just look pretty freaked out."

Creep nods.

"I'm fine," I say again. I rub my arms to smooth down the goosebumps. Deep breaths. The headache sits on my eyelids.

Mia rocks back. Her chair squeaks. At first I count the seconds before she answers, but after a while I lose track. Her gaze gathers on me. Eyes softer in the dim light.

"Eleanor," says Creep in a nightmare Mia-voice. "You're just too weird. At first I thought we could be friends, but whoa."

Mia finally blinks. She swipes her fingers through her bangs. "Okay, so you're fine. It just seemed like there was something going on that was more than just The A-Team."

She doesn't call me names or say there's something wrong with me. Hope sprouts. *Maybe she'll stay.*

Creep's eyes roll. Dry snarls rattle behind his teeth.

Mia sighs. "Look, Eleanor. I think you're cool." She smiles. "You came dressed all in black. I'm the only one who does that around here without a funeral. You laughed in witness meeting and you knocked Levi on his back. Everyone else might think that's fucked up, but as far as I can tell, we might have been separated at birth."

I imagine me and Mia standing side by side: breadstick straight and toasted marshmallow round.

A smile tries to crawl across my face.

"I'm just trying to get through the day," I say.

Mia laughs. "Aren't we all, *Sister* Eleanor?"

WE NEVER GO BACK TO YOUTH MINISTRY. INSTEAD WE SIT IN the breastfeeding room and talk about our favorite sci-fi shows. Mia's a Trekkie, and I'm not sure how I feel about that. But she doesn't bring up what happened with The A-Team again, and she doesn't ask me any difficult questions.

When meetings are adjourned, she says. "New kids usually meet back up with their siblings at the colonizer Jesus painting." She leads me back to the sanctuary doors, looking around corners for Levi and signaling the all clear.

Before we part ways in the foyer, Mia says, "We should hang out".

I nod. "Maybe you could come over sometime this week."

"What's your Snap?" she says, pulling out her phone, medium-sized with a black sparkly cover that says *That B!tch* in gold letters.

"I don't have Snap," I say. She looks at me for a moment.

"Okay. What's your Insta?"

"I don't have Insta," I said. "I don't have a phone."

She looks at me again, longer this time. She looks around and then back at me. "Okaaaay," she says when I don't offer an explanation. "You have a home phone right? Like a... landline?" I nod.

She grabs a church program from the table by the sanctuary doors, along with a pen from a charity sign-up sheet.

"Here," she says, scribbling. "I'll write down my email address and my number. Write or call me whenever."

I take the sheet from her. "Sorry."

She shrugs. "That's okay. Just email me or call me from home."

I try an explanation. "My mom's kind of . . . traditional. She thinks kids shouldn't have phones until they're older. We do have a family computer though."

She hands me the paper. "I'd die without my phone. Call me whenever, or email me? And I'll come over. See ya."

She bounces away.

One new friend.

"Who's that?" asks Joshua as we walk down the blinding sidewalk toward the car.

"Mom's goal," I tell him.

<u>Things I like about Mia:</u>

She waits for me to say something.
She wears all black.
She said "asshole" and "fuck" in church.
We're friends?

TEN

T hunder mutters in the distance. Faraway flashes of light try to part my newly hung curtains. Summer rains approach.

A crack of yellow from the bathroom door trembles across my ceiling.

Flat on my bed, I stare up at the ceiling fan. It's after eleven and my eyes feel like glue.

Don't fall asleep.

From under the bed, Creep hums. His voice is a heavy sheet pulling me into the mattress, so I concentrate on the fan. It whirls a clean down-draft of air. I try to follow the blades with my eyes, to freeze them for a moment, but I can't quite keep up.

Spin spin spin – freeze. Spin spin spin – freeze.

The fan's breath sits light on my lashes. I close my eyes, start to drift, sink into Creep's voice, slide under the slow-moving oil sound.

Don't fall asleep. No dreams. No dreams, I think.

Again a rumor of thunder.

Tap. Tap tap tap.

I drag myself out from Creep's humming web.

The noise again. I open my eyes, blinded by a photo flash of lightning against the walls.

Tap.

The door. I have a sudden thrill of anxiety.

He's here. He's coming in. I have to remind myself, *He's not here. It's just Josh.*

I sit up. Creep is quiet. Thunder growls.

My feet cross the carpet and I turn the doorknob. Through the open door gap I see Joshua. He has a flashlight pointed at the floor, a book under his arm and the other hand behind his back. He smiles.

I open the door wider and he comes into my room. The hand behind his back crinkles.

"Hi," he says in a whisper.

"Hi," I say. I rub my eyes and shut the door. "What are you doing awake?"

"I was reading," he says. He drops the book and sits down on the edge of my bed, the flashlight between his knees. "Plus, the thunder is getting louder."

I yawn.

"And," he says, "I have something to show you."

His dimples make me smile back. He pulls out the hand from behind his back and shines the flashlight on it. I laugh when I see what's clenched in his fingers: a ruby red, one-pound bag of Skittles.

I sit next to him on the bed with one leg folded under. "Where'd you get that?"

He holds it out for me. It's heavy.

"I won it in Children's Ministry today."

"How?" I ask.

His teeth reflect the flashlight. "I answered a question nobody else knew."

"What was the question?"

Joshua takes a deep breath, pushing out his chest. He impersonates the children's minister in a scholarly voice. "Who tried to burn Shadrach, Meshach, and Abednego in the fiery furnace?"

Thunder rattles the window.

"What's the answer?" I say.

"C'mon, Eleanor," he says. "You don't know? It's Nebuchadnezzar."

"How did you know that?"

"I remember his name because it was the name of Morpheus' ship in *The Matrix*."

Joshua scoots back on the bed and crosses his legs. "Nebuchadnezzar also went crazy for seven years and lived like a dog in the desert." He holds the flashlight under his chin, lolls out his tongue and rolls his eyes, creating a grotesquely panting portrait in black and white.

I laugh and push his shoulder. He falls over onto the bed. Another smattering of thunder as rain begins to plunk on the deck.

"So, you wanna?" he says, sitting up.

"Wanna what?"

"Build a fort." His tone says, *Duh*.

I built the first thunder fort when Joshua was a baby, awake and screaming during a heavy nighttime storm. I pulled a blanket across the walls of his crib and read books to him until the storm passed. We've done it for every nighttime storm since. The last thunder fort was almost a year ago, since storms like that only happen in summer.

Joshua sits on the floor, straining with both arms to open the Skittles bag as I pull all of the bedding off the mattress.

The Skittles bag suddenly surrenders and Joshua is showered in an explosion of multicolored candy pieces. We stifle a laugh while he tries to put handfuls of candy back in the torn bag.

He helps me push the mattress from the foot of the bed up against the wall where the pillows usually go, forming a triangular cavern underneath. We push the pillows and blankets into the space to soften the box spring. Then I scoop Skittles into the hammock made when Joshua pulls out the front of his oversized t-shirt. He gathers the fabric up in his hand, the pound of Skittles hangs like a bag of marbles below his fist.

We climb into the fort as a brilliant streak of lightning brightens my room. Thunder hammers at the window.

We prop the flashlight in a wrinkle of bedspread.

"What book did you bring?" I ask him. He trickles a handful of Skittles into my palm and then holds up the gray-covered volume.

"*The Children's Encyclopedia of Many Lands*," he reads.

We look at each other. I almost choke. "Those books are from the 50s."

"So?" he says. "We haven't read this one yet."

A peal of thunder makes us jump.

He thumbs through the book while we chew. He reads about tribal rituals in Kenya, political parades in Ireland, and the one-child policy in China. When the thunder gets too loud to hear his voice, we invent things to do with the Skittles.

We toss candy in the air and try to catch it between our teeth, bounce pieces off of the mattress ceiling, and see how many we can fit in our mouths. I give up at thirteen. I just can't fit any more in without feeling like I'm going to throw up. I chew as Joshua gets to twenty-seven and starts to giggle. He can't close his lips. I laugh at the colored drool sliding down his chin. He tries to chew them, but he can't get his teeth to clamp down. Eventually he runs to the bathroom, and I watch him spit the crunchy wad of sugared cement into the toilet.

We gasp for breath, the laughter convulsing in our stomachs. Stumbling back to the fort, I have to wipe tears away. By the time we stop laughing, the storm has passed. Rain patters on the deck, barely audible. My abdomen aches. The candy sits like a rock in my belly.

I hold the flashlight up for Joshua to practice shadow puppets on the wall. We lie side by side in the thunder fort.

"My stomach hurts," says Joshua. His fingers form a crude dog shadow.

"Yeah," I agree.

"I heard you knocked down a boy in church."

I raise my eyebrows. "Where'd you hear that?" I ask him.

"In the hall after church. Two boys were talking about it."

"Hmm," I say.

"So did you?"

"No," I say. "His chair fell backward and I just got up to see what happened."

Creep would be proud, I think. *Lie.*

"Oh," says Joshua. He makes a long-necked bird shadow. "Hey, Eleanor?"

"Yeah?" I watch the bird open and shut its beak.

"What are you scared of?"

I watch the shadow bird grow several smaller heads and writhe toward the mattress ceiling.

"I dunno," I say. "What are *you* scared of?"

He shrugs, his shoulder skinny next to mine.

"What's that supposed to be?" I ask. The shadow blob undulates.

"An alien," he says. We both laugh.

The alien oozes upward. I watch the finger tentacles.

"Sharks," I say.

"What?"

"I'm scared of sharks."

He makes a big mouth with both hands. Blunted fingertip teeth. It opens and shuts, a blind shadow predator.

"What about you?" I ask.

He drops his hands. "Um, Chihuahuas."

I press my lips together to keep from smiling. "Like.. tiny dogs."

"Yeah," he says. "Chihuahuas."

"Huh," I say. Because if I don't make some kind of noise, I think the laughter will start again.

"Remember that old Chihuahua that Aunt Julia used to have?"

"Yeah," I say. Speedy, the fat, white Chihuahua with the black spot over one eye that sat on Aunt Julia's lap. The dog bared its yellow teeth, snarled and snapped. It barked savagely whenever one of us moved during our visits.

"I hated that dog," says Joshua. I nod. The shadow turns into a dog's head in profile. It sticks out its tongue, panting. "Dad said we could get a dog," he says.

"Have you asked him about it?" I ask.

He shakes his head. "We should get a big giant dog."

"The opposite of a Chihuahua," I say. He laughs. "A Great Dane," I say.

"And we could name him…" Joshua pauses.

"Nebuchadnezzar," I say.

He rolls his eyes. "No, Eleanor. You can't name dogs after the Bible. You have to name them after cool things, like video games. Or shows." He takes a deep breath and then yawns.

"Tired?" I ask.

"Yeah," he says. "I'm gonna go to bed." He sits up and scoots out of the opening. I follow him.

He stretches his arms above his head. "Thanks for the fort." He leans in and gives me a hug.

"You okay?" I ask him.

He nods. "Thanks, Eleanor," he says.

We tell each other goodnight. He slips out into the hall with the flashlight and *The Children's Encyclopedia of Many Lands.*

After he's gone, the room seems empty. I wonder where Creep is. I crawl back into the fort and he's there, a denser shadow in the dark.

"Have fun?" he asks.

I waggle my hand at him to make him move. "Go away."

I lie down on my side. Blankets adjust to form a cocoon of warmth. I can smell Joshua on my pillow. It reminds me of his curly baby head.

"Why didn't you answer him?" asks Creep.

I yawn. "Answer what?"

"What you're scared of." He squats near my head in the opening.

"I did," I tell him.

"Sharks?" Creep says. "That's it?"

Creep sounds grumpy. He melts back into the shadows, back under the bed. Humming.

I wish Joshua would have stayed in here to sleep. I sit up to switch on my bedside lamp and then curl into the bedspread nest. The lamp turns the thunder fort into a warm den of light. Every once in a while, I can still hear the echo of thunder, very far away.

It sounds like the echo of a herd, galloping. I yawn again.

One eye is buried in a cool pillow, so the other eye traces the blanket folds by my hand. The bunched fabric becomes hills and wrinkles of land, covered in wind-bent grass. A high sun dives through scudding clouds. Winds carry the smell of pollen and rain, and the faint thunder of hooves sounds across distant valleys.

I can't see the horses, but I can hear them.

Over Creep's humming, I can barely hear them.

<u>Fear #1: Sharks</u>

They push themselves through the water in gray
sandpaper skins full of teeth and muscle.
They are built to hunt. But you're not built to escape.
Sharks can smell blood in the water. If you're hurt,
they'll find you.
They'll find you and they'll tear you apart.
Down in the water where you can't even scream.
And then they'll eat you.
Until there's nothing left but a cloud of blood
dissolving under the waves.

The Angel Room

I sit at the playground, sand piled around me. Baby Joshua naps in his crib at home. The sun beats down from a white ceiling sky and the horizon is a smudge of black far away. I can barely see it if I squint. With a kitchen spoon I dig a hole down to layers cool and dark. Creep lies propped on his black elbows. He looks into the hole with his flat feet stretched out behind.

"What are you doing?" he asks.

I tell Creep that I like to dig deep enough to poke the black plastic that covers the hard part of the ground.

"What's down there?" he asks.

I don't answer. The playground is deserted. I look at the swings, with the tracks where kids drag their feet to stop. I look at the upended teeter-totter. I wish Baby Joshua was old enough to play with me. I get tired having only Creep to talk to.

Cloud shadows pass over us.

Creep sticks his wrinkled face down in the hole. "What are you looking for?" he asks. I can see the top of his bald head.

"Treasures," I tell him.

"What kind of treasures?" asks Creep.

The spoon clinks against something in the hole. I put my hand in and feel a cold disc about the size of a nickel. My fingers close around it.

I pull it up into the light. A crust of sandy mud comes clean as I rub the coin. I can tell it's a coin now. It flashes in the sunlight, gold.

"Like this," I say to Creep.

Creep sits up on his haunches. His long toes curl over the edge of the hole.

"What is it?" he asks.

I hold the gold coin in the shadow of my bent head. It has a picture of a train engine on one side. I turn it over to see the word: Token.

"Money," I say. "From Token."

"What's Token?"

Excitement pushes into my throat. "There's a picture of a train on it." I show him. "I bet there's a place where I could give this coin and take a train to Token."

Another shadow hides us from the sun for a moment. Creep sticks his finger in his ear, one eye squinted shut. "What's Token?" he says again.

A strong breeze picks up sand.

I close my eyes and hold the coin tight in my fist. "I think Token is a place where no one knows who I am. No one knows my name, so I don't have to pretend to be the girl with that name. I don't have to be a girl at all. I can just be . . . whoever."

Creep laughs. "That's dumb!"

Ignoring him, I put the coin in the pocket of my white dress. I jam the spoon into the sand. "I'm going to find another one, so I can take Joshua."

"You can't go somewhere no one knows your name because I'll be there and I know your name." Creep pulls his finger out of his ear and looks at it.

I want to tell Creep, **I really hate you**. But I don't. Instead I turn my head to avoid another wave of sand that dashes across the surface of the playground.

"What's that?" says Creep.

When I look at him, he is skeleton-in-skin, standing. His hand is held up to shield his eyes from the glare. He blinks fast at the horizon. I turn to look too.

The dark smudge on the horizon has become a giant hulk of darkness. Clouds boil toward us, their undersides like thick green soup. The sun is covered in a brown haze. The wind begins to howl. I put my hands up to my ears to block out the sound. Past the edge of the apartment complex I see a black finger of whirling smoke thrust downward from the cloud bank.

"What is that?" asks Creep.

"Tornado!" I yell. I stumble up from the hole. The sand catches at my shoes and I feel like I'm moving through water. I run across the crumbling asphalt toward my apartment building. I have to get home. Mom will know what to do. Creep lopes behind me on all fours.

I am deafened by the noise. I open my mouth to yell, to ask Creep how close it is, but the noise covers everything. My heart flaps as I pass neighbor doors. I find mine, run through the front door, down the hall. The noise is quieter now that I'm in the apartment. I slam open Mom's door. Creep crowds in behind me.

Mom stands with bare white shoulders in the filtered light of the curtains. Her hair is wrapped in a towel, so I know she has just finished showering. The golden music box on the tall dresser stands open, playing tinkling music. Tiny bottles of perfume in rows. Light casting rainbows through them across the top of the dresser. Soft lacy things float in an open drawer. I want to touch everything at once, to memorize it and keep it. As my head explodes with terror, I see all of these things in an instant and want to remember them.

Mom jumps at the sound of the door and turns, her arms up over her chest as she gasps. I realize that I am crying; that there are tears on my face. I can't hear my own voice, but I can hear Mom's: "What are you doing? Eleanor, get out!"

"Mom," I yell. "A tornado!"

"What have I told you?" Mom says. Her eyes are steely. "Always knock."

I watch the twisting black cloud loom through the window behind her. I point.

"Mom!" I scream.

"Go out and try again," she says.

The building sways as I turn to leave the room. Giant creaking and the tearing of concrete. Creep ducks as the doorway buckles.

The insane roar of wind.

ELEVEN

I open my eyes. Creep is curled next to my head where I huddle in blankets under the mattress fort. He breathes me in, his eyes closed.

I jerk backward and he opens his eyes.

"What were you dreaming about?" he asks.

My head feels heavy as I sit up, shreds of rock behind my eyes.

"Tornado," I mutter.

"Ooh," says Creep. "I like that one. Tell it to me."

I shake my head.

"C'mon Eleanor," he pleads. "You used to tell me all your dreams."

I fall back onto my pillow and look up at Creep. I want to tell someone. I want to talk about it. He's the only one. The only one who knows everything.

"We were at the playground," I say. I close my eyes and see the bleached sky again, the harsh light. "I found the token and we saw the tornado."

He inhales long through his nose. Then: "There wasn't really a tornado. Remember?"

"I know," I tell him. I think about the day that jetliner flew over, the roar scaring me into a panicked run home. I think about Mom's room, how it looked to my seven-year-old eyes. With the sunlight and the perfume bottles and the tinkling music box. It looked like what I thought rooms in Heaven must look like. I didn't know how to feel about not being allowed in a room like that.

"You called it the Angel Room," says Creep, like he can read my mind.

"We argued about it." I remember.

Creep laughs. "You called me ugly."

I open my eyes. "You *are* ugly."

He shakes all over, the shiver of a dog flinging water off of its coat. "We can't all be as beautiful as you, Ellie," he says in a candy-coated voice.

I swallow a sour taste. Stare up at the line where mattress meets wall.

Creep reminisces. "You said I was too ugly to be a guardian angel. You said I wouldn't be allowed in Heaven because I was so ugly." His voice pitches higher, a little-Ellie imitation. "You're not allowed in Mom's room and I think Mom's room must be like Heaven."

I don't tell him that I remember. I don't tell him that I remember what he said back: ***You're*** *not allowed in there either.* I don't tell him that I still think about the Angel Room.

No unclean thing...

"You haven't gone in her room since then," says Creep. He wants me to answer. He wants me to talk about it. I don't tell him that I wish I could see it again. I don't tell him that I haven't asked because I'm afraid she'll say no.

Instead, I slide out of the opening feet first and stand up, stretching.

"Looks like a tornado went through *here*," observes Creep.

The nightmare images flicker. Creep standing with his hand raised against the glare. The vortex of wind twisting toward us. The Angel Room, speckled with light and music. My mother's eyes. *Eleanor, get out.*

I pull on jeans and a t-shirt, push my bed back into place. I toss the wadded bedspread and sheets onto the mattress. I can feel Skittles under my feet. The stray pieces of candy gather in my fingers. I find them in corners, scattered parts of a rainbow, which makes me miss my teardrop crystal.

I tried hanging it, but the deck blocks direct sunlight.

I drop the remnant Skittles into the bathroom trash can. In the mirror, the reflected Eleanor remembers the fort and smiles. I wish every night was a thunder-fort night. Joshua at my elbow, laughter instead of fighting sleep, sharing giggles with a little boy instead of sharing memories with Creep.

I stare at my reflection. Long hair: black. Flat eyes: blue. Paper skin: white. Outlines: invisible. *Why don't they run all over the floor?* I think. I've always thought of reflection Eleanor as a 'they.' *Black and blue and white and red red red all over the floor? A puddle of colors without an outline. What makes them stay together?*

"Nothing's changed," says Creep, behind me.

The scraggy Eleanor reflection stares back. *You can be different,* I tell them. *Nobody knows. You can pretend. Pretend until it's real. Pretend you're new. Pretend until you forget you're pretending.*

"What are you thinking?" asks Creep.

When I look at Creep in the mirror behind Eleanor's reflection, Eleanor looks at him too. *You can pretend, but he'll never forget.*

WITH TWO FLUFFY OVEN MITTS, I UNFOLD THE OVEN DOOR TO retrieve the frozen pizza. A blistery wash of pepperoni air hits my face. Creep sits up and sniffs. His hum dances around the kitchen floor while we make dinner. I step around him to set the table.

Joshua tears lettuce leaves as I chop two long carrots. He sprinkles the orange discs into the salad. I slice the pizza and we sit at the corner end of the table. Dad's chair is empty, as usual. We talk about the new *Star Wars* movie. Creep snuffles between my feet. I kick at him and he chuckles.

In the other room, we hear the front door unlock itself and swing open. We both stop chewing. Joshua takes a big swallow of milk. We stare at each other.

"I'm home!" Mom's voice. We both breathe again. "Kids?" she calls. Her footsteps on the stairs.

"In here, Mom," yells Joshua.

Mom stands in the kitchen doorway in her skirt and heels. She looks tired.

"We made dinner," Joshua says.

After she drops off her bag and shoes in the bedroom, she joins us. At the table with two slices of pizza on her plate and a pile of salad, she asks us how our day went.

"My day was awesome," says Joshua.

"Don't talk with your mouth full," says Mom.

He works his jaws fast and then swallows. "Sam came over and we sold Kool-Aid to the neighborhood."

Mom raises one eyebrow at me.

"I watched them the whole time," I say.

"Yeah," says Joshua. "And there was this girl across the street who was also selling it, but she had a price lower than ours, so we lowered our price. Then she lowered her price. Then we put *free* on ours and she brought all her little brothers over and drank all our Kool-Aid."

Mom laughs.

"What about you?" she asks me.

I break my crust into pieces and arrange them on my plate. "I unpacked books in the family room."

She nods. "Good. I'm glad you were productive."

Creep snorts.

"So I was thinking," says Mom. "Should we make some cookies?"

Joshua bounces in his chair. "Yeah, yeah, yeah! What kind?"

"Chocolate chip," she says. "I bought some on the way home." She pulls out her phone. "I have a good recipe in my photos."

"Cookies," says Creep. "What's the occasion?"

I chew the inside of my cheek.

The doorbell rings.

"I'll get it," says Joshua.

Mom gets up. "Thanks, sweetie," she says. "Let me get it." She hands me her phone, open to a picture of an old hand-written recipe. "Why don't you get things started?"

We hear her walking down the stairs. We hear the door open.

"Oh," says Mom. "Hi!"

"Hi, Jill," comes a voice. "We just wanted to drop this off and say congratulations on your new place!"

Joshua and I look at each other. It sounds familiar. I get up to dig in drawers and cabinets for measuring cups, spoons, and a mixing bowl.

Mom says, "Thank you! That's so kind. We've already had dinner, but we'll save this for tomorrow. Would you like to come in?"

"Oh, no. No," another voice says. It's a man and a woman. "We don't want to intrude."

I'm leaning on the counter to scroll through the recipe directions when a third voice says, "What do Ellie and Josh think of the new house?"

I freeze.

Mom says, "You can ask them. Eleanor, Joshua, come say hello!"

Joshua jumps up. I shove the phone into my back pocket and follow. Joshua is bouncing on the stairs when I come around the corner. I walk a few more steps to see the Taylors standing in the open doorway. The Taylors and Ian. His smile makes my stomach flip-flop. Mom waves me down the stairs. "Don't be rude," she says. "Come say hi."

I slowly walk down the stairs. Josh doesn't join me. He sits about three stairs down. I step around him.

"So many houses for sale in this neighborhood," says Mr. Taylor. "And this one is lovely."

"Yes," says Mom. "We're very blessed. A friend of a friend owns it and is giving us a deal on rent. Of course, we'd like to buy when we're positioned a little better."

Ian steps onto the landing while our parents talk about real estate. I stand close to the banister, gripping it tight with my right hand.

"Hi, Ellie," he says. He does a small wave.

"Hi," I say. We look into each other's eyes. He steps closer. Mom stands with her back to us. His parents are on the stoop.

"How's the house?" he asks.

"It's fine," I say. "My room is huge."

He puts his hands in his pockets. I'll sometimes put my hands in my pockets when I want to stop myself from touching something. Is this what he's doing?

"Going to have a lot of sleepovers?" he asks.

"I don't have any friends," I say. I think of Mia.

A smile tugs at his mouth. His bottom lip looks extra pink, like he's been biting it. I try not to think about how I know what the freckle under his left eye feels like. I put my hands in my pockets.

I watch his mouth say, "You'll have friends in no time. Boyfriends too, I bet."

My eyes slide up to his and I think of The A-Team. I think of Virgil. I can feel myself turning red.

Joshua says loud, "We're going to make cookies!" I know he says it because he's tired of waiting. Mom and the Taylors laugh.

"Okay. Okay," says Mom, turning around. "Why don't you two go get the batter started?" She starts saying goodbye to the Taylors.

Joshua scrambles up the stairs and runs into the kitchen.

I take the first two stairs backwards, holding onto the banister again. Ian's smile doesn't drop. "Bye, Ellie," he says. There are fingers in that smile, touching me.

"Bye," I say, taking the rest of the stairs two at a time. When I glance back on the way to the kitchen, his eyes are the last thing I see, before losing sight of the top of his head completely.

Joshua stacks the dishes. I stand next to the mixing bowl and swipe open the phone again. The fingers are still there, along my skin. My vision blurs. I have to keep blinking to put things back into focus. We hear the door close. I jump. I'm unwrapping a stick of margarine when Mom puts the yellow bag of chips on the counter. "I'll wash the dishes," she says.

Mom fills the sink while we assemble the cookie ingredients. Joshua cracks eggs into the bowl. My head swims. I take over stirring when Joshua's arm gets tired. As I stir, I feel like my arm belongs to someone else.

Mom sings to herself, rubber gloves buried in hot water. I look over at her. A lock of hair twists down her forehead in front of her eye. She blows at it. Sweat beads on her brow and her eyes look heavy. I reach over to tuck the hair behind her ear.

"Thank you, Eleanor." She smiles at me.

Joshua starts adding the dry ingredients. I watch Mom wash a bowl.

"Mom?" I ask.

She looks up, eyebrows raised.

"Can I have a phone?"

Her eyebrows fall, mouth flattening. "No, Eleanor. You know the rule. You can have one when you're sixteen, if you've proven you're responsible enough to handle it."

There's an eye roll in my voice. "How can it be a rule when I'm the oldest?"

Mom looks at me again. "Is that really a question you want to ask?"

"Sorry," I mutter.

"Help me, Eleanor," says Joshua. The dough is thicker now, so I take over stirring. Joshua pours in the chips. He snatches two and hands one to me. The dark chocolate warming across my tongue makes me feel less jittery.

Mom pulls out two cookie sheets and I sit down.

"Why don't you go get your pajamas on?" She tells Joshua when one pan is in the oven.

Joshua bounds down the stairs. From my kitchen chair, I watch Mom put the cookie utensils in the dishwater.

"Come talk to me, Eleanor," she says.

I move to stand next to her. I dry the plates with a dish towel while she talks.

"How was your day?" she asks.

"Fine," I tell her. *And then the Taylors stopped by*, I don't say. I open the cupboard to put away dishes.

"Do you want to tell me what happened on Sunday?"

"Uh oh," sings Creep. He climbs up onto the counter next to me to watch.

I dry another plate. "What do you mean?"

"Someone called from the congregation to tell me you knocked down a boy in Youth Ministry."

I don't answer.

"Well?" says Mom.

"Well what?" I ask.

"Did you knock down a boy in Youth Ministry?"

I shake my head.

"Then what happened?"

"Nothing."

Mom sighs. "Eleanor, parents don't call to talk about when nothing happens. Your habit of disruption in social settings is a problem."

I dry one cup for a long time. The dish towel is damp under my fingers.

"He was bugging me," I say finally.

She drops the measuring cups into the rinse water. "Eleanor, you can't just knock people over because they're bugging you. You have to be humble. You have to turn the other cheek. It's your job to set an example."

My heart lurches in my chest. I put the cup on the shelf and grab another.

"So what should I have done?" I ask.

"Ignore it," says Mom. "Just let it go and eventually they will lose interest. That's how boys are."

Creeps opens his black mouth. A croaking laugh. "Good advice," he says.

"Okay?" Mom asks.

Ignore it. Turn the other cheek. Just let it go. He'll lose interest. The tornado spins through my forehead.

Timer buzzes. "Oh," she says. "Perfect timing."

Melted chocolate and sweet dough exhale from the oven. Mom uses a spatula to transfer the cookies to a cooling rack. "Joshua!" she calls.

Once we're sitting at the table with a plate of cookies and glasses of milk, I watch Mom break her cookie in half. I always do the same thing; I never noticed before. We all bite into our cookies at about the same time.

Something's wrong with mine. I make a face and swallow. The bite goes down rough in my throat. Mom takes hers back out of her mouth.

Joshua coughs. "Ew!"

Mom looks across the table at me. "What happened, Eleanor? Didn't you follow the recipe?"

"Yeah," I tell her. "Just like it said."

"Yeah," says Joshua. "We did!" He grabs the phone from the counter and starts to read the ingredients out loud. When he gets to the dry ingredients, Mom stops him.

"How much salt did you say?"

"Twelve teaspoons," says Joshua.

"Let me see," says Mom.

Joshua hands her the phone and she glowers at it. "It says half a teaspoon of salt, Joshua. Not twelve."

"But the numbers looked weird," he says. "They weren't on top of each other like real fractions."

"Why weren't you watching him?" Mom asks me. "How did you not notice him adding twelve teaspoons?"

"I *was* watching him," I say. "I guess I got distracted."

Mom stands up. She pushes her chair back and grabs the plate of cookies. She slams open the cupboard door under the sink and dumps the cookies in the trash. She grabs the cooling rack and dumps those in too.

Joshua has tears on his cheeks.

Mom mutters to herself, "What a waste."

"I'm sorry, Mom," Joshua tells her. "I didn't know."

"It's okay," she says. She leans down and puts her arm around his shoulders. "It's not your fault."

Creep sits in Dad's chair with his elbows on the table and his chin in his hands. The smile stretches all the way across his face.

Mom finishes her milk. "Oh well." She sits back down again. "I have something to talk to you two about. I was going to wait for your father, but maybe we'll just start without him."

Joshua and I look at each other. He wipes his eyes, sniffling.

Mom dabs at her mouth with a napkin. "I wanted to talk to you two about a big change that's going to be happening. It will take a lot of work and patience from all of us, but I know you are up to it."

This sounds like one of Mom's *goals*. Big Change with capital letters.

"I'm going back to school," she says.

I look up at her. Her puffy eyes with circles underneath. "College?" I ask.

She nods. "I'm going to do a two-year nursing program at the community college."

"Why?" asks Joshua.

Mom sighs. A long sigh that rolls across the table. "Because we can't live on my wages anymore. Dad's having a hard time finding work, so I need to be able to make more money for the family. The best way to do that is for me to get an education."

"Do nurses make a lot more money than secretaries?" asks Joshua.

"Administrative assistant," I say absently.

"Yes," says Mom. "It makes a lot more money."

"Enough that we can eat sugar cereal for breakfast every day and go to all the movies?"

"Yes," says Mom. "But I'm still not going to buy sugar cereal. It's not good for your teeth. That's why we don't eat candy."

Joshua and I share a pound-of-Skittles glance.

"And we still won't go to many movies; they're a worldly influence."

Joshua groans.

"Anyway," says Mom. "I'll be going to classes after work. That means that Eleanor will be in charge of dinner every night. When Dad isn't around, she'll be in charge of everything else too."

Creep claps. "Yay. Ellie's in charge."

I toss him a glare.

She turns to me. "We'll plan a menu and go shopping. It won't be too hard right now, but once school starts for you, it will be more of a challenge. I'll need you to be my go-to girl."

A whirlwind moans between my temples. I don't want to be anybody's go-to girl. I don't want Mom to be not-around even more than she already is. I don't want it to be me and Joshua alone with Dad. I don't want to be in charge.

"Eleanor? You won't be able to let things happen like tonight with the cookies. You'll have to pay attention and be responsible."

Like it's my fault Joshua can't read ½ in tiny lettering. I just want to stay in my room and read books. I just want to work on forgetting we ever lived anywhere but here. I just want to be left alone.

I am dizzy. They're both watching me.

"Eleanor," Mom says again. "I'm going to need you to do some growing up this summer. You're going to have to be responsible and take care of the family when I'm not around. Am I going to be able to count on you?"

No.

"Yes," I tell her. "You can count on me."

<u>Fear #2: Tornadoes</u>

Tornadoes are formed by a meeting of
hot and cold air.

The meeting creates a vortex roar of wind that can
pick up an entire building and break it into splinters.

Black funnels tear things apart that people thought
would last forever.

The chaos of drinking straws punched through the
side of a house, cars dangling from trees.

A tornado can blast through anywhere.

And in the end there is only empty wind, a broken
doll, the sound of someone crying, the rubble of
once upon a time.

I am lying in the marigold garden. Late morning, warm with sun, settles over me. The blossoms meet above my head. I can see sky, bleached by heat, between the orange and yellow heads. They sprinkle pollen over my cheeks. When I close my eyes, my eyelids show scarlet and white dots, as if the sun is so close it could blind me with my eyes closed. It smells like earth under here – dry, hot, sleepy. An ant crawls across my thumb.

I hide here when I don't want anyone to find me. The marigolds are tall enough that I can lie flat under them and no one can see. I don't want anyone to see. People forget how small children can make themselves. How invisible.

The screen door opens, then swings shut with a bang. I turn my head to the side and watch the red Chuck Taylors pass by on the front walk. They stop at the end of the walk and wait there. I hold my breath.

Don't find me. I'm not here. If I'm not here, you can't find me.

They turn and come back, stop even with where I'm hiding. When the shoes skip over the garden stepping stones, they rattle the marigolds. Dust and petals rain. I look up into his face.

"Found you," he says.

TWELVE

"Eleanor!"

I open my eyes. They focus on a picture of a bay mare. She leaps in a frozen instant across a pasture fence.

Creep's steady stream of rancid humming pauses. His face pokes up over the edge of the mattress so that all I can see is his disembodied head.

"Eleanor!" It's Joshua's voice far away.

I blink, slow. My knees are pulled up to my chin. *Where was I? Before I opened my eyes... where was I? The warm dust of marigold pollen. Playing hide and seek.*

"Eleano-or!"

Creep smiles. He sniffs long and hard. Sniiiiiiffffff. "Someone's calling you."

I push the blanket off. I didn't realize how hot I was underneath, sweat sticking my legs together. I stumble out into the hallway. Creep follows.

"Eleano-o-o-o-or!"

"What!" I yell as I walk up the stairs.

Joshua leans around the kitchen entry grinning. "Phone."

I take the receiver and he moves out of the way. This vintage phone was here when we moved in. Mom said it was "perfect for our family." She means because we can't have any privacy while using it. The handset is heavy. The long coiled cord hangs to the floor, wrapped around itself. I'd like to wrap it around Joshua.

"Hello?" I say.

Creep sits at my feet. "Who is it?"

The voice on the other line: "Hey. It's Mia. What are you doing?"

I yawn.

"Were you sleeping?"

"Yeah."

Mia pauses. "Oh. Sorry. So wanna hang out?"

It's been two weeks since Mom announced the Big Change. Mia and I have talked on the phone almost every day.

Joshua slides open the arcadia door. Creep ambles over to follow him outside. The door rumbles shut. Phone cord stretches after me as I walk across the kitchen. Joshua hops down the deck steps and disappears. Creep waves at me. Echoes Joshua's shadow.

"Eleanor?" Mia's voice asks.

"Sure," I say. My eyes strain out the window. Down through the slats of the deck. I can't see either of them. Fear coats my mouth.

"Yeah?"

"Yeah. Come over," I tell her. "I'll see you whenever you get here." I hang up the receiver and push open the door.

"Joshua?" I call.

No answer.

I step out onto the deck. Raise my hand to shade my eyes. The brown peeling paint is hot and crumbly under my bare feet.

"Joshua?"

I step down the stairs, stand at the bottom on the threads of prickly grass.

"Raargh!" His hand snakes out from between the steps to grab my leg behind my knee.

I scream and fall backward. My heart threatens to leap from my chest. Joshua laughs behind me, dusty under the stairs. Creep hangs from a strut by his fingers and toes. He watches.

"Oh, man," says Joshua. "You should have seen it. That was awesome."

I sit on the steps. They burn the palms of my hands. I wait for my heart to fall back into place, instead of filling my throat. I blink back tears.

Joshua crawls out from under the stairs, grin stretched wide. He stands in front of me. His smile fades when he sees my face.

"Eleanor?" he says. "You okay?"

I take a shuddering breath.

"I'm sorry," he says. "I didn't mean to scare you so bad."

Creep laughs, quiet under the deck shadows.

"It's okay," I say at last. "Just don't do that anymore." I don't finish my thought: *Don't go off alone with Creep.*

Joshua offers a hand to pull me up and I take it.

JOSHUA WATCHES CARTOONS IN THE FAMILY ROOM. HE LAUGHS down the hall. They're old-school Warner Brothers cartoons. The violence of anvils dropped on heads. Bombs labeled *TNT*

exploding; blackened faces blinking in surprise. Hammered thumbs throb. Birds circle, tweet in a teasing unison.

Creep crouches in my closet. The hems of my church dresses hang around his shoulders. He sings low, teeth clicking: *You Are My Sunshine.*

I lie on my back, thinking about Mia while I blow bubbles up into the ceiling fan. They swirl into the downdraft. Some burst in midair, releasing their hold in a silvery shower. Others pop when they hit things, leaving wet little circles all over my room. When the tornado in my skull starts to howl, this is the only thing that helps to blow the vortex into nothing. The only thing besides drawing.

I track the iridescent shapes, thinking about the first time Mia came over. She was wearing black-striped thigh socks and a checkered miniskirt and a shirt that said *The sun is trying to kill me.* She asked for the WiFi password and when I told her I didn't know it, she shrugged. "I'll just use my hotspot." The three of us ate stove-top popcorn and lay around the living room watching two seasons of *She-Ra* on her tablet until she had to go home.

Mom's already started summer classes. She takes the bus after work to campus and stays until eight or nine o'clock. She sits at the kitchen table with a stack of books, chin in hand, biting her bottom lip. She brought home her first math quiz: A+ written in red on top. "See what you can do when you put your mind to it?" she says, proud. I make dinner every week night: spaghetti, chicken casserole, tacos, macaroni and cheese, hotdogs. Dad hasn't been around much. Leaves early to work on cars, gets home after we're in bed. There are worse things.

I blow another line of bubbles into the breeze. Dance, swoop, glide; they cling to the air, crystalline, perfect, gone in moments. Creep's voice dips in and out of my ears. I imagine each bubble with a tiny person inside.

The A-Team. They kneel together in a floating prison. Hands push on the sparkling walls. Mouths open in soundless screams.

Dad. Bulk scarcely contained, the ineffectual pounding as he tries to escape. Brow lowers. Muscles bunch.

Ian. Perfect neighbor boy, no air inside the bubble except what I breathed out. *Help*, I see his mouth say, *help*!

Creep. Ugly insect squatter. He tries to kick the bubble walls. Too late.

Me. I sit. Quiet. Alone. No one can reach me, floating away.

The bubbles start to burst, starting with The A-Team, and the tiny people disappear in a series of miniature explosions, one by one. Pop, pop, pop! Dad, Ian, Creep. And me last of all.

Pop.

The doorbell chimes and Joshua runs to get it. I hear Mia's voice on the landing. Two pairs of footsteps on the stairs. And then they're both standing in my doorway staring at the bubble breeze. Mia wears a long red skirt with zippers all over it and a t-shirt that says *I'm Only Wearing Black Until They Make Something Darker*.

"Dope," says Mia.

"Hey," says Joshua. "I wanna try."

He jumps onto my bed. I sit up and hand him the bottle. He scoots back toward the pillows. Globes stream from the wand. They lift and spin. Mia watches their progress around the room. She sits on the edge of the bed next to me.

"I like your room," she says.

I look around at my room now with Mia-eyes. Horse wall, bookcase, a cloud of bubbles.

She points at the horses. "Virgil has a wall like that."

I wonder what Virgil's room looks like.

"So let's do something," she says. "I've been in my house for a week and I've rewatched all the seasons of Red Dwarf and the 80s episodes of MST3K and I am going crazy, so can we just go do something?"

"What are we gonna do?" asks Joshua.

Mia purses her lips to one side. "I know," she says. "Let's walk to Seven-Eleven."

I shake my head. "No way. Too hot."

Mia shrugs. "We'll get Slurpees."

Joshua perks up. "Slurpees? Can we go Eleanor? Please?"

"We don't have money for Slurpees," I tell him.

"I'll pay," Mia offers.

Joshua bounces. He sloshes bubble liquid on his leg.

"Don't get my bedspread all sticky," I tell him.

"C'mon, Eleanor," says Joshua. "Please? Slur-peeeees? Pleeeeease?"

"Okay," I say.

"Woohoo!" Joshua yells. He puts the bottle on my dresser and jumps off the bed. "I'm gonna get my shoes."

"Wow," says Mia when he's gone. "Maybe he should switch to decaf."

<u>More Things I Like About Mia:</u>

Nice to Joshua
Sci-fi geek
Red lips, like something you'd see in Dracula
(they're super shiny too)

THIRTEEN

We walk along the searing sidewalk. I can feel it through the soles of my shoes. Cicadas drone. My hairline drips sweat. Joshua walks between Mia and me, and loping on all fours behind us like a dog, Creep traces the edge of each yard, pausing here and there.

Cars whip past us on Southern Avenue. The buffet of wind as they pass lifts my hair. I wish I had a hair elastic. I usually keep one on my wrist. I watch our shadows, stunted on the sidewalk in front of us. Mia swishes in her heavy skirt. Joshua pelts her with questions.

"What's your favorite color?"

"Black."

"Black? That's not a color."

"Sure it is. Things that are black absorb all colors. So maybe you could say my favorite color is all colors mixed together."

Joshua looks at me, like he wants me to tell him if she's joking.

"Okay. What's your favorite color that's not all colors mixed together?" he asks her.

"I dunno. Red I guess."

"What's your favorite food?"

"Sushi."

Joshua makes a face.

"What's your favorite pair of shoes?"

"These." Mia stops and holds up one foot for him to see.

"Those look like army boots," says Joshua.

"They are," she says. "I got them at the army surplus store."

"My dad shops there," says Joshua. "Why do you wear army boots with dresses?"

"I like them. Plus you should see the look on my mom's face whenever I put them on."

Joshua laughs. I squint down the length of sidewalk and road. Sizzle waves distort my vision, creating a mirage of watery reflection on the distant blacktop.

"How much farther is it?" asks Joshua.

"It's at the end of the next block." Mia points. "So," she says without warning, "what's up with your parents?"

I glance at Joshua. "What do you mean?"

"You're not allowed to have a phone. Your only computer is a family desktop. I've never even seen your Dad."

"Our dad doesn't come to church much," I say.

"Or ever," says Joshua.

"What does he do for a living?"

Joshua shrugs. "He fixes cars right now. He's gone a lot."

"You probably miss him when he's gone so much."

"It's okay," says Joshua. "He told us we could get a dog."

"What kind of dog do you want?" asks Mia.

"I want a Rhodesian Ridgeback."

Mia blinks. "What the hell is that?"

Joshua says gravely, "You shouldn't say hell."

Mia says, "Why? Christians say it all the time. Like, if you don't follow Jesus, you're going to Hell."

Joshua looks thoughtful. "I guess."

"Look," says Mia. "I'm gonna swear sometimes. That's just how it is. Swearing is, like, my first language. I'll do my best to avoid it, but sometimes they'll slip out. So let's make a deal. I won't judge you for talking about military aircraft all the time, and you don't judge me for saying words your mom wouldn't like."

Joshua nods slowly. "Okay," he says finally. He holds out his hand and Mia looks at me, smiling as they shake on it.

She says, "So tell me about these Rhodesian Ridgeheads."

Joshua laughs. "Ridgebacks! It's a lion hunting dog from Africa. They're big and red-brown and their hair grows backwards on their spine so that it stands up like a mohawk."

"Mohawk dogs, huh? That's pretty cool."

I imagine Creep as a dog. I see us at the dog park, toy poodles sniffing Creep's butt under drooped summer trees. I throw a stick for him. Joshua tosses a Frisbee for his Ridgeback, but it goes after Creep instead. It clamps down on Creep's neck until his black eyes bulge out of his head. He scrabbles against the dog's wide chest. His mouth opens and closes like a gasping fish.

I laugh.

"What's funny?" asks Mia. They both smile at me, questioning. Creep stops his sniffing to stare.

"Mohawk dogs," I say.

Mia looks at Joshua. He shrugs. "Your sister is weird," she says to him.

"I know, right?" He grins. "She does that all the time."

When I lunge to grab him, he skips out of the way. Mia's laugh follows us down the sidewalk. We wait for her to catch up, walking for a few moments in silence after she does.

Then Mia says, "My first girlfriend had a mohawk."

I look sideways at her. Joshua says, "You had a girlfriend? I thought girls were supposed to have boyfriends."

Mia says, "Some do. I'm lesbian."

Joshua says, "What's lesbian?"

"A girl that likes girls," says Mia.

"Likes girls," muses Joshua. "You mean LIKE likes?"

Mia laughs. "Yes, LIKE likes."

"Like kissing girls," says Joshua. "You like to kiss girls?"

"Uh. Yeah," Mia says. "I like kissing girls. There was one really special girl that I *loved* kissing."

"The girl with the mohawk," says Josh.

"Yes," says Mia.

"How many girls would you like to kiss?" asks Joshua.

"Yes," says Mia. She laughs.

"All of them?" says Josh.

Mia nods.

"Would you ever marry a girl?" Joshua asks.

"If I ever got married, it would be to a girl. But I'm never getting married. I'm against it."

Joshua falls quiet. He drags a stick along a chain link fence as we pass, our steps punctuated by a staccato of metallic clinks.

I say, "What are you against, exactly?"

Mia says, "The whole institution of marriage. It's a hetero-supremacist tool of patriarchal oppression."

I look at her.

"What?" she says.

"You just don't talk like any fifteen-year old I've ever met," I tell her.

"Both my parents are teachers." She holds up one hand in front of her, flaps her straightened fingers down so they touch her chest, and says in a British accent, "They impressed upon me the importance of being well-spoken." She drops the accent when I laugh. "My real education has been feminist Twitter."

I don't want to talk about not having a phone again, so I say, "So about marriage. What did you call it? A hetero something."

Mia grins. "A hetero-supremacist tool of patriarchal oppression. That's going in my TED Talk." She laughs at her own joke.

"Okay," I say.

"If I decide to commit myself to a woman for the rest of my life, a piece of paper saying the government approves my relationship doesn't magically make it valid." She puts her hand out again, this time palm up, the other on her chest. She closes her eyes and says, "Only God can judge me."

"Do you really believe that?" I ask her.

"No," she laughs. "I'm an atheist."

"What's an atheist?" asks Joshua.

"Someone who doesn't believe in God," I tell him.

Joshua says to Mia, "Why do you go to church if you don't believe in God?"

Mia says, "It's really important to my parents. They've done everything for me, and they're also pretty cool about letting me be myself, so I figure if it doesn't hurt me to go, why not? It makes them happy."

Joshua trails behind us to pick up a coin.

"I can't ever seem to make my parents happy," I say.

"Maybe they're already not happy," says Mia. "Maybe it's not even about you."

"Girls marrying girls," Joshua suddenly interjects, jumping between us and looking up at Mia. "My mom says that's an abomination."

Mia stops. She looks at me, then at Joshua. The sun reflecting makes a white crown on the top of her glossy hair. "Look at me, Josh," she says. "Do I look like an abomination to you? Would an abomination buy you a Slurpee?"

Joshua squints his eyes at Mia and then shakes his head. "Nah," he says. "You're not an abomination. You're nice."

Mia laughs. We lock eyes for a moment. "What about you?" she asks. "Do *you* think I'm an abomination?"

I shake my head. "No," I tell her, my face hot. *Hotter?* I want to say, *You're the coolest person I've ever met.* I say, "You're nice."

Mia eyes me, and then laughs again. "Okay. Then it's settled. I'm nice and no one is an abomination."

Creep is there at my side, staring at me. I know what he's thinking. He echoes Mia in a laugh that sounds just like her.

Dear Jesus,
I've met a gay atheist.
As far as I can tell, she is not an abomination.
What else is your book wrong about?
Amen.

FOURTEEN

The 7-Eleven doors part in a bleachy, hot-dog breeze as electronic bells announce our arrival. Drink machines and refrigerators hum along the back walls. Aisles are lined with shelf after shelf of multicolored candy wrappers, chocolate bars, and packs of gum

"Hey, girl!" says a voice from behind the register. We follow Mia to where the attendant leans over the counter.

"Hi, Nicole!"

The woman has black spiky hair, a mouth outlined in red, like Mia's. Her brown eyes smile at us. Her name tag says *Sharon*.

"How's your summer goin', Mia?" she asks.

Mia shrugs. "Okay, I guess. I'm super bored. These are my friends. They just moved in."

"Hi. I'm Nicole." She holds out her hand. Joshua shakes it. I don't.

"Why does your name tag say Sharon?" asks Joshua.

"I can't find mine today, so I figured Sharon wouldn't mind if I pretend to be her." She winks. "Just don't tell her, huh?"

Mia says, "Our secret."

"So what are your names, friends?" Nicole asks.

Mia points to us. "That's Joshua. That's Eleanor."

Nicole snaps her gum. "I like that. Old school. When I get enough money, I'm going to change my name to something old school, like Victoria or Abigail. How cool would that sound? Abigail Ashton. So what are you in here for?"

"We're here for Slurpees," says Mia. "My treat."

"Well," says Nicole, "aren't *you* the best?" She gestures to the drink machine.

Joshua grabs a 32 oz cup with the picture of a polar bear wearing a sweater. "I'm gonna get a suicide." I hand him a rounded lid.

"Do it through the lid," I tell him. "Then you can fill it past the top of the cup."

"I know how to do it, Eleanor," he says. He fits the lid onto his cup and holds it under the first Slurpee spigot. He reads the flavor label. "First, White Cherry." He grabs the handle.

We both watch as the noodle of Slurpee splats into the bottom of the cup. He names off every flavor as he adds it. When his cup is a cylinder of stripes, he plunges a straw in and sucks while he waits for Mia and I to fill our cups; Peach Mango and Strawberry Kiwi.

We push our cups across the counter for Nicole to scan. "What'd ya call that?" she asks Joshua.

"A suicide," he tells her.

Nicole winks at Mia and me, and then pops her gum. "Death by Slurpee."

Mia digs in the side of her boot for a black coin purse. While she's paying, Joshua and I flip through a spinning rack of Arizona postcards.

"Look at this one." Joshua holds up a jackalope card. The large jack rabbit sits upright, silhouetted against a perfect sky and surrounded by prickly pear and ocotillo. Antlers sprout between its ears. The postcard says in white lettering: *Arizona Wildlife.*

I find one with a rearing mustang. Its hind hooves are hidden by creosote, its head haloed by a white cloud in a panel of blue.

A voice behind me: "I have that one."

I turn to find Virgil behind me, close, but not too close. He points. "They have a whole series, but this store only sells the desert ones." His hand pivots back and forth once. "Hi."

"You collect horse postcards?" I ask him.

He shrugs. "Horse pictures. Anything with a horse on it. I have a wall collage. You have that one?"

I shake my head. "Where did you come from?"

He smiles. "My older sister says I come from a chrysalis. You know, like a pod person."

His eyes are apple-candy green.

I say, "*Invasion of the Body Snatchers.*"

He smiles. "Yeah. Sometimes I feel like coming from a chrysalis makes more sense than where I actually came from."

This is a very strange sentence and I'm not sure how to respond, so I don't say anything.

"He came from there," Joshua says around his straw, pointing to a door next to the drink fridges.

Mia steps over. "You still work here, Virgil?"

"Nicole is paying me to unload boxes."

"Nicole and his mom are cousins," Mia explains.

"It's supposed to keep me out of trouble," says Virgil. He leans between us to pluck a horse postcard from the rack. "You said you don't have this one, right?"

I shake my head again.

He goes over to the counter.

Mia looks at me. "I think he likes you," she whispers.

I roll my eyes at her.

I hear Nicole talking to Virgil. "Don't you have this one already?"

"It's for Eleanor," he says.

Mia raises her eyebrows. Joshua watches without comment, his mouth full of Slurpee.

"Leave it to me," says Mia.

"Leave what to –" I start, but Virgil's back.

He holds out the postcard. "Here you go." My hands are behind my back. Mia coughs. I stare at the picture. Finally I take it.

"Thank you," I say. I glance at him. His mouth twitches.

"Hey, Virgil," says Mia. "You have horses, right?"

"You know I do. This job goes to their feed."

Mia looks at me. "Eleanor loves horses. She's obsessed."

Now they are both looking at me. Joshua too.

"I wouldn't say obsessed." I look down at the postcard.

"I would," says Joshua.

Miraculously, he doesn't wither under my gaze.

"Cool," says Virgil. "You should come see them sometime. We could go riding. I stable them on my granddad's property near South Mountain. There're trails all over the place."

Riding?

"When?" asks Mia.

"When what?"

"When can Eleanor come and see the horses?"

I want to kick her.

"Uh," says Virgil. "I was gonna go over on Friday and spend the day." He turns to me. "You can bring Joshua. I know he and Sam like to play."

"You're Sam's brother?" I ask.

"Duh," says Joshua.

"He and Sam can play Xbox while we go. My mom will watch them."

The doorbell chimes. A wash of hot air.

"Hey, look, it's The Midget." We look over to see The A-Team silhouetted in the doorway. The one called Levi says, "And she brought The Freak."

They move into the store. My arm drops around Joshua's shoulders.

"Who's this?" one of them says. "Mini-Freak?"

"Cut it out, guys," says Virgil.

"Or what?" says Levi. He steps very close to Virgil, and Virgil has to tip his head up to look him in the eye. "You'll sic your ponies on us?"

"I'm serious, Levi," Virgil says. There's a pause while they stare at each other.

Then: "Hear that? The Virgin is serious." Levi steps back as he laughs. His friends join in.

Mia says: "You guys are like a pack of feral dogs. You only stop barking long enough to stick your nose in someone's crotch."

"Bet you'd like that, huh Mia?" says Levi.

Mia snorts. "Not from a walking definition of toxic masculinity like you."

Nicole's voice sounds from over at the register. "Hey! You guys can't come here and harass my paying customers. Please leave."

Mia smiles.

"But *we're* paying customers," one of them protests.

"Not today," counters Nicole. She throws one thumb at the sign hanging behind her, above the cigarettes: *We reserve the right to refuse service.* "Get out."

"That blows," says one. "C'mon," says another, and they shuffle out. "We'll see you later, Eleanor." My name in Levi's mouth sounds dirty. They toss smiles over their shoulders. I shiver. We watch as they all pile into an idling SUV. An older boy puts the car into gear and they squeal out of the parking lot.

We stand in a circle. Joshua sucks once on his straw. "Those guys are jerks. Especially Levi."

Mia says, "That's the one who got his ass knocked down in Youth Ministry by Eleanor."

"That's the one?" says Joshua. "Good job, Ellie."

They all look at me admiringly. "I know, right?" says Mia. "My hero." I start to turn pink. Then she tousles Joshua's hair. "Just promise me you won't turn out like them." She points. "Be more like Virgil here."

Joshua tips his head to one side to look at Virgil. Virgil puffs out his chest, his hands in his pockets. He turns so that Joshua can get a good look at his profile.

"What do you think?" he asks.

Joshua raises his eyebrows. "Meh."

This time we really do laugh.

"I'm surprised you didn't cuss them out," says Mia to Virgil.

Virgil says, "I'm trying to make a good impression."

Mia laughs, "Yeah, you've been leaning hard into that choir-boy energy." Then she looks at me. "So what makes a better impression, Eleanor?" She puts on a mock Virgil-voice. "*I'm serious*, or *Fuck off*?"

I take a sip of my Slurpee to stop myself from laughing when Joshua's eyes widen at Mia's swearing. "Depends," I say, "on which one is the real you."

He and Mia look at each other. She raises her eyebrows. "They're both the real me," says Virgil. Then he grins. "I'm serious about wanting them to fuck off."

Mia snorts. "We're gonna go. Bye, Virgil." She grabs Joshua's arm. "C'mon," she says. "Let's go run through the sprinklers or something."

"Bye, kids!" calls Nicole.

<u>Virgil:</u>

Nice to Joshua
Likes horses
Doesn't touch me
Knows Invasion of the Body Snatchers

FIFTEEN

Joshua cavorts through the arc of water as it shifts back and forth across the grass. Mia and I sit under the tree. The branches are low enough that they almost touch our heads. Creep's shadow feels cold on my neck. He watches from an overhanging limb.

"Eleanor, Mia!" calls Joshua. "Watch me!" Starting on one side of the lawn, he runs at the wall of water. He holds a plastic airplane high with one hand. Joshua leaps over the sprinkler with a sound of a swooping jet.

Mia claps. "That's sick, dude," she says to him.

He flashes a grin. Water droplets cling to his hair. "I'm gonna find a stick," he says. He runs to the other end of the yard.

"So you're going to Virgil's on Friday," says Mia.

"No," I say. "I'm not."

"Aw," her face falls. "Why not?"

"Why *would* I?" I say. "I don't know him. He's *your* friend. Not mine."

"He *could* be your friend."

"That's what everyone said about Ted Bundy too."

A laugh explodes out of Mia. "Virgil? A serial killer? The only thing Virgil's killed is a bucket of chicken wings at the church potluck."

I don't answer.

"What are you worried about specifically?" Mia says.

We both watch Joshua cartwheel through the sprinkler. Mia smiles. He slices at the water with a long stick, stabbing and swiping like it's an invisible foe.

"You said according to Brother Chad, Virgil needed to concentrate on his spiritual growth." Mia nods. "And adults don't usually say stuff like that unless there's something wrong. Like he's a bad kid they're trying to fix." I don't tell her that's what my mom means when she talks about me that way.

"Oh," says Mia. "No. Well, yes." She sees my expression and then says, "Sorry, let me start over."

I'm watching Joshua. He's letting the water chase him, splashing just his toes as he dances away. His smile catches the sun.

"When he was younger he had a lot of problems with," she pauses, "family stuff, and Brother Chad said he would help him back on the——," she uses air quotes. "… 'straight and narrow.' Okay. I feel weird telling you this, because it's his story to tell."

I wonder what she means by family problems. Does the straight and narrow feel like the tightrope I feel like I'm walking? One toe out of line and you'll fall to your death, disappointing everyone on the way down.

Mia continues. "He actually does a lot of censoring around church people now, or new people. He's really super sweet, especially next to that sausage fest Levi swags around with. They have history too, Virgil and Levi. I dunno. He's trying to make a good impression because he has a crush on you."

I roll my eyes. "He doesn't know anything about me."

"Maybe *you* made a good impression," Mia says.

I scoff.

"Honestly," says Mia, "I set it up because he has horses and I knew you would be too shy to ask. He's actually a really great guy. Like the kind of guy you could have water your plants for you while you're on vacation and you could come back and they wouldn't all be dead. Like the kind of guy straight Christian girls will be fighting over because he'll be a *valiant man* and change diapers and stuff. Like the kind of guy—"

"Okay, I get it," I say. "He's a *great guy*."

"Okay, one more," she says. I roll my eyes. "He's the kind of guy who tells you what he's really thinking and listens when you talk. I thought you could use another friend like that."

"Another friend," I say.

"Uh, yeah," she says, "I'm the first one. Just to be clear."

Creep sniggers. "Two whole friends."

Mia waits for me to answer. We both watch Joshua. He's attempting to walk on his hands, legs waving.

Finally she says, "I'm sorry if it was too much."

"It's okay," I say. I really do want to see the horses.

"You can cancel, if you really don't want to go." She brightens. "Or I can go with you if you want. If you don't want to be alone with him. I promise though, he would never do anything rapey or murdery. He's—"

"I know. I know," I say. "A great guy."

"Where have we heard that before?" muses Creep.

I squint up at him.

"So do you think you'll go?" Mia asks.

I say, "What would we even talk about?"

"I'll go with you," she says. "Then I'll fill all the conversational gaps with my glittering personality and you won't have to worry about it."

"No," I say, suddenly resolved. New place. New me. New life. *I'm going to see those horses.*

Mia sighs loudly. "Oh, thank God," she laughs. "I hate the stables."

"You don't like horses?"

She gestures to herself. "Have you *seen* this? Can you imagine me next to a horse?" She shakes her head. "No thanks, I'll leave the horsemanship to taller folks."

I start to smile. I lie back in the grass and gaze up into the branches. "I'll think about it," I say. "He can't be that hard to talk to, I guess." Creep peers down at me. He smiles, slow. I can hear his teeth click.

Mia nods. "You could tell him about your old neighborhood. Tell him about where you used to live. There were weird people there, right? You could tell him stories about the weird people in your neighborhood."

"No." I shake my head, put one arm over my eyes. The world goes dark. *No.* My head crushes down into the grass, a burr biting into my scalp.

Mia's still talking. "Like this couple that lives across the street from me. They have these tiny barrel cactuses in rows in their front yard and they rake the gravel into perfect lines and if someone steps one toe in their gravel, they go ballistic."

I'm dizzy, like the world is spinning and I can feel it, like at any moment I might go flying off into outer space. But I don't, because gravity pushes me down, down, down into the earth until my head feels heavy as lead and my arms and legs like anvils and I'll always be here, too heavy to move forever. I can feel it, the whole Earth spinning and orbiting and it's like the worst carousel in the universe.

"Eleanor?" says Mia.

I move my arm. The sun through the leaves hurts my eyes. "What?" I say.

"You okay?"

I swallow. Joshua is standing over me. Water drips from his sagging swim trunks into the thirsty ground beside me. I can feel an ant crawling along my other hand.

"Fine," I say.

Mia purses her lips. "Joshua was talking to you and you didn't answer."

"Sorry," I say. I sit up. I'm still dizzy. I look up at Joshua. "What do you need?"

"Macaroni and cheese," says Joshua.

"Okay," I say. I look up at Creep. He lounges like a house cat, across the branch, one arm swinging. His eyes slit down at me.

Joshua jumps back toward the water. I stand up and brush the grass from my jeans. Yellow pieces cling to my thighs. I brush them over and over. Harder, harder until I'm slapping my legs trying to get rid of them.

"Eleanor," says Mia.

I look up and my eyes are watering. She reaches out and plucks a sliver of grass from my knee. "You okay, girl?" she says.

I want to say, *Don't call me girl.* "Fine," I say. "I'm fine." *Aren't I always?*

"Can you watch Joshua for a sec?" Mia nods.

Creep jumps down from the tree when I go inside to start the water boiling. He chuckles all the way up the stairs.

"Eleanor," he says in Mia's voice as I open a cupboard door. "Eleanor, are you okay? Eleanor, what's wrong? Eleanor – "

I spin around. "Will you just shut up?"

Creep cackles. I slam a saucepan into the sink and fill it with water. The stove ticks to itself as it warms up, the burner growing red as I cover it with the pot. I wonder what it would be like to cover it with my hand instead. Would it stick to the burner? Would concentric circles be branded into the skin of my palm? I imagine my fingers smoking, black flesh peeling back from the bones. I imagine the smell of heated blood. I imagine the sear of pain.

"What are you thinking about?" asks Creep.

I realize that I'm staring into the pot of water. Tiny bubbles run up the sides of the scarred metal and break the surface of the water with no sound.

"Hurting myself," I say out loud. Not to Creep. Only because he asked. I don't tell him about what kind of hurt. I don't tell him about the charred muscle and snapping tendons.

"I know," says Creep. "I know everything about you, Eleanor."

Like he needs to remind me.

I wash my hands in very hot water. I wish no one knew. But if someone has to, I suppose I'm glad it's only Creep.

"Maybe that's what you should talk about to Virgil," Creep says. He jumps up to the kitchen counter, rocks back and forth on his heels so I have to follow him with my eyes. I can see my reflection in the black marble rounds under his brow. My face looks elongated, my eyes hollow oblong pits. "Tell him you think about hurting yourself. Or Mia had a good idea — tell him all about your old neighborhood, about the people there. Tell him how much you miss your old friends and neighbors."

Water boils. I tear open a box of macaroni and cheese and dump the noodles into the pot. They tumble from the ripped cardboard into the roiling water. I imagine myself as one of them, turning end over end until I'm covered in blistering heat. My story boiled away, rising like steam. Caught by the overhead fan and carried above the roof, into the sky, rising weightless while I lie in the bottom of the pot and watch the surface of the water roll and bubble like a storm waiting to break.

With a wooden spoon I stir the noodles once.

"I really hate you," I say to Creep.

<u>Things to Talk About:</u>

Books
Movies
Whatever comes up that's NOT the old neighborhood

SIXTEEN

That night Mom calls us into the living room. She looks tired. More tired than usual. She says she has something really important to tell us. I sit next to Joshua on the sofa and think about the last really important announcement she made. This time Dad's sitting next to her.

He looks deflated, like a balloon that's lost its buoyancy, but hasn't gone completely flat yet. Joshua fidgets, his hair wet after his shower. He's in his pajamas. Creep hunkers in the corner under the end table. He drums his fingers together.

"I called this family meeting to discuss something important," says Mom. She and Dad are holding hands. Her eyes are red.

"Are we talking about our week plans?" asks Joshua, "Because I want to play at Sam's every day. That's my plan." His legs bend at the knee and then move in a bouncing rhythm against the front of the sofa. Sticking out straight, bouncing against the sofa, straight, bounce, straight, bounce.

Mom shakes her head. Dad sighs.

"We need to talk about your father. He's sick." Mom coughs the words like they're stuck in her throat. Creep begins to hum.

"What kind of sick?" I ask.

Dad closes his eyes and opens them again. He looks at me. He seems different. Smaller.

"Cancer," he says.

Mom covers her mouth. She blinks over and over again. My body starts to prickle, like when someone touches my shoulder.

"Could you die from it?" Joshua asks Dad.

Mom says, "Sometimes people die from it. But we want you to know that we're hopeful that this cancer is fixable and that the doctors will do everything they can to make sure Dad gets better."

Joshua's legs keep swinging upward, bouncing down again. I put my hand on his thigh.

"What?" he says.

"Stop it," I say.

He stops. "Why?" he asks.

Because something is happening, I want to tell him. *Something big.* But I can't tell him. I can't say anything. My mouth feels glued shut. I just keep my hand on his leg while Creep's humming cuts through my forehead.

Mom wipes her eyes. "We just wanted you kids to know what's going on," she says. "Dad is going to go to the hospital twice a week for chemotherapy and radiation. It's very important that we pray every day for his recovery. Doctors and medicine are very important, but God is the only one who can heal him."

Joshua leans against me, somber now. "I'll pray for Dad," he says. "I'll pray all the time."

Mom smiles. It's quavery and small, but it's a smile. I wonder if it's fake. Of course it is.

"Good," she says. "That will help."

"Maybe we should pray right now," says Joshua.

"Good idea," says Mom. "You're right."

Mom slips from her chair onto her knees. Dad does too.

Joshua and I curl onto the floor, facing our parents. We are in a circle with our knees almost touching.

We bow our heads. Joshua's hand snakes into mine. We're all quiet for a second.

"Our Father," says Mom. She stops then and I wonder if she'll continue, but I know she has to. She never leaves a prayer incomplete. I always do.

She prays, begging God to help. I feel like I'm receding. Like I'm walking backwards without moving, like my brain is sliding out the back of my skull. She starts talking about being healed, and treatment. I feel like I'm behind myself now, that my body is just kneeling there in the circle, empty and dead-still, held up by Joshua's hand. Mom prays for a long time.

I float somewhere near the ceiling, bobbing in the down draft from the ceiling fan.

When she says, *amen*, I feel my shoulders droop. Joshua's the only one who says amen after Mom. He pulls his hand out of mine. He leans toward Dad, puts his arms around Dad's neck.

"It's okay, Dad," he says. "God will fix it. He'll make the cancer go away." He kisses Dad's dark cheek. Dad hasn't moved.

Joshua stretches. "I'm tired," he says. "Night."

He trips down the stairs, yawning.

"Eleanor," says Mom.

We're all still kneeling: Mom, Dad and me. I know I should say something, like Joshua did. I don't know what to say. I don't know what's going to happen and I realize that my parents don't know either. I look into my mother's blue eyes. I'm afraid to say the wrong thing.

My father looks up at me. His eyes, usually dark with anger or impatience, are soft, wilted like fallen petals from a dead flower. They search mine. I know he wants me to say something.

"I'm sorry you're sick," I say.

I stand up and run downstairs. Creep somehow follows me into my bedroom even though I shut the door quick. I fling myself onto the bed and put a pillow over my head. I can feel Creep next to me. I curl my legs up and blink into the darkness under the pillow, hoping he won't say anything. Hoping he'll leave me alone.

But of course, he doesn't.

"Wow," he says. "Big news."

Tears leak onto the bedspread. I'm breathing too fast and my face is hot. I pull my head out from under the pillow and stare across Creep's knees at the horse wall.

"Do you think he'll die?" asks Creep.

I don't say anything. I don't even *think* anything. I just stare at the horses. The winged unicorn that rears in front of a cloud nebula backdrop, back hooves planted on a wind-swept mountaintop, feathers outstretched for an unseen wind. I think about the aurora borealis – colored light brushed across the sky and just the cold cold cold all around me. I imagine the unicorn beating its wings once. One giant push as it leaps into the air. Would it just leave the ground and continue into space? Surrounded by the infinite abyss, cold light and distant stars and the vacuum of space. Just drift into the nothingness.

"What are you going to do?" asks Creep. I look up into his face as it hangs over me.

"About what?" I ask.

"About your dad?" he says.

"What do you mean? There's nothing *to* do. All I can do is what I've always been doing. Pick up the slack. Act like nothing's wrong. Be the Go-To Girl. Pretend everything's fine. "

"Why?" says Creep. "Isn't everything fine? I thought you hated your dad. You always used to talk about how you wanted him to go away. Here's your chance. If the cancer kills him, you won't have to worry about it anymore."

I close my eyes.

"Sure," I say to Creep. "Everything's fine. Now leave me alone so I can sleep."

Creep leaves me alone, but he hums and hums a headache between my ears until I open my sketchbook and fill ten pages with endless spiraling lines that disappear into black dots at the center of each paper, before I can fall asleep.

Dear Jesus,
In heaven, we should be able to be whatever we want.
If I get to choose, I'll be a winged unicorn.
Dappled gray.
I just realized this might be pointless to talk about.
People who have things like Creep don't
get into heaven.
Amen.

I'm in a hallway, impossibly long corridors stretching out to either side. Regularly placed lamps attempt to combat the gloom, but the murk seems to creep and crawl from the baseboards. I shiver under a cold draft.

I've been here before.

My father's voice issues from the darkness, "I'm waiting, Eleanor."

He's waiting. I can't keep him waiting. Waiting makes everything worse.

I push at the nearest door. It opens to my father's bedroom, a shadowy space illuminated by one lamp on a bedside table. The light barely reaching to the closet. He is waiting.

He is wearing the face that means I've been naughty. But I can't recall exactly what I've done. It doesn't matter -- I know what comes next.

I've been here before.

My father will pull back the closet door. Once he pushes his shirts aside, his collection of belts will be displayed, hung in a row — there are twelve. Different colors, sizes, and lengths, on pegs against the wall. He will pull back the closet door and tell me to choose.

I already know which one I will choose, because I have been here before. It's black, thick leather, with a silver buckle on one end that has slipped and bitten into my thigh only once before. This belt doesn't sting as much as thinner ones. Doesn't leave the piles of welts that burn for days afterward. This belt is dependable violence: bone-rattling impact, and reliable solidity, but no visible bruises. It is the belt I always choose now.

He is sitting on the bed. This is different. Will it be different? He rises when I enter, his black-flag shadow unfurling over me. He moves to the closet. I watch him grasp the knob. My hands are shaking.

The door pulls back and he uses one arm to swipe at the shirts on hangers. They slide back, and he says, "Choose."

There on the wall, instead of belts, are hung figures, like marionettes. Their heads slumping, faces in shadow.

One is red-haired and lanky. He is clutching a tiny horse.

Another is small, wearing shorts and sneakers. Messy hair and a shirt with an airplane on it. He holds a stick sprouting two leaves.

There is a set of three, indistinguishable from one another. They all wear matching rings that flash from their left hands.

Then one with black hair pushed back from his forehead. This one is longer than the others. I can just catch the hint of a dimple in one cheek. His right hand holds a doll by one arm. She hangs, unceremoniously, glassy-eyed, stringy hair and a piece of black electrical tape over her mouth

The last figure is colored like coal, bony and hunched. Long ears and ribs poking out. His hands are empty.

"Choose," my father says again, "or I will choose for you."

SEVENTEEN

Joshua leads me down the street.

"Sam's house is around the corner," he says.

I follow him, the sun on my neck. Creep slinks along the edge of the sidewalk. He sings, the sound rising like heat from the concrete, a musical round our mother taught us when we were little: "Horsie, horsie, on your way. . ." I aim a kick at him. He dodges out of the way.

"Is Virgil your boyfriend?" Joshua says.

I run my hand over the top of my head. My hair burns my fingers. "No," I say. "I don't have a boyfriend."

"But you're going on a date."

I say. "This isn't a date."

We pass under the shade of a mesquite tree. Cicadas buzz. "What is it then?"

"It's not a date if you bring your little brother. Besides, I'm not allowed to date until I'm sixteen." *Thank God.* "Anyway, Mia's the one who set it up. This is all her fault."

Joshua whacks a fence with the stick he's carrying. "What's her fault? I thought you liked horses."

I feel like growling. "I *do* like horses," I tell him. "I just don't like boys."

"Why not?"

"Yeah, Ellie," says Creep from behind me. "Why not?"

I wish then I could stomp on Creep's head. I wish I could split it open like a rotten apple, the insides bubbling on the hot sidewalk. Black steam would rise. Noxious fumes.

I take a couple of big steps to catch up to Joshua. "Boys are gross," I say, hoping this will shut him up.

"Except me." He grins.

"Except you," I say. "You're only a *little* gross."

"Probably because of my farts," says Joshua, grinning wider, almost laughing.

"You're probably right," I say, shaking my head.

He turns up the front walk of a yellow single-story house. "It's this one."

Goosebumps prickle up my arms. I wipe my palms on my jeans to dry them. I feel suddenly sick. Joshua stands on the doorstep.

"C'mon." He waves me up to the door and then presses the bell.

I stand a little behind him. Creep squats next to my ankle. A few seconds after the chimes fade, the door opens and Sam lunges out to grab Joshua by the arm. While he says something to Joshua about Rocket League, Creep slinks around the two boys, through the doorway, and into the house. I peer after him. There's a tiled entryway. After that, the hall opens into a living room.

Virgil walks across the tile in socks. "Hey," he says to Sam. "Don't just make them stand out there." He gestures to us. "Come in."

I follow Joshua over the threshold. Virgil closes the door behind us.

The two boys run down the hallway and into another room.

"Hi," says Virgil behind me.

I turn around. He's wearing a green shirt the same color as his eyes. He runs one hand through his hair.

"Hi," I say. I put my hands behind my back.

"You want some lemonade?" he says.

"Sure," I say.

He walks down the hall. I follow him into the kitchen. It's white with white cabinets and a black stove and oven and red fridge. On the wall is a painting of a bowl of tomatoes. The floor is white tile and it smells like Pine Sol. Virgil gets a glass pitcher out of the fridge, sets it on the counter, fills two glasses and hands one to me. It's fridge cold with bits of pulp floating between ice cubes. It's so tart, my jaw aches. I wonder if Virgil made it.

"How was your week?" he asks.

But I am busy looking at the fridge. It reminds me of red Skittles.

"What?" I say.

"Your week," he says. "How was it?"

I don't know how to answer. Joshua and I haven't talked about Dad yet. And instead of thinking about it, I've filled my sketchbook, or started reading another novel, or looked at the horse wall. Creep's face appears from the other side of the bar counter. He leans over the pitcher, looks like he's about to spit into it.

"Um," I point at the lemonade. "You should put that back in the fridge before it gets warm."

Virgil raises one eyebrow at me, like a cartoon character. I just drink from my glass with my eyes pointed at the ceiling. The ice bounces against my teeth.

Sam and Joshua hoot from the living room. They jump and fall together on the floor, clutching Xbox paddles. They stare, smiling at the television where digital cars accelerate as a giant ball explodes into a goal. They laugh crazily. Lean against each other.

Virgil turns back from the fridge with two water bottles and a bag of carrots. He holds the carrots out to me. "So," he says. "You ready to go?"

No, I want to say. But I just take the carrots and nod.

He smiles, steps past me. I don't realize my shoulders have tensed until he is out of the kitchen. I lower them and drain my glass. The carrots are cold. I swing the bag a little.

"What a nice boy," says Creep. He smiles at me. Tilts his head to the side. Tilts it farther and farther until his ear touches the counter top and he falls into a sideways somersault. Then he laughs and laughs, holding his stomach like he can't stop, sprawled out like a bony puddle of ink. I stare at him, clenching my jaw. I wish I could scream. Right now. Hear my voice bounce off all the white tile and candy-red fridge. Drown out Creep's laughter. I take a deep breath.

Virgil reappears carrying a few things. "My mom's gonna drive us."

Virgil's mom has auburn hair pulled back into a ponytail, glittery sandals, and a ruffled purse over one shoulder.

"Hi, Eleanor." She smiles at me with whitened teeth. Creep snaps his jaws at her elbow. "Ready to help Virgil with some chores?"

I nod.

"Hey," she calls over the sound of the video game. Sam and Joshua lie on their stomachs, both staring up at the booming television, thumbs working furiously over their paddle buttons. "Hey," she says again.

The game pauses as Sam turns to look at her.

"I'm taking Virge and Eleanor over to the stables. I'll be back in ten minutes."

"Okay, Mom," says Sam. The game restarts, cars revving loud.

"And turn it down," she says. The volume lowers minutely.

I follow Virgil and his mother toward a door that opens into the garage.

"Have fun," calls Joshua.

"Yeah," Sam replies. "Have fun on your *da-a-a-ate.*"

They both make kissing noises and then roll on the floor laughing. Creep joins them. His grating giggle scratches at my eardrums. Virgil rolls his eyes. "Whatever," he calls back.

The stables are only five minutes away. His mother is rambling about how we could have walked here, but it's going to be hot enough to fry a dozen eggs on the sidewalk and our family doesn't hold up against the sun very well, you look like your people can take the sun, what's your ethnic background? And are you all ready for the new school year? I'm sure Virgil will be happy to know he'll have friends there. I just nod, holding the carrots in both hands.

"She's a quiet one," she says to Virgil. Then to me: "Do you always talk this much?"

I look over at her. Virgil told me I should sit in front with his mom, and she's smiling at me. I smile back.

She pulls off onto a dirt road near the foot of South Mountain. A series of low buildings, sagging fences and a sign arching over the road: Foothills Ranch. She stops the car under a towering pine.

"Okay, I'll be back in a few hours."

Virgil climbs out of the car, so I do too. Creep hops down into the dust. He squints into the blistering sun, then smiles at me. Virgil is holding a tan-colored cowboy hat upside down like a basket, to carry the water bottles, some work gloves, and another black baseball cap.

"Okay, Mom. See you."

She drives away.

Virgil holds out the hat basket to me and I take a water bottle and a pair of gloves, holding the carrots under my arm. The gloves are leather, worn slippery with age. "The hat is for you," he says. I pick up the baseball cap. It says in embroidered letters, *Ride The Wind*, and shows the white silhouette of a horse in full gallop.

I take it, trace the embroidered design with my thumb.

"You like it?" he asks.

I nod. "Yeah."

"I got it at the feed store. They have Western stuff there, but this seemed like an Eleanor thing." He shoves the other pair of work gloves into his back pocket and puts his own hat on, grinning at me from under the wide brim. "More than a cowboy hat anyway. C'mon."

He turns to walk toward the nearest building. I follow him, pulling my ponytail through the back of the cap, settling it into place. Creep skulks beside me.

"Huh," he says. "An Eleanor thing. I wonder if he would be able to figure out what other things are Eleanor things."

I kick dirt at him. He coughs. Waves a clawed hand in front of his face, and the dust hangs in a cloud that coats his eyeballs.

Virgil walks around the corner of the nearest building. I jog to catch up. I find him pulling a wheelbarrow from where it's propped against the wall in a clump of yellow weeds.

He maneuvers it across the dry ground. It bumps over a hummock of dirt.

"I've gotta muck out some stalls," he says. I nod, follow him through the dust. He pauses to unbar the stable entrance, a metal gate painted green.

The stable is dusk-dark after the relentless sun outside, and quiet, but the quiet is only a waiting stillness. I blink to adjust my eyes. Misters run across the ceiling, releasing a cloud of cool spray over the hard, tamped ground. The air filled with the scent of hay and the tang of animals. When Virgil whistles low, a bird call through forest trees, four horses put their heads over their stall doors, two on each side of the center aisle. One of them nickers a greeting. Virgil stops the wheelbarrow inside the door and puts on his gloves. A pile of hay waits in the corner. Virgil lifts a few armfuls to fill the wheelbarrow.

"Wanna meet the gang?" he asks me.

I nod. I watch Creep climb up into the rafters while Virgil wheels the barrow toward the first stall on the right.

A white mare with a long wavy mane nods at our approach. The silky hair rounds over her shoulders like silver, falls into her blue eyes. She shakes it aside to look at us.

"This is Lady," he says. "She's my mom's. She's a mustang mare that my mom adopted, like, fifteen years ago."

"She looks like a unicorn," I say.

"You can pet her," says Virgil. He adds hay to the rack in Lady's stall.

I hold my fingers under her muzzle and she whuffs into my hand, her lips like wet velvet.

"She's looking for a treat," he says. "You can give her a carrot."

I pull a carrot out of the bag. She breaks off the end and I get a glimpse of her square teeth. She crunches. Virgil leans against the stall door, watches Lady crunch away on the carrot, watches me slide my hand along her neck. I twist my fingers through her mane, the coils bright around my knuckles.

When I look at Virgil, he's smiling.

"What?" I say.

"C'mon," he says. "There are a few more to meet."

The next stall houses a buckskin gelding. He tosses his head and snorts. The straight black mane stands up like a mohawk and then flops over onto his neck.

"This is Cricket," says Virgil. He dumps hay in the rack. "He gets mad when his lunch is late."

I offer Cricket a carrot. Instead of biting through it, he clamps down and jerks his head back. I laugh when the carrot is pulled from my fingers.

"Like I said," says Virgil, "he's very impatient."

I scratch Cricket between the ears, his coal-black forelock coarse and thick under my fingers. Across his shoulders, the skin twitches at flies. I watch the swish of his tail around his flanks. When Cricket has finished crunching, he lowers his head over the stall door and pushes his face against my hip so I unbalance sideways into Virgil. Virgil puts up his gloved hands to stop me from falling.

Virgil laughs and steps back to make room. "He's looking for another carrot." He smells like chlorine and hay and sunscreen. I don't look at him, just down at Cricket's hooves. I have to stop myself from brushing the Virgil-feeling off my arm and shoulder. He seems to notice I've gone still, but he pretends not to.

"Here we have Luke Skywalker," he says, dipping into the wheelbarrow for an armful of hay. He steps across the aisle to the next stall, where a small black mare with a delicate face nods toward us. She lifts her chin, smacking her velvety lips together.

I laugh. "Luke Skywalker?"

Virgil leans across the stall door, picks a piece of hay out of the mare's mane.

"Sam named her," he says. "I tried to tell him it didn't work, but . . ."

"No," I say, pulling out a carrot. "I like it." Luke Skywalker nibbles the end. "She's very pretty," I say, pushing her forelock aside so that I can see the white diamond on her forehead.

"Yeah," says Virgil. "Really pretty."

I glance at him, but he isn't looking at the horse. He's looking at me. I concentrate on the carrot, on Luke Skywalker's rubbery lips as she breaks off small pieces. I don't look back up at Virgil, even though I want to. Heat rises into my cheeks.

Cricket snorts. Luke Skywalker tosses her head and the carrot goes flying. It hits Virgil in the head. He squints one eye, wipes his face and bends down to retrieve it. I cover my mouth to stifle a giggle, but when Virgil stands up, he's smiling.

We both laugh.

He hands me the carrot. Our fingers touch. I catch a glance of his grass green eyes before I wipe the dusty carrot on my leg and offer the rest of it to Luke Skywalker.

"Thanks for inviting me," I say to Virgil, but I'm looking at my own reflection in the mare's black pupil. I see Creep drop to the floor behind me.

I can hear the smile in Virgil's voice. "I'm glad you came," he says. He moves to the last stall. "This is Pancake."

Pancake is a deep chestnut red with white socks and a white blaze on his face. His mane shines in the shadowed light. He whuffs and pushes his head against my shoulder.

I turn to Virgil, "So who named Pancake?"

Virgil smiles at me.

"What?" I say. I feel Pancake's breath on the back of my neck. I turn around to realize the horse is nibbling on my ponytail. I pull the wet strands out of Pancake's mouth. His lips stretch back and he looks like he's smiling. He shakes his head at me. I hold out a carrot.

"He's a comedian," Virgil says. "I think he has a better sense of humor than anyone I know. Except maybe Sam, who laughs at everything. Let me grab some shovels."

I lean against Pancake's door, watch his tail swish through dust motes. "Must be nice," I say. Creep's shadow dances through the horse's legs.

"What?" he asks.

I turn away from him, cross back over to Lady's stall.

"Laughing at everything," I say. Lady blinks at me through her feathery eyelashes. Her nostrils flare under my palm. I want to braid her hair.

"It *is* nice," says Creep. I hear the click of his teeth. "I laugh at everything. I find this world delightful."

"Obviously," I say.

I pull three sections of Lady's wavy forelock apart and start to braid them. They're soft as corn silk. Creep hums to himself in Pancake's stall. I breathe deep the hay-warm-life smell of the horses, the mist drifting down from the shadowy rafters, sunlight cutting through the windows in regular swaths of yellow. I feel a part of me go quiet. Not just hiding, like usual – but quiet, still. The calm munching of the horses, their large and small shiftings as they move. I close my eyes, my hands still on Lady's forehead, wrapped in her mane.

"Here," says Virgil.

I jump.

"Sorry." He holds out a shovel. "I like it here too. It's peaceful."

When we turn the horses out, Virgil lets me lead them. They're so big, walking behind me. I can feel in the ground the impact of their hooves, all heavy muscle and bone and organs bigger than my head. I imagine Creep getting torn and trampled by their iron hooves and it makes me smile. But then they whuff and whicker and I forget to think about Creep.

The horses dance. They toss their heads and prance around the corral. Virgil says they just love the feeling of stretching their legs, and leaves me to watch. Pancake rolls in the dirt. Lady and Luke Skywalker start to race back and forth, loping along the fence rail. Dust rises. Lady's mane streams after her like a silver flag. After a while they all move over to a patch of grass under a stand of eucalyptus trees. I want to watch them all morning, but I know Virgil brought me here to help, so I go back to the barn.

He puts me to work moving things out of each stall. We rake, shovel, rake again. Sweat pours down my neck. We stop for water breaks, and other than making sure I didn't fall over in the barn, Virgil doesn't touch me once. By the time Virgil's mom is back, I'm covered with dust, hay, and sweat.

I wave to the horses as we walk to the car.

"So what do you think?" asks Virgil.

I take off my hat and use it to fan my face. "I guess I didn't ever really think about this part of having horses."

"Yeah," he says. He pulls the car door open for me. "It's a lot of work."

Virgil's mom doesn't talk to me this time, instead singing along to Patti LaBelle on the radio. I catch Virgil's eye in the side mirror and he shakes his head, but still smiles.

We're almost at Virgil's house when I realize I haven't seen or heard Creep in over an hour.

<u>New Friends:</u>

Mia
Virgil
Lady
Cricket
Luke Skywalker
Pancake

EIGHTEEN

"So how was it?"

Mia's got a pillow over her crossed legs. Mom said she could spend the night, and Sam is spending the night with Joshua. It's the first sleepover I've had since I was seven. Even Mia's pajamas are black — a spaghetti-strapped top with a picture of a winged goat holding a teddy bear and loose bottoms printed in pentagrams.

"It was fine." I can feel Creep watching us from the closet. He hasn't said anything since we got back from Virgil's, instead choosing to fill my head with that gargley humming.

Mia throws a piece of popcorn at me. "C'mon dude, you know what I mean. How *was* it?"

I smile, because I do sort of know what she means, even if I don't know exactly what she means. "It was fine." I pick at my quilt. The smile won't seem to drop off my face. "He was nice. He showed me around and we talked."

"Okay, okay. But did you go riding? You know, sitting behind him on a horse. Your arms wrapped around his stomach. Like the cover of one of those romance novels you see in the grocery-store checkout, except you're wearing jeans instead of baring a thigh under layers of petticoats. Virgil's one of those secretly hot guys. Like the kind that has to wring out his shirt at the church car wash and all the girls are like, 'Whaaaaat?'"

I roll my eyes while she chews some popcorn.
"So?"

I grab a handful of popcorn. It's buttery. Real butter, not the stuff you get out of a plastic tub like the one in our fridge. Mia brought it over along with her sleeping bag and a tote full of what she called "sleepover essentials."

"So, what?" I ask as I lick my fingers.

"So how are Virgil's abs? You touched them right?"

"Abs? C'mon!" I yell. I grab Mia's pillow and hit her across the head with it. She hits me back and popcorn goes everywhere. In the middle of the pillow fight, we hear Joshua's voice.

"Ellie, can we have some popcorn?" He and Sam stand in the doorway, their empty mixing bowl slick with butter.

Mia says, "Sure," and pulls out another two gallon ZipLock filled with popcorn. She tosses it to Sam.

The boys turn to each other, hold up and then pull back their fists in unison. "Yesss."

"Just a sec," I say to Mia as I follow Joshua and Sam back to their room. Creep pokes his head out between my skirts and skulks after us.

Joshua's room is a study in destruction. Legos are strewn. Every jet Joshua owns is lined up along the edge of the bed. I notice all of his clothes are off the hangers too, each drawer in his dresser emptied. Books are off the shelf in piles.

Creep laughs.

"What the –," I start. I shake my head. "What were you looking for?"

Joshua looks around. "Something to *do*." He says it like it was the dumbest question in the world.

"Okay," I say, wondering if I sound like Mom. "You gotta make sure this is cleaned up before Sam leaves tomorrow. Otherwise Mom will kill me."

Sam laughs. Josh nods.

"Seriously," I say to Sam.

"Okay," Sam says. He pulls open the bag of popcorn and dumps it into the bowl, getting a good part of it on the floor. Creep clicks his teeth together.

Back in my room, Creep jumps up onto the bed behind Mia. He crouches there so that when I look at her I can see him. She is cleaning her face with makeup remover. The cotton ball leaves a streak of wet on her dark skin that almost sparkles in the yellow light. Her lips are brown and pink now, instead of lipstick red. I scoop popcorn from the floor back into the bowl.

"You never answered my question," she says.

"Yes, Eleanor," says Creep, "tell us about Virgil's abs."

Mia doesn't notice my look at Creep as she wipes the black from around her eye.

"We didn't ride. We talked and mucked out the stalls."

She stops and stares at me. "Wait," she says. "You mucked out stalls. You *mucked*?"

Creep giggles.

Avoiding her eyes, I sweep my hand across the carpet to find stray kernels. "Yeah," I say to the dark space under the bed.

"Your first date and you mucked?"

Creep's laugh rakes into my ear.

I kneel up and fold my arms, eyes narrowed. "It wasn't a date."

"Uh, yeah. It was. And I can't believe you mucked on the first date." She's smiling now.

Creep falls over, arms wrapped around his stomach. He laughs and laughs, rolling back and forth.

"Shut up," I say as much to him as to Mia. "It wasn't a date. He needed help, so I helped him. Besides, *you* set it up."

"*I* set up a date." She points the cotton ball at me and laughs. "But you're the ones who mucked. Did you at least let him buy you dinner first?"

I start to smile.

"I bet it was hot," she says.

"It *was* hot," I say looking into the popcorn bowl. "... And dirty."

Mia laughs. Loud. I laugh too. Creep sits up. He watches us with one brow lowered. I like the effect my laughter has on Creep, so I laugh louder.

"How long did it take?"

"A couple of hours."

"You and Virgil mucked for *hours*?"

We're doubled over now. I have tears leaking and the makeup around Mia's remaining eye makes her look like someone punched her in the face.

My door flies open. Mom stands in the doorway, her mouth pressed into a thin line.

As the laughter fades, Mia and I both sit up. I wipe my cheeks.

"Here it comes," says Creep. The smile is back in his voice.

"Do you realize how loud you are?" says Mom. "Your father is trying to rest."

"Sorry," I say.

"Sorry what?" she says, her eyes hard. "You know how hard the chemo is on him."

I swallow. "I'm sorry, Mom. We'll be quieter."

She shakes her head and exhales. "You won't be *quieter*. You'll be *quiet*. Or Mia will go straight home."

"Okay."

"I'm serious, Eleanor."

Are you really? I couldn't tell. How serious are you? Are you serious as a heart attack? Are you serious as cancer?

"I know, Mom. Sorry."

She closes the door.

Mia cleans the makeup off her second eye and says, "Whoa."

I climb up onto the bed and fall back into my pillow. "I know."

"No. Eleanor, why didn't you tell me?"

I stare at the ceiling, looking for the spackle shaped like an upside-down whale. "Tell you what?"

"Um. That your dad has cancer."

I shrug. "I dunno. We don't really talk about it."

I can feel her watching me. I don't look at her. Instead, I find the spackle whale. Its tail touches a pattern resembling two birds in flight.

"Sorry," I say again.

She chews on her bottom lip. She fishes around in her sleepover tote. I hear the crinkle of paper and foil. "You don't talk about it in the family, or with anyone?"

I trace the birds with my eyes. "I dunno."

"How long has he had it?"

"I dunno."

"Dude, that's messed up. What *do* you know?"

She's never asked me this many questions all in a row. My heart starts to pound. I roll onto my side and lean up on one elbow. Creep hunches up behind Mia. He stares at me. I can see us reflected in his eyes.

"I don't know what I know. Okay? I know we moved here and I was glad to leave, because I didn't have any friends there and I could get away from—" I stop. "But it's like everything is still the same. I'm the same – he's the same." I stop again.

"Who? Your dad?"

I shake my head. I can feel tears starting to form, that familiar tightening in my chest. I don't want to cry in front of Mia. I've cried in front of Creep a million times, but it's not the same thing. I clench my jaw and put my hand over my eyes.

Mia taps me on the shoulder. I open my eyes. She hands me a square of dark chocolate. I want to laugh. Or scream. I put the chocolate in my mouth and lay back on my pillow again.

"Look," says Mia. "I know how you feel. Cancer is crazy. My aunt had it and my grandma, too. Lots of times, people will just be okay. You know?"

The chocolate begins to dissolve. It's creamy and bitter and tastes dark like being caught in a dream you can't wake up from.

You don't know how I feel.

"I don't know if I *want* him to be okay," I say.

"Dude, that's messed up," says Creep in Mia's voice.

Mia just chews the inside of her lip. She breaks off another piece of chocolate and then balances it on my nose.

I smile. A tear runs out of the corner of my left eye. I add the chocolate to the melted piece on my tongue, biting down this time, and it splits between my teeth.

"Things *are* different, you know," she says.

I sniff. "What do you mean?"

Mia lays down next to me and our shoulders touch. We both stare at the ceiling.

"You've moved into this rad neighborhood. Mostly rad because this is where *I* live. Knowing me is already changing everything. I mean, think about it. Here we are having a sleepover and… how long has it been since you've done that? And thanks to me, now you know Virgil. And I'm sure he'll have you over to muck again very soon."

I snort.

We lie next to each other on my bed, staring up at the ceiling. Mia says, "See that spot right there?" She points. "It kinda looks like a shark… or a …"

"Whale," I finish. "And right there next to it? Two birds." She eats another piece of chocolate and passes one to me.

Creep moves to sit between our heads. I close my eyes so that I can't see him hovering over us.

"Hey," I say into the blackness behind my eyelids. "Can I ask you a question?"

"Sure," she says. "It's only fair."

It's just her voice and the touch of her shoulder and the breeze from the fan and my mouth full of warm rich bitterness, and I feel like if I never see Mia again after this night, dark chocolate will always make me think of her. I swallow.

Creep ruins the moment by saying, "Ask her when she's finally going to get tired of you and leave."

I ignore him. "What's your girlfriend's name?"

Mia says, "Ex-girlfriend. Celeste." She pauses, like she's remembering Celeste. "We met at school. We were in theater together. She put on this amazing gender-bent one-act version of Hamlet in the black box."

"She sounds cool," I say. "When did you know you were…."

"…an abomination?" Mia finishes.

I cringe. "Sorry about that."

Mia laughs, but it does sound strained. "It's fine. Josh was just repeating what he's heard. In this community, I'm used to it. I'm not exactly out at church, but my parents know."

Creep starts to hum

"How did you come out to your parents?"

"I had thought for a long time about the best way to do it. Best words to use. Best time to bring it up. I was waiting for the perfect moment, to kind of make it easier to swallow. Turned out to be much easier to bring up the subject than I thought it would be."

"How's that?" I ask.

"They caught us making out the night she stayed for a sleepover. They didn't know it was a *girlfriend* sleepover."

"Wow," I say. I still have my eyes closed. I imagine Mia and Celeste in bed, kissing, touching. I imagine Mia's fingers in Celeste's electric-blue mohawk. Celeste's tongue in her mouth.

I open my eyes. Creep is leaning over me, staring into my face. He's smiling. I close my eyes again.

"Yeah," Mia is saying. "They thought the worst. We were in my bed. They thought we were having sex."

"Would you?" I pause. "Have had sex? If they didn't catch you."

"Not everyone is you, Eleanor," says Creep.

"Nah," Mia says. "I'm not ready for that. I would have played with her boobs though. I love boobs." She stops. "You asked me something that I don't think I answered. What was it?"

"When did you know?"

"Oh," she says. "Right. I always knew on some level, I guess. When they started talking about marriage and the role of women and being a worthy wife for your valiant husband, you know, in twelve-year Sunday school? That was all so gross for me. Like it's the absolute worst thing I could think of to marry a man and touch a penis." She shudders.

Her reaction makes me snort again. But then I stop laughing to think about her words.

She changes position. I open my eyes. She is lying on her side, facing me, propped up on one elbow.

"Are you straight?" she asks.

Yes, I want to say right away. *Of course.* But I don't answer. I just refuse to make eye contact while she watches me watch the ceiling fan.

"You don't have to tell me," she says, "just because I told you." She lies back down again, her shoulder and hip pressing into mine now.

"No," I say, "It's not that. I just… don't know. I don't know what I am."

"I know what you are," says Creep. He slinks across the top of my pillow and drops off the edge of the bed.

"That's okay," Mia says. "You don't have to know. You can just be Eleanor."

What if I don't want to be Eleanor? I think.

"How do you know?" I ask. "If you're…"

"Queer?" says Mia. "Some people just know, from the beginning. Others it takes longer. Because we're all programmed to think straight is the default."

"Isn't that a bad word? The way I've heard it…" I say. "It's not nice."

"Queer? We've reclaimed it," says Mia. "Girl, we need to get you online."

I don't say anything. After a while Mia says, "What's wrong?"

"I'm not sure how to say it," I say.

"Just say it," she says.

"Can you not call me that?"

Mia pauses, probably running the conversation back in her mind. "Oh, 'girl?' Okay," she says. "No problem."

"Thanks," I say. We're both quiet. Then I say, "I still don't get how people just… know." I don't tell Mia that I was always taught that queer people were sick or confused.

Mia laughs. It's just a small sound. More of a puff of air through her nose a few times.

"You'll know. You'll figure it out. But you don't have to label it if you don't want to. A lot of people do because it helps them figure themselves out, to name things. Trans, bi, ace, pan, enby. Some people just use queer. But you can just be Eleanor," she says again. "Or you can just be whatever. Even straight." She laughs. "Whatever you are is cool with me." She sits up. "Hey," she looks down at me. "You can tell me stuff you know. Eleanor stuff."

I really can't, I think. I sit up too, my eyes sweeping the floor for Creep.

Then Joshua knocks on the door and pokes his head in. "You guys wanna play Ninja UNO?" He opens the door wider. Sam stands behind Joshua. He produces a bag of Skittles and origami throwing stars made of colored paper.

"What's Ninja UNO?" asks Mia.

Josh says, "We don't know." He and Sam look at each other and erupt into giggles.

I shush them while Mia says to me, "What do you think?"

I look at the ceiling, pretending to think about it. "Well, they obviously need our help."

"Obviously," Mia agrees. "And we are clearly game experts."

"Clearly," I say.

We go into the farthest corner of the family room with flashlights and bowls of popcorn and set to work inventing a new game. Everyone contributes random rules, Sam uses a Sharpie to change one of the +4 cards into a +10 card, Joshua keeps telling everyone to switch their hands with an opponent, a lot of wrestling between the two boys ensues and Ninja UNO is born. "No," says Josh. "*Ninj-UNO.*"

Played silently, of course. Because as Sam says, "Ninjas are silent, but deadly."

And then Joshua says, "I thought those were farts."

And then we all have to cover our mouths to keep from waking Mom up again.

Dear Jesus,
Am I straight?
It would be really helpful if you would just...
let me know.
Amen.

NINETEEN

Around 3am, Mia digs in her sleepover tote. She hands me a smart phone with wired earbuds wrapped around it.

"So my dad got me a new phone and I thought you could use my old one. Until you get your own. It won't have data, because you don't have a phone plan, but you can take pictures, and if you can get the WiFi password, you could use apps for messaging and video calls."

I reach out to pluck the device from her hand.

"I've signed you into my Spotify," she says. "So you can access my playlists." She turns it on, shows me how to find the app, and then passes it back to me.

I scroll through the music list. Morrisey, Bjork, David Bowie, Michael Kiwanuka, Counting Crows, The Smiths, Lupe Fiasco, The Decemberists, Sigur Ros. And there are more.

"I don't know any of these bands."

"Are you kidding me?"

"Okay, well I know Coldplay because they're on the radio."

Mia laughs. "These other guys are on the radio too, you just have to listen to the right stations. 80s, 90s, disco, post-grunge, jazz fusion, trap, industrial. Not that top forties crap." She stops. "Okay, maybe this stuff isn't on the radio anymore."

"I don't really ever listen to the radio unless we're in the car or on the bus. My parents listen to oldies and classical and church music. Mom says everything else is too worldly."

Mia looks nonplussed. "Okay, well, consider this your musical education. My child, you have issues and you need music."

I want to hug her. "No one's ever given me something like this."

She bumps her shoulder against mine. "You're welcome. There's a charger too."

She shows me the playlists:

Rock Out. "Lots of Queen, The Clash, Van Halen, Nirvana, Led Zeppelin. You'll dig it."

Cerebral. "For studying. It's all instrumental. Chillwave, trance, lo-fi, and those stupid string-quartet tributes. I mean, really, how many versions of *Smooth Criminal* do we really need? But I love them."

Covers. "Cuz covers are rad. *Boys Of Summer* by The Ataris? *I Will Survive* by Cake? *Crazy* by Daniela Andrade? Sick."

Love Mix. "Al Green, Marvin Gaye, The Temptations... a lot about relationships. You can listen to it and think about all the ones you've loved and lost." I elbow her in the ribs.

Dubstep. "This is, like, angry robot music. My dad calls it *screamo for nerds.*" The look on my face prompts her to say,

"Just listen to it while reading some old-school sci-fi. It will freak you out."

All Black. "Prince, Binki, Janelle Monáe, KAMAUU, Megan Thee Stallion, Isaac Dunbar, Childish Gambino, Stevie Wonder, Unlike Pluto. Good luck finding a cooler playlist."

Goth. "Bauhaus, Cocteau Twins, Dead Can Dance, Type O Negative, Lacuna Coil. Arise your inner darkness."

Indie. "Bands you've never heard of."

Issues. "Put it together just for you. It's really random."

There are more, but she yawns. "I'm so wiped. Night."

Then she curls up, still facing me, and instantly falls asleep. I don't know how I feel about another body in the bed with me, but since there's a pillow wedged between us, I suppose it's okay.

Creep sits next to my pillow, licking his hands until they drip and then rubbing them all over his face.

"Do you mind?" I whisper.

I scroll through the list of bands and songs. There are hundreds. I sit up.

"What are you doing?" asks Creep.

"I'm going to find that WiFi password," I tell him.

"Mom won't like that." Creep smiles widely. "Let's do it."

I roll my eyes. "You're not invited," I say.

Creep laughs. "You could print that on a shirt and wear it, Eleanor. It wouldn't make any difference."

I slowly get out of bed and tiptoe to the door, slipping the phone into my pocket. Creep follows me.

"What do you think she wants?" he says.

I ignore him.

Out in the black hallway, he asks again. "What do you think she wants?"

"What do you mean?" I whisper.

At the base of the stairs he says, "Mia." He snaps his teeth. "What do you think she wants from you?"

"Would you shut up? I'm trying to concentrate."

Creep doesn't shut up. I take the stairs one step at a time. I try to ignore him. I don't remember which stairs squeak, so I go very slowly. Counting to ten after easing myself up onto each step, Creep sitting next to my feet. He is talking about Mia and how she obviously wants something from me because who would be friends with *you*, Eleanor, unless you had something they wanted and on and on and on.

The entire house is dark, quiet. I can hear the hum of the fridge, the whisper of the air conditioning. I turn left at the top of the stairs, pausing to listen. Creep does the same, quiet for a moment. When I move to the hallway, he starts talking again.

"You know what I'm talking about. No one gives you something like that without wanting something in return."

I push open the study door. The room is pitch black. I pull the phone out and turn on the flashlight, putting it on the lowest setting.

"Not Mia," I whisper.

"Yes, Mia," he says as I move to the filing cabinet where Mom keeps all of her important papers. I click open the heavy top drawer and it creaks. I stop, listening for any movement in my parents' room at the end of the hall. Creep's voice starts up again when I slowly pull the drawer out the rest of the way.

"Yes, Mia," he says again. "She's just like everyone else. Like Ian."

Stop talking about him, I want to say. I'm looking for a folder marked Internet/Cable. I find it and pull it out of the drawer with one hand. A yellow sticky note just inside says *WiFi password: JesusSaves777!* I take a picture of it.

"You remember Ian," Creep is saying. "Your special friend. He wanted lots. And your parents practically paid him for it."

His voice bites. A headache starts to form around my eyes. I stuff the folder back into the drawer.

BACK IN MY ROOM, I CLICK THE DOOR SHUT BEHIND ME. CREEP hasn't stopped talking about Ian, and what Mia will take from me. I crawl into bed next to Mia. The headache has begun to stab. I enter the password to access our network, which my mother has named *Josh.24:15*. I cram the earbuds in my ears, open the playlist, and click on the first song that pops up. It's called *Winter*.

A lyrical piano begins to sound and then the wavery voice of a woman. I can't hear Creep. His mouth keeps moving, but I might as well be deaf to him. The piano and the voice fill my ears completely. It's like a miracle.

The woman sings about snow and drifts and gloves. I stare at the horse wall and think about the barn and Virgil. I imagine snowflakes caught in Lady's mane, piles of glittering snow and an ice-cold wind sweeping around the horses' fetlocks. I see their breath steaming, crystals forming around their nostrils. Virgil has an outstretched hand, fingers pink with cold. I take it.

The wavery-voiced woman is asking someone when they will make up their mind. She sings about things changing. I think about Mia. *Things are different*, she said. The music swells.

I still can't hear Creep. I close my eyes.

I think about Mia in the snow. A black beanie pulled down to cover her ears. Nose nipped red. I think about her wrapped in a long trailing scarf. I pick up the end of the scarf and hand it to her. I think about her under the naked branches of winter trees, looking up into a cool twilight as snowflakes sparkle on her lipstick. She pulls a red mitten off and interlaces her fingers with mine.

I open my eyes to look at Mia. Her lips are parted a little, her tank-topped chest rising and falling in the regular breaths of deep sleep, her hair a curly black tumble across the pillow. I roll over, warm and self-conscious.

Creep is watching me. Knowingly. Nastily. He says something, but I still can't hear him. I close my eyes.

<u>Things That Change:</u>

Different neighborhood
New friends
I met horses
Me?

The Box

We are in the car. Mom drives. Joshua sits next to me on the backseat bench. The sun falls on everything outside. Blinding brilliant white. I have to squint my eyes almost shut to see. Peer through eyelashes and I wonder where we're going

Where are we going?

In front of us, I can see a truck filled with boxes. Each box has a name on it. The box with Dad's name overflows with belts. Black, brown. Some thick, others thin like ropes. Mom's box is filled with flowers. Marigolds, sunflowers, daisies. Joshua's box rattles with model cars and trucks, toy airplanes. My box is filled with clothes I used to wear. Stuff I haven't worn for years.

As we drive, clothes begin to drift out of my box. They float back to our car and flap against the windshield.

Mom turns on the windshield wipers.

"Eleanor," she says. "You were supposed to pack that box so nothing would come out."

Wipers sweep back and forth. The white frilly church dress flutters, a yellow shirt with a scalloped collar, flowered cotton underpants. They *move across the windshield in a slow-motion breeze. Some of them get caught on the wipers. Red overalls from first grade, undershirts and pink panties.*

"Eleanor," says Mom again. "People shouldn't see this. How could you let everyone see this?"

TWENTY

"**E**leanor!"

I sit up tangled in earbud cords. My eyes feel glued shut, pressed together by the heaviness of a normal night of bad dreams. It has to be just past dawn. When I squint at the clock, it reads 9:00 am. Joshua calls down the stairs again.

"Eleanor!"

Dirty laundry. My mother's disapproving voice.

Sprawled next to me, Mia snores softly. I rub my eyes. I can sense Joshua winding up to scream my name again.

"Yeah," I shout back. "Yeah. Coming."

Mia doesn't even twitch.

I stumble from the bed, tripping over Mia's shoes and then stepping in the popcorn bowl, which makes me growl. Saturday morning cartoon sounds drift down the hall and I can see Sam's back as he sits cross-legged in front of the TV, rocking back and forth. His voice joins in singing, "Who lives in a pineapple under the sea?"

My back hurts. I use my hands on the stairs, walking like Creep. By the time I reach to take the receiver from Joshua, I'm less happy than I started. "Are you crazy? Mom and Dad'll kill you, screaming like that."

"Duh," says Josh. "They're gone."

I scowl at the wall as Joshua runs back down the stairs.

"Hello?"

"Hi. Eleanor?" It's Virgil.

"Oh. Hi." I smooth my hair with one hand.

"It's Virgil."

"I know."

"Oh."

There's a long silence. I doodle on the wall with my finger and bite the inside of my cheek. Then we both start talking at the same time.

I say, "How did you get my number?" and he says, "So I was wondering – "

We both laugh.

We both start talking again.

I say, "You first." He says, "Go ahead."

We both laugh again. I wonder if he's wearing the green shirt that matches his eyes. There's another long silence. He coughs.

I finally say, "You first," again.

"I got your number from Mia," he says.

"Oh," I say.

"Is that okay?"

I smooth my hair again. "I guess so. Yeah."

He exhales, like he's been holding his breath this whole time. "Okay. Cool." He pauses. When he speaks again, it's all in a rush. "So I was wondering if you had any fun the other day. I mean, if you didn't, I can understand that because mucking isn't really fun and it was kinda too hot to go riding even though I would like to take you riding sometime. I was just hoping that you would still want to go riding even though we had to muck last time. I mean if you wanted to come see the horses again, we wouldn't have to muck if you didn't want to, we could ride or whatever instead. Or just hang out. Or we could muck if you did have fun doing that. I just wanted you to know that if you want to come again, it doesn't always have to be about mucking. So do you want to?"

I laugh.

He says, "What?"

I shake my head. "It's just Mia."

"What about her?"

From behind me I hear Mia's voice at the same time. "What about me?"

I turn around and she's on the couch, yawning under a jungle of hair.

She says, "Who is it?"

I cover the mouthpiece. "Shut up."

Her face lights up. "Is it Virgil?"

The invisible lasers I fire at her from my eye sockets have no effect.

"Eleanor?" says Virgil.

"It *is* Virgil! Tell him I say hi," she says. She bounces off the couch.

"No," I tell her. I hold out one hand, trying to stop her approach.

"What?" says Virgil.

"Oh, c'mon," says Mia, at my shoulder now. "Is he asking you to go mucking again?"

"No," I say to Virgil. "It's Mia. She's here."

Mia reaches for the receiver. "Let me talk to him."

I pull away. "No. Mia. Virgil, sorry. Just a sec."

We wrestle over the phone. She pulls on my shirt to reach it. I elbow her in the stomach. She kicks me in the back of the knee. We both fall on the floor. Luckily my arms are longer than hers.

"Virgil," she says. "Virgil! Eleanor wants to muck with you again."

I sit up and say into the phone, "Call you back."

Mia lies on her back, giggling breathlessly. She lets go of my leg and I stand to hang up the phone.

I sit next to her on the carpet. My nerves are on fire after wrestling. I have to shrug my shoulders and rub both arms to get rid of the slithery feeling.

"Sorry," she says. "I was in the moment."

"Me too," I tell her. And I was. "But maybe don't do that again."

She nods. "Sorry," she says again.

"It's okay," I tell her. "But we can't be so loud."

"What do you mean?" she asks.

I pick at the carpet. I wipe my hand one way across the fibers and then the other. "My parents are weird about noise. Also–," I look down the hallway toward my parent's room.

"I thought your parents weren't here," she says.

I stand up and gesture for her to follow me. We go into the kitchen. I pull out two boxes of cereal, one Frosted Mini-Wheats and one Honey Nut Cheerios. I put them on the table. Mia gets the milk out of the fridge. I get two bowls and two spoons. She sits in Joshua's chair. I slide a bowl over to her and pour Mini-Wheats into mine. When I look at her, she is watching me. Still waiting for an answer, but not stepping all over me for it.

I tell her, "I like how you just wait."

She pours Cheerios into her bowl. "It *is* kind of nice to have a friend that doesn't dominate the conversation," she says. "As you've probably noticed, I'm very reserved. It's hard for me to get a word in edgewise sometimes." Milk splashes over her cereal. She wrinkles her nose at me. "Seriously, though," she says, pushing her Cheerios down with her spoon so they all get wet. "Elle, you're weird and whatever, but I know you've got a story just like everybody. I just figure you'll tell me whenever. Or not." She takes a bite and looks at me, chewing.

Elle. No one's ever called me that before. It's calm. Soft. Open. Like the breath you take after a sip of lemonade.

"What are you thinking?"

"Elle," I say.

"Oh, sorry," she says. "I'm always giving people nicknames."

"No," I tell her. "I like it." I spoon a Mini-Wheat into my mouth. Milk squeezes out the sides of the square, across my tongue and down my throat. I pull the cereal box close and lean over my bowl. Mia does the same. It's like a fort between the boxes.

"About my parents," I say low, "they don't know that I went with Virgil."

"Why are you being so quiet?" asks Mia. "They're not here."

I look into my bowl. Could I scream down the stairs, even without my parents around? "Just, habit, I guess."

"Wait. They don't know you went to the stables?" Mia furrows her eyebrows. "Why not?"

"Because I didn't tell them." I scoop more squares into my mouth. They're softening fast.

"Why not?" she says again.

"Because they would freak out."

Mia smiles. "Well, you did muck on the first date."

I smile. What if I dumped the soggy Mini-Wheats over her head? "Seriously," I say. "They would freak out if they knew."

"Really?"

I nod.

"But you guys just shoveled horse crap. You didn't even touch his abs."

I almost choke. Mia laughs.

Joshua and Sam come into the kitchen.

"What are you laughing at?" asks Joshua. He boosts himself up onto the counter, opens the cabinet and hands two bowls to Sam.

"Virgil's abs," says Mia. I haven't finished almost choking the first time, and it happens all over again.

"Gross," says Joshua. "You touched Virgil's abs?" He jumps down from the counter.

"What're abs?" says Sam.

"No," I say, finally swallowing. "I didn't touch Virgil's abs."

The boys reach across us for the cereal boxes. They fill their bowls and start eating.

"What *did* you touch?" asks Sam between mouthfuls.

Mia laughs.

"Um, *nothing*," I say.

Mia points her spoon at me. "They did muck though."

I smack her arm.

"Ew!" say the boys together. They share a look.

"What's muck?" asks Joshua.

Sam says, "Shoveling horse poop."

"Gross," says Joshua again. "That's worse than I thought."

Sam says to me with his mouth full, "Virgil really likes you."

Mia elbows me. She raises her eyebrows three times. I kick her under the table.

"Oh, yeah?" she says. "What did he say?"

"He talks about her all the time." He sticks his tongue out. "Yech."

I can't help smiling into my bowl.

Mia pats my arm. "You need to call him back."

I shake my head. "Um. No. Not with you around."

"No, I was just playing before. I'll leave you alone. Promise. Just do it. Ooh, wait! I have an idea." She pulls out her phone. "You can call him from my phone."

Butterflies erupt in my stomach. "Maybe I could call him from mine," I tell her. "I got the WiFi password."

"You got the password?" Mia squeals at the same time that Joshua exclaims, "You got a phone?"

Mia jumps up and runs downstairs. I tell Joshua, "Yes, and you can't say anything to Mom or Dad about it."

Joshua considers this. "Can I play games on your phone?"

Sam says, "*My* older sister has tons of games on *her* phone."

Mia is back, out of breath and grinning, she has my phone and hers.

"They want to know if there are games on this phone," I tell her.

"Oh yeah," says Mia, swiping open her phone and navigating through apps. "Lots." She looks at me. "What's the network called?"

I tell her and she rolls her eyes. "What's the password?"

I tell her it's in the photos on my phone and she opens up the most recent picture. She reads it aloud and then looks up at me, completely straight-faced in amused irony.

"My *God*," she says, typing it in, shaking her head. "Christians." Then she puts her phone down and picks up mine again. "Okay, now that I can bogart your WiFi. Let's set you up to make calls." All three of us wait, watching her. "What's your email?"

I tell her and she types and swipes and furrows her brows.

My face feels hot. The butterflies have multiplied. "Okay." I point at the boys. "You guys be quiet. Don't say anything."

They look at each other. Joshua makes a face at me.

The phone begins to chime. Mia shoves it at me. "It's ringing."

"Wait." I take it with sweating hands. "What?" I hold it up to my ear.

The chiming stops and there's a click. "Hello?" says Virgil.

Josh, Sam, and Mia are staring at me. I turn my back. "Hi," I say. Mia is whispering something. I glance over my shoulder.

"It's a video call," she hisses.

"Hello?" says Virgil. "Who is this?"

I pull the phone away from my ear to look at it. Virgil's face, outside, branches and leaves behind him.

"Oh," I say. "Sorry. It's me."

"Eleanor?"

"Yeah," I say. "It's me. Eleanor."

"Oh hi," he says. "I couldn't really tell who it was. I'm kinda just looking up your nose."

"Oh!" I lift the phone up and away from my face, horrified. Mia is stifling a laugh. I glare at her.

"Ok," he says. "That's better. Hi, Eleanor." He smiles.

"Ok," I say. "Sorry. Hi." There's a small box in the corner, showing Virgil's view of me. I try holding the phone above me, but then I can suddenly see my whole body and I whip it downward again. I try holding it out at arm's length directly at eye level and that seems to be better. I can't ignore Mia and the boys staring at me. I turn my back again, but then they're suddenly visible behind me. I spin back around. Mia is laughing now.

"Hey, sorry about earlier," I tell him. "Mia was distracting." I'm trying to look at him instead of at me. He's moving through a doorway into the dark. Then the picture adjusts and I can see walls and a ceiling and a door filled with light behind him as he walks through rooms.

"Why's she over there so early?"

"She spent the night. Sam's here too."

"Bet that was fun." He's moving down a hallway.

"It was actually," I say. "We invented a new card game."

"You and Mia hung out with the boys?" he asks.

"Sure," I say. "Sam shared his Skittles." Virgil stops. There is a painting of a tree behind him.

Sam ducks his head behind a cereal box.

"That brat," laughs Virgil.

"What?" I say.

"Tell that brat-hole he owes me a bag of Skittles."

I point at Sam. He and Joshua exchange a high five.

Virgil enters a new room. He moves around and I can see band posters, and a mobile hanging from the ceiling, blue and red planets rotating.

"Where are you?" I ask him.

"My room," he says. He switches the camera and then slowly sweeps it around the room. I can see shelves of books and movies, a desk, a dresser with photo frames, a bed with a green cover.

"Wait," I say. "Go back."

The camera drifts back to the dresser.

"I want to see your pictures," I say.

The camera moves closer. There are snapshots of Virgil and Sam together riding horses, one of a young Virgil holding a baby wrapped in a blue blanket. He's sitting next to an older girl with long orange hair.

"Is that your sister?" I ask.

The camera stops. The older girl has her arm around little Virgil, one hand supporting the baby, like she's making sure Virgil doesn't drop him. She and Virgil have the same smile.

"Yeah," he says. "Clare. She lives in Utah."

The camera moves on. There's a photo of Virgil's mom with Lady, two photos of Virgil and Mia. One photo shows them about Joshua's age, sitting together on the back of an elephant, and a more recent photo, probably taken at school. They're dressed as Doctor 10 and River Song. A final frame on the end shows Virgil young again. He looks like Sam, sitting in stadium-style seats with another little boy. Both boys have tubs of popcorn. They squint against a high-noon sun. The camera moves to swing away.

"Wait.. who's that?" I ask. The camera moves back to the last frame. "Yeah," I say.

Virgil sighs. "That's Levi."

My mouth drops open. "Why do you have a photo with Levi?" I look over at Mia, who has been obviously listening. She is looking at the ceiling and shaking her head.

He switches back to the front-facing camera and he's shaking his head too, a chagrined look on his face. "It's a long story," he says. "I'll tell you sometime if you want, but I want to show you my collage."

"Okay," I say, swallowing all of my questions.

When the camera flips again, it shows Virgil's horse wall. But it's not just a piece of the wall, like mine. It's the entire wall. Hundreds of pictures, every single one different.

I walk into the living room, holding the phone out in front of me. I sit on the couch at the same time the camera switches back to Virgil's face.

"Wait," I say. "Go back again."

He switches the camera again to show me the horse wall. I can't even see the whole thing, it's so big. "That's so cool." I tell him.

His face appears. I think he's sitting on his bed. "Thanks. I started it when I was eight."

I don't tell him that I started mine when I was eight too. I think about how we're in Virgil's room. Sitting on his bed. I start to blush.

"What are you guys doing today?" He asks.

I want to cover my face. "I dunno," I tell him.

"Wanna go to the Seven-Eleven? I'll spring for Slurpees."

I jump up and walk back to the kitchen, "You guys wanna go to the Seven-Eleven?"

The boys pop out of their chairs. Sam knocks over his bowl. They throw their dishes in the sink and rush downstairs to change.

Mia gestures to her face. "I need at *least* half an hour," she says.

"Come over in an hour," I tell him.

He falls back on his bed and I'm looking down at him, his hair on the pillow, and I'm imagining him with eyes half-lidded, holding my name in his mouth and he's pulling at me—

"I gotta go," I say.

He waves, smiling. "Bye."

<u>Things I know about Virgil from looking at his room:</u>

He likes music.
He reads.
He likes space.
The color green.
He has a sister.
He used to be friends with Levi.
He collects horses, like I do.
~~His hair falls back from his forehead when he's~~

TWENTY-ONE

I sit on the toilet lid and watch Mia apply her makeup. Creep squats in the tub. He comments on everything Mia does. It's like watching a live demonstration of fine art, with a scathing critic giving a play by play. Mia's process is a long one involving colored liquids, powders, pencils, and brushes.

She's wearing a large black tee that's been cut into a crop top. It shows a black dragon, wings outspread, engulfing the words *BURN THE PATRIARCHY* in flame. The dragon flashes a rainbow of belly scales. It looks angry. She has a plaid pleated skirt this time, like a kilt. Maybe it *is* a kilt. Black and red striped knee socks. Little black Mary Jane shoes with flames stitched in red.

"I like your shirt," I say. I'm turning my phone over and over in my hands.

She outlines her eyes in black with a tiny brush.

"Thanks," She says, "I bought it from an indie artist online." She eyes me. "I think you're a closet goth."

I look down at my jeans, my black v-neck not filled out by anything.

"Look at that skin," she says. "You're practically white. I mean, you're white, but you're actually white. Like, literally white."

I turn around to look at myself in the mirror. Sunken eyes, black curtain of hair. The usual.

"My dad is brown," I say. "I tan really easily. I guess it's mostly because I usually spend most of my time reading or drawing. Inside. Too much of my time, my mom says."

"Take it from me," she says, spreading dark gray shadow across her eyelid. "You've already got the whole mistress-of-the-night thing going for you. There are goths who would kill for your complexion. Guess how many people think Afro-Latinas can be goth? It's like a rule or something. Goths can't be people of color."

"That's dumb," I say.

She adds a deep red and blends the color toward the corner of her eye. I open the camera app and set it to black and white. I frame Mia on the screen, leaning toward the mirror, lips parted, painting her lid with a delicate brush. I take a photo and she flicks her gaze over to me for a moment.

"How did you like your first video call with Virgil?"

"Um," I say, putting the phone in my pocket. "Please, never do that again. I've had video calls with my grandparents on my mom's phone, but that's it."

"So you've never had a boyfriend?"

I shake my head. "No." *I've never had a girlfriend either*, I want to say. I say instead, "I still don't get how people know."

"Know what?"

"That they're…" I pause.

"Queer," says Mia. She looks at me in the mirror. "You can say it." She starts working on her makeup again. "Some people say even just wondering whether you're queer is a sign that you're not straight."

"What if I'm straight," I say, "but broken… or confused, I guess?"

She turns around and leans against the counter. "What would you be confused about?" She asks. "Are you attracted to girls?"

"No," I say, not meeting her gaze. Then, "I don't know."

She looks at me for a long moment and says, "Fair enough." She turns back to the mirror. "Try not to worry about it too much. You'll figure it out. And I'll be here to help, if you need it." She says to her reflection and then to me, "I wish you could have seen yourself dancing around trying to figure out how to hold that phone. Classic."

"Classic," repeats Creep in Mia's voice. "Classic Eleanor."

"Great," I say. "Glad I'm so entertaining."

She giggles. Then steps back to regard her face in the mirror. "You really are," she says to her reflection. Then she turns. "Dude," she says. "You should totally let me do your makeup."

I shake my head. "My mom wouldn't like it."

"C'mon, Elle," she says. "She's not here."

I look in the mirror again. I can feel Creep watching me. "C'mon, *Elle*," he says. "You can make yourself all pretty for the new boy."

"Don't," I say, but stop myself. *Don't call me that. Don't turn my new name into something bad.*

Mia shrugs. "All right."

"No," I tell her. "Do it."

THE BOYS LET VIRGIL IN. I CAN HEAR HIS VOICE ACROSS THE hall in Joshua's room.

"Are you okay with me touching your face?" she asks.

I nod, steeling myself.

Mia paints my eyes, paying extra attention to the outer corners. Every touch thrums a chill down my spine. I take deep breaths, imagining Virgil's horses as they canter around the corral. The strokes of her tiny brush tickle at the top of my cheekbone, up to my brow. She curls the lashes, adds a dusting of fine glitter. "Look up. Look down. Close your eyes. Open." She outlines my lips, fills them with color.

"Wish I had something for you to wear," she says. "Oh, wait!" She goes out into my room and then comes back in with a black shirt. I hold it up. It reads *CARPE NOCTEM* in white block letters, with a small illustration of the moon underneath. I look at her.

"Well go ahead," she says. Then she rolls her eyes and turns her back. "Alright, go ahead."

I quickly change shirts, careful to protect the makeup. I pull my hair out of the collar and tell her to turn around.

Finally she lets me look in the mirror. "Done."

I turn to look, expecting to see the me I always see. But I don't. Mirror Eleanor is not even there. It's like I'm wearing a mask. I open my mouth and turn my face sideways to see if the reflection matches. It does.

Creep laughs.

My eyes are lined heavily in black, the strokes sure and elegant. Shadow diffuses softly across each eye, two charcoal clouds that fade into pale pink near the brow. Coiled designs spread from the outer corners, curlicues and spirals growing tiny leaves and flower buds. My upper lip is darker than the bottom one, almost black against deep pink.

I blink. The person in the mirror blinks back.

"It's probably too much," says Mia. "But your skin is so great. And your eyes are..."

She pauses and I look at her reflection. "Gorgeous," she says. She starts cleaning off the counter. "You have pretty eyes." I watch her putting colors and brushes back into her makeup bag. She glances at me and then seems to be concentrating hard on her task, so I look back at myself.

How can I be the same person but look so completely different? I feel like I'm hiding in plain sight. No one who sees me will even know who I am. I can be Elle. I stand up and lean closer to the mirror, examining the details around my eyes.

I can feel Eleanor shrinking inside, disappearing down a dark hallway. I feel something expanding inside of me. Something bright, like sunflowers blooming inside my chest. I turn to Mia.

"I love it." She smiles and I turn back to the mirror. "I look so different. Thank you."

I tie my hair back and put my shoes on. Mia stops me to pull a lock of hair out of my ponytail and drape it down the side of my face. We step into the hallway.

Virgil is scooping handfuls of Legos into a storage bucket. The boys are folding clothes and lining toy airplanes on the shelf.

Joshua sees me. "Whoa," he says.

Virgil turns around. His jaw drops a little. I feel the pasted-on face smile. The Eleanor eyes that normally drop are replaced by the Elle eyes that stare right back.

"What do you think?" says Mia.

Virgil nods.

Joshua says, "What did you do to your *face*?"

Mia puts a hand on her hip. "*I* did it, Cracker Barrel."

Sam laughs. "Cracker barrel!"

Mia looks at Virgil. "Well? What do you think?"

Virgil puts a hand on the back of his neck. "It's cool," he says.

"Cool?" says Mia. "*Cool?* This is *art*. This isn't just cool. This is amazing."

He just nods again.

Joshua grabs my hand to pull me down the hallway. "You look weird. Let's go."

SAM AND JOSHUA WALK IN FRONT. WE FOLLOW BEHIND, ME IN the middle with Virgil and Mia on either side. Sometimes Virgil's arm almost brushes mine, but it never really does. It's almost like the air around his arm touches the air around mine and it makes me tingle. Mia's arm does the same thing. I spend the entire walk awash in an electric bubble. Mia spends the whole walk telling us about her preparations for Bible Camp. I don't pay much attention. Virgil catches my eye every so often, throwing me a half smile or rolling his eyes at Mia's detailed explanation of what she hates most about camp.

"You should totally come!" she says suddenly. "It would be so awesome. Then me and Virgil wouldn't be the only kids there with half a brain."

I look at Virgil. "You're going to Bible Camp?"

He nods. "Yeah, it's kind of a thing. My mom sent my sister every year after she turned twelve, and now I go. But I like it. The weather's nice, and we learn survival skills."

"Would your parents let you?" Mia asks.

"I don't think so," I tell them. "My mom says I need to be supervised in social situations."

Mia and Virgil look at each other. "That sucks," says Mia, before launching into a description of the skunk that visited camp last year.

Virgil's arm almost brushes mine again. I watch the boys, walking about fifty feet ahead of us, and I slide my phone from my pocket. They wave their arms as they talk, bumping into each other, yelling and laughing. I wonder what it would be like, to just let people touch me and not feel what I feel. Then I remember that Eleanor's hiding. Elle's in charge today. She might like it. I take a picture.

"Lemme see," says Mia when I lower the phone. I lift it up to show her. The boys are silhouetted against the white sidewalk, Sam caught mid-jump. "Virgil, look," says Mia. "She gets a phone and twelve hours later she's a damn street photographer."

Virgil barely has time to look before I'm pushing the phone back into my pocket. "Okay," I say. "Okay."

"I'm serious," says Mia. "It's really good. Isn't it Virge?"

"I'm not an artist," says Virgil. "But yeah."

"Elle's an artist," says Mia. "She draws all sorts of stuff into a sketchbook."

"Yeah?" asks Virgil.

"No," I say. "I mean, no, I'm not an artist. I just doodle."

"You are so totally an artist," says Mia. "That must be why you're good at photography. You have an eye for it." She grabs my arm. "You should set up an account and fill it with drawings and photos. You could document your new neighborhood, and your—," she pauses to purse her lips and flutter the long feathery eyelashes, framing her face with her hands, "—amazing new friends."

"I'd follow you," says Virgil.

I look at Mia and Virgil. Back and forth between them. Wondering what I did right to be walking between this bubbly goth girl who gave me a phone, and this lanky sweet boy who shares his horses with me. Wondering how I came to be here, with these Amazing New Friends. I walk along, and on either side of me: two of the best goals mom has ever had.

WHEN WE CROSS THE PARKING LOT, I PULL MY ARM AWAY FROM my side, let it brush Mia's arm. The hand too. I feel her knuckles against mine as her fingers twitch. A jolt runs up my spine and I almost laugh. Mia glances at me, describing the feeling of watching 200 Christian kids bolt for the hills to escape a small striped mammal. I smile back. I brush Virgil's hand too. He immediately puts a little more distance between us, probably thinking it was an accident.

The 7-Eleven is like an oasis after the hot street. Cool air spills over us as we follow Joshua and Sam through the double doors. The boys are already exclaiming over candy, holding up brightly-colored containers and action figures, comparing them. Their voices carry across the aisles. Mia leans on the counter. Nicole looks up from washing the side of the drink fountain.

"Look who it is," she says. "The three musketeers. Virgil, I haven't seen you around for a few days. What's cookin', boy?"

He glances at me, unconsciously I think, but Nicole looks too, and her eyes light up. She puts one hand on her hip.

"Ooo, gorge! I hardly recognize you. Has our Mia here been working some of her magic?"

I nod. "Hi," I say. "How are you, Nicole?"

"Check her out," she says to Mia. "Like we've known each other forever." She says to me, "I'm good, hot stuff. Can't complain."

No one's ever called me Hot Stuff before. It makes me laugh.

Mia and Virgil smile at me. Nicole does too. Does Elle's laugh sound so different from mine?

"So what's it going to be today, kids?" asks Nicole.

"Slurpee run," says Virgil.

"His treat," says Mia.

"What a gentleman," says Nicole. "I'll get out of your way then."

Joshua and Sam pick out giant cups. I tell Joshua to choose a smaller one, but Virgil says it's no problem, so the boys fill up with every flavor. "Suiciiiiide!" They yell together. I get a peach mango. Mia fills hers partway with Coca-Cola, dribbles in some White Cherry Blast, and tops it off with Coca-Cola again. She plunges in the straw.

"I call it the Oreo," she says.

Virgil gets sour apple. The same color as his eyes, I notice.

When he pays for the drinks, Nicole gives me a thumbs-up. "I like the new look, Eleanor," she says. "You going to make it permanent?"

"Maybe," I say. It feels nice to think that I can be something other than me for a change.

<u>Ideas for a Photo Account:</u>

A series of Mia portraits
The stables
Joshua and his airplanes
Nicole
Sunsets
Virgil
The tree out front

TWENTY-TWO

We sprawl on the basement carpet to watch a movie. We still don't have any furniture down here, just bookshelves and the TV. I have Virgil on one side of me and Mia on the other. Sam and Joshua choose *The Last Unicorn*. Sam's never seen it.

"*What*?" says Joshua. "Eleanor's made me watch it a bajillion times."

"What?" I say. "No."

But he plows on, explaining the movie to Sam. "It's cool. There's this bull made out of fire that chases all the unicorns into the water and a tree with huge boobs and a skeleton that can't stop laughing and a pirate cat."

Virgil raises his eyebrows at me. "Tree with boobs?"

I take a pull on my straw. "I don't know what he's talking about."

Virgil is wiping the condensation off of his cup in vertical stripes. "So you *haven't* seen it a bajillion times?"

I look at the ceiling. "Well, not a *bajillion*."

. He laughs. Sitting next to me, his knee is almost touching mine. He puts his cup to one side and leans back on his elbows, so I do the same. Our shoulders are so close, the fabric of our sleeves touch. Mia is lying on her side, perpendicular to me, head propped in her hand, Slurpee straw in her mouth. If she moved toward me a few more inches, she could use my thigh as a pillow. I could put my hand out and run my fingers through her hair. I feel light with possibility.

The makeup makes the skin on my face feel tight. I keep wanting to wipe my eyes, but then I remember that it's Mia's artwork making the rigid sensation on my eyelids and cheeks.

The opening credits start to roll.

"Aw man," says Sam. "This is *old*."

Mia sits up and taps Sam with the toe of her flaming shoe. "It's not *old*. Dude, you think everything's old."

"Everything *is*," complains Sam. He unwraps a Snickers. He and Joshua split the candy bar, so they're quiet for a while. Mia moves to sit closer to me, leaning back on her elbows the way Virgil and I do. No one talks during the opening song.

I can see Creep, a cut-out shadow in the corner. He is strangely quiet too, glaring at me from across the room. I ignore him. The basement is cool and dark, but it seems the sun is still rising off of Virgil and Mia. Warmth emanates, me in the middle. I can smell the summer on them.

We watch the unicorn talking to a butterfly. She is perfectly white, sculpted out of curves, with a mane dashing in waves across her shoulders. She has eyes like amethyst. The butterfly tells her she is all alone in the world, so she decides to go on a dangerous quest to recover her people. A forest of forlorn woodland creatures watches her departure. She trots down the road to a folk-music soundtrack.

Virgil bumps my shoulder with his. I look over at him. His head is turned toward me, his chin on his shoulder. His eyes are closer than they've ever been. I can see myself in them.

"So," he says. "Why do you like this movie so much?" His voice is low, almost a whisper.

I feel my cheeks redden. His eyes are so green.

"Who says I do?" I say, looking back at the screen.

"C'mon," he says.

I look back at him, but I can't hold his gaze. So I look out the window over his shoulder. Leaves tremble. Black branches, and high clouds suspended behind everything.

"I don't know," I say. "After she gets turned into a human, it's like she forgets herself, what she wanted, even where she came from or why she started out in the first place. It's like she's lost for a while." I notice a hummingbird flit through the tree branches outside. It darts from twig to twig for a moment, emerald and flashing. Then it zooms away. I look at Virgil. "But then she remembers. She finds herself."

Virgil is looking directly into my eyes, like he's looking for something. I wish I didn't have to look away. But then I remember that I'm Elle today, and I don't have to look away. So I don't. I can hear the witch in the movie, casting a spell on the unicorn. I wonder what it would be like to be enchanted. I suppose this doesn't feel very far off.

The front door opens. Joshua and I look at each other. Footfalls on the stairs going up to the kitchen, the rustle of grocery sacks.

"Hello?" calls Mom.

"Down here," says Joshua, before I can stop him.

She comes down the stairs. I should have gone into the bathroom while I had the chance. I sit up, grab my drink. Turn more towards the television.

"What are you up to?" says Mom as she comes in the room. She stands behind Virgil and me.

"Just watching a movie," I say, watching the screen.

"You shouldn't have those drinks over the carpet," she says.

"Okay," I say.

"You need to ask me before you have friends over."

"Sorry," I say without looking at her.

"Sorry what?" she says.

"Sorry, Mom," I say.

I see Virgil's feet twitch. Then he pulls them in and sits up. "Hi, Mrs. Moreno."

"Hello, Virgil," she says. "Sam."

Sam waves without taking his eyes off the television.

"Eleanor, can you help me put groceries away?" says Mom.

"Can it wait?" I ask. "Kind of in the middle of something."

"You're in the middle of a movie you've seen a hundred times. Come and help me."

I sigh and drag myself up. Creep bounces over to me, suddenly happy. Mom has already turned away. She starts up the stairs.

"I'm just going to the bathroom real quick." I head down the hallway.

"Just come upstairs," she says. "It won't take long."

I clench my jaw. Creep follows.

I stare at the back of her head. I can see the hair clinging to her neck under the ponytail. Her ears are red. There are bags of groceries on the counter. She says something about school and the kitchen is bright with afternoon sunlight. She opens a cupboard, fills a green plastic cup with water from the fridge, talking all the time. When she finally turns around, she gets the first look at my face.

"What on earth," she says. The cup hits the floor, splashing both our feet with icy water.

Creep laughs. He claps his long-fingered hands, clicks his teeth together.

"I want to go to Bible Camp," I say. I move to the counter and start pulling boxes and cans out of the sacks.

"Eleanor," she says. I look back at her. She grabs a dish towel from the oven handle with a flick and moves to wipe it across the floor. Creep skitters out of her way. She squints up at me. They both do.

"Who did that?" she points at my face.

"So can I go?" I say.

"Who *did* that?" She's turned back to the floor, mopping around my feet. I pull out a container of spinach, and another of strawberries.

"You better answer her," says Creep. He's climbed up onto the counter next to me. He sits next to a box of spaghetti, legs curled on either side. He leans forward onto his elbows, chin in his hands. He blinks his eyes innocently. His grin is wider than ever.

"I did," I lie.

Creep laughs loud, like it's the funniest thing ever.

"You did that," she says. It's not a question. I turn to face her. She stands, throws the towel in the sink, and crosses her arms in front of her.

"Yeah."

"Where did you get it?"

"Get what?"

Creep won't shut up. Still laughing.

"The makeup," Mom says.

"I borrowed it," I say.

"You know you're not allowed to wear makeup until you're eighteen."

"I'm not *wearing* it," I say. Creep guffaws, a sudden blasting screech. "I mean, I'm not *really* wearing it. It's just for fun."

She looks at the ceiling, the adult version of rolling your eyes. "Is it on your face?" she says.

I don't answer. She waits. Sighs. Creep laughs harder.

Finally I say, "Yes."

"Then you're wearing it," she says. She waits.

"So can I?" I say.

"Can you what?"

"Go to Bible Camp," I say.

"You need to apologize," she says.

"For what?" I say.

She raises her eyebrows. I can feel the air tightening between us. "For your disrespectful attitude, for your tone, for your disregard of house rules."

I can see Creep out of the corner of my eye. His eyes flick back and forth.

"What house rules?" I say.

Creep covers his mouth. "Ooooh." His voice rises at the end, like a little kid mocking someone for getting in trouble.

Mom looks like she's going to slap me. She licks her lips, rubs them together, closes her eyes for a moment. She takes a deep breath. Then she starts ticking off rules on her fingers.

"No makeup until you're eighteen. No friends over without permission. No drinks but water leave the kitchen," she says.

I fold my arms like she did. "Sorry," I say. "So can I go?"

She shakes her head. "Eleanor, where is this coming from?"

I'm not sure if she means the attitude, or the Bible Camp.

"Mom," I say. "Please just answer the question."

"It depends," she says. "Are you going to go wash your face? Or am I going to do it for you?"

We stare at each other. I can see the fine lines around her eyes, the puffy skin, sagging under the hard blue irises. A frown tugging her mouth downward.

"Tell her to do it for you," says Creep. "I would love to see that."

I imagine my mother, fist full of my hair, plunging my head into a full sink of cold water. I imagine myself spluttering, drowning, the black makeup running into my eyes, blinding me.

"I'll do it," I say.

"Good," she says. "Do it now. I'm going to study group. I won't be home until late."

I turn toward the stairs.

Her voice comes after me. "Go to Bible Camp, Eleanor," she says. "Maybe it will fix your attitude."

Creep follows me down the stairs. "Not very likely," he says.

WHEN THE MOVIE ENDS, MIA GATHERS HER THINGS. "CALL me," she says. "Next time I'll bring some clothes for you to try on. I have tons I don't wear anymore."

Virgil doesn't move. Joshua and Sam plug in our ancient gaming system and start playing *Super C.*

Virgil laughs as the pixelated soldiers jump around the screen dodging bullets and enemies. "I don't think I've ever seen a classic NES in person," he says.

"Yeah," I say. "Joshua bought it at a garage sale for five dollars. He's obsessed with retro stuff like that. It came with a box of games. Half of them don't work."

Joshua bounces, falls onto Sam as they both wave their paddles around, used to Sam's motion-sensing games. "They do so work," says Joshua.

We watch the boys play for a moment. "He got the TV and VCR at a garage sale too. My mom was mad about it at first. Said we didn't need the worldly influence. But Josh said he would just watch cartoons on it. Now he and Dad get VHS tapes by the box at Goodwill."

"And *The Last Unicorn* is Eleanor's favorite," says Joshua.

Virgil is watching them play. I can tell he wants to play too. He's leaning forward a little to see better, lips parted, a half smile on his face. I wonder what it would be like to kiss him. *Different*, I think. *Better*.

I can feel my skin turning pink under the makeup.

"This console sucks," says Sam. "Let's go back to my house."

Virgil stands up. He offers one hand to help me up. After the smallest millisecond, I take it. It's warm and dry. The fingers are calloused. Probably from all the mucking.

After I stand, he puts his hands in his pockets. He says, "Are you coming with us?"

"I can't," I say. "I have to wash my face."

It must sound like a joke, because Virgil laughs.

Dear Jesus,
I'm coming to Bible Camp.
Mia thinks it's full of brainwashed disciples.
Virgil thinks I'll learn survival skills.
Mom thinks it will solve my problems.
Does it work that way?
Amen.

TWENTY-THREE

I sit on my bathroom counter. I drew in my sketchbook after everyone left. Listened to one of Mia's playlists. Imagined what it would be like to kiss Virgil. Then imagined what it would be like to kiss Mia. Made a quick dinner for Joshua and let him eat while watching *Legend of Korra* on my phone. I heard Mom and Dad get back, separately. I heard Mom check on Joshua, heard her murmur a quiet goodnight to him. I was relieved when she didn't knock on my door.

The house is quiet now, with everyone in bed. Except for me. As usual. I take a picture of my face, up close, my eyes looking directly into the camera. I want to preserve this face Mia gave me for a day. Elle's face. Creep is sitting on the toilet lid. He watches me do it.

I put the phone down with a sigh. I lean my forehead against the mirror.

"When are you going to see Virgil again?" Creep asks me.

"Why?" I say. I run lukewarm water over a washcloth, wring it out.

"Does he remind you of Ian?" says Creep.

I look at him. I know I shouldn't. I know it only makes things worse.

The black globes of his eyes reflect the shape of my head, a tiny silhouette in a square of light. He smiles, wide. I wish I could punch his teeth in. I imagine my knuckles splitting as the shards of teeth splinter. Creep reels backward. Chunks of bone and blood and saliva spray the wall. I shake the pain out of my fingers and Creep drools blood onto the floor, his smile just ashy gums and a few broken teeth. The thought makes me grin.

I turn back to the mirror, wipe the lipstick off first. My lips are strangely pale without it now.

"Virgil's nothing like Ian," I tell him.

Creep chuckles in the back of his throat, a grating sound. "Sure he is," he says. "They're all the same."

"They're not," I say. The outline of my eyes doesn't come off easily. I scrub at one corner.

"Yeah," says Creep. "They are. They only want one thing."

The washcloth slowly turns black. I run water over it again, add soap. "Virgil's different," I say. "He's not like that."

Creep puts one hand on the counter, like he's going to touch my knee. I automatically lean away from him. "Dear, sweet Ellie," he says. Then in Ian's voice, "My special girl." The words slide in shivers down my back. I roll my shoulders. Will the feeling to pass. "They're all like that," he continues, in his own voice again. "You'll see."

I shake my head. I'm scrubbing hard across my eyes now, digging deep, pushing them into my skull. The rough terry cloth smells faintly of mildew and chlorine.

"No," I say.

"Yes." Creeps drums his fingernails on the counter top. Clickclickclickclick. Clickclickclickclick. "Why else would he be friends with you? What else are you good for?"

"Stop it," I tell him. I look at my reflection. Makeup trails down my cheeks, like I'm crying black oil. I turn the faucet to hot. The water starts to steam. I put my hands under it. They turn pink.

"You can't answer it, can you?" he says. "You don't know what else you're good for. Nothing."

"Stop it," I say again. I say it through clenched teeth. I bite down hard on nothing, my jaw aching. I cup the hot water in my hands, bring it to my face. "Stop it," I say into my hands, into the water, into the sink.

"Nothing," says Creep. His voice burns like the water. "Nothing nothing.." He keeps repeating it.

I shout. "Shut up!" I slam my hands onto the counter, splashing dirty water everywhere. I throw the washcloth at Creep. He dodges it laughing, still saying *nothing* over and over, until it's a pulse between my temples. I press my hands to my head and squeeze my eyes shut.

Nothing nothing nothing.

Creep's not touching me. Just his voice. But I feel like he is. His long fingernails scraping my skin. Clawing through my hair. Pulling at my clothes.

Nothing nothing nothing.

A hand on my shoulder. I scrabble away from it, across the floor. *When did I curl up on the floor?*

"Ellie?"

"Don't call me that," I yell.

"Sorry. Are you okay?"

I open my eyes. Joshua stands in the doorway. He's wearing Mario Bros pajamas, his hair sticking up. He stares down at me.

We hear a thump upstairs, the sounds of feet coming down. We look at each other. Creep claps his hands.

I pick up the washcloth. I sponge it across my face. My hands shake.

"Don't tell," I whisper to Joshua. "Don't tell."

He reaches over to turn off the water. The mirror is cloudy.

Then Dad's in the room. I feel like I haven't seen him in months. He's thinner, dark circles under his eyes. He shaved his head after clumps started falling out. He leans against the door jamb, a hospital bracelet hanging loose on his wrist.

"What's all the noise?" he says. His voice is subdued. Joshua and I share a glance again. I wonder if he shares my shock at Dad's lack of mass.

Joshua has his hands behind his back. "Eleanor saw a scorpion," he says.

Dad sniffs. One long slow blink. "Where?" he says.

Joshua points by the baseboard under the cabinet. "It slipped under there."

Joshua and Dad both look at me.

"What's on your face?" says Dad.

"I was washing off some makeup," I tell him. "Mia and I were playing around today."

Dad doesn't say anything. I can't tell what he's thinking. This makes me more nervous than anything else.

"Josh," he says. "Go back to bed."

Joshua looks at me. I know he wants to stay, just in case. "Goodnight, Joshua," I say. He leans in and I put my arms around his shoulders.

"Night, Eleanor," he says. "Night, Dad."

I avoid looking at Dad. I can feel his eyes on me in the mirror. I pull a towel off the rack and start drying the counter.

"If I ever hear about you disrespecting your mother again," he says. "There will be hell to pay."

Whatever, I think. "Okay," I say.

"I'm serious, Eleanor. She has enough to worry about without your shitty attitude making things worse."

"I don't have an attitude," I say.

"You better cut it out," he says. "She has a lot on her plate. She doesn't need you causing trouble."

"We all have a lot on our plates, Dad," I say.

He raises one hand. "Don't talk back to me."

"I'm not--" I start to say.

He points one finger at me. The hospital bracelet jumps on his wrist whenever he moves his hand. "You will obey your mother. You will show her the respect she deserves. Or you will regret it. Do you hear me?"

I nod. I wipe mechanically at the counter.

"And stop yelling and screaming in the middle of the night. Your mother and I need our sleep. I don't care what's happening. You keep it down."

He turns away from the door, disappears into the hall.

I drop the washcloth in the sink. I wipe my face with a hand towel and fall into bed. I curl on my side. *I don't care what's happening — never yell. Never scream. Never cry. Never fight. I don't care what's happening. Keep it down. Down. Down.*

Creep lies in the same position facing me. He folds his hands under his cheek.

"Your dad might want you to keep it down no matter what, but you can talk to me about anything, Ellie. Anything at all." He reaches one clawed hand toward me, traces the air around my cheek. "Dear, sweet, Ellie, what a troublemaker," he says. "Nobody understands you."

I put the pillow over my face. I whisper, "Just stop."

Creep. Never. Listens.

<u>Fear #3: Disappearing</u>

I do my best not to draw attention to myself.
I'm not as good at it as I used to be.
I'm getting taller.
I'm getting louder.
I feel things moving inside of me, and I don't
know what they are.
I used to do my best not to draw attention to myself,
but that never seemed to matter to him.
He always noticed me.
Sometimes I think, now that he's not around to notice
me, I'll disappear.
If Creep wasn't here to remind me
to color in my lines, to move like a rabbit
chased by a fox,
to feel the phantom handprints along my skin,
maybe I would.
Maybe I would vanish.
Maybe that's not a bad thing.

The hallway. I turn back and forth, looking for an end to the narrow expanse of carpet and bulbs and featureless doors. Nothing.

I've been here before.

Creep is at my feet. He looks up at me. He points. I see a door open on its own, soundless. The doorway is a black cavity. I turn back to Creep. His finger hangs in the air.

That one.

I move toward the yawning doorway. It seems to expand the closer I get. Creep follows me, grinning that shards-of-bone smile. I stand in front of the tall, black square. I can't hear anything in the hallway and the darkness in the doorway seems inky and muted, like it may pour from the abyss as black smoke. Creep steps up to the doorway. He waggles his fingers in invitation and crosses the threshold. He vanishes.

I step back from the doorway.

I'm not going in there.

I turn around to the door opposite, but I feel myself sliding backward. Toward the blackness. I scramble forward and grab the handle of the opposite door. The portal behind me pulls with a strong gravity. Braced on the smooth carpet, I lean into the doorknob, struggling to turn and push it open. It clicks and I wedge my fingers over the door jamb. The drag from behind is so great that I feel I'm pulling myself up and into a trapdoor overhead. My feet dangle as somehow I haul myself through the doorway, like I'm climbing out of a pool. I yank my legs after me and the door slams shut.

It feels like a victory to have gone the other direction. To not have followed Creep. I am sitting on the floor in the new room. A doctor's examination room. A girl with black hair sits on the tissue-covered table. She is wearing a paper-thin gown. She stares at the ceiling, her hands on her knees.

The white-coated doctor bustles in, wearing a surgical mask and carrying a tablet. Creep follows at his heels, wearing a mask as well. The doctor taps on the tablet briefly with a stylus, then puts it aside.

"Good morning," the doctor says. "It's nice to see you again. I've brought my assistant." He indicates Creep. "Let's see what the problem is, shall we?" He pulls on latex gloves with a snap.

He takes the girl's temperature, her blood pressure, peers in her ears, nose and throat, he holds a light up to her eye and leans in close. He holds a cold stethoscope to her chest. She winces. He listens at her chest and back.

Finally he stands back, picks up the tablet, and taps for a moment. Then he says, "I'm pretty sure we've figured it out. You're empty."

"What do you mean?" says the girl. Her eyes are sky blue.

"You're completely empty. That's why you've been feeling this way. Here, I'll show you."

He pulls a dark, plastic sheet out of a manila envelope.

"Here's your x-ray," he says. The film shows the girl's ribs, collarbone, vertebrae, pelvis, glowing white against the black background. "See," he holds up his pen, pointing at the photo. "In a normal film, we would be able to see distinct, if cloudy, shapes that indicate organs." He points. "Lungs, heart, stomach, liver, colon, kidneys. There's nothing there. You're just skin, muscle, and bone, nothing in between."

She's confused, eyebrows furrowed. Staring at the x-ray. "That can't be right," she says. "How am I alive? There must be some mistake."

"Lie back," says the doctor. "I'll prove it to you."

She lies back on the table, paper crinkling under her. Creep jumps up and sits next to her head. The doctor cuts away the girl's gown with a pair of scissors, exposing her chest. Her flesh is white and goose-pimpled, her figure bony and boyish. The doctor raises a scalpel and cuts into her. A red line appears as he presses down. Creep dabs away the blood, throwing the used gauze on the floor. Red-stained fabric pile grows.

The girl stares at the ceiling. She sighs.

They peel back the girl's skin. Creep hands the doctor a power tool and he saws through the girl's sternum.

"Retractor," the doctor says. He wedges the tool between the two halves of her breastbone and slowly cranks it open. "Here," says the doctor. "See for yourself."

The girl looks down into her own chest. Just an empty, dripping cavity.

"Huh," she says. "I still don't get how I am alive."

"We have no idea," says the doctor. He steps back and pulls down his mask. I gasp as I see that the doctor is Ian. He gestures to Creep, who spins the crank on the retractor and pulls it off, jerking her body.

"You're just a freak of nature, I guess," says Ian as Creep pushes the two halves of her ribcage back together. "My assistant will use state-of-the-art sutures. There won't be a scar and we'll keep it a secret. So what if you're different? People don't have to know."

"But I'll know," says the girl. "How will I keep it a secret?"

"Just pretend you're like everyone else." He smiles. "No one will ever know." He rips off the gloves and tosses them into the trash with his mask. "Now I've got other patients to see."

TWENTY-FOUR

Virgil is saying on the phone, "Wear your horse hat." He's invited Joshua and me over. My parents aren't home, so I tell Joshua he gets to play at Sam's. I change my shirt and pull my ponytail through the back of my hat. We walk to Virgil's house.

When we get there, Pancake is saddled and tethered, cropping grass in the front yard. Joshua and I laugh.

"Your steed, milady," says Virgil. He's wearing his cowboy hat. He holds a hand out. I don't take it at first. But I want to feel the warmth of his fingers wrapped around mine. He leads me over to Pancake. I pet her nose and Virgil gets up in the saddle. Again he offers his hand.

"Let us ride," he says.

"What about Joshua?" I ask.

"He and Sam have plans," says Virgil mysteriously. Then: "My mom'll watch them."

When he pulls me up behind him, I am surprised how far off the ground Pancake's back is. I've never been on a horse before. Her massive skeleton moves under us, her rope muscles tying everything together, lungs like bellows. I put one hand behind me on her rump, sure I'll slide off the back.

"Here," says Virgil. He reaches back, grabs both my forearms and pulls me gently forward. "Hang on to me. That way you won't fall off."

I hold Virgil around the middle, my fingers meeting at his navel. I immediately think of Mia. Virgil's back is warm. I can feel the movements of him too, under his skin. Vertebrae and shoulder blades and how he twists to maneuver Pancake out of the yard. His hair smells like lemons. My vision starts to swim and I am sure I'll fall off. Then Pancake stamps and everything snaps back into focus.

"Ready?" says Virgil.

"For what?" I say.

He swivels his head to look at me, but doesn't get all the way around. His ear touches my lips. My head jerks back.

"Your first horseback ride," he says. He shakes the reins and Pancake moves us out to the sidewalk.

We ride through the neighborhood, down 48th street. We use the crosswalk at Baseline Road, six lanes of traffic stopped at a red light, honking as we pass. My arms around Virgil's waist the entire time.

When it's over, but before Virgil grasps my forearm to help me slide from Pancake's back, he digs in his front pocket and pulls out his phone.

"Mind if I get a photo? For Pancake's Insta."

"Pancake has an Insta?" I say as he swipes open the camera app.

"Yeah," he says, sheepish. "It's for all the horses, but it's really Pancake's account." He hasn't raised the phone yet, waiting for my permission.

"Okay," I tell him.

He holds up the phone at arm's length, the front camera showing us our own faces. He smiles, one hand on the pommel. I lift my head a little higher, tucking my chin over his shoulder. I smile too.

After he snaps it, I ask, "Can you get one with my phone?"

Our fingers touch as I pass it to him, but it hardly matters, not with my arms wrapped around him, my chest pressed against his back. My chin over his shoulder, close enough to touch his cheek with my lips. Our hats shading our faces. When he takes the picture, I look into the eyes of the Virgil on-screen, instead of the camera lens, my fingers laced together in front of his secretly-hot abs.

VIRGIL PASSES ME THE SPONGE. I PLUNGE IT IN THE BUCKET. IN the shade of a giant eucalyptus, I run the sponge, fat with dripping water, across Pancake's wet flank. She snorts, whickers.

"She loves the bath," says Virgil. He is wearing green again and his cowboy hat. I have my horse hat on. We meet eyes over Pancake's back.

"What do you think?" he says.

I run the sponge in circles on her large side. Washing a horse is like washing a car, only leggy . . . and breathing.

"About what?" I ask.

"Grooming," he says. He lifts the hose, sprays Pancake's back. Water splashes in my face. I laugh.

"Better than mucking." I wipe my face with my arm. "At least it's wet. Cooler."

"What about riding?" he says.

I look down at Pancake's hooves, smile as she shakes her mane, spraying me with water. I wipe my hand on my jeans and pull out my phone. A black and white photo of Pancake's front hooves in a mirrored puddle of water. I think about my arms around his waist, about the horse moving underneath us, her bunching muscles, the clop of her shoes on the concrete, the clean smell of her sweat. The sunshine pushing down heavy on everything.

"It was great," I say.

"Next time," he says. "You can ride Pancake and I'll ride Cricket." My stomach flutters at the thought of next time.

He rinses Pancake and then we use scrapers to squeeze off the excess water. We towel her mostly dry, me on one side, Virgil on the other. He brushes out her tail, and I work on her mane, gently pulling through tangles. I lead her around the yard until she's dry and back into her stall while Virgil puts the grooming tools away. She whuffles into my hand, looking for treats. I lean my forehead between her eyes, my fingers clasped around the curve of her jaw. She smells like shampoo. I close my eyes. "Is it so easy to be you?" I whisper.

Pancake is very still and I wonder if she knows what I'm thinking.

"What are you two talking about?" says Virgil behind me. Pancake looks over my shoulder at him.

Virgil laughs.

He fills the bottom of a bucket with oats. He holds it with two hands as Pancake lowers her head and over the sounds of crunching I watch Virgil.

His hair looks darker inside, sweeping across his forehead in red strands. The green of his eyes looks darker too. I put out one hand to pet Pancake's forelock. It falls over the horse's long eyelashes and when I pull my hand away, even though she's just been bathed, it smells like dust and sunlight. The horse shuffles, heavy shifting steps I can feel in the ground itself. I raise my head and Virgil's looking at me. We're standing close. Close enough that I can smell his sweat too. It's not bad though, reminds me of Playdoh.

"What?" I say.

He shakes his head.

"Nothing," he says. "Just that you're pretty."

I watch his mouth say the words. I don't know if I believe them. Or maybe I believe them but I don't want to. And now that I've looked at his mouth I can't stop looking at it. His lips are almost coral pink, surrounded by a sprinkling of freckles. He chews on his bottom lip. Ian used to say I was pretty. *Pretty girl. Special girl. Why did I have to think of Ian right now?*

I shake Ian out of my head.

"You are," says Virgil.

"No," I say, meaning *No, I wasn't contradicting you,* but I know it's not enough so I say, "I mean, thank you. I guess."

When I say it, I think, *I'm going to kiss him.* It's like he knows what I'm thinking because he looks at *my* mouth.

"Why don't you – ," he starts. But I lean toward him and press my lips to his.

The kiss is soft, dry, with the horse's head munching and snuffling between us. His eyes are wide in surprise before they close almost thoughtfully. My nose brushes Virgil's cheek. He inhales. And then he doesn't move, doesn't even breathe out, like I'm a butterfly he doesn't want to scare away.

I lean back. Virgil exhales and I want to turn around and run before he opens his eyes. *No,* I think, *he's safe. Virgil's safe.* I force my body to remain still. My chest tightens. My head starts to spin.

Virgil blinks. He looks dizzy. Or is that just me?

He says, " – think you're pretty?"

I laugh. A bubble pops inside of me and I sit down in the dirt. My hands are shaking.

He drops the bucket. "Are you okay?" He crouches and almost touches my shoulder, then pulls his hand back. He scans my face.

I laugh again. "I wanted to run," I say. "After."

I don't tell him why.

He smiles, "I'm glad you didn't. That would have been weird."

I hold out my hand. He looks at it for a second and then stands and slides his fingers past my palm. His hand is warm on my wrist. He pulls me to my feet.

We stand looking at each other until Pancake nudges Virgil, looking for the bucket. He picks it up again and we stand as we were, on either side of Pancake's head.

My lips tingle. I want to touch my mouth. The slithery feeling crawls up my back, but I still want to kiss him again.

Virgil says, "I wish –," and then he stops. He's looking down into the bucket.

What does he wish? Does he wish I was shorter? Rounder? Does he wish I had boobs? Blonde hair? A different smile? Does he wish I was more outgoing? A better kisser? More grown up? Less grown up? Different than I am?

My face is hot, running through all the possible wishes. I suddenly wish I was somewhere else. My eyes start to water. I can't cry in front of him.

"Eleanor," he says.

I don't want to look at him.

"Hey," he says.

I look at him. I blink fast. I have one hand on Pancake's neck.

"That was my first real kiss," he says. "I wish it was in a more special place than an old horse barn."

I shake my head. The tears fly off my face. I swipe my cheeks. I lean forward again. This time when our lips meet, we both close our eyes and the anxious thrumming in my body changes to thrill and all I can hear is the munching of horses and all I can feel is the gentle press of Virgil's lips and his breath on my cheek and all I can smell is his hair and his skin. He moves his mouth just a little, interlocking our lips. He takes my hand and his fingers brush my palm and then intertwine with mine. He pulls away from me this time, takes a deep breath, and smiles.

"I love the barn," I say. I look down at our fingers, still weaved together.

LATER, WHEN I'M LYING IN BED, I REPLAY THE KISS IN MY HEAD. Creep is turning in circles on the bedspread like a dog. I close my eyes and I can see Virgil in front of me, sunshine in his hair and I feel warmed by the memory, instead of smothered or crawly. I turn away from Creep and look at the horse wall, imagine Virgil and me riding horses on a beach. The water sprays up as we splash through. We race down a stretch of white sand and it feels like flying. My mouth feels like it forgot to do anything but smile.

"Yuck," says Creep behind me. "You look cheerful. What are you thinking about?"

"I am not telling you," I say.

"You must be thinking about Virgil," he says. "I saw you kissing in the barn."

"So what?" I say. "You see everything I do."

"No," says Creep, "you're right, it's not a big deal." He hops down off of my bed and crawls underneath. His voice is muffled. "It's just nice to be right."

I roll my eyes. "Right about what?"

"Remember when I told you about how boys only want one thing from you. And Virgil's no different. I told you. Remember?"

I do remember what Creep said. But he's wrong. He has to be. Virgil is different. He feels different. He's got to be different.

Creep keeps talking. "I told you. I was right. You won't have to wait long for the rest."

I kissed **him**, I think. I want to tell Creep, but I also want to frustrate him with my silence, so I don't say anything.

He just keeps going. "I know you said he's different, but really Ellie, I wouldn't get my hopes up if I were you. Ian showed you how it's going to be. With all of them. You might as well get used to it."

My skin prickles. My head feels like it will float off the pillow. Why does he have to do that? Why does he have to talk about Ian?

I throw the covers off and run for the bedroom door. I shut it quick, but Creep still follows me. The hallway is dark. I lean into Joshua's doorway. The nightlight in his room shows me that he fell asleep with his arms wrapped around one of his jets. If Joshua were a girl, I would wake him up and tell him about Virgil. Then I realize I *do* have someone I could tell.

Back in my room, I pull up the video call app. The phone sounds its calling alert and I sit on my bathroom floor, in the corner where the edge of the tub meets the wall. Creep clambers over the edge and then sits in the tub to watch me.

When Mia finally answers, her face is close to the camera in dim yellow lighting. I think she's lying down. "What's up, Elle?"

"Did I wake you?" I whisper.

"Nah," she says, "I couldn't find my phone. I was binging *Firefly*. Do you think River could ever have a functional relationship? She's like, seriously deranged. But she's super-smart and talented. It's just sad, because Kaylee has Simon, Zoe has Wash, and Mal has Inara. But who could ever love River, what with all the crazy? She actually kind of reminds me of you–"

I cut her off. "I have to tell you something."

"Okay," she says. "Where are you?"

"In my bathroom. Virgil took me to the barn today."

"Wait," she says. Then, smiling: "Don't tell me. You mucked."

I wave away her joke with one hand. She laughs.

"Your face," she says.

"Mia," I say. "I have to tell you something."

"Sorry," she says. "Go."

"We kissed."

She squeals, sitting up. "Seriously?" I can tell she is holding the phone with both hands. it's below her face, her hair hanging into the camera.

I nod.

"You seriously kissed? Did he kiss you or you kiss him? Well, obviously he kissed you, because you would *never* kiss him," she says.

"*I* kissed *him*," I say.

"What?" Her mouth is hanging open.

"Twice," I say. My face in the little corner box covers her smile.

Mia starts talking very quickly. "Well?" she says. "How was it? Did he touch your face? Was there tongue? How was his breath? Did you close your eyes or keep them open? Tell me everything." The camera is bouncing.

"No face touching. No tongue, ew. His breath was fine, he actually smelled like cinnamon. I closed my eyes the second time."

"But they were open the first time? Awk-waaaard." She puts on a pained grimace.

"No," I say. "It wasn't. Which was weird. It was totally comfortable. I felt like . . . safe. It was way different than–" I stop myself.

"Way different than what?" she says.

Than Ian.

"Than I thought it would be," I tell her.

"Wow," she says. "I'm proud. Oh my God, Elle, what did I tell you about things changing?"

I don't tell her she's right. I don't want to hope about things changing. The last time I did that, Creep followed me to what was supposed to be my new life.

"Okay." She falls back onto her pillow again, the way Virgil did. She turns on her side. She props the phone on something and tucks her hands under her chin. Her face is clean, no lashes, no eyeliner, no lipstick. She looks open and sleepy and it's like I'm lying on my side too, facing her, about to tell her my deepest secrets. She yawns. "Our moms planned us getting together for camp prep. You can tell me all about Virgil tomorrow."

We hang up. I sit blinking in the dark, then look over at Creep, or at the shadow where he should be. He doesn't say anything, but I can feel him watching, watching, watching. Always. My fingers curl around the phone. I wonder what Virgil's eyes look like, lit by a phone screen in a dark room.

<u>Things I Like About Virgil:</u>

Eyes
Mouth
Freckles
Smell
Voice
Hands
That he loves horses
That he opens doors for me
That he doesn't ask questions

Mom is standing in front of me holding out her key ring. We're on the porch of our new house. Her arms are filled with boxes, stacked so I can't see her face. She reaches around the load, leaning, off-balance. "It's this one," she says. A silver key winks.

"Well?" she asks me. "I can't hold this much longer."

I take the key, look up at the blue door. "Joshua wants to do it," I tell her

"You do it," she says. "Joshua is too little and I have too much to do."

"Where's Dad?" I ask.

Mom's voice gets louder. "Eleanor," she warns.

I lift the key. The dangling ring seems very heavy. I try to push the key into the dead-bolt lock.

"It won't fit," I tell Mom.

She sighs behind the boxes. "Eleanor, just make it work."

I decide to try the doorknob. I turn the key upside down, right side up. I wiggle the knob. Nothing works.

"Mom," I say. "It's not working."

Another voice says, "I can make it work."

I turn and there's Ian, standing close. I back away from him, but Mom is behind me. I bump into her load of boxes.

"Eleanor," she says. "What's taking so long?"

"Here." Ian holds out his hand. He wants the key.

I put the key ring behind my back. Not here, I think. Not my new house. Not my new life.

"What's wrong?" he asks.

I just shake my head.

"Eleanor," Mom snaps. "I don't care what you have to do. Get us inside that house."

Ian's eyes are on me. I put the key ring into his big hand.

"Here," he says. "Watch. It's easy."

He slides the key into the lock. It sounds wet, like someone getting stabbed.

"Trust me, Ellie," says Ian.

Can't breathe.

TWENTY-FIVE

I sit up straight, choked by bed linens. Keys shoved into locks. The sense of suffocation, pressed into blackness. Eating something that stuck in my throat. Someone saying, "Ellie. *Ellie.*" Heat.

I untangle myself from the sheets, throw the blanket off in the dark, and go to the door. The wall is cool where I lean against it, my forehead sheened with sweat. The face. His face hangs in front of my eyes. I try to bat it away, but only hit the wall. The dull thump drives me into the hallway. I'm smothering in all this silent blackness.

I take the stairs two at a time. Luckily the front door doesn't squeak.

Standing on the concrete porch, the door quietly shut behind me, the top of my head feels like it's burning. I want to scratch at my arms. I feel like there's something behind me. Like I'm a gazelle and there's a cheetah, stalking me somewhere in the darkness. My legs feel ready to spring from the porch, carry me racing under street lights across the city and into the black desert.

It's muggy, city lights reflecting off a swath of low clouds. No stars are visible. The lamp on the corner casts a yellow pool, the electric buzz mixing with the sound of cicadas. My shadow shifts as I walk under it. I forgot my shoes and the sidewalk is warm. I tie my hair back.

The night smells of rain. I imagine a gathering of clouds over my patch of sidewalk. They split open. Lightning flashes. A deluge engulfs me, washing my dreams into the gutter, black and clotted, where they tumble along with twigs and dust and dry leaves until they reach a sewer grate and disappear forever. I imagine myself washed clean by summer thunder.

"Where are we going?" asks Creep. He lopes beside me. I shake my head. I'm not wet or clean or dressed in goose-bumps. I'm walking fast down a dry sidewalk. Nearly running.

Cars whiz by. A couple of them honk.

"Where are we going?" Creep asks again.

"Walking," I say. "Don't talk to me."

"That's dumb," says Creep. "Who else am I going to talk to?"

"I don't know," I say. The wind from a passing car flings my ponytail to one side. "I don't care. Why don't you go find someone else to bother?"

Creep laughs. "Ellie," he says. "You know you're my favorite."

I don't realize I'm walking to the 7-Eleven until I stand outside the door. I stare in through the glass. It looks deserted. Then Nicole emerges from a doorway and walks back behind the counter. She's singing along to the overhead music. She writes something in a binder. I wonder if she'll see me.

"What are you doing?" says Creep. "She's gonna think you're a stalker."

Right then, Nicole looks up. She sees me and waves. When she opens the door, a cool breeze breaks over me. I blink.

"Hey sweet pea, what are you doing? Everything okay?"

I just nod.

"You wanna come in?" she asks.

I look down at my bare feet. She leans over to me and whispers, "I won't tell if you don't." She holds the door open for me.

I step onto the cold linoleum. I feel suddenly strange, here in my pajama pants and old shirt.

I watch her straighten small displays on the counter, line up cigarette lighters, restock cups and napkins. I think she's waiting for me to say something. Eventually she gives up waiting.

"Just my night schedule," she says. "I'm just gonna wipe down. Wanna sit and talk to me while I work?" She pulls a chair up behind the counter. I walk over the springy floor mats and sit in the chair. She works with her spray bottle and wad of paper towels. Blue droplets mist across every surface. Her right arm polishes in circles. Spaces shine. She whistles.

"So what's up?" she says. "I've never seen you without your entourage. Come from a slumber party to get snacks?" She knows I didn't come for snacks.

Creep climbs up onto the counter to watch us. He lies on his back and then starts chewing his toenails. I eye him and then say to Nicole, "Just out walking."

She shakes her head. "Not exactly safe out there this time of night for someone your age. Your parents know you're out?"

I shake my head back at her. "Who cares? What difference does it make?"

Nicole clicks her tongue. She sprays the hot-dog warmer's glass front. "Of course it makes a difference. What if something happened to you?"

I shrug. Glass squeaks.

"So if you aren't on a midnight snack run, why are you out walking so late? And barefoot."

"What time is it?" I ask.

She moves the towels down the front of the display. "About two."

I pull my knees up and wrap my arms around them. "Bad dreams," I say.

Nicole nods. "Oh, yeah, that'll do it," she says. "I used to dream about aliens. Like, I was so scared of aliens that I would have these crazy nightmares about them. They'd float me right out of my bed; kidnap me and do experiments on me. My parents didn't know what to do. I'd be in their room every night crying about aliens. What about you? I bet you're not the type to crawl into your parents' bed in the middle of the night."

I shake my head.

Nicole moves around the store. She keeps up a stream of questions as she cleans. I don't answer most of them, because after a moment, she'll answer them herself. I just sit and watch her under the warm tide of her words. They surround me – soothing, buoying me up. After a while, I'm nodding. She doesn't seem to mind my silence. It doesn't discourage her from making jokes and laughing alone at the punchlines.

I drift off. Lean with my elbow on the counter. When Nicole taps me on the shoulder, I jump.

"Sorry," she says. "Looks like the insomnia is wearing off. Do you want a ride home?"

I blink up at her. "What about the store?"

"Cheryl's here. She'll cover for a few minutes."

Cheryl stands behind Nicole, her bright red hair twisted into a long braid over her shoulder.

"Is she okay?" she says.

Nicole nods. "Sure, she is. C'mon, Eleanor."

I rub my eyes and follow Nicole out to her car. The night is even quieter than before, with only the occasional passing car. Nicole's SUV is black. She holds open the passenger door for me. I am dragging, heavy with drowsiness. Her car smells like a pineapple air freshener.

"Don't forget your seat belt," she says before she pulls out of the parking lot.

I can see a sliver of moon just above the line of roofs. It slides in and out of passing branches. In less than a minute, I'm home. The house is still dark when Nicole pulls up to the curb. I unclip the seat belt and it retracts with a hiss.

"Eleanor," she says. I look over at her. Her face is bleached of color in the black and white of the night city, the spikes of her hair outlined. "You don't have to tell me your story. But it would probably be good if you found someone to tell. It can get really lonely being the only one carrying a secret."

I stare at my front door, green in the wan streetlight. "Why do you think I have a secret?" I say it without looking at her. I have one hand on the car door handle.

"Everybody has secrets," she says. "But more than that, I've had to carry a lot of secrets in my life. I know what it looks like." She pauses. I want to shrink into the shadows.

I release the door handle. I look down at my hands, wondering how she can see. Am I marked somehow?

I think about what they would say; what would happen if I told. My thoughts are inflating my skull. Light-headed, I will drift upward from my shoulders, leaving the heavy, dragging body behind. My chest constricts. Am I holding my breath?

I stare at my front door. I imagine the secret under my bed. Vile crouching secret. Pushed and prodded into the deepest corners. I see the secret start to spread, to leak out from under my bed, like a heavy black liquid soaking into the carpet. It oozes outward, reaches the walls of my room, soiling the carpet, licking at the bed skirt. The sludge moves into the hall, into Joshua's room. He sleeps, curled into his bed. The black oil spreads, deepens. It fills the house. Presses against the windows, coats and covers everything.

I see the front door bulge, strain. I watch it burst, releasing a tide of black that roars onto the lawn. I see the bodies of my parents, of Joshua – slack-limbed and white – carried in the churning rush. They sink onto the blackened grass as the liquid drains away. They look flat and empty, staring, like plastic grocery sacks on the beach. Creep steps through the puddles. Around the still forms of my family. He laughs. A headache spreads between my temples. Stomach knots. I rub my eyes.

"I can't tell anyone," I say.

"Oh, now," says Nicole, "I don't think that's true. There's gotta be at least one person on this planet who could help carry your secret."

I shake my head. When I look back at the front door, Creep is sitting on the stoop. He is a hump of shadow in the night. He could be a large cat, sitting there waiting for me to come home.

I shake my head. "I can't tell anyone," I say again. "Ever."

Nicole sighs. "The way I look at it, the only reason to keep a secret like that is fear."

I want to tell her I don't know what she means, but I can't make it sound true. Even in my head.

She goes on. "Fear of what people will think. What they'll say. What might happen to you. What might happen to them. How your life might change."

I put my hand back on the door handle.

"I have to go," I say.

"Alright," she says. "I'm glad you came to hang out with me tonight. You can always talk to me. You know, if you decide you need to talk."

"Okay," I say. I push the door open and run across the lawn. It's dry and prickles under my bare feet. On the porch, I look back at Nicole's car. She waves. I open the front door and close it behind me. I watch through the curtains next to the door. She waits until the door is shut and sits there for a minute before she drives away. I wait on the landing. The house is quiet. I can hear a hum as the refrigerator clicks on.

I tiptoe down the stairs. Creep follows me through the darkness back to my room. I fall into my bed.

Creep hunches next to me. He hums and clicks his fingernails together.

"So who are you going to tell?" he asks between hums. I cover my head with a pillow.

"No one," I say into the feathers and fabric, my voice muffled.

Creep stops humming. He clicks his fingers together three times. C-r-r-r-r-ick. C-r-r-r-r-ick. C-r-r-r-r-ick.

"That's good," he says. "You remember what he said."

I close my eyes against the stifling blackness. "Yes," I say. "I remember."

<u>Things He Said:</u>

Hi, Beautiful.
Let's play a game.
Pretty Girl.
Our Secret.
They wouldn't understand.
I love you.

It's dark in my room, quiet. I am small in the big bed from Mom and Dad. When they got their new one, Baby Joshua graduated from his crib and got my bed, and I got their old one. Mom says it's a queen, but I don't think it is. I think a queen bed would have posts and gauzy curtains hanging from the top. The wind coming in the turret window would blow them and I would lie there under my satin quilts and fall asleep watching how the moonlight glints off the rubies in my crown on the bedside table.

But I'm not a queen, or even a princess. I am a small person in a dark room. I have my big flat teddy bear, the one I got for Christmas, lying next to me. It didn't used to be flat, but I laid on top of it so much that it got as flat as an old pillow.

Sometimes when I close my eyes, I feel the world getting bigger and bigger, until I am tiny. So tiny I start to be afraid that I will disappear. And then the world starts to shrink, and I feel myself expanding. My limbs swell, bulbous and grotesque, until I'm sure I'll touch the walls any moment. Then my body shrinks down again, faster, and back out, dizzying in its speed. I'm afraid to open my eyes, because I'll see the horror of this bizarre transition. But I have to open my eyes, because I know it's the only thing that will make it stop.

I open my eyes. I'm still in my dark room. A small person in a big bed. The house is quiet. I am surprised, somehow, that I am so small. I expect to be bigger, and I don't know why. I lie perfectly still under the covers, my arms to either side of my body. I move my eyes around, to see every wall, every corner of the room. The horse collection is small, just started. My books are all picture books, a collection of stuffed animals on the highest shelf. My favorite purple dress is hanging in the closet. I can see it because the door is partly slid open. I want to get up and close it. I want to pull the covers over my head, but I can't move. Moving just reminds people you're there.

My bedroom door is cracked. Just enough so that someone can put their face there and see if I'm sleeping. I close my eyes again, to make myself brave enough to turn over. In one quick movement, I turn toward the wall, and I lie there staring at the kitten poster that says, "Hang in there!" It's a ginger tabby kitten, dangling by its front paws on a leafy branch. I stare at the kitten. I know what it feels like, hanging, hoping someone will catch you, but knowing no one is there. The cracked bedroom door makes a line of light on the wall, right over the kitten's face.

Then I hear footsteps in the hallway. I make sure not to move. A shadow covers up the line of light because someone is looking through the doorway. He wants to know if I'm asleep. I pretend to be asleep, try not to move. Try not to breathe.

He comes into the room, pushes the door all the way open for a moment and then cracks it behind him again. His feet are whisper soft on the carpet. I can feel the side of the mattress sink down where he sits next to me. I close my eyes.

"Ellie," he says. He puts his hand on my head.

My skin covers itself with goosebumps. I want him to move his hand away, or put it somewhere else. I want to wrap my blanket around both our necks and pull it tight. I want to say something

His hand slides over my hair. Down my neck. Over my shoulder. The touch is light, but it feels heavy on my skin. Prickly. Like it's stuck to me, magnetized, and I couldn't get it off if I wanted to. I want to. I don't want to. My throat closes up. Words, any words I might have said, are stuck just below the swallowing point. My eyes blink fast. I can feel myself receding, pulling away. Farther. Farther.

"Ellie," he says again. He pulls on my shoulder, turning me toward him. "I missed you."

Suddenly I'm bigger, not a small person in a big bed anymore. Like his hands made me grow somehow. I'm bigger. I'm fifteen. I feel different. The bigger body feels different, like not all the goosebumps are bad. He missed me.

He missed me.

Part of me missed him too.

I stare into his face. His hand is warm. He parts my lips with his thumb. I can't tell where one heartbeat begins and another one ends I shouldn't be alive it's hammering so fast my chest should be explodingnownownow

He leans closer, like he'll kiss me. Closer.

I feel myself flatten, contract, disappear. I'm all gone.

There's nothing left.

"Why is he still touching her," I think, "when she's already gone?"

I missed you too.

TWENTY-SIX

I wake thrashing. I run to the bathroom, stumbling over my shoes on the floor. I fall to my knees and vomit into the toilet. My hands are shaking as I lean back against the wall, a headache stabbing between my temples.

Creep crouches, a black shadow in the dark doorway. He is featureless. The darkness makes me blind. There is only his voice like deep, slow, chains dragged across stone.

"What is it, Eleanor?"

I don't tell him. I don't say anything. I curl slowly over until I am lying on the bathroom rug. I am folded, contracted in on myself.

Creep crawls closer. "C'mon, Ellie," he says. "You can tell me." He reaches out like he'll touch me, so close that I can feel the air around me change under the cracked blackness of his hand. My throat is still full, tightened down on itself, there's no way I can make any sound, but if he touches me, I know I'll scream.

He doesn't touch me. Instead, he curls up next to me like a cat. There's no purr though — there is only that hum. That sound digging out my eye sockets.

So I don't say anything. I close my eyes against the sound and I don't tell Creep. I don't tell him that in the dream, when I turned over to look into the face, when the fear washed over me like a wave, the face was Virgil's.

I WAKE TO MOM KNOCKING ON MY DOOR. WHEN I OPEN IT, SHE has a sleeping bag, a suitcase, and several grocery sacks full. She comes in to put them on my bed. "Here are your supplies for Bible Camp," she says. "Let me know if Mia remembers anything else you need."

"Okay," I tell her.

"Joshua is going to stay with Sam's mother while I'm at work and school," she says. "So we will be able to make do without you." She smiles at me. "It won't be easy though."

She puts a hand on my shoulder, but I move away from it. I act like I'm investigating the supplies on the bed, so she doesn't notice.

"Thanks, Mom," I say.

"Okay," she says. "I have class. See you later."

Once she leaves, I head back into the bathroom. I splash my face with water and rinse the sour taste from my mouth. I'm brushing my teeth when Joshua appears in the bathroom doorway with Sam standing behind him.

"Eleanor," says Joshua.

"Hey," I tell them around my toothbrush. "You can't just come into a person's bedroom without knocking. People need privacy, you know." I point my toothbrush at them and spit in the sink. "You have to ask to come in here. Don't just come in whenever you want."

"The door was open," says Joshua.

"Well, it shouldn't have been," I tell him. "Mom left it open." I spin him around by his shoulders and push him out of the bedroom. Sam follows. When both of them are standing in the hallway, I shut my door. As soon as the latch clicks: *knock knock*.

"Who is it?" I say. I pull a shirt out of my closet.

"Me," says Joshua.

"Me who?" I say. I drop the shirt I'm wearing on the floor and shrug into the new one.

"Me, Josh," says Joshua.

"Are you alone, Josh?" I say.

There's a pause. "No," he says.

"Who's with you?" I ask. "What's his security clearance?" I grab my bottle of bubbles.

Another pause.

"Sam," he says. "Security clearance alpha."

I flop down on my bed next to the camping pile.

"What's the secret password?" I call. I blow a line of bubbles toward the ceiling fan.

Pause.

"Captain-Chihuahua-shark-pants," says Joshua.

"Enter," I say.

When the door opens, Mia is standing behind them, a large duffle bag over her shoulder.

"You guys are so weird," she says to me.

"Hey," I tell her. "Turn on the fan."

She clicks the switch, and sits on my bed to go through the bags. Joshua and Sam borrow my colored pencils.

"We need paper too, we're going to make a book," Joshua tells me.

"What's it about?" I ask him.

Sam shakes his head. "Top secret," he says.

I throw a pillow at them and they retreat, shutting the door behind them. As soon as they're gone, Mia pushes the bags onto the floor, kicks off her shoes, and rolls onto her stomach.

"So," she says. "Tell me everything."

"I told you everything," I say. I exhale through the bubble wand. The iridescent globes whirl around the room.

"You're so boring," she says. "Give me specifics."

"Didn't I tell you specifics last night?" I blow another set of bubbles. She reaches up to catch them, but the fan shoots them off in different directions.

"No," she says. "All you said was you kissed and there was no tongue."

"Ew." I make a face. "Don't say that."

"What? Tongue?"

My stomach twists. "Yeah."

"Why?"

I can't tell her why. No one knows. Only Creep. And that's just because he knows everything.

"I don't know. It's just gross."

She rolls her eyes. "What are you, twelve? Okaaaay. So how did it happen?"

I blow bubbles upward. They fly away from the wand, their path erratic.

"We were grooming the horses," I say. "And we were talking."

"Before that," she says. "Tell me *everything*."

"Okay." I watch the flight of surviving bubbles. "He took me riding."

"Sweet," she says. "Where?"

"Just down the street," I say.

"On the sidewalk?" she says. "In the neighborhood? Like, next to cars?"

I nod. She laughs. "I bet a lot of cars honked."

I nod again.

"Was he in front, or you?"

"He was in front," I tell her. "He's the one who knows how to drive."

She rolls over to her back, watches the bubble galaxy. "What else?"

"Then we just hung out at the stable. We groomed the horses and fed them and we were just talking and I kissed him."

"That's it?" she says. "You were talking and you just kissed him all of a sudden."

"Yeah," I say. My fingers are wet with bubble liquid. It drips on my shirt.

"What were you talking about?"

I shrug. "I dunno. He told me I was pretty."

"Well, you are," she says. I look at her, but she pretends not to notice. "But that's it? You went on a romantic horseback ride, with him in front. So you basically had your legs wrapped around him for hours." I make a face, so she says, "Okay, for an *hour*. Then you end up making out in the barn, and I don't even get to hear about his abs?"

I laugh. It's a short burst of sound, taking me by surprise. "Um, no," I tell her.

"Okay, then," she says. "Just give me this. So here's the real question – is Virgil a good kisser?"

I raise my eyebrows and blow another line of bubbles. "I guess," I say.

Yes, I think. But I can't tell her why. *He was quiet and gentle and shy. He didn't trample me, or smother me, or act like he wanted anything else.*

"I've been thinking about what you said," I tell her. "About figuring myself out."

"Yeah?" Mia reaches for the bottle of bubbles. I hand it to her and wipe my hand on my jeans.

"What if there's something in the way… of figuring yourself out?" She blows and the bubbles scatter. One pops on my forehead. Soft, like the brush of a moth. It leaves a damp circle, cool under the fan breeze. I think about the way Virgil's lips felt. Then I think about the dream, his face leaning over me. I feel sick again. I close my eyes against sudden dizziness.

"What kind of thing?" asks Mia.

"I don't know," I tell her. "It's hard to explain."

"There are lots of things that can get in the way of queer people living their truth." She blows another string of bubbles. "Sometimes we'll dress a certain way to increase our visibility as queer. Like at Pride. Oh, my God," Mia says. "Speaking of clothing. I come bearing gifts." She grabs her bag. "I brought over a bunch of stuff for you. Stuff I used to wear before I grew boobs."

"Well. Thanks," I say, flatly.

Mia laughs as she pulls out a wad of clothing, almost everything black. "Hey," she says. "No body shaming here." She gives me an appraising look. "Actually, with the right haircut, you could totally pull off the androgynous-babe look. Anyway…" She spreads the clothing on the bed. There are skirts, shirts, long socks, and at the bottom of the bag, a pair of black combat-style boots. I look through the shirts. One says, *This **is** my smile.* Another says, *I'm practicing for your funeral.*

"Wow, Mia," I say. "These are so cool. Thank you."

She nods. "You seemed to dig the makeup the other day, so I thought you might want to try a different look."

I hold up a shirt. "A look that says '*Dead Inside*?'"

"Hey," she says grinning. "That vibe is so *you.*"

Different look. Different me. Maybe it could *be a different life.*

The doorbell rings and we hear the boys on the stairs, falling over each other to get to the door first. They start yelling something about Slurpees and pound back down the stairs again, whooping and laughing. There's a knock.

"Who is it?"

"Virgil."

I sit up and look at Mia. My stomach drops. She grins and smacks my arm. I smack her back. She pushes me off the bed.

"Virgil who?" says Mia.

"Um – ," says Virgil.

"Are you alone?" Mia cuts him off.

I scramble back up onto the bed and smooth my hair.

"Not really," says Virgil.

We hear Joshua and Sam giggle.

"What's the password?" asks Mia.

A pause. "Captain." Virgil waits. "Chihuahua." He waits again. "Shark pants?"

"What's your security clearance?"

Silence. Then: "Ten out of ten?"

"You may enter," says Mia.

The door cracks open. "Eleanor," whispers Joshua through the crack. "Your boyfriend is here."

"Joshua!" I hiss.

He and Sam erupt into giggles as Virgil pushes the door open. The two younger boys go back into Joshua's room, they're both carrying Slurpee cups. Virgil stands in the doorway. He raises one hand.

"Hi," he says.

I look at his mouth forming the word.

"Hello, Virgil," says Mia. She elbows me in the side.

I feel like I'm part of a TV sitcom. *Is that a laugh track? Or just Creep?*

"Hi," I say. Virgil and I lock eyes for a moment. Cheeks warm.

Mia blows a line of bubbles upward. "To what do we owe the grace of your presence, Virge?"

Virgil's eyes scan the whirling bubbles. He sees the horse wall and his gaze passing over the pictures make me wish my collection was bigger. "I promised the boys I would help them beat Contra before I take Sam home."

"Great," says Mia. "That leaves Elle and I alone to talk about secret things that have nothing whatsoever to do with you."

Virgil raises his eyebrows.

"Go on," says Mia. "Go have your boy time." Then she is shooing him out and closing the door behind him. She turns to look at me. "You were staring at his lips the whole time, weren't you?"

I throw a pillow at her and she catches it and tosses it back. "Actually," she says. "That brings me to my question." She looks mischievous.

"What question?" I say.

"Do you think you'll kiss him again?" She presses her lips together, trying not to smile. "No tongue, obviously."

I roll my eyes, almost smiling too. "I don't know," I say.

I don't tell her that I'm worried if I do, he'll show up in *all* my dreams.

<u>Things Mia is Obsessed With:</u>

Movies
Makeup
Politics
The color black
Music
Tongue
Virgil's abs

TWENTY-SEVEN

At bedtime, Mia and I have a long discussion about *Star Wars* versus *Star Trek* versus *Battlestar Galactica* versus *The Expanse*. She says *Star Trek* is superior, because of its ultimately positive outlook on the future.

"Roddenberry was full of hope!" Mia practically shouts. We're whisper-yelling at each other, while Mia paints my toenails.

I argue that while *Star Trek* is full of positivity, *The Expanse* is much more realistic.

"Don't you mean fatalistic?" Mia says. She's working on the second-to-last toe on my right foot.

"Come on," I tell her. "*Star Trek* is at the bottom of the list. *Star Wars* is way more fun. It's spaghetti-western space-opera telling The Hero's Journey. *Trek* is just preachy social commentary."

"What's wrong with social commentary?" says Mia. "The first interracial kiss on broadcast television? Roddenberry was a visionary!"

"If we're going to talk about visionary television," I counter. "Let's talk about Rod Serling and Jordan Peele."

"*Twilight Zone* isn't on this list—," begins Mia.

I interrupt her, "A list which reads thusly: Number one—"

Mia cackles, "THUSLY!"

I don't stop. "Number ONE, *The Expanse*. Number two, *Star Wars*. Number three, *Battlestar*. And a distant fourth, *Trek*."

Mia holds my pinkie toe steady. "This list should really include *For All Mankind*," I say, thoughtful as I watch her hands on my feet, trying not to shiver at the thrills that keep moving up my legs. I am constantly tempted to jerk my legs away.

"How is it," she says, leaning over my foot, "that you're not online, and you don't know music outside of churchy shit, and you don't have a phone, and you have a prehistoric TV that barely gets local network channels, but you seem to know everything about sci-fi and fantasy? Movies, shows, books. It's like you lived under a rock for almost everything, except for this. You're like a sci-fi-trivia savant."

Creep who fell silent during the last hour, bored by the Han-Shot-First convo, has perked up at this question. I look at him and then look back to see Mia put the last brushstroke on my toe. She blows on my foot. I watch the shape of her lips pushing the air out, feel it tickling lightly over my skin.

"Oh," I say. "My dad takes us to movies when he's in a good mood and mom isn't around. And a guy I used to know… was really into sci-fi."

She stops blowing. She looks up. "A *guy*… you used to know. A *GUY* you used to know?"

Oh no.

Creep sniggers.

"A guy, Elle?" She starts waving her hands, and getting louder. I'm worried she'll splash nail polish on the carpet. I take the bottle and the brush from her. I shush her and she whisper-screams, "WHAT… GUY??"

Creep joins in, waving his hands. "What guy, Elle? Tell her about 'the guy'."

"Shhh! Please," I say. "Nothing. It's no one. Someone I used to know."

"Who?" Her eyes are wide and after I put the securely-closed nail-polish bottle down, she grabs both my hands. "Who? Why did I think Virgil was your first guy?"

"Virgil is not *my guy*." I pull my hands away.

She says, "Sorry," and then, "but WHO. IS. IT??"

"Really," I say. I get up, stepping over her in the toe spacers she put on my feet before she started painting. "It's no one. We just…" She and Creep get up to follow me into the bathroom. Mia watches me fill a glass at the sink and swallow some water before I say; "… used to watch everything together. He… showed me all the shows and kinda…" I take another drink. "He's just a big fan," I finish.

Mia's mouth has been open. She closes it now. She folds her arms and leans against the counter. Creep crouches next to her on the rug.

I pull open a drawer and start brushing my hair, pretending to look at myself in the mirror. Mia watches me. I watch the Eleanor reflection. They run their fingers through long black hair, ruthlessly brushing tangles out. Mirror-Eleanor draws me closer to the glass. I examine their pores. I glance at Creep's reflection. He's grinning.

"So that's it, huh?" says Mia. "Some guy you used to know is a big sci-fi fan."

Mirror-Eleanor puts down the brush. I turn to look at Mia. "Yeah," I say. "Sorry."

Creep watches our exchange, his eyes flicking back and forth. "This is it," comes his guttural whisper. "This is the moment you lose her."

Mia narrows her eyes at me. We stare at each other. Then she says brightly, "Alright. That's fine." She turns back to the bedroom. I find her sitting on her side of the bed. She has her legs crossed. "Kinda disappointing though."

I'm standing in the doorway of the bathroom. "What's disappointing?"

Mia says, "We almost had a whole conversation that could pass the Bechdel Test." And then she laughs.

"What's the Bechdel Test?"

"Oh," she says. "That's when two women in a movie or book have a conversation that doesn't revolve around men for once. But then you had to mention The Guy."

"I just mentioned him," I say. "You're the one who jumped all over it."

"Hey," she says innocently, "it's not my fault that you're such an enigma I need to grasp onto every detail I can." She bats her eyelashes at me. "But like I said, it's fine."

"It's fine?" I ask her. I crawl onto my side of the bed, and sit facing her, carefully protecting my toes. Creep clambers up to hunker at the foot of the bed. I fold my legs up and wrap my arms around my knees.

"Yeah," she says. "It is. Because," she gathers her hair over one shoulder and starts winding it into a loose braid. "I'm determined to become worthy of your story."

I pluck at a stray thread poking up from my bedspread. "Worthy?" I want to cringe.

"Yeah," she says again. "I'm going to do whatever it takes to get you to trust me. So that when you're ready to talk about yourself, you know you're safe with me." She pulls the braid out, fingers running through the thick locks, tosses her hair back, looking at me. I can feel it.

I wind the thread around my index finger. I watch it pull loose from the other stitches holding it in place. "What if I never feel safe?"

She reaches out to take my other hand. Her touch zings up my arm and sparks snap, crackle, pop in my head. She's looking directly into my eyes when I look up. "That's fine too," she says. "I'm here for whatever you want to share with me. We're friends."

My eyes fall on our hands. I weave my fingers between hers. *Is this what friends do?* Her mouth is saying words. I watch the lips moving, but I don't hear what she's saying. Everything slows down. I look over at Creep. His smile gets wider and wider and wider until it seems his whole face is made of broken-shard teeth.

Mia is still talking. Her eyes are soft and sympathetic. I think about laying back with her on the pillows, tracing the curve of her chest with one fingertip while her hands are in my hair. I think about our mouths fitting together the way Virgil's did with mine. I wonder what her lipstick tastes like. She squeezes my hand.

"You okay?" she asks.

I blink. "Yeah," I say. "Thank you. That's… really nice of you to say. Thank you."

"It feels weird: you're always thanking me for basic courtesy," Mia says. "But you're welcome? Anything else I can help you with?" She laughs.

"Actually," I say. "Yes. Can you help me set up the account you were talking about? For photos and stuff?"

"Oh my God, yes," Mia says. "Get your phone."

We're lying on our stomachs side by side as she helps me set up a Twitter account. "Tons of creators left Tumblr when they started censoring content, and Instagram is so dead since the Zuckerbot took over. They shadowban queer creators all the time. It's like … all middle-aged white women now, posting pictures of their oatmilk lattes and heather infinity scarves."

I say, "Virgil has an Instagram for his horses."

Mia quirks her mouth to one side. "Well, I don't want to say that Virgil has the aesthetic of a middle-aged white woman." She makes a sound like she's trying not to laugh and it's escaping through her nose. "But he would clearly be comfortable on *Facebook*." She lets the laugh out, and it's so infectious, I'm laughing too, even though I'm not sure what she means.

She glances over at me and says, "Okay, you Luddite, we'll set up an Insta too. So you can tag Virgil in your romantic horse pictures."

I roll my eyes. But I'm thinking about Virgil opening his app and finding a picture of mine and what his face will look like when he sees it.

She shows me how to make a post, how to use tags, and how to "at" someone. I watch her thumbs blur over the phone keyboard. Her hair tickles my arm. She smells like coconuts. Then she's yawning.

"Uuuugh," she says. "I just remembered how early we have to get up. It's gonna suck."

She gets up and goes into the bathroom and shuts the door. Water runs. Creep moves on all fours to take her place on the bed.

"You like her," he says.

I shake my head.

"Uh huh," he says. "You LIKE her, like her."

"Shut up," I tell him.

He chuckles, deep, a sound I feel like a vibration in my organs. "My favorite part is how she is trying to be a good friend and all you can think about is doing naughty things to her."

"Would you just shut UP?" I hiss.

"It's alright, Ellie," he says. "You can be abominations together."

When Mia clicks the light off, I'm facing the horse wall. My eyes are closed, but I'm not asleep yet. I just don't want to talk anymore, and it seems like that's all Mia wants to do. I feel the bed shift as she climbs back in. She adjusts the covers. Finally, she's quiet and still. I open my eyes. The room is very dark. I don't usually sleep in complete darkness like this. I feel better knowing where Creep is, and this way he just blends into all the shadows. But he's here, crouched on my pillow, humming a lullaby. Well, his version of a lullaby, a slow and rasping Creep-cover of *I'll Be Watching You* by The Police.

I fall asleep staring at where the horse wall would be if I could see it, Creep's voice like the ebb and flow of distant city traffic.

THE DREAM IMAGES FILL MY VISION AS I'M NUDGED AWAKE. They fade quickly. The first thing I see through them: the alarm clock, 3am. My entire body is a drumming heartbeat, and a wave of shame crashes over me. The impressions in my flesh, the scent, the sound — those fade more slowly. His hands. The sensitive fingers, generous with gifts, heavy with demands. His voice, deep, throaty with longing. My name whispered, falling from the heat of an open mouth ready to consume me.

His hands are still on me still on me stillonmestillonme and I'm rolling over to find him until I realize it's Mia leaning over me, saying my name, her hand on my shoulder. And I push her hand away at the same time I realize *everything* and sit up suddenly, hot with humiliation.

She falls back to rest on her heels. She drops her hand.

"Sorry," I mutter, pressing my palms into my eye sockets.

"Don't be sorry," she says. "I thought you were having a bad dream." I can't see her face in the dark like this. But I can imagine the look.

"I was," I say. *Was I?*

She lets those two words sit in the silence for several breaths. She yawns. Then: "Are you okay?"

"I'm okay," I say. "Sorry. You should go back to sleep."

She's lying down again, and I want nothing more than to curl up in the gap between her arms. Instead, I wait until the easy regularity of her breathing tells me she's asleep. Then I grab the copy of *Dandelion Wine* from my bedside table and my sketchbook and take them with my pillow and the phone into the bathroom. Creep is stalking across the edge of the tub on all-fours. Back and forth, back and forth.

I slowly click the door shut.

"Which one was it?" Creep asks. "Didn't sound like a bad dream to me."

"You're disgusting," I tell him, thumbing through my book to find where I left off. Creep giggles.

"Excuse me, Eleanor," he says. "I think you'll find, of the two of us, the disgusting one is *you*."

I put my earbuds in.

"Which dream was it Ellie?" He whines. "C'mon, just tell me. It's one of my favorite games to play with you." When I don't answer, he sulks.

I scroll down the playlists and find *Issues*. I tap it and a song by Linkin Park begins to play. The music buoys me, a man singing about being more like himself, and I can feel it washing the dream away. Creep is still talking. I don't answer.

When he realizes I'm not going to play his game, Creep says, "You used to be so fun."

I turn the volume setting all the way up and though he's talking, I can't hear him over the crash of the music — Linkin Park singing and howling and screaming in my ears, turning Creep into a silent film, scored by *Numb*. His mouth opening and closing, but no sounds coming out.

Creep finally gives up. He curls up in the sink and watches me like a grumpy cat, his chin on the counter, slow-blinking those eyes like polished obsidian.

<u>Things I Hate About Creep:</u>
Everything

<u>Things I Hate About Me:</u>
*See above

TWENTY-EIGHT

The buses mumble to themselves, waiting in a corner of the church parking lot. This is the coolest part of the day, with the sun drowsy just below the golden horizon and purple clouds streaking over our heads. A smell of fallen rain, but the asphalt is dry. Lines of vans, SUVs, and family sedans drop off more and more teenagers – kids dressed in pajama bottoms, hair mussed, clutching pillows. Everyone yawns, stands around rubbing their eyes. Except for me.

I stand next to Mia, buzzing with sleeplessness, and stare at the clouds and listen again to all of her reasons why camping is the worst. She wears a black shirt that says *NO*, Jack Skellington slippers, and her hair in pigtails. She has what she calls a "full face." She got up an hour and a half early to do her makeup. I want to hold her hand. I don't like crowds.

Virgil is standing at my other side, shoulders almost touching. He doesn't say anything. He just watches a Hacky Sack circle across the crowd. Levi and The A-Team have joined, with a large amount of name-calling and jostling. They're loud. Creep curls up on my sleeping bag and his gargling hum scatters through Mia's words until I tune them out.

After a while, Mia falls silent, scrolling and texting and Virgil picks up a conversation we started at the barn, the five best sci-fi heroines of all time, and after twenty minutes I realize that I haven't thought about Creep or Ian since Virgil started talking.

Brother Chad finally takes roll. I swat at Creep, we put our bags in the pile to be stowed, and climb onto the bus. I wait for Creep to mount the steps before I follow.

Mia and I sit next to each other, Virgil a row ahead of us. Luckily, The A-Team is on the other bus. I have the window seat. Mia leans her pillow against my shoulder and closes her eyes while Creep curls up under my seat. I hear him humming, so I put in the ear buds. I get out my sketch book and start doodling.

As the bus pulls onto the freeway, the sun peeks over the horizon, a bright disc of yellow-white. Downtempo electronica beats fill my ears and I take a black and white picture of the paths of gauzy clouds already starting to dissipate. Sunlight washes through the tinted windows. I yawn.

A folded piece of notebook paper slides backward between the seats in front of me. It sticks out. I stare at it for a moment, then it wiggles and I look up to see a sliver of Virgil's face suspended above it. He smiles. I take the paper and unfold it.

Hi.

I look back up to where Virgil's face had been. It's turned forward again.

Hi, I write.

I fold the paper back up, stick it through the crack. It disappears.

A moment later, it reappears. I unfold it.

That's the most I think you've ever said at one time, he writes. He's talking about our movie-heroine discussion.

Was I talking too much? I write back. The note disappears again.

No, he writes. *I wish you would talk more. Seems like the only way to get you to talk is NOT to ask you about yourself. You'll monologue about Joss Whedon, but you won't even volunteer your favorite color.*

I write back: *Blue.*

When I unfold it next, the note says, *Green. How are you?*

Tired, I write.

I pass the note back. I hear Virgil laugh.

See?

I think about hanging out with Virgil and Mia at camp. I think about Creep following me around, just like at home. I shiver. I want to respond, but I don't know what to say. I remember those notes from fourth grade, the ones passed around with boxes to check. *Do you like me? Check yes or no.* I return the note without writing anything.

The note stays with Virgil for a while. So long that I start drawing again, Mia's form heavy against my arm. I have drawn a stick figure trapped in a bottle, a girl sitting under a dead tree, and a fish when the note appears again. I unfold it.

Remember that day at the barn?

There have been lots of days at the barn, but I'm pretty sure I know which one he's talking about. I write, *Yes.*

The note comes back more quickly this time.

Was that your first kiss?

I need to lie. I *have* to, but I don't want to lie to Virgil.

I write, *You said it was **your** first real kiss.*

Yes, he writes. *I kissed my best friend's sister in third grade. But I don't think that counts. What about you?*

I hold on to the note for a long time. My hands start to sweat. Creep crouches behind my ankles. Fingers ache around the pen. *No, not my first kiss. But maybe mine doesn't count either.*

Can I write that? *Did* it count? It feels like it counted. My mouth feels bruised when I think about it. I press my lips together. My teeth catch the inside of my cheek. I almost crumple the paper, but take a deep breath and pass the note back before I change my mind.

When the note comes back, I'm afraid to open it. *He must know. How can he not see it when he looks at me?*

I unfold the paper to find another smiley face. The knot in my stomach unravels. I release a breath I didn't know I was holding. My sketchbook falls to the floor and when I bend over to pick it up, Mia groans and Creep peeks out from under the seat.

"How's your boyfriend?" he says.

I don't answer him. Mia sits up. She yawns, rubbing her eyes.

"Sorry," I say. I pull one ear bud out and tuck it into my collar.

She stretches. "I gotta pee."

She moves down the aisle toward the back of the bus and I'm drawing a smiley face in response when Virgil sits down next to me.

My heart almost jumps out of my chest as I fold the paper in a hurry and hand it to him.

"Thanks," he says. His arm brushes mine. The tingle makes me shift a little more toward the window, away from him.

"I wanted to ask you a question," he says. His voice is low.

"Okay," I say.

He leans closer. "Will you meet me?" he whispers.

"What?" I whisper back.

He gestures and I sideways-lean toward him, my eyes on the front of the bus. His breath is warm on my ear. Goosebumps spread. "At camp," he says. "There's a testify night. We can sneak away."

He waits for me to answer. I just nod.

"There's a place by the creek," he whispers, "with a little waterfall over rocks. There's a huge tree with this branch that hangs out over the pool. You'll see it during Glory Hike. Will you meet me there on testify night?"

I turn toward him and our faces are close enough to touch. His eyes this close are green within green, darker toward the pupil, lighter at the edge of the iris, with flecks of gold. I drop my eyes.

"Okay," I whisper.

"Um." We both turn and Mia is standing in the aisle.

"Virgil," she points. "You're sitting in my seat."

"Sorry," says Virgil. He doesn't move. Our hands are next to each other on the arm rest. His pinky moves and touches mine.

"Vacate," says Mia.

Virgil scrambles up. "Sorry," he says again. He shoves the note in his back pocket, his eyes on me. "See you guys there."

Mia sits down and gives me a pointed look.

"What?" I say. I open my sketch book.

"You guys aren't going to be one of those cute couples, are you?" she says. "You know the ones that are all '*O-M-G we are so cute we make everyone want to vomit*'?"

"We're not a couple," I say.

"Sure," she says. She pulls out a pack of gum and offers me a piece. "Please, Elle. Please promise me you and Virgil won't be one of those couples."

"We're not a couple," I say again.

"Right," she says. She fluffs the pillow in her lap and folds over, face down into it. After a minute, I realize she's asleep.

I spend the better part of an hour drawing a stick-figure couple sitting on a branch under a full moon.

Dear Jesus,

I will be skipping testify night.

I hope this won't reflect poorly on my standing with you.

Brother Chad says you understand everyone's feelings.

so I'm sure you'll understand why I would rather hang out with Virgil

than listen to everyone cry about how happy they are to be saved

because they have you inside them.

Amen.

TWENTY-NINE

We get to the camp before lunch, a series of cabins in a wide clearing with concrete bunker bathrooms and a huge ramada, all surrounded by a forest of towering ponderosa pines. Mia and I carry our luggage up the dusty path to our assigned cabin. It has a wide farmhouse Dutch door, open to the air. A concrete floor. Bunks in rows. An open ceiling of visible support beams. Mia chooses a bunk at the back of the room, next to the one window – "So that if a bear comes in, it'll be chewing on the girls nearest the door and we can escape," – and tells me I'll be on the top bunk.

"What if I want the bottom?"

She snorts. "Are you serious? You're going to make me try to climb up there?"

We unroll our sleeping bags. Six other girls – the twins Hope and Grace – and four older ones I don't know – unpack around us. Creep climbs up into the rafters and hangs upside down above me.

Our youth leader is Sister April, Brother Chad's wife. She stands by the door and her pasted-on smile makes camp announcements. I sit on my bunk and draw her as just a face on a balloon. Mia stands in front of me, so I'm looking down at the top of her head.

"We are here to grow together in Jesus. To develop friendships with each other and with Him," Sister April says. Her teeth are an unsettling white. She tells us to take turns introducing ourselves.

When it gets around to our turn, Mia says, "I'm Mia. And I am pretty sure that my mom is going to send me here every summer for the next three years."

"And that's bad?" says Sister April.

"Anywhere you have to swat bugs out of your hair, can't connect to the internet, and walk outside to pee is bad. Especially when it's full of conservative Christians."

Sister April's smile doesn't waver. Like a Stepford wife. "You're not a Christian?"

"I'm a secular humanist."

Sister April blinks. After a pause she says, "Hopefully we'll change your mind, Mia. We're so glad you're here with us. And what about you?" She raises her eyes to me.

I would rather stuff my head in an oven than talk to a room full of people. "I'm Elle," I say.

"Ellie," Creep corrects.

Sister April waits. "And tell us something about you."

I shrug. "I dunno."

"She likes to draw," says Mia. "And she's a photographer."

"See?" says Sister April. "That's something. Art is a talent. We all have gifts and talents from God."

She tells us that Bible Camp is a great way to unplug and get closer to God. She tells us we have free time until lunch. The girls follow Sister April outside, until Mia and I are the only ones left. I poke my sketchbook inside my pillowcase. Creep hops off the bunk and wanders out.

Mia is reapplying her lipstick using a compact mirror. She says to me, "Everyone has such a hard-on for Jesus here. But it's not all bad."

I hop down. "Gross," I tell her.

She presses her lips together and then grins at me.

"I dunno," I say. "It's okay. I don't mind the Bible stuff. I like to think people can feel better when they think about Jesus."

"I guess it can work that way," Mia says. "Come on. I wanna show you something."

I follow her out the door and then around the side of the cabin and into the woods. We crunch across a thick layer of pine needles, between ferns and scrubby bushes. The ground is littered with large jagged rocks. After we cross a fallen log, the ground flattens out and a trail appears.

"This leads to the creek," she says. I think of Virgil.

We walk side by side in silence for a minute. I hear the flutter of birds, the patterned tap of a woodpecker. Insects drone. The air is cool and fragrant, with the dry scent of wood, the green smell of growing things, of a billion pine needles. I trail one hand along the sienna-on-black tree trunks as we pass, their thick-layered bark rough under my fingers. I look up through the branches. A high wind weaves the boughs in and out of the sky's sparse cloud. It's a light and airy forest, full of sunlight and sound. I take pictures as we walk along.

"What are you thinking?" Mia asks.

"About what you said," I say. "Do you really think it's bad for people to like Jesus?"

Mia says, "As long as religions don't oppress, murder, or marginalize people, they can believe whatever they like. But too many people in this country use Jesus to treat people like shit. That sucks. I'd like it so much better if everyone was atheist."

I don't answer. We keep walking.

"What are you thinking now?" Mia says.

"Maybe some people need Jesus. To be good."

She pauses and puts out one hand to stop me. I pull away reflexively and she says, "Sorry." Then she says, "Do you feel like one of those people?"

I don't answer. I look down at the powdery trail dust around our feet.

"Elle," she says. "You're not bad. You're the opposite of that. You're like, the nicest person I know. I mean, you obviously have issues, but you don't talk about people behind their backs. You take care of your little brother. You never complain about your parents. I've never seen you do a single bad thing. Like, *ever*."

I am looking at her shoes. They're black Converse All-Stars with a red paisley print. She has a skull ring on her right index finger. The long, wavy pigtails curl over her shoulders. She blinks at me.

"What did you want to show me?" I ask her.

She lowers her eyebrows for a moment. Presses her lips together. "Elle, I'm hoping one of these days, you'll trust me." She waves one hand. "C'mon."

I crunch along after her. "How do you do that?"

She turns around. "Do what?"

"I dunno," I say. I pick up a pebble. It's smooth on one side and rough on the other, cool in my palm. "Always know what to say." I cock my arm back and throw the pebble as hard as I can. It hits a tree trunk ten feet away and ricochets off.

Mia puts her hands in her pockets. She starts walking again. I jog to catch up. "I was adopted," she says. "From a Mexican orphanage when I was five. I don't remember anything about it, like from before I got home, but my parents were worried I had attachment or behavioral problems, so they put me in therapy. They went too. For years."

"You've been to therapy for years?" I kick at a stone, but it turns out to be a tree root and I end up tripping. I almost fall and Mia laughs.

"You okay?" she says. When I nod, she continues. "Yeah, basically my whole life. They just wanted me to have the best chance I guess. At least they didn't put me on drugs."

"So did you have problems?"

Mia shrugs. "I guess. I don't remember anything about my life before I got adopted. If I did have problems, the therapist worked them all out. My parents and I are very good at communication now. And listening. And boundaries. Blah blah blah."

"Are you *still* in therapy?"

"Yep. I go every other Tuesday."

"Why do you still go if you don't have any problems?"

"I guess my parents think it will keep me from getting any new ones."

I pick up another rock. "Why do you come to Bible Camp if you're an atheist?" I throw it into the trees.

"It makes my parents happy," Mia says. "They've done so much for me, it's the least I can do. Honestly, I don't get why they believe it. Like, they're *educated*. Whatever. They accept me with all my quirks. I accept them with theirs. Plus, I find it very entertaining to come here and challenge Christian confirmation bias."

I don't know what she's talking about, but I'm pretty sure it has to do with how she argues in Sunday School all the time. "Do your parents know you don't believe it?" I pluck a green pine needle from a passing twig. I bend it in half and then in half again.

"Yeah," says Mia. "They think it's just a phase. So they're just waiting until I grow out of it. Same thing with my clothes. But they *did* tell me they accept my 'same-sex attraction' as part of the real me though. That's what they call my lack of interest in penises: same-sex attraction." She does air quotes.

"They don't care that you're a lesbian?"

"They did at first," Mia says. "Because they were worried at *how hard my life would be,* they said. But they got used to the idea."

The pine needle has been broken into a long jointed chain of perfect segments. I undulate it like a snake. "What do you talk about?"

"Me and my parents?"

"Your therapist."

"Oh. I dunno. Everything. Anything. I binged all the episodes of *Lost* last month and we had a whole session discussing our theories. Brian says that all the people on the island are just aspects of Jack's psyche. I told him only a psychiatrist would see it that way." She laughs.

"What did he say?"

"Brian said, '*I'm not a psychiatrist, Mia. I'm a licensed clinical psychologist.*' And then I said, 'My point exactly.'" She laughs again. "It's okay though. It's nice to have someone to talk to about anything I want. I can complain about my parents. You know, whatever."

She pushes through a stand of ferns. I wonder what it would be like to be able to tell someone anything I want. Someone besides Creep.

"It's over here," she says.

I follow her to a stand of trees about forty feet from the path. She squeezes between two trunks. I do the same and we're completely surrounded by tree trunks in a circle about ten feet across. The branches jumble above our heads, casting a thick shade. She points. In the center of the grove is a perfect ring of large, white mushrooms. Their caps poke upward – wide, irregular discs. Ferns are scattered around the ring, but within, nothing sprouts through the bed of pine needles. The needles lie flat and gathered, dark in the shadow of the copse.

I crouch to look at the mushrooms. "Cool."

Mia says, "My parents used to bring me here for family reunions. People can rent out this campground for private parties and stuff. I found this when I was a kid. Sometimes dumb kids come and rip them out, but they always grow back the same way. It's like some weird natural phenomena."

I reach out to touch one. It's cool and damp, fleshy under my fingertip. "Weird," I say.

"Yeah," she says. "It's like a real, live fairy ring."

"Yeah," I agree.

"When I was a kid, I used to come out here in the middle of the night and sit right in the middle of it and wish that the fairies would kidnap me and take me away."

We both laugh. Mia watches as I take a photo.

"That's how boring my life was," she says. "Now, I come out here and just sit and wish for something."

I stand up. "Do your wishes ever come true?"

"Try it," says Mia.

I roll my eyes at her.

"Seriously," she says. So I step inside the ring and sit down on the cushion of needles. There's plenty of room to cross my legs.

"Close your eyes," says Mia.

I look at her.

"Do it, Elle. How many times have you sat in a fairy ring?"

I close my eyes.

"Now," she says. "Take a breath and make a wish. Make it the deepest wish from the basement of your heart."

I open one eye. "The basement?"

"You know what I mean. Just do it."

I close my eyes again. The smells are crowded here: pine and bark and the scent of earth. Birds and the chatter of squirrels a few trees away. The distant voices calling to each other. Just me and the trees and a bed of pine on solid ground. I wipe my hands on my legs and then rest them on my knees.

The deepest wish from the basement of my heart.

One long inhalation.

I wish I were someone else.

<u>Ways That Bible Camp Could Solve my Problems:</u>

Getting eaten by a bear
Getting lost on a hike and never being seen again
Jesus literally doing anything to help

THIRTY

A sudden breeze drifts between the trees, lifting my hair. It feathers coolness over the back of my neck and I imagine some fairy queen blessing my wish. When I open my eyes, the distant tree-bouncing voices have become more distinct. Definitely boys. Multiple. I jump to my feet. At the same time, Creep slides between two trunks and bares his teeth at me.

"Miss me?" he says. "I brought some friends."

And then the voices are at the edge of the copse. A hand and arm follow Creep, a leg, a torso. I step backward out of the fairy ring.

It's The A-Team.

"Hey, look who it is," says Levi. The two others follow until they're all standing inside the circle of trees. "The Midget and The Freak."

They all laugh. I know they must look different. Different colors of hair, of eyes. Different t-shirts and shoes. But at this moment they look the same to me: mean and strong, with hard eyes and Creep-grins.

"Come here to make out?" says one of them.

Mia rolls her eyes. She's standing closest to them. How is she not afraid? I've retreated until I can feel toothy bark pressing into the back of my head. And then I feel like I'm trapped in a giant mouth, in danger of being swallowed. My chest closes in on itself.

"Jealous?" says Mia. "You're not my type. How are you such a dumbass?" She smiles. "Oh, I'm sorry. I forgot you can't help it."

A distant hand bell clangs through the woods.

Levi glowers at Mia. "You better watch your mouth."

"Hey, Mia," says another. "*I'll* tell you what you can do with your mouth. It would be a lot more exciting than making out with The Freak."

Mia groans. "Your three IQs *combined* aren't enough to excite me, much less any other parts of you. C'mon, Elle. That's lunch." She grabs my arm. I resist pulling it away from her. I follow her through the cleft in the trunks, feeling their eyes on me the whole time.

"Aw," says Creep as we leave. "You girls are no fun."

We're back on the path back to the cabin when I realize my fists are clenched. I relax my fingers and rub my palms on my jeans.

Mia tosses her hair. "Those guys are total sheep. They only function in a herd. Don't let them freak you out."

"Why don't they bother *you*?" I will my heart to stop its racing.

"Um, maybe because I've known them since kindergarten." She starts ticking them off on her fingers. "Braxton used to eat paste." She glances at me. "I mean *a lot*. Colby used to collect Beanie Babies. And when Levi didn't get what he wanted, he used to hold his breath until he threw up."

I laugh.

"See?" she says. "Don't worry about it."

I look behind me, sure their eyes are on my back.

THERE ARE THREE HUNDRED KIDS AT LUNCH, FROM MULTIPLE congregations. The ramada is huge, a low roof covering a floor of concrete, open to the air with a stage on one end. A food station is set up along one end of the ramada. I try not to touch anyone, but we are jostled and nudged as we line up for a sack, grab a drink out of ice-filled buckets, and sit at one of the rows of tables. I see a familiar face here and there, but it's mostly strangers. I take bites of my sandwich, three-cheese on grilled sourdough. It's hard to feel hungry with the rock in my stomach since the tree circle.

Mia pops a grape into her mouth. "Hey!" she waves, and Virgil detaches from the line. He weaves through the crowd to sit across from us.

"How's it going?" he asks with a smile. He tears into his sandwich.

"Fine," says Mia. "I showed Elle the fairy ring."

Virgil nods. "Cool, huh?"

"Yeah." I push baby carrots around my plate. "Until The A-Team showed up."

Virgil raises his eyebrows.

"Levi and his minions," says Mia.

"Oh," says Virgil around a mouthful of sandwich. "Don't let them bother you. They're a bunch of lemmings."

"Thank you," says Mia. "That's what I told her."

"Lemmings with sharp teeth," I say. "They're bullies. You're not worried they'll do something serious?"

"Yeah, they're bullies," says Virgil. "But the biggest thing they've ever done is knock over a few mailboxes."

"I don't know," I say. I bite a chunk out of my apple and then nibble on it. "I'm afraid they'll do something dangerous, like hurt somebody." I don't say, *I'm afraid they'll hurt* **me**.

Mia touches my arm. When I move away from her hand, she says, "Sorry. Look, don't worry. They're all talk. Trust me."

"I guess," I say.

"She's right," says Virgil. "We've known them forever. It's all just a big act." He smiles at me again, warm. I look out to the edge of the woods, wondering when I'll be able to see the fairy ring again.

I feel a hand on my shoulder. My skin shudders. I look up and it's Brother Chad. He leans over me, smiling, but his eyes are sad.

"I heard about your father," he says. "How is he?"

I want to shrug away from the hand. It's heavy, pressing through my shirt.

Dad. I haven't thought about him all day. A series of images fly across my vision: Dad holding up the second-hand bike so I could learn how to balance, Dad handing me my first dog-eared Ray Bradbury book, Dad in church sketching animals for me to trace on the back of the program. The dad with his eyebrows lowered, the explosive voice, the dad for whom it was never good enough. The dad in chemo, in radiation, in the bathroom throwing up for five hours straight.

I cover my face with my hands. The sobs come unexpectedly, shaking my shoulders.

"Brother Chad," says Mia. "She doesn't like that." She moves next to me and the weight of the hand disappears. "She doesn't like to be touched."

"Oh," he says. "I'm sorry, Eleanor. And I'm very sorry for your family. We are all praying mightily that your father will be healed."

I push away and stand up, tripping over the bench. I grope between tables. Tears blur. I run across the dirt packed path, across the clearing, and into the woods.

"Eleanor!" I hear Virgil calling after me.

I don't stop. I cut across the woods toward our cabin. I trip over branches, stagger between boulders. I see the fallen log and vault over it. The path seems edged with brambles now, tearing at my ankles as I run. It winds through the trees. My lungs clench and I fall twice. I see the tree stand and veer off the path, crashing through the underbrush.

I squeeze between the tree trunks and slump to the ground, gasping in the sudden shade.

"What's up?" It's Creep.

He sits in the middle of what used to be the fairy ring. The mushrooms are in pieces, torn, shriveled, scattered. The flat bed of needles churned and broken. He rocks back and forth on his heels.

"What did you do?" I yell.

He looks around. "It wasn't me."

"Yes, it was." I get up and move to kick him. He scurries out of the way. "You did this. you brought them here. You ruin everything!"

He clicks his teeth. "It wasn't me, Ellie. It was your friends. You know, those nice boys who just wanted to play with you."

"It *was* you! You told them to do this. And they're not my friends," I yell, my voice hoarse with crying. I stalk him around the tree circle, kicking and swinging at him.

He dodges every one. "C'mon, Ellie, you know you're the only one that can see me."

I scream, "Stop calling me that!"

He bounces away from me, snickering. A flash of that broken-glass smile.

"Eleanor?"

I whip around to see Virgil push his way into the copse, Mia is behind him.

They look around, taking in the carnage. We stand there for a moment, Creep between us. I run my fingers through my hair, wipe my face.

"You okay?" asks Virgil.

I don't say anything.

He pushes a broken mushroom cap with his toe. "What happened?"

"The A-Team," says Mia.

He sighs.

"Why can't people just leave things alone?" I ask them.

Virgil shakes his head. "I don't know," he says at the same time Mia says, "Because they're assholes."

I move to stand between them. Creep shuffles out of my way. We look down at the ruined fairy ring.

"Why can't things just *be*?" My voice catches. "Why can't they just be left alone?"

"I don't know," Virgil says again. "I'm sorry." Mia is quiet.

My eyes won't stop watering. I swipe at the tears, angry to be crying in front of someone.

"Can I hold your hand?" asks Virgil.

I look at Creep. He stares back up at me, his unblinking eyes perfectly black. I nod at Virgil.

He slips his fingers around mine. His hand is warm and dry. He doesn't move any closer, just stands there next to me. He squeezes once. Then I feel Mia at my other side, her fingers gently grasping my free hand. I can feel her looking up at me.

"Mia told me about your dad," he says. "I'm sorry. Is he going to die?"

I take a shuddering breath. "I don't know," I say.

"How's your mom?" he asks.

"I don't know," I tell him. "I don't know."

Creep moves to sit in the middle of the ruins. He starts to hum, watching me. The spines of a headache sprout in my right temple.

Words build. Both of my hands are taken, so I can't cover my face or block my mouth. The words roil in my stomach, climbing up my throat and choking me until they're all spilling out.

"I don't know. I don't know anything. Nobody talks about anything in my family. It's like this unwritten rule." I spit the words at the wreckage of the fairy ring. "You don't complain, because, guess what? Somebody always has it worse than you, and you should be thankful for your blessings. Just pretend that everything is okay." My lips and chin are wet.

I feel Virgil nod. "So no one talks in your family?"

"People talk all the time," I say. "But no one ever talks about anything important. I don't really know how my parents really *feel* about anything. They have like two settings: annoyed at me and not-annoyed. The only reason they told us about the cancer was because they knew they wouldn't be able to hide it."

Neither of them speak for a minute. Then Mia says, "What are you going to do?"

"It's just my life. I'm trapped in it and I'll never get out." I tell her. "What am I even doing at *Bible Camp*? I don't belong here."

He turns toward me, clasping both his hands over mine. "You belong with your friends. With Mia and me." He glances at Mia. She nods. "People who care about you."

I pull my hand away from Virgil to wipe my eyes. Mia squeezes the other one. She threads our fingers together and raises our hands to her sternum, holding mine tight in both of hers. "It'll be okay," she says.

I look at her. She nods. Virgil is nodding too.

"It's just my life," I say again miserably. "It's just one more thing."

I don't say, *Maybe he'll die. Then it would be one less thing.*

<u>Things About Camp</u>

Activities: ropes course, survival tutorials, glory hike, skit night, campfire songs, scavenger hunts, orienteering. All "faith promoting," which Mia says is another word for indoctrination.

Classes: modesty, humility, obedience, virtue, service, sacrifice, faith, chastity. Mia says this all means rape culture and toxic patriarchy.
Best Mia quote during class: "You know Jesus wasn't Christian, right?"

What Mia says they SHOULD teach: The Council of Nicaea, her "Gay Jesus" theory, comparative mythology, Hebrew, Aramaic, and Greek translations, actual unconditional love.

Mia's shirts this week: Down With Our Robot Overlords, DISSENT, Intersectional Feminist, Not Today Jesus.

Favorite parts of camp: fish tacos, trees everywhere, spending all my time with Mia.
Least favorite parts of camp: cold showers, the other girls giggling at all their inside jokes, Sister April reminding us to pray, Creep commenting on everything, everyone telling me how SORRY they are about Dad.

Mia's awesome. No one can pay attention to anything else when she's around. I keep thinking about her holding my hand when the fairy ring got messed up. I wish I could crawl into the bottom bunk with her and listen to her talk all night about movies and music and dismantling systems of oppression. I feel like if I could just lie under the covers with her, and inhale all the breaths that she breathes out and let them clean me, they would fill me up with the way she sees me until that's all that would be left.

Mia snores. Lol.

THIRTY-ONE

It's the last day of camp. After lunch, we are encouraged to wander the woods with our Bibles and prepare for witness meeting.

Mia grabs her Bible. She's been busy making notes about the first inclusion — in 1946 — of the word 'homosexual' in the King James. She told me all about it over breakfast. I ignore my Bible and grab my sketchbook.

I haven't felt anything at these meetings except not good enough.

"Let's go to the creek," she says.

We head through the trees, Creep close at my heels. I lift my fingers toward the tree stand as we pass. A silent greeting. Mia says that the mushrooms will take a while to regrow, but I'm tempted to go and see if they're grown back yet.

We follow the path all the way down to the creek. We can hear people moving up and down stream. The forest is muted, as if it's listening.

Mia leads the way to the tree. She sits on the big branch, close to the trunk and opens her Bible. I don't talk to her, but I do take a picture of her. Then I crawl up the branch over the water and stretch out along its length. Feathery ferns and water grasses gather along the edges of the creek. I watch the water slip over the short waterfall into a small, placid pool. The water is clear and ice cold. Creep climbs up to the highest rock in the waterfall and sits gazing into the pool like a cat watching fish.

I look down into the water too. I imagine it full of piranhas. I imagine Creep falling in. He strains to keep his head above water, but the fish school around him, picking him apart, piece by piece in a maelstrom of blood. The thought makes me smile. I open my sketchbook, draw Creep's hunched form, a few leaves, the twisted pattern of the bark under my hand, and then rest my head on my folded arms. The last thing I see when I close my eyes is Creep's mouth. It lingers behind my eyelids like the suspended grin of the Cheshire Cat.

I don't know how long I've been asleep when Mia wakes me. Creep is gone. Shadows are longer, leaning sideways.

"Hey," she says. "I just heard the dinner bell."

I scrunch my face and yawn. "How long was I asleep?"

"I dunno. Hours? C'mon, let's go."

I massage a crick in my neck as we follow the path back to main camp.

"Virgil wants me to meet him there," I tell her.

She stops in the middle of the path. "What? When?"

"After dinner," I tell her. I am smiling. I can't help it. "During testify meeting."

She starts walking again. "Holy shit. How do you feel about it? How do you feel about meeting Virgil in these romantic woods full of magic?"

"Magic." I say.

"Elle, you felt the fairy ring. Woods are magical."

"Okay," I say.

"So when are you going to sneak away?"

"I don't know," I say. "When's the best time?"

She thinks for a moment. "Right after dinner," she says. "They have everyone fold up the tables and then set up a million chairs, so it's more like church. You can get away during all the shuffling. I'll cover for you." She looks at me. "Will you admit you're a couple now?"

"Mia," I say, "seriously? Why do we have to call it something? Can't we just be friends or…" I don't know how to finish.

"Or *more* than friends?" Mia finishes for me. She elbows me in the side.

I push her off the path and we're both laughing.

DINNER IS SPINACH SALAD WITH CARAMELIZED PECANS AND poppy seed dressing. I'm surprisingly hungry. We go through the line and add what we want from the salad bar. Virgil is ahead of me in line, Mia behind. They're arguing about the best episodes of classic *Twilight Zo ne* as we load our plates and find a place to sit.

"*To Serve Man* is clearly one of the best episodes," says Mia, adding roasted chicken to her salad.

"No way," says Virgil across me. "It's clearly one of the most *popular*. Even *Five Characters In Search of an Exit* was better than *To Serve Man*." He smiles at me. My breath gets caught for a moment.

"Are you kidding? That episode wouldn't even get into my top forty."

We follow Virgil to a table.

"What's your favorite episode, Elle?" asks Mia.

"I dunno," I say, forking spinach into my mouth. I chew for a moment. "I like the one where that kid uses his brain to torture people."

Mia shudders. "*It's A Good Life*." Virgil nods.

"Or the one where Shatner sees a creature outside while the plane is flying."

Virgil puts on his best Shatner impression, staring out of an imaginary airplane window in horror. He starts to deliver the episode's famous line when Mia interrupts him, spluttering into her lemonade with a laugh and then coughing violently. Virgil whacks her on the back until she waves her hand. "That almost came out my nose."

Virgil and I laugh. Mia then tells us her concept for an episode. Something involving a haunted phone and repetitive texts that drive the main character crazy. I stop listening. The salad is sweet and crunchy. I keep checking the path of the sun as it falls lower and lower. I can't stop thinking about my rendezvous with Virgil. He glances at me throughout the meal, smiling down into his plate. My heart stutters every time he catches my eyes.

At one point, Mia says, "O-M-G, you guys. You *are* going to be one of those couples." She makes a gagging face.

Virgil just grins.

The half hour flies by. We throw our plates away and wait, my legs bouncing under the table as my anxiety builds. Mia kicks me.

"What?" I tell her.

She rolls her eyes.

Brother Chad makes the announcement that we're going to convert the ramada for testify meeting and the crowd becomes a confusion of squeaking tables rolled away on casters and armies of chairs unfolding all at once. Mia nudges me and tosses her head. I walk away as nonchalantly as I can toward the bathroom, then veer into the woods and skirt the clearing. I pick over boulders and kick through fallen leaves until I find the path. It will be dark soon, so I go as quickly as I can. I look around for Creep, but I haven't seen him since after lunch.

I get to the creek just after sunset. It looks different in the twilight. Blue-black shadows are woven into the dark green of shrubs lining the creek. The water looks purple and silver. The air, heavy with cricket song, is tangibly cooler next to the water. I stand listening to the waterfall and watch the sky turn from lavender to cobalt blue. The scent of wet rock and damp earth. I edge out onto the branch and lean back so that I can watch the stars come out.

When Virgil steps out of the dusk, I almost lose my balance.

"Hi," he says. He's a black shape against the darkening sky.

"Hi," I say.

"Can I sit?" he says.

I sit up. He scoots out on the branch next to me, letting his legs hang down.

"I really like this spot," he says.

"Me too," I tell him. I look up at the wash of stars. "I can't believe how many stars we can see here. It's so much easier to remember that we're just so tiny in the middle of a whole galaxy. A whole universe."

"Yeah, Phoenix sucks for stargazing," he says, pointing. "Look, you can actually see the edge of the Milky Way, like it's splashed across the sky."

When his arm comes down, his hand touches my knee for a moment. I jump.

"Sorry," he says.

"No," I tell him. "It's okay. I'm trying to learn not to be so sensitive."

He shifts on the branch, scooting a little away so that he can face me more.

"I like how sensitive you are," he says.

"Me too," I say. "I mean for you."

The moon is getting higher, a mottled white circle casting a dim light onto Virgil's face.

He reaches out. Hovering. "It's okay," I say.

He takes my hand. He holds it in both of his again, lightly. His thumb strokes back and forth. I don't even feel like pulling away.

"Virgil," I say. "I don't know if I ever told you how much it meant that you brought me to the horses."

"You're welcome," he says. "It was no big deal."

"It kind of was though," I tell him. "I came to this new neighborhood not thinking that I would even be able to make friends. I'm not good at making friends. And the ones I do make don't usually stick around very long."

"What, *you*?" says Virgil. "The girl who yelled at me the first day in Sunday School and then knocked down Levi during Youth Ministry?"

"That's me," I say, embarrassed.

"I'm just joking," he apologizes.

I nod. "But really, you and Mia were so cool to me. And you bringing me to the barn." I look down at my hand resting between his. "Horses have always been my safe place. But just in my head, I guess. I had never even met one until this summer."

He doesn't answer at first, his silence filled with the gurgle of water and a choir of crickets. Then he leans toward me. I look for his mouth. Hold up my free hand and touch his lips. They're slightly parted under my fingers. He freezes.

"It's okay," I whisper.

The kiss is so light, it's barely there. I lean into it and our teeth bump.

I pull away, mortified. Virgil just laughs, rubbing his front teeth with his index finger. I smile at him.

"I love you," he laughs.

The smile falls off of my face. My heart palpitates. "What?"

"I . . . love you?"

I shake my head. "No."

"No, what?"

"No, you can't love me." I pull my hand away.

His hands fall into his lap. "I didn't mean it that way... I meant.. like I love how funny you are. I love how ... What do you mean?"

"I'm not good." What do I tell him? How do I make him know *without* telling him? "I'm not a good person to love."

He looks mystified. "Wait.. What do you *mean*?"

I look off into the trees, into the patterned patches where the moon breaks through the branches to the forest floor. The water ripples underneath us.

"I don't know," I tell him. "I can't explain it. There are just things you don't know about me that would change your mind."

Virgil takes my hand again. I don't pull it away. "I didn't mean it that way when I said it, but what if I did? I don't think there's anything that could change how I feel if I love someone."

I feel tears starting to well up again. "Trust me," I say. "This would." I'm glad for the dark, so that he can't see me crying. My throat constricts.

"Why don't you tell me?" he says. "Then you would see that it won't make any difference."

I shake my head, swipe the tears off my face. "I can't tell you," I say, the words hitching my voice. "I can't tell anyone."

"Eleanor," he says.

"Please don't ask me," I say.

He leans forward and kisses me again. It's certain, but not rough. I know he can feel the tears on my cheek. I keep my mouth absolutely still. *DON'T BE SCARED. Don'tBeScared. don'tbescared. don'tbe…* His head moves a little to one side, fitting our lips more firmly together. I start to move too. He squeezes my hand and I only want to remember this moment – the moon, the pine trees, the dark stillness, our shadows cast on the glittering water. The sound of the waterfall, of crickets. He tastes like peppermint.

A sudden sound on the bank startles us, we pull away from each other and turn toward the sound, only to be blinded by an intense flashlight shining. *A counselor!* I think.

"Check it out," comes a voice. "The Virgin's finally getting some."

Other voices laugh. And even though I can't see them, I know that it's The A-Team.

Virgil shields his eyes. "Get rid of the light, Levi."

The light doesn't waver. "Or what?"

I can't see anything, only the bright circle of white and the glare around it. The A-Team are just vague outlines of black.

"What do you want?" I say.

"Just looking for some fun," says Levi. "Hold this."

The light shifts to one side and Levi steps onto the bank and into the beam of light.

"Isn't that why *you* came out here, Virgin?" He grins, his face lit from below. "To have some fun?"

"We're just talking," says Virgil. "So why don't you leave?"

"Didn't look like talking to me," says Levi. "Is she a good kisser, Virgin? What else does she do?"

My hand clamps down on Virgil's. I am frozen onto the branch.

"Levi," says Virgil. "Would you kindly shut the fuck up?"

"Why don't you make me?" Levi splashes forward and grabs Virgil by the shirt collar, pulling him upward. I lose my grip on Virgil's hand. He stumbles through the water as Levi pulls him close.

"Tell us, Virgin," Levi says into Virgil's face. "Did she suck your dick, or did you suck hers?"

Then things slow to a crawl as Virgil brings up his arm and punches Levi in the ear. Levi recoils and swears, but he doesn't let go. Instead he swings Virgil around and pushes him toward the other boys. The flashlight hits the ground, pointed across the water and away from the figures in the dark. I can see a rippling moon on the surface of the pool, bending water grasses, and dust motes floating in the beam of light. I can't move. I hear a scuffle of leaves and grunting. The boys are just a jumble of shadows. I hear the smack of fallen blows, the thud of kicks, and an *Oof!* Then a popping sound and Virgil's voice crying out.

His voice breaks the spell.

"Virgil!" I shout. I slide off of the branch, shattering the moon's reflection. The cold water closes over my knees. I splash to the bank, yelling Virgil's name, and grab the flashlight. It's long and heavy. Like something a security guard would carry.

When I turn the light around with shaking hands, I see Virgil on the ground, blood on his face. He cradles his right hand. Levi is bloody too. It flows from his nose, dripping off his chin. One of the other boys pulls on his arm. Levi aims a kick at Virgil's back.

"No!" I yell. I do the only thing I can think of and throw the flashlight at Levi's head. It hits his shoulder and neck, making him stagger. The flashlight bounces to the ground and goes out. All I can see are swimming shadows.

"C'mon, let's go," says one of the boys into the darkness. Everyone is panting. The sound of their feet in foliage. Virgil moans. Then they are moving into the trees.

As the A-Team crunches away through the forest, I kneel to feel around for Virgil. My eyes are starting to adjust, but he's just a black form. I find his shoulder. He's lying on his side.

He coughs. "Are you okay?"

"Me?" I say. "Are *you?*"

He doesn't answer, but I can feel him trying to sit up. I pull at him, putting one arm around his shoulders. He grunts, upright. "Thanks. Grab the flashlight," he says.

I doubt it will turn on, but I search for it in the dead leaves. I shake it once and press the button. A beam of light shows me Virgil. It's hard to tell how bad it is with all the blood.

"What happened to your hand?" I ask.

"Someone stomped on it," says Virgil. "I think something's broken. Let's go back to camp."

He limps next to me. Left arm circling his ribs, right hand held against his chest.

We're halfway down the path when a counselor jogs up.

"What are you doing out here?" he says. He trains his flashlight on us, taking in Virgil's face. "What's going on?"

"I got into a fight," says Virgil. "It shouldn't have happened."

"You've got that right," says the counselor. "Where's the other guy?"

"Guys," I say.

"What?" says the counselor.

"Guys," I say. "Plural. They took off."

"Uh huh," says the counselor. "Okay. You never told me what you were doing out here."

Virgil and I glance at each other. His left eye is swelling, his bottom lip split open, face smeared with blood.

"Nothing," says Virgil.

"Right," says the counselor. "C'mon."

I keep the flashlight trained on his heels as we continue down the path. The forest is darker than ever, black on all sides. Virgil limps next to me. I want to take his hand. Dust puffs up around our feet when I slow down to let the counselor get ahead of us.

"Thank you," I say. "For defending my honor or whatever."

"You're welcome or whatever," says Virgil. He pauses. "Sorry about what we said earlier."

"What who said?"

"You know," he says. "What Mia and I said, about them being all talk and not to worry about it. Obviously, I was wrong."

"Obviously," I say.

I look around us, trying to see Creep's outline in the darkness pressing in on all sides. The night is thick and black. No sign of Creep.

"Such a magical forest," I mutter, tears welling.

"What?" says Virgil.

"Nothing," I tell him.

<u>Fear #4: Fear</u>

Some US President said the only thing we have to
fear is fear itself.
People say fight or flight, but for me it's
always freeze.
Like my body has grown roots and I'm
trapped inside.
I don't know how to stop being afraid.
I don't know how to go from freeze to fight.
Is there a switch inside me I can flip or something?

THIRTY-TWO

Virgil leans back in the chair, his head resting against the bare wood wall behind us. He clutches a bag of ice to his injured hand. The index finger is already a swollen pink, the same shade as the bruises over his eye. We were taken directly to the nurse's station. After checking Virgil's allergy record, the gray-haired nurse gave him two Tylenol, the Ziploc full of ice, and carefully cleaned his face. She examined the cuts on his brow and his mouth, shined a bright light into both eyes, and left the room. We haven't seen her for twenty minutes.

"Don't tell them," he says.

"What are you talking about?" I ask him.

He rolls his right shoulder back and winces. "Don't tell them about Levi. I don't want to make things any worse than they already are."

"Virgil, are you crazy?" I say. "Look what they did to you."

He tongues the split in his bottom lip and I have to make an effort not to wince. A deep blood-red gathers around the apple-green iris of his right eye.

"Are you okay?" I ask him for the fiftieth time.

Virgil does a slow blink and I wonder if he's concussed. "I'm okay," he says. "Please stop asking. Don't worry. I'm fine."

"Sorry," I tell him. My knee jiggles. I feel like I've just sprung out of bed after a nightmare.

"Are *you* okay?" he asks.

I nod. Just as I'm about to answer, the nurse bustles back in, along with Brother Chad.

"Oh my gosh," he says as he sees Virgil. "What the hell happened?"

"I think his finger's broken," says the nurse, "but it doesn't look serious."

"It looks plenty serious," says Brother Chad, gesturing to Virgil. "Who did this?"

Virgil shakes his head.

Brother Chad looks at me. "Eleanor?"

Virgil looks at me. One eye is swelling, the other shot through with red. "Elle," he says.

Brother Chad squats down on the floor to be at our eye-level. I feel like I'm five and sitting in the principal's office.

"Eleanor," he says. "You need to tell me."

Virgil shakes his head again.

"It was Levi," I say.

Virgil sighs. Brother Chad takes a deep breath and lets it out slow. "I thought," he starts, but doesn't finish. "Just Levi?"

"Levi and his friends," I say.

"I need names," says Brother Chad.

I struggle to remember the names Mia told me. "Braxton." *Which one ate paste?* "And Colby." I glance at Virgil. His eyes are closed.

Brother Chad looks like he's going to punch something. A vein stands out on his forehead. He takes another deep breath.

"I called your mother," he tells Virgil. "She's coming to get you." He turns to me. "Eleanor, since you were involved in the altercation, your mother asked that you get a ride with Virgil's mom."

I groan inwardly.

"She wasn't involved in anything," says Virgil. "None of this is her fault."

Brother Chad says to me, "I'm afraid she insisted." Then to Virgil, "Don't worry. We'll take care of this."

He goes back outside with his jaw set.

Fifteen minutes later, Brother Chad escorts Levi through the door and into the adjoining room. Levi's eyes slide across me and then land on Virgil as he passes through. His face is clean as well, but his nose is pink. I notice that Creep slinks in as the door opens. The nurse follows and shuts the door behind them. Sister April comes in. She goes over to Virgil.

"Let me see your hand."

He holds it out. It's starting to turn bluish purple, the swelling has spread. She takes it and turns it over, studying it. Virgil sucks in a breath. Creep sidles up to the chair and leans over Virgil's hand.

"Oooh," says Creep. "Tenderized virgin. My favorite."

Sister April hands Virgil another bag of ice wrapped in a paper towel. "You should have this on your face," she says.

She makes him lie down on the cot and positions the ice on his forehead. Then she sits in his chair. Creep crouches under the cot, humming to himself.

"I'm sorry this happened," Sister April says.

"Why is Levi here?" I ask her in a whisper. "Shouldn't he be in the back of a police car?"

"He claims that Virgil threw the first punch," she says. "Is that true?"

Virgil doesn't move. He doesn't say anything. I can't see his eyes under the bag of ice.

"I don't remember," I say.

"Liar," says Creep.

"Yes," says Virgil to the ceiling. "I threw the first punch."

"Levi was threatening him," I tell her. "He had Virgil by the shirt."

"Okay," says Sister April.

Brother Chad comes in. He and his wife look at each other. Sister April nods.

"Virgil," says Brother Chad, "you said you were done with fighting."

Virgil sits up with a groan. "I *am*," he says.

"Oooh," says Creep. "The Virgin has a *history*."

I stand up. I want to cave Creep's head in. He just flashes his teeth at me.

"Then why did you instigate this?" asks Brother Chad. He glances at me. I shove my hands in my pockets.

"I *didn't* instigate this. *They* did. You should have heard the shit they were saying," says Virgil. "To Eleanor. About Eleanor. It was fucking disgusting." My cheeks are hot. I look at the ground, hoping the curtain of my hair will hide my face.

"Watch your language. The things they were saying… they were just words," says Brother Chad.

I want to say, *You're telling Virgil to watch his language, but when Levi does it, it's just words?* I don't dare speak up.

"It was verbal assault," says Virgil. "Brother Chad, they can't just run around saying whatever they want."

"Eleanor," says Brother Chad. "Did you feel threatened by what the boys were saying?"

Don't answer. Don't draw attention. Don't get involved. "Yes," I say.

"So why not tell a counselor?" says Brother Chad. "What makes it *your* job to stop it, Virgil?"

"Because no one else *will!*" yells Virgil. "You never do anything about it, and neither do the other leaders. He and his asshole bros just run around acting like they own the place!"

Brother Chad sighs. He and Sister April share a look again. "How many times did Jesus turn the other cheek?" he asks Virgil.

"That's a good question," says Creep. "How many times was it exactly?"

Virgil sighs in disgust and lies back on the cot, replacing the bag of ice over his eyes and folding his arms, injured hand on top.

"If you didn't already have a history of fighting," says Brother Chad, "it would be easier to swallow."

"I haven't gotten into a fight in like two years," says Virgil.

"Okay," says Brother Chad. "I guess we'll just have to let the police sort it out."

My heart tilts in my chest. "You're going to tell them that it was Virgil's fault?"

"They'll hear both sides," says Brother Chad. He gets up and he and Sister April go into the other room where Levi is.

"You just bring out the best in people, Ellie," says Creep.

I sit back down, willing my heart to slow.

A minute later, the three adults bring Levi into our room. He steps in front of them.

"I can't believe you told on me," he says to Virgil. Virgil moves the bag of ice again. They stare at each other. The space between them winds itself tight and suddenly I'm worried that Virgil will jump off the table.

"He didn't say anything," I tell Levi. "*I* did." I grip the sides of my chair, my knuckles bearing down into the hard plastic.

His eyes move from Virgil's face to mine. Brother Chad clears his throat.

"I think it will go easier if both of you apologize to each other," he says.

"I am *not* apologizing to him," says Virgil.

"I'm really sorry," says Levi. His eyes are locked onto mine. "I shouldn't have fought back when you hit me, Virgil. I should have walked away. I feel terrible." Because they are standing behind him, the adults can't see that he hasn't shifted his gaze away from me.

"And Eleanor?" says Brother Chad.

For a moment I think he wants me to apologize.

"I'm sorry, Eleanor," says Levi. His eyes drill directly into mine. "I shouldn't have called you a freak. You are obviously a very normal person."

"Levi," says Brother Chad.

"I'm really sorry," Levi says again.

I look over at Virgil. He has his eyes closed under the bag of ice.

"Thank you, Levi," says Brother Chad. "I think that you'll find a sincere apology begins to change your heart. Just like forgiveness does, Virgil."

"Whatever," says Virgil.

Levi's eyes fall back to Virgil as he turns to leave. I can't read them and it makes me shiver.

"I just love making new friends," says Creep. "Don't you, Ellie?"

AN HOUR LATER, AS THE NURSE FILLS OUT PAPERWORK IN THE adjoining room, Mia arrives on the station stoop with Hope and Grace behind her. When I open the door, moths swoop through the lamplight. Cool night air floats in. All three girls are carrying my packed belongings, along with Virgil's, as well as our sleeping bags and pillows. Mia piles our things in the corner and Hope and Grace take one look at Virgil and leave again. I can only imagine what kind of stories will be circulating at church on Sunday.

"Holy shit," says Mia. Virgil is still lying down, Creep on his back under the cot. Creep's in the same pose, injured hand held across his chest, the other arm pressing an invisible bag of ice to his temple, like a smaller repeated image of Virgil.

"It's not as bad as it looks," he tells her.

"That's a relief," says Mia. "Because it looks pretty bad." She sits on the chair next to mine. "What the hell happened?"

Virgil laughs and then moans and closes his eyes.

"Headache," he says.

"That's the same thing Brother Chad said," I tell her.

"Whoa," says Mia. "Brother Chad said *hell*? He must have been P-I-S-T."

Virgil laughs again. "Mia," he says. "Stop it."

"What?" Mia tells him. "I can't help it. It's not *my* fault you got the shit kicked out of you and now you can't laugh without going on life support."

Virgil laughs and grunts at the same time.

"So what happened?" she asks me again.

"I don't even know," I tell her. "We were sitting at the waterfall pool – "

"Doing what?"

I squint at her.

"Oka-a-a-ay," she says. "Go on."

"And then The A-Team showed up and started running off their mouths and –"

"Lemme guess," says Mia. "Virgil took offense."

"I guess you could say I raised their ire," says Virgil from the cot.

"He asked Levi to kindly shut the fuck up," I tell Mia.

"I don't blame you," Mia tells Virgil. "That's pretty much one of my constant states of existence: annoyed, hungry, and wanting-to-rearrange-Levi's-face."

"But then Virgil punched him," I say. "After that I couldn't really see what happened because they had blinded us with their flashlight."

"Vir-g-i-i-i-i-l," says Mia. "You *started* it?"

We both look over at Virgil.

He puts his arms in the air. "What do you want from me? *They* started it!" And then he groans again and lowers both arms slowly.

"I bet Brother Chad had something to say. He was the one who did that whole intervention for you last time."

"Intervention?" I ask.

"If he wants me to turn the other cheek, he's gonna be waiting 'til the Second Coming," says Virgil.

"Listen to you," says Mia. "You should write Christian thriller screenplays." She turns to me. "Elle, Virgil totally fought for you. How do you feel about that?"

I eye Virgil's bags of ice, the bruises, the wince as he shifts position. "Like crap," I tell her.

"So what now?" says Mia.

"My mom's coming," says Virgil.

"Yeah, I thought so, because of packing your bags and stuff. But what are you going to do about The A-Team?"

Virgil just looks at me.

"Dunno," I tell Mia. "Brother Chad was saying something about calling the cops and assault and battery charges. But after Levi started talking I heard him telling Sister April something about self-defense."

Mia shakes her head. "You're a mess, Virge," she says.

Dear Jesus.
Such a great camp you've got here.
I'll leave a glowing Yelp review:
Stunning views.
Great food.
Attentive staff.
Bodily harm.

⭐ ⭐

Amen.

THIRTY-THREE

Virgil's mom is mostly quiet in the car. She asks Virgil what happened. I'm in the backseat, but even with the air on and her 90s pop hits, I catch most of it. He leaves out the part about the kissing and his *I love you*, but mostly he's honest with her. He doesn't downplay his involvement in the fight, telling her that he hit Levi first.

I slide across the backseat, so I am sitting behind the driver's side. Creep crouches on the floor behind Virgil's chair. He tried to curl up on the seat next to me, but I swatted him off with my sketchbook. I watch Virgil's profile, outlined in blue light from the dash.

"I know I shouldn't have done it, Mom, but you should hear the things these guys say about girls. And they were talking about Eleanor specifically, and… it wasn't nice."

"Those boys are reprobates," says Virgil's mom. "But fighting them only brings you down to their level. You shouldn't have lost your temper."

"I know," says Virgil. "But I've been listening to them all summer and I just couldn't stand it anymore."

Virgil's mom sighs. "I can't believe they ganged up on you like that. I have half a mind to go talk to their mothers."

"Please, don't," says Virgil.

"I don't know what I can do for you," says his mom. "I told Chad that I would do everything I could to make sure this doesn't happen again, but that's what I told him *last* time. If he decides to get the police involved, that's up to him. And honestly, Virge, I wouldn't blame him."

"Okay, Mom," says Virgil.

She goes on. "Seriously, Virgil. The man just wants a safe place for the youth to gather. You and Levi fist-fighting isn't really conducive to the kind of atmosphere Chad is trying to foster."

"*Okay*, Mom," says Virgil. "I get it."

After that, she's quiet for the rest of the ride. She turns up her music and sings along with the radio. It's dark in the car. She opens the moon roof and I turn my face up to watch the field of stars, dense, clinging to the black sky, rotating above me with every turn of the car as we wind our way back down to the valley.

Eventually my eyes start to droop. I prop my pillow against the window and I'm drifting… drifting… and then suddenly choking on a breath. The hot pillow falls into my lap. City street lights show through with windows, throwing down shadow patterns. I don't know where I am for a moment. Dream images like the broken end of a film reel. I look over and see Creep grinning at me, his splintered smile curling upward from the floor.

"Eleanor." Virgil reaches his left arm back between the two front seats. He taps my knee. "You okay?" he asks.

I rub my face.

"Fine," I tell him. "Bad dream." I notice the car is stopped. "Where's your mom?"

"Getting gas," he says. "We're almost home," he says. "She wanted to stop at urgent care to get my hand x-rayed, but I convinced her that we should just do it tomorrow. I mean, however much it's torn up, it's going to be the same in the morning, right?"

"I guess." He's cradling the injured hand cradled in his lap, the bag of ice is gone. "Does it hurt?"

"Yeah," he says. "So my mom called your mom, before she even left home, and your mom said it was okay for you to sleep at our house, since she's going to be at the hospital with your dad."

Something lurches in my chest. "What's wrong with my dad?"

"What isn't?" says Creep.

"Your mom said to tell you it wasn't serious. He just got dehydrated. So they're keeping him overnight," says Virgil.

"Nothing serious," I say. "Just cancer."

Virgil doesn't say anything. Then: "Yeah."

"What about Joshua?" I ask.

"He's at our house with Sam," says Virgil. "My mom got her friend to come sleep on the couch."

"Okay," I say.

"Okay," says Virgil.

We're quiet for a moment, just looking at each other, when his mom opens the car door and gets in. Virgil coughs and turns back to the front. His mom hands me a bottle of water.

As the car starts moving again, Creep asks, "What was it this time? The hallway? The castle? The garden?"

I don't answer him. I just look out the window.

"Something new," says Creep. "I wish you would tell me. You always have the best dreams, Eleanor."

Virgil's house is quiet, with none of the lingering tension I've become accustomed to at home. After sending the neighbor home, Virgil's mom makes a bed for me on the TV-room sofa. The cushions are deep and wide and I lie on my back and stare up at the ceiling fan like I do at home, trying to catch the spin of the blades. It clicks softly, a patterned rhythm that could put me to sleep. The house smells lived in, but clean — a mixed scent of faint Italian-food-garlic and vanilla. The sofa cushions smell like lavender.

Creep circles the rug, tracing the design with his black knobby hands and feet. He talks in a steady drone.

"You really should be careful, Eleanor. I warned you about Virgil. I told you to be prepared. All men are like Ian. I told you that. He'll ask you for more, and if you don't give it to him, he'll take it."

He continues around and around the rug. Even though I'm not watching him, the circular pattern of his voice makes me dizzy. He says the same thing over and over, his voice getting closer and farther away, turned away from me, turned toward me.

"Tonight's the perfect night," says Creep. "He'll wait until his mother is asleep, and then he'll come out here. He knows your type, Eleanor. He knows you won't say anything. You won't make a sound. You know you won't, and so does he. He can see it in your face. Just like Ian could."

"Shut up," I hiss.

He sidles up next to the sofa, his voice in my ear. "You'll see. You'll see."

I turn over to look at him. His teeth are an inch from my face. He slowly lowers his chin and focuses one black, marble eye on me. "Virgil's not like that," I say.

"You'll see," says Creep. "You'll see, Eleanor. You'll see." He keeps saying it as he resumes his track around the rug.

I reach into my bag and pull out my phone. I fall asleep to the sound of Morrissey singing about how tired he is.

<u>Best Part of Camp:</u>

The Fairy Ring

<u>Worst Part of Camp:</u>

"I love you."

Virgil and I are walking through the woods. One of those brilliant days when the air is just cool enough for a hoodie and the sun strikes a perfect balance between light and warmth. We walk hand-in-hand, his fingers loose between mine. I look up and the trees go on forever until their tops disappear into tiny black pinpricks, lost in cloud. Their branches are long, gnarled, twisted like mesquite trees, black and furred with pine needles. Leaves crunch as we step between ferns. We climb over fallen logs.

Virgil talks easily about his horses. He laughs about something Luke Skywalker did and I smile at the flawless air, at Virgil's laugh, at the smell of orange blossoms. He leads me through the narrow gap between canted, lichen-covered boulders. When the crevice is at its closest, in the shadowed space, he stops. I wait, one hand in his, the other on the rock face, wondering if he's seen a deer where the path opens back up. He turns around.

"Eleanor," he says. "You're so beautiful." His voice sounds different. Older.

"Thank you," I say. I want to ask him not to say that, but I can't remember why I don't like it.

He leans toward me. Puts his mouth over mine. The kiss is hard. It pushes me back against the rock. He's taller than me. When did that happen?

He takes my other hand. And then I am pinned between him and the wall of rock. His mouth moves to the side of my face, trailing heat along my jaw and then down my neck. I feel the familiar stirrings low in my belly. An electric sensation that makes my skin crackle.

"Please," I say.

And when his voice breathes out, pinched over my collarbone, I realize why it sounded familiar. "Oh, Ellie." The words are hot on my skin in Ian's voice. And I can't move. And I roll my eyes up in their sockets, but all I can see above is the place where the boulders meet over our heads. And I wonder, Is this what it means to be between a rock and a hard place? *Blackness closes over me and all I know is I can't I can't Ican'tIcan't*

"Oh, Ellie," he says again. "So beautiful."

I open my eyes over his shoulder and there is Creep, sitting in a nook of rock just across from me. "It's all you're good for, Eleanor. You'll see," Creep says. "Why fight it?"

Why fight it? Why? Why? Why fight? Fight?

Fight.

I bring my knee up between Virgil's legs and as he grunts, I push him backward and break away from his grasp.

THIRTY-FOUR

I open my eyes.

My eyes focus on Virgil standing over me, his face a swollen mess of bruises. Like something from a horror movie.

I scramble away from him into the corner of the sofa.

"It's okay," he says. "It's okay. It's just me."

I am wedged between the corner cushions with my knees up to my chest. My hands are shaking.

"What are you doing?" I ask him.

"My hand was throbbing, so I got up to get some Tylenol," he says. "I was getting a drink from the kitchen and it sounded like you were talking in your sleep or something."

Tears well. I cover my mouth.

He sits on the other end of the sofa. "Another bad dream?"

I don't say anything.

"Told you so," says Creep. He climbs up onto the back of the sofa, sitting between Virgil and me.

I want to smack him across the room. I wrap my arms around my knees instead.

I swallow down the compulsion to cry. "You startled me," I say.

"I'm sorry," says Virgil. "Do you want to talk about it?"

"No," I tell him.

His voice and Ian's voice bounce between my ears. Creep's laugh.

"Okay," says Virgil. "Do you want me to just sit here with you?"

"No... I don't know. What do you *want*, Virgil?" I say. I think about his hands, the big Ian-hands, pressing me up against the rock. His breath, warmth in the hollow of my throat. A shudder buries itself deep and I lift my shoulders and cover my face to flex my skin away from the sensation.

"That's the big question," says Creep.

He looks surprised. "I don't know," he says. "I just want to help."

"Sure, he does," says Creep.

I blow the breath I've been holding out through pursed lips and say without looking at him, "Why don't you tell me about Brother Chad? Tell me why he got so mad when he found out you hit Levi."

Virgil leans back. "Okay," he says. "You want the long version, or the short version?"

"The long version," I say. I watch him gingerly touch his eyebrow and his cheek. He licks his bottom lip.

"Maybe you noticed that my dad is never around."

I don't say anything. But I don't drop my eyes this time.

Virgil continues. "He took off when I was eleven and my mom was a wreck for a while. My mom said he's an addict.

I guess he was hooking up with other women and stuff, bringing nasty, dangerous shit into the house. It brought up a bunch of stuff from her childhood, and I guess that sort of thing really messes with your head, because my mom just kind of lost it. She was even hospitalized once. Sam was pretty much a baby still, so I had to take care of him a lot. I kind of took care of all of us a lot of the time."

While he's talking, I run my finger nail across the textured fabric of the couch under my hand. I think about Virgil as just a kid taking care of another little kid. Taking care of his own mom. "Mia told me about some of this," I say.

"My mom's gone through a lot of doctors and medicine and therapy," says Virgil. "Things are a ton better. But for a while, I had a lot of rage. About my dad leaving. About my mom being sick. About having to take care of everybody." His voice turns a little muted, like his throat is clenching down on his words. "Sometimes I think it would have been nice to just be a kid, you know?"

I nod. *I know.*

"So I got into fights all the time. I had detention a bunch at school, but because of how it was at home, they kept giving me second chances. Things kept getting worse and worse for a couple years. Eventually I got suspended and they almost sent me to juvie." He turns toward me, folds his legs up underneath him, and rests his head on his forearm. "You know, Levi used to be my best friend. When we were kids. But after my dad took off, and my mom got sick, and we got a little older, he got kinda mean. One day he was making fun of me and I lost it. We got into a huge fight. It happened a few times. And then he had a growth spurt and he and his friends joined Pop Warner football and that was it." He looks sad about it.

"I've been suspended," I say. I don't tell him that dad whipped me black and blue for it. For all I know, his dad would have too.

"For what?" asks Virgil.

I use air quotes. "Disruptive behavior." He waits to see if I'll go on, so I say, "When I was ten, I stabbed a boy in the leg with a pencil."

"Some of Ellie's best work," Creep laughs.

Virgil raises his eyebrows. "I'd like to hear *that* story."

"Maybe some other time," I tell him. "I want to hear the rest of yours."

He lifts one shoulder in a half shrug. "There's only the last part. Brother Chad kind of took me under his wing and made a bunch of promises to keep me under control so I didn't have to go to the jail for children." A laugh bursts out of me when he says *jail for children*. He smiles, but I think it's just because I'm laughing, and not because it's funny.

"Sorry," I say again.

He goes on. "Once I realized that it was making things worse for my mom, I promised I would stop. My grandparents gave my mom her inheritance, which turned out to be a lot I guess, so she paid off the house and she took over the horses and then she made *me* take over the horses because she thought it would teach me responsibility or whatever."

"Which it did," I say.

"Yeah," he says. "I guess. And my mom took me to the Seven-Eleven, because Nicole is her cousin and then Nicole taught me how to run the store and stuff, so I could learn life skills and be a productive member of society."

"You seem pretty productive now," I say.

"I guess," he says again.

We're both quiet for a second.

I say, "Mia says you're going to make some Christian girl very happy by changing diapers and being a valiant husband in Jesus, or something."

Virgil snorts. "Why the hell would she say that?" He starts to laugh.

"I was worried you might murder me in the barn," I say.

He laughs harder. "Valiant husband in Jesus," he says. He leans forward, curling his good arm protectively around his ribs. His shoulders bounce.

I start to laugh too.

He tries to say something again, but it comes out squeaky because he's laughing so hard. He tries again. "I suppose now that I've lost my looks…," the words trail off into a long bouncing exhalation as he points to his face, the laugh becoming a wheeze. I cover my mouth to stifle my giggles. He's gasping. "…being a valiant husband in Jesus is all I have left!"

We're shaking. Virgil's eyes water. My legs are curled against my body, my mouth pressed against my knees to stifle the noise. All of the tension and fear drain away with the laughter, until we're left sighing the last of it out.

"Uuugh," says Virgil, pressing lightly at his ribs. "I'm going to regret that in the morning."

I straighten out my legs and put my hands in my lap. I let out a long breath. Virgil is quiet for long enough that I think he might be done talking. We smile at each other.

Then he says, "About what I said before."

"About what?" I say. My shoulders immediately tense.

"Are you going to make me say it again?"

"I guess I am," I say.

His mouth forms a straight line, and he exhales loudly through his nose. The whirling breeze from the ceiling fan sounds like a distant wind.

"About when I said that I love you," he says.

"Oh," I say. "That." I look at my hands.

"I'm sorry if it freaked you out," he says. "Since my mom has been in therapy, she's all about authentic living or whatever and we all have just gotten used to saying what we're thinking. I forget, sometimes, that other people don't have that."

"It's fine," I say, glancing up at him.

Virgil quirks his eyebrows, and then exhales when the pain hits. He touches his forehead. "It didn't seem fine."

I don't answer. He watches me for so long that my face starts to turn hot.

"I'm sorry," I say finally.

"No," says Virgil. "It's just–" But he doesn't finish.

I wait. When he doesn't say anything, I say, "Your mom went to therapy? Mia was telling me at camp that she's in therapy too. Forever."

Virgil laughs. "Yeah. *I* had a few sessions, mostly just to talk about my dad and why I was so angry. But it didn't last long, because I got my shit together and everyone figured I was fine."

"*Are* you fine?"

He touches his cheek with two fingers. "Yeah," he winces. "I'm fine."

"How long have you known Mia?" I ask him.

"Since kindergarten," he says. "We all grew up in this neighborhood. Mia only spoke Spanish when she first came here, but went to half-day kindergarten with us because her parents wanted her to transition smoothly. The other half of the day she had a nanny because her parents are both professors at ASU. The nanny was supposed to teach her English, but Mia says she learned it from MTV and YouTube."

I nod, thinking about Mia and Virgil growing up together. On the playground, having movie nights, barbecues with parents. The pang of jealousy surprises me.

We don't say anything for a while. My eyelids are starting to droop again when he stands up.

"I better go back to bed," he says. "My mom would birth a bovine if she found us sleeping together in the morning."

Creep cackles.

"Um," I say.

"I mean," says Virgil. "Not sleeping together. Sleeping. Out here. Together. Not together. In the same room. On the –" He stops.

"Night," he says abruptly and walks back down the hall.

"I told you," I say to Creep once Virgil is gone.

Creep flashes a nasty smile. "We'll see." He slinks off the sofa and disappears, his voice fading. "We'll see"

Joshua and I eat breakfast at Virgil's house. Whole-grain pecan waffles and fresh orange juice, which his mother juices first thing in the morning. Sam and Joshua line up their superhero action figures on the table and talk about versus scenarios for twenty minutes. I rinse the dishes and Virgil puts them in the dishwasher, one-handed. When his mom asks me how I slept, Virgil and I exchange a glance.

"Fine, thanks," I tell her.

Virgil's mom plans on taking him to get x-rays, so Sam is going to spend the morning at our house. Mom's car is still gone when we get there. I breathe a sigh of relief that I don't have to answer any questions yet. Virgil waves at me as we stand on the porch. I wave back. He mouths: *I'll call you.* Sam and Joshua help me carry my luggage into the house. They turn on the Nintendo and settle in.

In my room I drop my things on the floor and fall onto the bed. I can't believe how tired I am. I am just drifting off when Creep climbs up next to me.

"Hi," he says.

"Go away," I tell him.

"Oh, Ellie," he says. "You don't mean that."

"I'm tired," I say. "Leave me alone so I can sleep."

"What do you think you'll dream about this time?"

"Your head on a stick," I say.

"Well, that's hurtful," he laughs.

"Good," I tell him. "Now go away."

"Okay." He looks over his shoulder. "I'll go see what Joshua's doing."

I imagine him sitting next to Joshua. Whispering in Joshua's ear. "No," I tell him. "You're right. I didn't mean it. Stay here and talk to me."

"Okay." Creep burrows into the pillow next to mine. "Tell me about your dream last night."

I sigh. "I dreamed about Virgil."

"What about him?" Creep puts his hands behind his head. His smile stretches across his face.

"We were in the woods," I say.

"Really?" says Creep. "How interesting. What were you doing in the woods?"

"Walking," I tell him.

"What else?" asks Creep.

I close my eyes. "He kissed me. Then he turned into Ian."

"Foreshadowing," says Creep.

"Shut up," I say.

I hear the front door open and shut again. Mom's voice calls down the stairs.

"Eleanor, where are you?"

"Oh, goodie," says Creep.

"Downstairs," I call.

Creep hops up and down on the bedspread. He giggles.

Mom appears in the doorway. Her eyes are tired, with dark circles. They look red.

"How's Dad?" I say. I rise so she's not standing over me. We face each other.

"They're keeping him another day," she says. "Why were you in bed?"

"I'm tired," I say.

"So what happened at camp?" she asks.

"Nothing really," I tell her.

"You wouldn't have been brought home early if nothing happened," she says.

I step around her to pick up my bag, and then move to put the bed between us. "*You're* the one that wanted me to come home," I say.

"Because you were in a *fight*, Eleanor," she says.

I unzip the bag. I need to give my hands something to do or I'll start to cry. "No, I wasn't, Mom," I say. "Virgil and The A– " I stop myself. "These other boys were in the fight. I was just there."

"What were you doing there?" She's standing in front of the doorway with her arms folded.

"I was just there," I say again. I'm pulling my clothing out of the bag and piling it on the bedspread. Everything smells like campfire. "You know how when there's a fight, sometimes there are other people there who aren't fighting?"

"No, Eleanor," she says. "Brother Chad told me there were four boys and *you*. What am I supposed to think of that?"

"I don't know, Mom." I don't look at her. I'm lining up travel-sized toiletries next to the clothing: toothbrush and toothpaste, shampoo, conditioner, body wash. "I guess you'll just think what you think." *Like you usually do*, I don't say.

"Why don't you tell me what happened?" she says, watching me. "Then I'll know what to think. When you're being evasive like this, it seems like you have something to hide."

Creep is watching our verbal volleys, his face turning back and forth.

"Fine," I sigh. I fold my arms in a matching pose to hers. "Virgil and I were talking—"

"Where?"

"In the woods."

"Who else was there?"

"Well, those three other boys—" I start.

"You were in the woods with Virgil and three other boys?"

"No," I say. "Maybe let me finish a sentence and I can tell you."

Her chin is set. She visibly clenches her jaw. "Go ahead," she says.

Creep giggles again.

"I was in the woods with Virgil. Those three boys came out of the bushes and started trash-talking us. Virgil told them to cut it out and when they didn't, he hit Levi. Then all three of them jumped on Virgil and beat him up. He's at the hospital now with his mom getting x-rays."

She waits.

"Are you done?" she says.

"Yes," I tell her. I pick up the pile of camp clothes and walk into the dark bathroom. Creep hops off the bed to follow me.

Mom's voice follows me too, though she doesn't move. "What were you doing in the woods with Virgil? Alone. At *night*."

"We were just talking." I drop the clothes into the hamper and then turn toward the mirror. Creep is on the counter.

"Lie," he says. I rub at my eyes. They're burning. *I just want to sleep.*

Mom's voice is raised, like she's worried I won't be able to hear her. Or maybe she's just angry. "Why couldn't you just talk to Virgil with the rest of the group?"

I want to snarl like a cornered dog. I step out of the bathroom and face her. "I don't know, Mom. Because we wanted to have a private conversation."

She holds one finger up at me. "You better watch your tone. Fifteen-year-olds of the opposite sex don't need to have private conversations. What did you talk about?"

I fold my arms again. I have to close my eyes to keep from rolling them. "That's why it's called private. Because no one hears it and you don't tell anyone about it afterward."

"Uh oh," says Creep.

Her eyes harden. "You're not going to tell me?"

"No," I tell her. "What would be the point of a private conversation if you told everyone about it later?" I don't even know why I'm arguing with her. Other than the kiss and the *I love you*, the conversation was totally innocent. *We talked about the stars and the horses and why he shouldn't love me.* A little voice inside suggests, *And maybe the kiss was totally innocent too.*

She sets her mouth into a straight line. "Did you do anything inappropriate?"

This time I do roll my eyes.

"Don't roll your eyes at me," she says. "Just answer the question."

"No," I say. "We didn't."

She doesn't seem to know how to answer. Instead she just fills the silence with a glare.

While she's staring me down, Creep says, "I can't decide if this is a lie or not. On one hand, by her standards, your behavior is very inappropriate. On the other hand, she doesn't even know that when it comes to you, the word *appropriate* loses all meaning."

I turn to look at him. He clicks his teeth.

"Look at me," says Mom. She puts her hands on her hips. That Mom stance. "You're grounded. You are not allowed to see your friends. Neither Virgil or Mia can come over."

"But–," I start.

"No." She puts up one hand. "No, Eleanor. No buts. Bible Camp was supposed to improve your attitude, not worsen it. Instead of coming back with a countenance of spiritual growth, you're more defiant and disobedient than ever. You're grounded until further notice." She turns away from the doorway, and then back again. I think she has tears in her eyes. Her voice shakes a little. "I'm going back to the hospital. I'm going to be there for the rest of the day. I expect you to handle dinner. Do you understand?"

"Fine," I say.

Once she's gone, Creep lets out a low whistle. "Harsh," he says. "What do you think she would have done if she'd found out about the kissing?"

"Who cares?" I say. "I'd do it again."

"I know you would," says Creep. "You're a naughty girl."

"Stop calling me that," I tell him. I fall on the comforter and put a pillow over my head.

I WAKE TO THE MUTED VIBRATING RHYTHM OF MY PHONE somewhere.

I sit up, eyes bleary. I stumble over to my bag to paw through it. I have to dump it out to find the phone. It's just a voice call.

"Hello?"

"Hi." It's Virgil.

"Hi," I say. "How's your hand?"

"Not bad," he says. "Broken in places, but I don't have to have surgery, which is good. My mom isn't happy about it though. Brother Chad called the cops and we all have to give statements and stuff. I'll probably have to do community service."

"What are you doing right now?" I ask him.

"Nothing," he says. "We're going to do that stuff tomorrow, because my mom is just *done* for today."

"My mom, too." *You're grounded until further notice.* I wonder what a countenance of spiritual growth looks like.

"Did you get in trouble?" asks Virgil.

"You could say that," I tell him. "Do you think your mom could drive us over to the stables? I'm guessing you have work to do, since you were gone at camp. I can help. Are you up to that? I kinda just need to be around the horses right now."

"Sure," he says. "She likes you, Eleanor. She thinks you're a good influence."

"If only she knew," whispers Creep.

"Okay," I say. "Do you think it would be okay for the boys to stay with her while we're gone?"

"They'll just play video games," he says. "They're pretty easy. I think she'll be okay with it."

"I'll bring them over," I say.

People who know the real me:
Creep

THIRTY-FIVE

Virgil orders me around the barn. He scatters straw with one hand, leaning his injured arm on the stall door. He's wearing a sling. His wrist and hand are immobilized in a white cast, two fingers splinted together. I like the rhythm we've fallen into. With the horses. With each other. The big animals are used to me. Virgil is used to me. I don't need to pretend here.

Creep skulks around in the shadows, but I just ignore him.

I feed and water the horses. They snuffle into my hands when I offer carrots. They don't ask questions. They don't push in. They just blink their long eyelashes at me and nudge my shoulders when they want to be petted.

I take pictures. I breathe deep their sunny, dust-pelted scent. The soft smells of hay and horse get into my hair. As I work, my muscles loosen, the tension falls away, the knot in my stomach unwinds itself. My skin feels more comfortable. Instead of being trapped inside of my body, I *am* my body, touching things with *my* fingers. I forget to think and I realize I'm not inside my brain for once. I'm just me.

In a couple of hours, I take off my gloves and I lean back on a bale of hay with my water, smiling at Virgil as he tries to open his bottle with one hand.

"Here." I take the bottle and unscrew the lid.

He thanks me. We sit for a while, the silence broken only by the occasional swish of a tail or clomp of a hoof. I study my hands. I'm thinking about being in my body, instead of sitting in my head like a pilot. The scent of summer in *my* nose. My eyes full of Virgil's smile. My ears catch the snuffling barn sounds, the slow-motion litter of hay bits as they fall through the air, the crunch of fodder between the horses' teeth. I wonder what it would be like to always feel this way. Just me without fear in my ribs and Creep in my ears. My sternum with something alive unfurling behind it.

"What are you thinking about?"

I look up and see Virgil watching me. I look around for Creep, expecting him to interject. I see him huddled in the rafters. He just watches. His face is slack, eyes blank like he's thinking, until he sees me turn around. Then his face cracks into two rows of jagged teeth. The chilly smile hardens something inside of me. The stirring movement inside me grinds back into solidity. The rock in my stomach. The cave in my chest.

"Go on," says Creep.

I look back down at my hands.

"Elle?" says Virgil.

"I can't—" I start. But *I can't I can't I can't tell him. I can't. Tell him.*

Tell him.

He waits.

I don't know how he knows to wait like this. He watches me. Picks at his cast.

When I speak again, it feels like falling into the waterfall pool. A sudden immersion into treacherous waters.

"Do you know what it feels like to have something you can't say?"

Virgil breathes out. Was he holding his breath?

"Sure," he says. "I've kept lots of secrets."

"Bigger than that. Darker, I guess. Maybe just something that would change everything. Change everything if people knew."

"This is the thing you were talking about before," he says. "The thing you said I didn't know about you that would change my mind."

I nod. The words crowd my mouth, clinging to the back of my throat. I swallow.

"I have something," I say. "Something I've never told anyone. There's only one person." I stop. Does Creep count as a person? Could I tell Virgil about Creep? I haven't said Creep's name out loud in so many years that I'm not even sure it's his name anymore. I don't know if I can talk about Ian. But maybe I can talk about Creep.

"Someone knows about it," I say. "But—"

I look up into the rafters again. Creep is stretched out, lounging like a cat. His mouth is drawn downward. A frowning grimace. He holds out one finger and wags it back and forth. *Don't*, the finger says. *Don't do it.*

Virgil follows my eyes. "What is it?" he says.

I look back at him and he raises his eyebrows. "I'm going to tell you something," I say in a rush. "And you're going to think I'm crazy, but I feel like something is changing. Or maybe I am? Or I want to? And maybe I would be able to change if someone knew. So I'm going to tell you."

"Okay," says Virgil.

I hear Creep scrambling along the rafter. I don't know what he will do, so I plunge ahead.

"When I was a kid I had this imaginary friend. But he was kind of... creepy, and my parents didn't like me talking about him, so after a while I stopped."

"Eleanor," says Creep behind me. I don't turn around. "Don't do it. He'll think you're crazy."

"You stopped having an imaginary friend?" asks Virgil.

"Eleanor." Creep climbs up onto the bale between Virgil and me. I edge away from him.

"I stopped... talking about him." My palms are slick. I wipe them on my thighs.

"Eleanor," says Creep. "Eleanor, stop. Eleanor, stop. ELEANOR." His voice rattles in his throat, the coarse sound of gargling with gravel.

"Okay," says Virgil.

"The thing is," I say. "I don't know if he really *was* imaginary. Or *is* . . . imaginary."

Creep gets louder and louder. I try to concentrate on Virgil's face, but I can see Creep on the edge of my vision. He rocks back and forth on his hands and feet; the knobs of his spine jut. The sharp contours of his shoulder blades. He clacks his teeth together between each iteration of my name, raking his fingernails along his arms and legs, until he's oozing black. I would close my eyes on this part of a horror movie. It takes all I have not to run out of the barn.

"What do you mean?" asks Virgil. I can barely hear him over the sound of Creep's screeding rant.

Creep is shouting now. He tells me to stop. Says my name over and over. He has fallen off the bale and he is a frothing ball of black chaos in the dust at my feet. Then I do close my eyes. A headache sprouts in my right temple. The more

Creep screams, the more I feel myself withdrawing. Folding back into the hiding place deep inside.

"He's still around," I say. Creep falls silent. I look at Virgil.

Virgil blinks.

"Now you've done it," says Creep. His eyes glint.

I cover my face, Virgil reaches out to pull one of my hands away. "Are you saying you have an imaginary friend?"

I nod, staring down at Creep. He lies curled, like a snake, staring back. His arms and legs are scored with black gashes. Virgil holds my right hand in his left.

"How long has he been around?" asks Virgil.

I shrug. "I don't know," I say. "As long as I can remember. I don't remember a time when he wasn't around."

"Is he *always* around?" asks Virgil.

"Yes," I say.

I glance at him and then back down. Can he feel how sweaty my hand is?

"Is he here right now?"

I nod again.

"Where is he?" asks Virgil.

I point at Creep. He points back at me. Virgil looks at nothing.

"You can't see him," I say. "No one can. Except for me."

"What does he look like?" asks Virgil.

I rub my eyes. "I don't know," I say. "He's small, like kid-sized. He's skinny. Tall spiky ears. And he has these teeth in a mouth that… it's gross," I finish.

"What color are his eyes?"

"Black," I say. *Black. Blank. Hard.*

Virgil stares hard at the spot where Creep lies. Creep slinks away from us, looking back over his shoulder to glare at me.

"He went over there." I point.

"What does he do normally?" Virgil says.

"He just follows me everywhere," I tell him. "It seems like the only times he disappears is sometimes when I'm with Joshua, or Mia, or you." I realize it as I say it, and I wonder why. "Otherwise, he comments on everything and basically just won't shut up. He's mean. He used to get me in trouble all the time when I was little."

"Is he the reason you stabbed a kid in the leg with a pencil?"

"Yes," says Creep. He sounds grumpy.

"I guess," I say.

Virgil looks at me for a long time, his gold-flecked eyes examining my face. His thumb runs back and forth across the knuckle of my index finger. I watch the movement across my skin. It's abstracted, remote – like he's touching someone else's hand. I watch his thumb like looking at the motion will help me remember what it's supposed to feel like.

"You think I'm crazy," I say.

He shrugs. "No," he says. "I wouldn't say crazy. Maybe there's a reason he's here."

"Why?" I ask. "And why can't anyone else see him?"

"I don't know. Maybe it's something just for you. You know, like in Matthew, how it says many are called, but few are chosen."

"Why would someone be chosen for this?" I think about how else I was chosen. Ian's face flashes and I take my hand back from Virgil and hold my water bottle with both.

"I dunno," says Virgil. "I've read about people who were possessed and God allowed it because he wanted them to be able to testify of the reality of the Devil."

The thin plastic of my water bottle crackles a little as I squeeze it. "Possessed."

"That's not what I meant," Virgil says quickly. Then his voice turns thoughtful. "But it does sound kinda demonic." He pauses. Then he looks at me, "You don't seem possessed. So maybe more like... mental illness?"

"Back to crazy again," I say.

"That's not what I mean," says Virgil. "People can have mental health problems for all kinds of reasons. People have hallucinations. Or… delusions?" He's going to go on, but I interrupt him.

"That's literally the definition of crazy."

"No," says Virgil. "Crazy is just a word that people use when they don't want to take the time to figure something out."

"So you're saying I'm mentally ill." This sentence coming out of my mouth makes me want to sink into the floor and disappear forever.

"So what if you are?" asks Virgil. He says it in a soft voice, like the kind you would use with an animal you're afraid to scare away. "Maybe you would need medicine and treatment. Just like someone with a physical illness."

"Therapy," I say.

"Maybe," says Virgil. "But let's just say you're not mentally ill. Maybe he's a ghost?" Creep guffaws. I shake my head at that and Virgil says, "Or a supernatural creature or something…maybe you're supposed to help him accomplish something. Or learn something from him. "

"Like how to feel like crap all the time," I say.

Creep laughs again, quieter this time. "C'mon, Eleanor," he calls from the other side of the barn. "It's not like that. We're besties, right?"

"Is he part of the reason you don't like to be touched?"

"Not really. Maybe." I look him in the eyes. "You're taking this really well."

"It doesn't change how I feel about you, if that's what you mean," he says. Virgil sits up straighter. "It seems like there's maybe more to this than you want to tell me, and that's okay. But I think you should tell somebody. It sounds important. Maybe dangerous."

I shake my head. "I can't tell anyone."

"Just think about it," he says. "Maybe Brother Chad could help." I make a face. Virgil says, "Or Mia's therapist, Brian? He's pretty cool. Oh, you know who would be good to talk to? Nicole. After my dad left and all that crap happened with my mom and how I ended up helping her at the store? It was mostly just to get me talking. I would sit in her office while she did her paperwork and I would just talk to her about everything. Sometimes I would yell and cry. And she never told me to chill out or be a man or whatever. It was way better than the anger management counseling. She's cool."

I shake my head again.

"Why can't you tell anyone?" Virgil asks.

I don't answer.

"You know," Virgil says. "One day, Nicole told me that what happened between my parents didn't just happen to *them*. It happened to me too. It was part of my story. She said, *You're allowed to tell your story. Don't ever let anyone tell you that you're not.*"

I just stare at the dust where Creep had his tantrum. His voice echoes. *Eleanor, stop.*

"Just think about it," Virgil says. "Promise me you'll just think about it. In the meantime, I'm here. And I don't think you're crazy."

<u>People Creep Says I'm Allowed to Tell:</u>

Creep

THIRTY-SIX

Virgil's mom offers to drive Joshua and me home, but I tell her we'll walk. Joshua invites Sam over to play Legos, so it's the three of us. Virgil stands on the porch and waves once, then just watches us walk down the street. Sam and Joshua both tease me, giggling and making kissing noises. And they complain about the heat the whole way, tugging at their collars, wiping their foreheads, gagging on the hot air. Creep lopes behind us, bare hands and feet on the burning sidewalk.

"Why would anyone live here?" Josh says. "I mean, why would people come here in the first place?"

"Cuz they were dumb," says Sam.

Joshua giggles.

"He's right," I say. "Those dumb pioneers came here in their covered wagons and they drove up and rolled down the window and said, *Wow, check out all the awesome cactus! Look there's twenty-seven varieties of scorpions here, cool! And what's that?*

*Let's call it a Gila monster. Let's **live** here! Sure, you'll drop dead in summer if you don't sit in the shade drinking plenty of water, but who else can say they live with actual monsters! Sounds great, right?"*

Joshua and Sam laugh as we reach the edge of our yard. "Eleanor, covered wagons don't have windows," says Josh.

He and Sam run around our tree, across the grass, and go into the house. *Weird,* I think. *I thought we locked the door.*

They don't notice the car parked on the curb one house down.

But I do. I stop on the sidewalk to look at it. The sun beats down, filling my eyes and making them water.

"What do we have here?" says Creep.

The car door opens and a figure gets out.

- - - I want to turn toward the house, but my feet are heavy everything starts to mush together I try anyway the world continues to spin after I've stopped turning and I can't get a grip on it moving through water too slow and everything is just wavy lines since my eyes haven't stopped watering I don't get any closer to the house than the edge of the shade cast by the tree when I feel his handonmyshoulder - - -

I pull away and his hand slides down to mine. It holds. I pull him behind me toward the protective shade, and then I'm under the umbrella of boughs. Some of the branches are so low, I have to duck. He follows me. I feel the weight of his hand. He pulls at my arm and I swing around to face him. I've grown this summer, closer to his height, but he still seems very tall. Creep dances around our feet.

"Ellie," says Ian.

No. Not here. You're not part of this place.

Creep says, like he can hear my thoughts, "But he's a part of *you.*"

I take a step back, but I only move into a crook of boughs protruding from the trunk. I watch him look around. But the branches hang so low, the leaves so dense, that we are shielded from view. Only our knees and feet will show if someone drives by. He turns back.

He hasn't let go of my hand. His touch is so familiar, I automatically grasp at it.

We're staring at each other. He moves the other hand up to my face. His fingers brush over my cheek. The caress stirs warmth under my stomach. *The basement of my heart.* My body replying to him, though he's only said my name. My body betraying me. My eyes are full. They'll spill over any moment.

"You're not supposed to be here," I say. My throat is tight. I'm surprised the words come out at all.

"Why didn't you call me? I missed you," he says. His dark hair is swooped up. It looks nice, like he just had a fresh haircut, his brown eyes shot with amber, his cheeks a little flushed in the heat. Leaf shadows move across his face.

"I miss you too," I say. Another betrayal. I can't stop it — twin tears fall, one from each eye.

He moves to wipe them away with his thumbs, holding my face in both hands. Then he pulls me into a hug. My face is buried in his arm, his voice resonant in my ear against his chest as he says, "God, I missed you."

I breathe in his scent. I know it better than I know my own. His breath in my hair makes me tingle.

"I heard about your dad," he says.

That's when my arms snake around his waist. I sink into him. I'm sobbing into his shirt. He hugs me tighter. Everything bubbles up at once: Mia holding my hand telling me I'm good, Virgil getting hurt, the Go-To Girl, Creep circling and circling, Ian being gone forever, Ian being back, Dad being sick.

He lets me cry for a while. "I know," he says. "I know, sweetie. It's scary. He's like a dad to me too." His arms loosen. He kisses my temple. His lips on my skin just above my brow.

It puts a sudden lid on my fear and my grief; the tears stop. I pull back to look up into his eyes, sniffling. They look a little sad — soft and sympathetic, the way Mia looked at me. My hands fall to his hips. His body as natural under my touch as my favorite book, and as easy to read, my fingers tracing pages I've read a thousand times. He came back from his service mission taller too, and strong — strong and confident and hungry. And mine, in a way he wasn't anyone else's.

He presses his mouth to my forehead. I think of the Wizard of Oz, Glinda blessing Dorothy with a kiss of protection. I close my eyes.

I lift my face to meet the kiss I know is coming. His lips are dry and gentle. A low throb pulses through me as I lean into it, my arms pulling him close again. My fists clench the fabric of his shirt. His mouth turns heavy. His tongue finds mine and he groans. I can feel all of him against all of me, pressing me into a cradle of branches.

I want him to stop. I want him to keep going. I want the Ian that draws a feather-light touch along my arm to make me laugh while we talk about *The Iron Giant*. The Ian that made mountains of popcorn for our *Doctor Who* marathon. That let me paint his toenails. That saved my tooth in a ziploc when I was seven.

I want him to keep going. I want him to stop. I don't want the Ian that groans while the smell of him gets in my nose and down my throat and in my hair — the hunger for me that comes out through his pores, that makes my blood race and my stomach turn. The greed that can't be filled. I've never been enough. And he was always too much.

I want him to stop.

But my mouth can't form the words. My throat rebels, not letting me breathe. Lungs burning for air, I taste bile and the salt from my tears. The heat. The suffocating heat.

I pull back, my hands moving to the center of his chest. I push him lightly.

Then: "Stop," I say. We're both panting. I'm hot everywhere. My scalp tingles, like it's about to catch fire.

He looks around. He says, "You're right. We should go inside."

"No," I say. "I'm sorry." *Why am I apologizing? I am though. Sorry.* "You should go."

He looks at me quizzically. "I texted your mom and told her I would be on this side of town. Since she's still at the hospital, she asked if I would stop by and check on you and Josh." He rubs my shoulders with both hands.

"I *missed* him," says Creep. "Didn't you *miss* him, Ellie?"

"We're fine," I say.

"Okay," says Ian. "You're not going to invite me in?"

"No," I say. Or I *mean* to say. The sound isn't even a sound. It's just the shape of my mouth and a little puff of air.

His hand lifts one of mine. Presses his lips to the knuckles. I try to pull the hand away, watching his mouth. He's always been stronger than me.

"Is this about Virgil?"

I freeze, looking into his eyes. Our hands fall, but he's still holding on.

"Uh oh," says Creep. He's climbed up onto a branch just beyond Ian's shoulder. I see him smile. He clacks his teeth together.

"Yeah," said Ian. "Your mom told me about your little boyfriend. How you got caught in the woods."

His grasp tightens. The bones in my hand creak.

"What were you doing out there, Ellie? Doing what you do with me?"

I shake my head slightly. *Virgil is different.* "No."

He's studying me. Looking into me. He's always seen into me. "You like him, don't you, sweetie?"

I don't answer. I can't breathe. I feel like a fish caught in a net.

"Do you *love* him?" asks Ian. His eyes burrowing.

I still don't say anything. He answers his own question. "No," he says. "You don't love him. Not yet."

"I love *you*," I whisper.

He smiles. Warmly. A real Ian smile. My chest feels like it might collapse. "I know, sweetie," he says. "I love you too. I really do." He tips my chin up and kisses me again. It's slow and tender and it could be Virgil kissing me. He could pull me down with him, could pull me down by both hands, mouth locked with mine, and I would follow.

Then he says, "No one will ever love you like I do," at the same time that I say, "You shouldn't come back here."

His arms around me. His taste in my mouth. His handprints all over me. He makes a sound of disappointment. "You're right," he says. "It's too dangerous." He's talking about *our secret*. "Oh, that reminds me. I have something for you." He digs in his pocket and then holds out a phone. "You'll have to hide it from your parents," he says. "But it will be easier to keep in touch."

I stare at the phone in his hand. It's purple. Visions of texts and midnight conversations and video calls with Ian scrolling through my imagination. My stomach flipflops in that familiar way.

"I already have one," I say.

He looks confused. "You already have a phone? You should have said." He pockets the new phone and holds out his hand. "Give it to me, honey, and I'll put my new number in. Do you have Telegram?"

I don't move. My eyes flick between his hand and his face.

"What?" he says.

My voice cracks at his expression. "I don't want to see you anymore."

Creep starts to laugh.

Ian's brow creases a little. "Ellie, are you... breaking up with me?" he says. He says it like he's holding back a laugh. Like I'm a kid making up jokes. Like the phrase "breaking up" is a joke. And then I realize what a ridiculous set of words it is. *As if "breaking up" could possibly capture anything I want after what Ian and I have done.*

"Yes," I say.

Then he *does* laugh. it's affectionate and familiar, only something I can hear. He steps back, not far. Just far enough to hold me at arms' length, his hands on my shoulders. "You're so cute," he says smiling. He's rubbing my arms from shoulder to elbow. "I missed you so much." He moves to kiss me again. My chest *is* collapsing, caving in on itself. I'm dizzy.

Then someone calls my name. Ian pushes away from me and we lock eyes.

"Eleanor?"

I turn around, and Mia is peering through the branches. She's come up the sidewalk. She probably heard us talking. I know I've wasted the second it takes her eyes to adjust. She sees me, and then she sees Ian. He steps further back and then turns away. I duck under the branches holding me in place and move toward Mia. My chest hurts. I take a deep quivering breath. She pushes under the branches to meet me in the shady canopy.

"Elle, why didn't you call me? I've been back for a couple hours. Are you okay?"

Ian has gone back out to the grass. He pulls out his phone as he walks toward the front door. It's black, and bigger than the one he offered me. I'm saying, "I went to see the horses," as Mia tries to adjust her view between the leaves and branches to see him better.

"Who is *that*?" she says. "He's hot." Then she sees my expression and says, "Wait."

Ian leans against the door frame, looking at his phone. His other hand in his pocket.

"Wait," says Mia. "Wait. WAIT." She looks at me and then back at Ian. "Is that *THE GUY*??"

I shush her as Ian looks up. *God, please, Jesus, anyone, if you're listening, please, please make her drop this.*

"Sorry," she whispers. "But is it? The GUY?"

"Yeah," I say. "Yeah, it is, okay? It's the guy." I'm trying to block her view. She leans around me to see.

"Wow," she says. "He's so hot. *He's* the sci-fi fan? Look at those eyelashes. Who has eyelashes like that?" Then her face changes. "How old is he? He looks old." I take her arm to drag her back to the sidewalk. She looks me up and down. "Are you okay? Are you *crying*?"

I swipe at my cheeks. "He's not *old*," I say. "He's twenty four."

She stops. "Elle," she says seriously. "You're dating a twenty-four-year-old?"

"NO!" I say loudly before lowering my voice. "No." I pull at her arm again. "We broke up."

"When," she demands, "*were* you dating a twenty-four-year-old?"

"Well, he wasn't twenty-four when we—"

The sound of a car engine and Ian pushes off the door frame and hops down the steps.

I wipe the sweat from my forehead. Mia says, "When you what?"

A car door and Ian is at the driveway.

"Hi, Mrs. Moreno," I hear him say.

"You have to go," I whisper to Mia.

"Hi, Ian," says my mom. "How are you?"

"I'm good," says Ian.

"He wasn't twenty-four when you WHAT?" Mia demands.

"Please, please, just go," I beg. "I'm grounded. We can talk about it later." I push her toward the sidewalk and then run towards Mom's car.

I burst out of the leaves just as Ian is saying, "Ellie was just showing me the hummingbird feeder. What a great tree. I didn't really notice it the first time we visited."

I listen to their conversation as I cross the lawn. Mom says, "Yes, Joshua wants to build a tree house. Maybe you could come over sometime and help him. Mike isn't feeling up to much these days."

"Yeah," says Ian. "That would be great. I heard about Mr. Moreno. How is he?"

"He's fighting," says Mom. "Will you stay for dinner?"

"No, I can't," says Ian. "I have a class."

"Oh, that's great," says Mom. "Getting a jump on summer school. Did you hear I went back to school?" Mom notices me. "Eleanor," she says. "Have you started dinner?"

I keep walking.

"Oh, they just got back," says Ian.

"Back?" says Mom. "From where?"

"I'll start dinner," I say. I pause on the porch to look for Mia. I don't see her anywhere.

"Bye, Ellie! Thanks for——," calls Ian, but I open the door and close it behind me, cutting off his farewell.

In the kitchen, I pull a pound of ground beef out of the fridge. I slap it into a skillet and turn the burner on. I chop an onion, not caring about the fumes, and soon the tears that had gathered outside are leaking down my face. A headache starts to pulse behind my right eyebrow. I dump the onion into the skillet and turn the beef over with a wooden spoon. It sizzles. I lower the heat, my face wet and flushed, trying to take deep breaths. Lungs burn.

"What are you making?" I jump. Mom is standing behind me, Creep just a little behind her.

"Tacos," I tell her.

She takes the spoon and turns the beef. It's still a little pink. She tears open a packet of taco seasoning. I pull the bag of lettuce out of the fridge, tearing pieces into a bowl.

"That was rude," she says. "Just walking away when Ian was saying goodbye."

"We already said goodbye," I say.

"He told me you went somewhere," she says.

"Okay," I say.

"So where did you go?" she says.

"To the stables," I say. My hands are still shaking.

She turns to look at me. "What stables?" She squints her eyes. "Have you been crying?"

"It's the onions," I say. "The stables where Virgil's family keeps their horses."

"Was Virgil there?" She is getting a stack of plates for the table.

I dice a tomato with a long chef's knife. The knife is sharp. It slices with no resistance through the tomato. The red fruit falls into perfect cubes, the seedy juice running across the cutting board. I wonder how hard I would have to press to cut into my own flesh. "Yes," I tell her.

"Were you two alone?"

"Yes," I say. I slice the ends off of a cucumber. The smell of frying meat fills the air.

She bangs the cupboard door shut. The plates rattle on the counter. "Let me get this straight," she says. "Even though you are forbidden to date until you're sixteen, as well as being grounded as of *this morning*, the first thing you do when I leave is go on a date."

The line of cucumber slices lean to the right. I stack them upright and quarter them. "I took a nap first thing after you left. And it wasn't a date." I pause. "But, yes."

I look at her. Her mouth is hanging open.

Creep cackles.

"It's burning," I tell her.

She turns back to the stove and pulls the skillet off the heat. She rubs her eyes.

"Eleanor," she says to the beef, "I really don't know what's come over you. I understand that you might be having a hard time with your father's illness, and I appreciate that, so I have tried to make allowances, but–,"

I cut her off. "What allowances?" I say.

"Excuse me?" She turns.

"What allowances have you tried to make? I haven't noticed any. Things are the same as ever, except now I'm expected to do all the cooking."

Her mouth is hanging open again. She points. "Go to your room," she says, "and stay there. You are not permitted to leave until you hear from me."

I drop the knife next to the cutting board.

Creep follows me down the stairs. "Dinner's almost ready," I call into the family room.

"'Kay," says Joshua.

As I stand in the doorway of my room, I watch Creep amble over to the bed and pull himself up. He turns in a circle, on all fours like a dog, before he nestles next to my pillow. He looks up at me with wide eyes. I step in and close the door behind me. I stare at my bed. At Creep. *New life.* I can almost smell the secrets, steamed into bedspread, into the pillows, into the sheets. I've washed my bedding since we moved here, but he'll never wash out. Of the bed. Of me. If I could light a match right now and touch it to the worn fabric, I would. I press one knuckle to my right temple. The headache mutes briefly. *New me.*

"What are you thinking?" asks Creep.

I don't answer. I gather up my sleeping bag, my sketchbook, and my phone and I take them into the bathroom. Light from the frosted window creates soft shadows. The sleeping bag fits into the bathtub perfectly. I use part of it to pad where I lean back in the tub. Creep perches on the toilet lid to watch me. I put the earbuds in.

"Too bad he didn't stay for dinner," he says. He says something else, but I can't hear him over the sound of the suddenly blaring music.

Head throbbing under the jagged bass of Korn's *Coming Undone*, I draw seven self-portraits before I fall asleep.

<u>Fear #5:</u>

That everyone will find out.

The bare hallway is empty.

I've been here before.

I move down to the next closest door. The knob is cold and slippery. It defies my grasp until I use both hands.

A bright, empty room. The walls and floor are white, a dazzling, spherical light fixture hanging down from the center of the white ceiling.

"Hi."

I turn around to see a figure in the corner. He is bent over something, head down, turned away from me. He sticks one elbow out and I can see the muscles in his arm flex as he moves to pry something. I hear the pop of a seal. "I'm glad you're here. Want to play a game?"

When he stands, I can see that it's Ian.

"C'mon, Ellie," he says. "You like games, don't you?" He has a paint bucket in either hand. The big paint buckets used for house interiors. He steps closer and holds out one of the buckets. It's filled to the brim with florid paint. "It's called Crimson," he says. "You have to mix it first." He holds out a ruler-sized stick. I don't take either the

paint bucket or the stick. He sets them on the floor in front of me and then bends to mix his own bucket.

After he doesn't move toward me for a minute, I pick up the stick. I sink it into the paint. It's viscous and smooth and bright, bright red. I turn the stick through the paint, absorbed by the separated shades that combine in swirling patterns. I forget that Ian is a few feet away.

I am startled when he finally stands up. "Okay," he says. "I think we're ready."

"For what?" I ask.

"To have some fun," he says. He twists then, and snaps the bucket to one side. Paint spatters onto the pristine wall. He holds the bucket in both hands and jerks it upward. An arc of paint glides through the air, showering down on the wall, the floor. Streaking the light fixture. He turns to look at me. His smile looks painted on, his eyes heavy-lidded.

"C'mon, Ellie," he says again. "Play with me." I watch him spray the walls with paint from the bottomless bucket. He leaves one section mostly white, gesturing me over. "Here," he says. "Try it."

I lift the bucket. It sloshes paint across the floor. I step around it, but my shoes are already splattered. I swing the bucket and the paint hits the wall with a slapping sound. It drips downward, trailing across the floor. I swing the bucket again and again, soaking my patch of wall. When I turn to look at the rest of the room, I am out of breath. Ian has covered everything in red. The floor squelches with paint. The light fixture drips red, making the room dark.

Ian leans against one wall. He is covered in paint – his face smeared. He smiles at me. "That was the best," he says. "My favorite game." He looks tired.

My eyes flick around the room. I imagine what my mother would say.

"How are we going to clean it up?" I ask.

"We don't need to clean it up," he says.

"But look at this," I say. "It's a huge mess."

"It's okay," he says. "It doesn't matter. We've done it lots of times. We'll just find another room."

My hands are sticky with red. I try to wipe the paint from my arms and face. It's starting to dry in place like a second skin.

I find the door. I look back at Ian. He waves. "I'll see you next time, beautiful," he says.

Back in the hallway, I look down at my shoes, but the paint has dried, so I don't leave footprints. I can feel paint hardening in my hair. There must be a way out. I move down the hall a little way and choose another door.

Another cold knob. It opens directly into a bathroom. Steam billows out of the doorway when I step inside. The room is long and narrow, with a tub at one end. The shower curtain is drawn. I can hear weeping. I call out.

"Hello?"

The curtain shifts at one end of the tub, the plastic drawn aside and a girl's pale face looks out at me. I can tell from the angle of her shoulders and head that she's lying in the tub.

"Help!" she cries. Her face contorts and she moans. The girl flails. She grabs the side of the tub and screams, the curtain crumpling under her hand. I approach the tub.

"Help," she says again.

I don't want to, but I need to look. I need to see to help her. I lean over her, peeking into the shower. She's maybe twelve, with slender, white arms and legs, no breasts yet, not really, delicate hands and feet. Her belly is distended, impossibly huge. She thrashes. Blood circles the drain.

The awareness of her pregnancy makes my legs weak. I kneel next to the tub. Wet tendrils of black hair cling to her forehead and neck, tangled across the porcelain. Her eyes are squeezed shut. She arches her back and groans. It comes from deep inside her – a sound like a trapped animal.

"Hey," I say.

The girl squints at me. Her eyes are ice-blue. She grabs for my hand, crushing my fingers in her grip. "I don't want it," she says. "I don't want it."

I don't know what to tell her. I put my hand on her slick arm. Try to swallow my horror.

"I didn't want any of this," she moans. She is grinding her teeth. The tendons of her jaw stand out as she clenches down.

"I'm sorry." I hold her hand in both of mine.

She screams.

"It's coming," she says. "It's coming." Breathless, her voice hoarse. "No, no nono. . .."

She sobs once, but any tears are lost in the shower's spray.

"No," says the girl again, but I can barely hear the word. Her legs are drawn up, thighs apart. The girl writhes and I'm afraid. I wipe water from my eyes as the shape of her belly distorts, as if something inside is pushing outward. The girl shrieks. She sits up, dragging on my hand and the shower curtain. There is a tearing sound. She collapses back into the tub. Her legs flop outward. A drop of blood leaks from the corner of her mouth. It turns pink as it joins a rivulet of water. I lean over her to see if she's still breathing. Her eyes are open, pointed at the ceiling.

Without letting go of her hand, I recoil against the bathroom wall. The girl's belly moves again. Its shape elongates toward her pelvis and the taut flesh goes suddenly slack. At the same time I hear a squelching sound and see a large black shape slither to the foot of the tub between her feet. Under the arc of water, it glistens, covered in blood and slime. I look back at the girl's face. She doesn't move, long hair trailing down her chest. I pull my hand out of hers — peer at the shape unfolding itself underneath the faucet.

Gaunt arms and legs, a soft round head. I lean forward. The creature squats over the drain in a circling pool of black, turns its wobbly head and blinks at me. I stumble backwards and fall, ripping the shower curtain from the rod. It tangles around me as I scramble back toward the door. The creature hooks its bony fingers over the edge of the tub, hoists itself up. Scrabbles toward me, leaving a dark, glossy trail on the linoleum.

I can't turn the doorknob. My fingers can't get a grip. I fight the entangling curtain.

I feel the weight of the creature behind me as it mounts my legs. I turn back to see it crawling, pulling itself by the wadded plastic up to my torso. Its claws pierce the fabric of my shirt. The angles of its joints stab into my stomach and ribs as it moves. It hunches on my chest, dripping oily fluid, inches from my face.

It coughs once and then smiles.

"Hi, Eleanor," says Creep.

THIRTY-SEVEN

I kick awake, banging my knee on the side of the tub. The ear buds are twisted around my arm and I yank them out of my ears as I jerk upright. A scream is pressed to the top of my mouth. I swallow it. The bathroom is midnight dark. The sudden absence of music makes the silence feel like a blanket. I rub the sleep out of my eyes and then lean against my knees. The panic floods over me and away. I'm limp.

"What was it this time?" asks Creep.

I startle. He separates from the blackness of my sleeping bag and climbs up to sit on the side of the tub. Just a shadow against the shower curtain. Was he lying on my feet? The thought makes me shiver.

"The hallway," I say into my hands.

"Oh, I like that one," he says. "So much variety. You've been having that one for years."

"No kidding," I say. When I stretch, I hear my vertebrae pop. I find the phone by touch and wrap the ear bud cords around it.

"Tell me about your dream," says Creep. "Tell me about the hallway." He leans close. He smells like laundry detergent and sweat and something else.

"Do you mind?" I twist my hair to the back of my head and use the hair band on my wrist to secure it.

"What?" says Creep. "You used to tell me all about your dreams when you were little."

"Well, I'm not little anymore," I tell him, "and I'd like you to forget about it."

I hear his teeth click together. "C'mon, Ellie," he whines. "Was it the bed? The birdcage? The bathroom? It was the bathroom wasn't it? Makes sense, since you slept in the bathtub." As he's talking, I stand up, slipping a little on the sleeping bag. I step out of the bathtub holding on to the wall. "Why did you sleep in here, anyway?"

"Shut up," I tell him.

"What happened in the bathroom this time?" He follows me out of the bathroom.

"Please," I tell him. "Please. Stop." I find my lamp on the bedside table. The light is overwhelming at first and I have to squint my eyes to adjust. Creep climbs up onto the bed.

"What was it? C'mon, tell me," he says. He rolls onto his back and waves his feet in the air.

I pull a pair of yoga pants and a large t-shirt out of my drawer. Creep questions me as I change. Was it the library? The movie theater? The school? Ian's house? It was Ian's house, wasn't it? I sure miss that boy. Blah blah blah.

I finally round on him. "If I tell you, will you shut up?" I hiss.

"Sure," he says. He rolls over and over on the mattress until he falls off the bed. He turns in circles and then sits picking his toes. He stares at me while I talk.

"It was the paint."

His smile lengthens. "Ah, the splattered white room. I love that image. Like a blood-spatter analyst's wet dream." He rolls his eyes and then closes them for a moment, as if he's visualizing the evidence of our violent red efforts. "What else?"

"The bathroom."

"I knew it," he says.

I shake my head, remembering the girl in the tub. "It was a new one," I say.

"What was it? Tell me." He clasps his hands like a child about to receive a gift.

I think about the Creep-creature, oozing and sliding across the floor toward me.

"No," I say. I open my bedroom door.

"Where are you going?" asks Creep.

"I'm thirsty," I tell him. I start up the stairs. Creep follows me, asking over and over about the dream.

At the top of the stairs I stop. "I thought you said you would leave me alone if I told you about it."

"But you didn't tell me about it," he says. "Not really."

"I told you enough," I whisper as we cross the dark living room. "Now shut up."

I am so preoccupied with our conversation that I don't notice the kitchen light is on until I actually step into it. I stop short at the line where carpet changes to linoleum.

Dad is at the table, sheets of newsprint scattered, an open box of vine charcoal at his right. He drags a piece across a large sheet of white paper, creating a swoop of textured black. He does it again and again, the black getting darker, grainier. He drops the charcoal and picks up a kneaded eraser. He rolls it into a point and starts to draw on the black, lifting out the charcoal to create white shapes.

I haven't seen him draw in years.

"What's he doing?" says Creep.

I look down at Creep and shrug. The movement draws my father's attention. He looks up.

"Eleanor," he says. His voice is quiet. Almost a whisper. "Come in. Come in." He holds up one arm, waving me into the kitchen. He's still wearing the hospital bracelet.

I step into the kitchen.

"What time is it?" he says.

I glance at the clock above his head. "Two-thirty."

He rubs his face, leaving a black charcoal smudge on his forehead. "I hadn't realized it was so late."

I get two glasses and pull the water pitcher out of the fridge. "When did you get back?" I fill the glasses.

"Your mom came to get me after dinner," he says. "But then I couldn't sleep. Sometimes drawing helps, you know?"

I know. He's so quiet. Tranquil even.

"Here." I sit at the end of the table and push a glass of water toward him. "How are you feeling?"

He smiles at me. A real smile with nothing hard behind it. "Thank you." He takes a drink. I watch his Adam's apple bob as he swallows. He's bald now, his arms smooth. No eyebrows even. Colored medical tape where they've been sticking him with needles. "I've been better."

I nod. "Yeah."

He starts drawing with the eraser again. "What about you? How are *you* feeling?"

I reach for the scattered papers, pull them toward me and start putting them in a straight pile. I look at each one. "I'm okay," I say. "I couldn't sleep either."

The drawings are all in black and white – charcoal on newsprint. A knife. A leafless tree. A figure falling from a cliff. A crescent moon over an empty landscape. A crucifix. I pause on that one. The cross is textured wood – wide and tall. The attached figure is lank, sagging, tattered. A pool of blood gathers under the cross.

He keeps drawing. A round white shape on a field of black. His fingers holding the charcoal delicately. I've never thought about my father's hands doing anything delicately.

"Did you have a bad dream?" he asks.

I put the drawings in a pile. We've never talked like this before. I'm not sure what to do. "Yeah," I say.

"You want to tell me about it?"

"No," I say. He nods.

"Your mom told me about what happened at camp. With those boys. They didn't try to hurt you?"

I shake my head again. "They were after Virgil."

"Okay," he says. "Is Virgil okay?"

"They broke his hand and beat him up pretty good. But he's okay, I think."

Dad nods. "You know, your mom worries about you. She doesn't want you to end up making mistakes that have life-changing consequences. She wants you to have the best chance to be happy." He pauses. "But then I look at you and I see that you don't seem very happy."

I don't say anything.

"Do you have bad dreams a lot?"

"Sometimes," I say. "I draw sometimes when I can't sleep."

He nods. "I do too," he says.

I didn't know that.

"I have nightmares too." He keeps drawing as he speaks, a slight pause between each phrase. "I saw a lot of things when I was deployed." A skull forms under his hand, a three-quarter view, with shaded eye-sockets and grinning teeth. "I could have died so many times in the field. But I was saved. Over and over." I watch his hand move over the paper. He draws a crack in the cranium, a hole at the very top of the skull. "And here I am now," he says. "Wasting away."

This is more than he's said to me in months.

His hand stops moving. "I stared Death in the face so many times before," he says to the skull. "But he never noticed me until now."

"Dad," I say. He looks up. "You're going to be okay."

He looks at me for a long time. Then he picks up the box of charcoal and puts it within my reach. "Remember when we used to finish each other's drawings?"

I nod. "That was a long time ago."

He gestures to the stack of images. "Go ahead."

I pick up a piece of charcoal. I'm not used to drawing with something so soft. It breaks when I press it to the paper. He laughs.

"Be gentle," he says. I can't stop picturing his hands doing… not this. *Be gentle.* This from the man who made me choose.

I pull out the knife picture and start drawing.

He puts the skull aside and tears a fresh sheet of paper from the pad. "You know," he says. "The one good thing about facing your mortality is that it makes you look at your life. Makes you take stock. Create an inventory, you know? For how you've lived so far."

"Okay," I say. He is watching me draw.

"I wanted to be a good dad," he says. His voice becomes thick. "When you were born and the first time I laid eyes on you. The light from the overhead lamp was so bright. You were crying. I looked down on you. You were so beautiful.

I raised my hand and shielded your eyes and you stopped crying. You looked at me. And you had the eyes of an old soul."

He touches my arm with black-stained fingers. I imagine them blocking a harsh light. I've heard this story before. He writes it in every birthday card. I don't like hearing it. It makes me feel like this is all he knows about me. That I had the eyes of an old soul.

"I promised myself I would be a good dad," he continues. "I promised *you*." This part of the story is new.

He pets my arms briefly with his fingertips, stripes of black trailing across my skin. I can't remember the last time he touched me like this. I can't decide if I like it or not.

"Are you on drugs?" I ask him.

He laughs. "They did top me off with some strong medication at the hospital."

I finish my drawing and as I shuffle to the next drawing, he pulls his hand away.

"My dad was strict," he says. "He was hard to live with. I promised myself I wouldn't be like him." He stops. He sniffles. He wipes his nose with the back of his hand.

"I'm sorry," he says.

I look at him. His eyes are red. Tears mix with the charcoal smudges and streak his face. The hardness inside me, the anger – what is it now? Looking into his eyes, glistening with tears, I believe him, that he feels it right now. *I* feel it right now, just looking at him. But what will it be tomorrow?

He wipes his eyes. "Can you try to forgive me?" he says. "I'm going to do better. I realize that I might not have that much time left. But I want to change. I want the time we have left to be a good memory for you."

My throat clenches. In my head, he says, *Choose*. A tear escapes my right eye. "I don't know," I say. "I guess I can try."

"Thank you," he whispers. He coughs, and I think it's to cover a sob, and then he lifts his glass for a drink.

I get the next drawing out. He doesn't talk anymore. We sit together for another hour, our charcoal sticks scratching across paper. Finally, my eyelids start to feel heavy. I slide the last drawing on top of the stack. I stand up and stretch.

"I think I'll go back to bed," I say.

"That's a good idea." He stands up too. He puts the lid back on the charcoal box, folds up the newsprint pad.

He flips through the stack of Eleanor-improved drawings. He looks at me.

"You amaze me," he says.

I wipe my fingers on my pants. I don't know what to say. "Thanks," I tell him.

"Can I have a hug?" he asks.

I stop myself from saying no right away, putting on a show that I'm thinking about it. But then I don't want to look like I'm thinking about it, so I nod and then stand still as he puts his arms around my shoulders. He smells like melaleuca oil and frankincense. The hug is brief and light, as if he senses my hesitation. He kisses the top of my head. It makes me think of Ian.

"Get some sleep," he says.

"Don't forget to wash your face," I tell him.

He gives me a thumbs up. I watch him disappear into the dark living room carrying the drawings.

A juicy lemon being sliced in half.

Birds covering the branches of a tree.

An angel diving from a cliff, wings spread in preparation.

A couple walking hand in hand under a crescent moon.

Rays of light exploding from a crucifix – a supernova of unconditional love.

And a cracked skull – chrysalis-white – venting the shape of a single, delicate butterfly.

<u>Things that I can always predict:</u>

Ian

Creep

Joshua

Mom

~~Dad~~

THIRTY-EIGHT

When I come out of the bathroom in the morning, I'm stiff from sleeping curled in the tub. I find an apple in my camp backpack and then get dressed in some of Mia's hand-me-downs. The clothes are black. The shirt is decorated with a line art ribcage and an anatomically correct heart. The skirt is long, with two buckles on one side. I wear it for a few minutes and then change into knee-length shorts with a red pinstripe. Creep sits on the windowsill watching me. I find a note on my pillow.

Eleanor, it says. *I have classes today. Your dad said you were up late, so I let you sleep in. He left early this morning. Joshua is at Sam's. No friends over and you're restricted to the house. Make sure dinner's on the table by six. ~ Mom*

"What's the plan for today?" he says.

"Mia's coming over," I tell him.

Creep holds out both hands. "What about the note?"

I shrug. "What about it?"

"She'll be pissed when she finds out."

"I don't care," I say.

Creep jumps down from the windowsill. "Why don't you invite some other friends too? Virgil. Ian."

I glare at him.

"What?" he says. "It's an idea. I thought it was really sweet of Ian to stop by. You two just pick up where you left off, don't you? Just like old times."

I pull my hair up. "You are a horrible person," I tell him.

He follows me out into the hall. "Eleanor," he says, "that is hurtful." I don't have to look at him to hear the smile in his voice.

Mia's phone rings four times before she picks up. "I'll be over in five minutes."

I answer the door with a bowl of cereal in one hand.

"Why didn't you call me yesterday?" she demands. "I waited all night."

She sits across from me at the kitchen table. Creep sits between us, obscuring my view. I wave my arm at him and he scoots away. Mia raises one eyebrow at me.

"Mosquito," I say. She looks around. Creep hisses at me.

"So the stables," she says. "Tell me everything. No wait, tell me about spending the night at Virgil's house. No wait, tell me about what happened with The A-Team. No wait, tell me about what happened at the waterfall."

I wait for another *No wait*, but she rolls her hand expectantly.

"Go on," she says.

I laugh. "I thought you might have something to add to the list."

"Whatever," she says. "Just tell me everything. No, wait. Tell me about *the guy.*"

Creep licks the back of his hand and uses it to rub his face. Ignoring him, I say, "There's nothing to tell."

She narrows her eyes at me. "There's nothing to tell about a very hot, twenty-four-year old sci-fi guy? Where did you meet him?"

I sigh. "He lived in my complex."

After a moment, Mia folds her arms. "That's all I'm going to get, huh?" She says. She has one eyebrow raised.

"I guess," I say. "Sorry."

She doesn't take her eyes off my face. "Alright," she says. "That's fine. We'll save this for later. Tell me everything else."

I start at the waterfall. She makes me describe every detail. She leans forward, completely absorbed by my story, asking, "And then what did he say?" and "And then what did you say?"

She squeals. "He told you he *loves* you?" She leans back and covers her face. "Oh, Virge," she says into her hands, "you didn't." Her eyes peek over her fingers, her voice muffled. "What did you say?"

"Nothing good."

"Oh my God, Elle," she says as I get up to rinse my bowl. "Did he kiss you again?"

I nod.

"What kind of kiss?" she says. "Was there tongue?"

My bowl drops into the sink. My spoon clatters. "Ugh!" I say. "You're obsessed. No tongue. Never tongue. Shut up about tongue."

Creep tilts his head at me. "C'mon Ellie, stop pretending you don't like it."

I spin around and say to him, "Shut *up!*"

Mia holds up both her hands. "Okay, okay, I won't mention tongue again."

Creep just smiles.

The phone rings and Mia watches me walk across to pick it up.

"Eleanor?" It's Mom.

"Yeah?"

"I'm just checking to make sure you're home," she says. She sounds out of breath, like she's climbing stairs.

"Well, here I am," I say.

She asks me what I'm doing and if I'm planning on inviting friends over. I lie, of course. She's quiet for a moment and then says, "I don't like the person you're becoming, Eleanor."

I swallow. "Okay," I say. "Gotta go, Mom."

I hang up. I turn to walk down the stairs.

Mia follows me. "So what happened with The A-Team?"

We sit on my bed. I lean against the wall while Creep disappears under the bed skirt. I tell her how The A-Team showed up. What they said. How Virgil punched Levi and then how they dragged him into the darkness. I feel the panic rise again as I talk about it. I unclench my fists and force myself to breathe deep.

Mia shakes her head. "They've never done anything like that before," she says. "I'm sure it won't happen again."

"That's what you said last time we talked about what they might do. You said, *Don't worry about it.* Remember?"

"Yeah," she says. "You called it. They're idiots."

"They're psychopaths," I say.

Creeps voice issues from beneath the bed. "Takes one to know one."

"They're just wanna-be bad-asses," says Mia.

I don't say anything. I just look at her. Creep starts humming.

"What?" says Mia.

I feel the words building. I've said so many things lately that I normally wouldn't say that it doesn't feel as strange to let them out.

"You don't know what it was like," I tell her. "I couldn't see anything. And all I could hear was Virgil's voice and they were *hurting* him. And I didn't do anything about it, because I was afraid they would hurt me too."

A chill comes over me and I shiver.

"Okay," says Mia. "I guess I didn't think about it like that. I'm sorry."

"Okay," I say.

The front door opens. I experience a moment of terror thinking that Ian is walking into the house.

"Hello?" Joshua's voice calls.

I put my hand on my chest. I've broken out into a sudden sweat. Mia eyes me. "Down here," she calls.

Two pairs of feet and Joshua and Sam stand in my doorway. They have collapsed cardboard boxes under their arms, and boxes of aluminum foil.

"Hey, Mia," says Josh.

"Hey, Josh," she says.

"Eleanor, we're gonna make throwing stars for NinjUNO. You wanna make throwing stars with us?"

I look at Mia.

"You get started," she says. "We'll come in a few minutes."

The boys go down the hall.

"So what was it like spending the night at Virgil's house?" she asks.

"Weird," I say. "I woke up from a nightmare and he was there."

"He was there," Mia says. "Like in the middle of the night? In your pajamas?"

"Yeah. And before you ask, we didn't make out. We just talked."

She twists her mouth to the side. "What did you talk about in the middle of the night?"

"He told me about his past. You know, about his dad and mom and the fighting and getting in trouble."

"Oh, yeah," she says. "Crazy, huh? You wouldn't know looking at him now that he was such a hard-core thirteen-year old."

"He told me about Levi too. That they used to be besties when they were little."

"I know, right?" Mia whistles from high to low, her eyebrows raised. "I never saw closer friends back then. And now they've beat the shit out of each other more than once. It's like an archnemesis origin story."

I nod. "I guess everyone has something they'd like to forget about."

"So what about yesterday? He took you to the stables. You're welcome, by the way, for setting that up for you in the first place."

I roll my eyes. "I *asked* him to take me."

"Look at you," she says, "all proactive."

"I just needed to talk," I tell her.

"Okay," she says. "What did you talk about?"

I listen to the ragged tones of Creep's voice. I haven't talked to Virgil since I told him about Creep. *What if he's changed his mind? What if he thinks I'm crazy? Or possessed?*

"*My* past," I tell her.

"Oooh," she says. "Juicy."

"It's not that interesting," I say.

"Did you talk about The Guy?"

"No," I say. "You're obsessed with *The Guy*."

She throws her hands up. "Can you *blame* me? He's hot A-F, and twenty-four, and you're FIFTEEN, and you won't talk about him."

There's too much to tell, I want to say. "There's nothing to tell," I say.

Mia narrows her eyes at me. Then she stands up. "Alright. Okay then," she says. "But you're going to have to talk about it soon. I'm worried about you. Let's go make throwing stars."

<u>Things I Wish I Had When The A-Team Attacked:</u>

Bravery
The ability to move
Actual throwing stars

THIRTY-NINE

We are screaming around the house, parkouring over furniture, and pelting each other with homemade throwing stars when the front door opens.

Mia is just sliding down the second story banister as Dad steps onto the landing carrying a box. He has to jump aside in order to avoid colliding with her. She loses her balance on the dismount, stumbles out the open door and off the porch. She somersaults into the grass and ends sitting up. I watch it all from the railing at the top of the stairs, a sudden stab of anxiety at the sight of Dad.

Sam whoops, "That was sick!"

Joshua jumps down the stairs. "Hi, Dad." He throws his arms around Dad's middle. Instead of yelling about running in the house, Dad pats Joshua's head. I watch them, something clenched inside of me.

"What's going on here?" he asks.

"Shuriken battle," says Sam. Both he and Joshua are breathless.

Mia gets up, brushing grass from her backside.

"Hi, Mr. Moreno," she says. Steps back onto the porch and holds out her hand. "I'm Mia."

He ends up shaking with his left because of the box under his right arm. "Nice to meet you, Mia," he says. "I'm Mike." He looks better today. Brighter. The thing inside me starts to unwind.

He waves at me. I raise my hand back. He asks us, "Is this what you guys normally do when we're not around?"

We all look at each other. "Not normally," says Joshua.

"Normally Mia doesn't land right side up," says Sam.

"Bruh," laughs Mia and smacks him on the back of the head.

"I have something for you guys," Dad says to Joshua. "Come here. I'll show you."

We all follow him up to the living room. Dad sits on the couch and we gather around him in the same spot where we heard about the cancer. Creep comes out from behind the couch. Dad puts the box on his lap and pulls off the lid.

There in the box, sitting on a bundled towel, is a puppy. Joshua gasps.

"For us?" he asks.

"Yeah," says Dad. "Go ahead."

Joshua picks up the puppy with both hands. We all reach to pet it and it's the softest thing I've ever felt. The reddish coat is smooth and warm. The puppy wiggles in Joshua's hands, but when he holds it close, the puppy settles down, leaning its head into the crook of Joshua's arm. It has floppy hound-dog ears, a black muzzle and a pale chest. Its eyebrows come together above its deep, brown eyes, forming a perfect set of quizzical wrinkles.

"Oh my God," says Mia. "That's the cutest puppy I've ever seen."

"It's a Ridgeback!" says Joshua. "Dad, you got us a Rhodesian Ridgeback."

"The mohawk dog?" asks Mia.

"Yeah, look," says Joshua. He holds the puppy out.

The hair along the puppy's spine, from the shoulders down to the back legs, is darker than the rest. It comes together in a small peak.

"Cool," says Sam.

"I told you guys we would get a dog when we moved in here. But then I was sick and I kind of forgot," Dad says. "But better late than never, right?"

He looks at me. I nod.

"Let me hold it," I say to Joshua.

He gives me the puppy. It squirms, tiny black toenails digging into my arm. It chews on my thumb and I rub its warm stomach.

"What should we name it?" I ask Joshua.

"Is it a girl or a boy?" he says.

"Check for a wiener," says Sam.

"Boy," says Dad.

"Raphael," says Joshua.

"No. Alfredo," says Sam.

"How about Freddie?" suggests Mia.

"Schmendrick," I say and then laugh at Joshua's face. "What? I thought we were suggesting character names."

"Yeah," says Joshua. "*Good* ones."

"Hitler," says Creep.

I put the puppy down and it sniffs around the carpet. We call out names as we watch the puppy investigate the drapes. Dad just laughs at first, but then joins in. The names stack up. *Vader. Caspian. Sweeney. Logan. Frodo. Spike. Ender. Gareth. Percy. Sherlock. Harry.* And pretty soon we're all laughing.

"Pumpkin," says Sam. "Mochi. Waffles."

We watch the puppy trot under the coffee table.

Rogue. Spock. Bane. Stitch. Dash. Hawkeye.

Dad says, "James Bond."

Creep says, "Manson."

"Potato," says Sam. "Beans. Marshmallow."

"What's with the food names, kid?" asks Mia.

Sam shrugs. "I'm hungry."

"I know," says Joshua. We all look at him. "Loki."

We all look at the puppy, who happens to be peeing on the carpet right at that moment. Joshua and I eye our father, expecting him to start yelling.

He watches the puppy, lips pressing into a thin line. We expect the eyebrows to lower, but he starts laughing instead. "Perfect."

Joshua and Sam set up a bed and a feeding station for Loki in the laundry room. Then they take the puppy out front to play. They sit in the shade of the tree and Loki bounces through the grass, tumbling, jouncing sideways, picking up sticks, gnawing on Joshua's shoe.

Mia, Creep, and I watch them through Joshua's bedroom window. The boys laugh and laugh at the puppy. They run in circles, let the puppy climb on them and giggle when it tickles. They try to teach Loki to sit and stay. All he does is fall to one side and gnaw on his own paw. I take a picture of them.

I smile at the boys and the puppy on my phone screen, safe in the shade and laughing. I feel a strange nostalgia for something I can't remember having.

"I wonder what it feels like," I say, putting my phone down. "To be a kid."

"What do you mean?" Mia asks. "Aren't we kids?"

I shrug. "I don't really feel like a kid. I mean, I never really did. I always felt like . . . just a smaller version of myself." I watch as Sam climbs the tree and Joshua hands the puppy up to him. "Like I was always the same size inside, just the outside changed."

"Huh," says Mia. "But you don't think Joshua has that?"

"Look at him," I say. He has climbed up next to Sam. He puts the puppy down his shirt. "He doesn't really worry about anything. He's totally in the moment. Like he feels everything."

Mia purses her lips. "And you don't?"

"It doesn't matter," I say. "But I'm glad it's different for him."

"What makes it different?" asks Mia.

I watch Joshua as he and Sam exchange jokes and then laugh like it's the funniest thing in the world. I imagine him pressed down and smothered and hating himself. *It would never happen,* I think. *It could never happen to him. He's good. He's so good. He's not like me.*

"You're right," says Creep to me. Like he knew what I was thinking.

"I don't know," I say. "He's just different than me. In a good way."

She watches me for a long moment.

"What?" I ask her.

She smiles wryly. "I want to give you a hug."

I say with mock suspicion, "Why?"

"I'm worried about you," she says. "I feel like you need some positive energy, absorbed by osmosis."

I look back out the window. "Okay," I say.

I feel her arms slide around my waist. I put one around her shoulders. We watch the boys. It does feel good. Mia hugging me. I feel like I could walk around strong all the time, propped up by Mia's arms. I look down at her. She looks up at me. She has thick glittery lashes on, and tiny jewels at the corner of each eye. Her lips are the deep crimson of paint splashed on a wall and I think about kissing her. Then I'm thinking about Ian looking down at me the way I'm looking down at Mia and I have to pull away from Mia to sit on the bed.

I'm seeing stars when my vision starts to tunnel. Mia sits next to me. She touches my wrist. "Are you okay?"

When I don't answer, she says, "I'll get you some water."

By the time she's back with the glass, my vision has cleared. Mia sits next to me again and I drink some water.

"Maybe you got dehydrated at camp," she says. "It happens a lot."

I'm staring at the floor. *No one will ever love you like I do.*

I look up at Mia. "Did you love her? Celeste."

She raises her eyebrows. "Didn't expect *that*," she says. She tugs at the cuff of one sleeve. She's wearing a red poet's blouse with flared sleeves, her cleavage spilling out of a black corset printed with spiderwebs. I can still see grass in her hair from when she catapulted off of the front porch. "I dunno," she finally says. "I cared about her. We had fun. She was awesome."

"Was she your first kiss?" I ask.

She shakes her head. "Oh," she says. "No. I've kissed many humans in my travels."

I watch her gather the fabric of her cuff, pull it tight around her wrist and release it.

"But you haven't had sex," I say.

"Nope," she says.

"Do you wonder what it's like?" I ask.

She laughs. "I mean… other than the obvious?"

"Just," I say, "being that close to another person."

She thinks about it, still playing with her sleeve. "Yeah, I guess that would be pretty intense. Which is why I'm not in a hurry to add that to my life," she says. "Being a kid is already intense enough. I mean, I don't think sex will change me as a person. Being a virgin or not doesn't mean anything. It's just … if it's going to be that intense, I want it to be with someone I already feel safe with."

"Yeah," I say. "That's pretty important."

After a long moment she says, "Are we talking about The Guy?"

I give her a watery smile. "Careful, or this conversation won't pass the Bechdel Test."

Mia quirks her mouth to acknowledge my joke. Then she turns toward me, one leg folding up, the other still hanging over the edge of the bed. "You can talk to me, Elle," she says. Her hands are in her lap.

I turn toward her too. "I want to," I say. "I'm trying." I reach out to take her right hand. It's easier than I thought it would be. "I just…"

I don't finish.

"You just…" she says. I watch her say it. Her lips are parted. I can see her teeth.

I kiss her, just like I did with Virgil, suddenly, without even meaning to. Her eyes widen in surprise like Virgil's did. Her mouth is different than Virgil's though, softer, waxy with lipstick. Her fingers curl between mine. Her eyes close. And it feels different from Virgil in another way. Our mouths feel like pieces of something split in half a long time ago that are finally coming together again. She kisses me back, but doesn't move to touch me. I want to suck on her bottom lip.

She says, "Um—" into the kiss and squeezes my hand. I sit back and we look at each other. She presses her lips together, and then runs the tip of one thumb around her bottom lip to correct any smudges. She raises her eyebrows.

"Sorry," I say.

She says, "How long have you wanted to do that?"

"Basically since we met," I say.

She starts to laugh. It's quiet at first. "What?" I say.

Then she laughs harder. I start to smile. "Mia, what?" I start to laugh too.

Soon we can't stop. We're both bent over, giggling and gasping. Finally she's wiping her eyes and I can breathe again.

"Mia," I say. "What *was* that?"

She's still smiling and another giggle pops out. "Elle," she says.

"What?"

She snorts. Her voice breaks. "Um… Elle," she says, giggling. "I don't think you're straight."

We both collapse into laughter again. She doesn't ask me what it means or how I feel or what will happen or what I want. We just laugh, and it's the best feeling I've had in ages.

Dear Jesus.
I'm an abomination. Lol.
Amen.

FORTY

fter Mia and Sam go home, I make chicken stir fry for dinner. Minced ginger in sesame oil, with cubed chicken breast. I add cooked rice and a raw egg. It yellows as the egg coats the rice and cooks into the oil. I chop green onions into the pan as Joshua sets the table.

We eat with Dad, Loki playing around our ankles. I can't remember the last time we've eaten together. Dad asks us what we've been doing with our summer while he's been in and out of the hospital. Joshua tells him about the Kool-Aid stand, the top-secret illustrated book, the Lego castles, video games, sleepovers, movie nights. I tell him about Bible Camp: the survival classes, the ropes course, the skit night.

"The counselors wanted me to let you know that people at church are praying for you," I tell him. I don't tell him how I broke down crying.

"That's nice," says Dad. "I need all the help I can get."

Dad does the dishes while I put the leftovers away and Joshua takes Loki out for a pee. Spending the entire evening with Dad is like holding my breath for five hours. I keep waiting for something to happen that doesn't.

Later, Dad puts on David Lynch's *Dune.*

"You know there's a new *Dune*, right Dad?" Joshua says.

"I know," says Dad as the narration begins. "I just really like this one."

Joshua and I lie on the carpet with our pillows while Dad sits in an old lawn chair and we all quote the movie together. When Sting steps out of the sauna, Joshua says something about a stainless-steel Speedo and Dad almost falls out of his chair laughing.

Before the movie ends, Joshua falls asleep with Loki curled next to him. I look to my side and see Creep curled up the same way.

As the end credits roll, Dad says, "I love that movie. I love that quote, the one about the sleeper needing to wake up." His face is awash in cool light from the TV.

"What do you think it means?" I say. I watch the character images superimposed over a blue unquiet sea, the list of actor names against a musical theme of synthesized piano and guitar.

"I think it's talking about awareness," says Dad. "We go through life half-asleep. And finding our purpose, discovering who we are is like waking up. In the movie, Paul realizes he's tired of the dreamworld."

"He lives in his head," I say.

"Yeah," says Dad. "Maybe that he's tired of waiting for something to happen that will make his destiny come to him. He knows he needs to wake up and live and go *find* his destiny."

I sit up. Creep grumbles and rolls over.

I want to ask Dad if this is real — the day we had with him — if it's okay to unwind completely. Or if I should just keep everything locked up, ready for him to go back to the way things usually are.

"You know what part I like?" I say to Dad.

He raises his eyebrows. His eyes are bloodshot, sunk into the sockets and surrounded by dark shadows.

"You should go to bed," I tell him. "You look tired."

"No," he says. "I want to hear the part you like." He smiles at me.

I'm not used to him wanting to hear what I have to say.

"I like the part where he has his hand in the box and he talks about how fear will destroy you."

Dad nods. "Yes," he says. "I thought about that a lot when I was in the service. Fear can change everything. You let a little fear creep in, and it will grow to control every choice you make. Every moment of your life will be ruled by fear."

The images fade to scrolling text. I nod.

"It's okay, Eleanor. You don't know what I'm talking about," he says. He blinks and then rubs his eyes. "You're right," he says. "I am tired." He stands up. "Can I have a hug?"

I let him hug me, thinking that it's nice to be asked.

"Thanks, Dad," I say before he climbs the stairs. "We had a nice day with you."

After I've tucked Joshua into his bed, he mumbles for Loki. The puppy is still asleep on the floor in the family room.

"I'm going to put him in the laundry room," I whisper to Joshua. "His pee won't be so hard to clean up in there."

"No, Ellie," says Joshua with his eyes closed. "He'll be scared in there by himself."

I have to agree with Joshua; I wouldn't want to sleep alone in the laundry room. I wrap Loki in a bath towel and then fold him into the comforter with Joshua.

Joshua murmurs, "Do you think this new Dad is real Dad? Or is old Dad the real Dad?" His eyes are closed. They both look so peaceful snuggled together in the covers. Joshua throws one arm over Loki and the puppy stretches and yawns.

"I don't know," I tell him. "We'll see, I guess."

He's asleep.

I hear a key in the lock and I move to the bottom of the stairs to see who it is. Bag over her shoulder, Mom closes the door behind her, locks the deadbolt, takes a deep breath, and then sees me looking up at her.

"Eleanor," she says. "How'd it go today?"

"Fine," I say.

"Please," she says. "The last thing I need right now is an attitude." She starts to climb the stairs. I follow her.

"No, really," I say. "It was fine. Joshua and Sam played all day and dad brought home a puppy."

She turns around at the top. "A puppy?"

"Yeah, a Rhodesian Ridgeback. We named it Loki."

"A real puppy?" she says.

"Yeah, Mom," I tell her. "A real puppy that eats and poops and everything."

She pinches the bridge of her nose. "I saw your dad's car in the driveway. Is he home?"

"Yeah, he just went to bed," I tell her. "You missed out. We had a nice time with the puppy and I made chicken fried rice for dinner and then we watched *Dune*."

"*Dune*, huh?" She turns toward the kitchen. "Glad I had study group."

"Goodnight," I say.

"Night, Eleanor," she says from the kitchen. "I want you up early for chores tomorrow, so don't stay up too late."

In my bedroom, Creep watches every movement. His eyes follow me as I choose pajamas. I go into the bathroom to take a shower, something I avoid as often as possible. I try to shut the door quickly, as always, but Creep somehow manages to get in. The water warms while I examine my face in the mirror. Same as ever. No awakening.

When steam starts to cloud the mirror, I peel my clothes off. I avoid Creep's gaze, his silent appraisal of my body. Stepping into the shower reminds me of the dream, and I go through the motions quickly. If I linger, I feel I'll be trapped there – in the dream, in my head, in a body slithering with memories. I lather my hair and rinse it immediately. The conditioner sits in my hair while I soap my body. I run the washcloth over my arms and legs as fast as I can, hard so that it almost hurts. If I do it gentler, my skin tingles, and my mind starts to circle, and I have to turn the water up so that steam rolls around me in clouds so that I can only think of how hot it is and how I'm going to boil alive. I rinse my hair again and take a peek around the edge of the shower curtain. Creep sits in the middle of the bathmat, staring. I rinse all over and after a brisk drying off with a large towel, I put my pajamas on with the wet soles of my feet still standing in the tub.

I wipe the mirror and then comb through my hair, staring at my reflection. Creep climbs up on the counter next to me. He says something about how some things never change, but I'm not listening. I'm thinking about Mia. Her white teeth, laughing after our kiss. Her giggles buoying me up. How she touched the corner of my mouth and said, "You'd better wipe that off," and when I checked, my lips were colored Mia-red.

I concentrate on thinking of Mia as I crawl into bed. I pull out my sketchbook, put the earbuds in and press play. Creep keeps crawling closer to me and I keep batting him away. I can't hear what he's saying, but he's there, on the edge of my vision, while I try to fill my mind with the softness of Mia's mouth pressed to mine. I draw four pages of unending spirals to *Colorblind* by Counting Crows on repeat before I finally give up, closing my eyes to block Creep out, pulling my knees up to my chest. I fall asleep to a voice crooning over pulsating piano and strings.

If I Didn't Have Creep:
Maybe I could think.
Maybe I could breathe.
Maybe I could be alone.

Again the open door in the distance. I don't walk toward it this time, but in the other direction. I choose a door.

Virgil's house. I sit on the sofa, but after a moment, I hear his voice.

"Eleanor," he calls. It's down the hall. I follow the sound and find myself in his bedroom. He is sitting on the edge of the bed. The room is dark, the shades drawn. I look around.

He has a horse wall like I do, but a lot of them are photos of his own horses. There are band posters and a slowly turning mobile of the solar system. On one shelf a Blu Ray collection of classic science-fiction films. I turn my head to look at some of the titles. Metropolis. Forbidden Planet. Invasion of the Body Snatchers. Soylent Green. War of the Worlds. I run my fingers along a shelf of books.

"Eleanor," he says again. He hasn't moved. I sit next to him on the bed.

"Nice collection," I say.

"I love you," he says. He's facing me.

I cover my mouth to hide my nervous smile. "I wish you wouldn't say that," I tell him.

"I can't help it," he says. "I love you, Eleanor."

This time I cover his mouth. He grabs my hand and kisses the fingers, then pulls me toward him.

"Please don't," I say. "You can't love me. I told you about Creep."

"I don't care about Creep," he says. He pushes me down on the bed. "I don't care about Ian. You're beautiful to me and I love you."

"Don't call me beautiful," I tell him as he moves to lie next to me. "I don't like that. It means you're not really seeing me."

"I am seeing you," he says, his face close to mine. "The real you." He touches my hair. "Not this." My cheek. "Not this. You're beautiful because of what's in you, not what I see out here."

"There's nothing in me," I say, remembering the girl on the table.

"There is," says Virgil. He lies on top of me. "I love you. You're my pretty girl. Let me show you."

He kisses me. I close my eyes. Can't breathe. He's hard against me.

Not Ian not Ian not Ian, I think. The kiss is smothering.

When Virgil pulls away, his mouth is black. I inhale one harsh breath. My brows furrow; eyes widen. The black starts to spread, like spilled ink soaking into a table cloth. He leans in for another kiss and I push away from him.

"Your face," I say.

And then Virgil is wearing Ian's face and he touches his lips and his fingers come away stained and the black moves up his arms and he looks at me.

"What did you do?"

FORTY-ONE

I open my eyes. Creep is leaning over me. I wave my arms and he backs away. I push out of the hot covers. My hair sticks to the back of my neck. I turn my pillow over so it's cool against my face.

"What was it this time?" he asks.

"Go away," I mumble.

Another door. A black-haired girl with no mouth.

Another door. A flock of ravens break through a window. They tear my flesh, screaming around my head.

Another door. Ian is leaning over Joshua's bed in the dark. I pick up Joshua's soccer trophy and use it to bash in Ian's head. He slumps over the bed, so I pull him by one shoulder until he flops back onto the floor. My hand is covered in blood. Joshua doesn't stir. I reach out to smooth his hair, leaving a smear of red on his forehead.

"He's not like me," I say to Ian's dead and open eyes. "Don't try to make him like me."

FINALLY I GET UP AND SPLASH WATER ON MY FACE. MY HEAD IS dull – unwieldy on my shoulders. My eyes are glue-sticky. I rub them as I walk back and forth by the foot of my bed.

"Tell me, Eleanor," says Creep. "Tell me all about it."

"Don't talk to me," I tell him.

"But Eleanor," he says. "You need someone to talk to. Someone who understands you." He licks his right eye with one swipe of his long tongue. "I understand you."

I pace the carpet, trying to stay awake. I slap my own face and pinch the back of my hands.

"It's okay, Ellie," says Creep. "If you go back to sleep I'll watch over you."

"That's what I'm afraid of," I tell him. I grab my phone and slip my shoes on.

"Where are you going?" he asks.

"For a walk."

I sneak up the stairs, taking them every other step.

I get to the landing and my hand is on the doorknob when I hear, "Where do you think you're going?"

"Uh-oh," says Creep.

I look up and Mom is at the railing above. She must have just come out of the bathroom. She's wearing the same thing she was when she got home. She looks as if she hasn't slept in weeks.

"What are you doing up?" I ask her.

"Studying," she says, looking down at me. "Are you going to answer my question?" It's a loud whisper, since the master bedroom is only down the hall.

"I'm going for a walk," I tell her.

She looks at her watch. "It's one a.m. Girls don't go walking around the city in the middle of the night. At least not good girls." Dim yellow light from the living room illuminates one side of her face.

"*I* do," I say. "Maybe I'm not the type of girl you think I am."

"That's for sure," says Creep.

Her hands clench on the railing. "Do you ever think about what comes out of your mouth before you say it?"

"Do *you?*" I ask.

Creep starts to giggle.

Mom grinds her jaw. "Your father told me Mia was over today."

"Yeah," I say. "She was helping me–"

But she cuts me off. "Don't lie to me. You are grounded. You are not permitted to leave this house."

"But–," I start.

"What is that?" She points at the phone in my hand.

"A phone."

"Where did you get it?" she asks.

"Mia gave it to me." I open the door. It smells like rain.

"Shut that door," she says. She moves to the top of the stairs, like she's going to come down. I don't shut it. She points at the phone again. "Hand it over," she says. "If I had known you had something like that, I would have confiscated it."

I could do it. I could walk up the stairs and hand it to her. But there's a canyon between us and I can't see a way across.

"No, Mom, I need it," I say.

She lets go of the banister to fold her arms. "You *want* it, Eleanor. There's a difference between wants and needs."

My hand tightens on the knob. The hot city night ebbs in, the humid buzz of cicadas like fingers on my skin. "Mom, it helps me work things out." I tell her. "The music I mean."

Her voice shakes. She steps onto the first stair. The hand drops to the banister again. "What do you have to work out?" she says. "What could you *possibly* have to work out? Because as far as I can see, the only things you've worked out are how to ignore me, lie to me, and set a horrible example for your brother." She waits. "Well?"

The doorknob is becoming slick under my hand.

She goes on, the tremble in her voice worsening. She advances down the stairs, slowly, one step at a time. "Do you have to work out how to deal with your rebellious teen? Do you have to work out going to school and having a job? Do you have to work out how to provide for your children once your husband is dead?" Her voice catches at the end and she gulps. I can see the words caught in her throat. I know how that feels.

She's stopped a couple stairs from the bottom. A small part of me wishes I could hug her right now. That I could sit down with her and tell her everything's going to be okay. We're close enough now that we could touch if we both stepped forward and reached out. But her words jab at that place inside of me that suddenly swells with outrage.

"No," I say, not bothering to keep my voice to a whisper anymore. "I have to work out how to take care of my little brother. I have to work out how to deal with three bullies who beat up one of my best friends." My throat constricts. My eyes well. "I have to work out what to feel about my dad dying. I have to work out how to be *perfect*, because whatever I am obviously isn't good enough for you."

I turn and run out onto the porch, across the grass, and down the sidewalk. Creep lopes alongside me. He howls like a coyote as we cut across the corner of a gravel yard.

"Eleanor," my mother shouts. "Come back here!"

She doesn't chase me.

I WALK FOR HALF AN HOUR, BARELY REALIZING IT WHEN MY FEET step up to the storefront of the 7-Eleven. I push open the door. The electronic bell dings and Nicole pops her head up from behind the counter. Creep slinks down the candy bar aisle.

"Hey there," she says. "How's my favorite nocturnal visitor?"

The tears have dried on my face, but I'm sure my eyes are red.

"Everything okay?" she asks. "I heard about what happened at camp. That must have been scary."

I nod. I put my hands on the cold counter top. "Can I talk to you?"

"Sure," she says. "Hey, Sharon?"

After a moment, Sharon comes out from a door marked *Employees Only*. She is dressed in a heavy coat, beanie, and gloves.

"Can you mind the front for a bit?" asks Nicole. "I have a meeting."

Sharon looks at me. "Okay," she says. "I hate the fridge anyway."

Nicole says, "C'mon, girl," and I follow her around the back of the counter, where she opens another *Employees Only* door. A desk is piled with papers and an old PC. Stacks of boxes, cleaners, cases of toilet paper and paper towels line the shelves. She grabs her jacket off a chair and gestures.

"Have a seat," she says. She rolls another chair around the desk to sit across from me.

"So what's up?" she says.

Creep's voice sounds from the back of the room. He mumbles to himself, out of sight.

I don't say anything. I pick at the corner of my thumbnail until the skin peels back and there's a bleeding gouge. Creep prowls around the edge of Nicole's desk, then he climbs up to perch on a stack of papers, his bony toes hanging over the side.

"I think I'm crazy," I say. I watch Creep. He runs his tongue over his long teeth. It makes a sucking sound.

"Why do you say that?" she asks.

Creep turns his back on me, the spurs of his vertebrae protruding underneath his peeling skin.

"I have these thoughts," I say. "They're always there. I can't sleep. And I'm scared of everything. Even myself."

"Why do you think you feel this way?" asks Nicole.

I don't answer. We wait for a while. She's quiet. Creep sits with his chin on his knees.

"Listen," she says. "I'm going to take a stab in the dark. And you can just nod if I'm anywhere close. How's that?"

I nod.

"I'm gonna tell you a story," she says, "When I was little, I had this grandpa. I actually used to live with him, after my dad died. Because my mom couldn't cope with the loss. So my grandparents took care of me. My grandpa was really fun to be around. One time, when we were camping, he offered me some candy if I would play a game with him."

My eyes drift from her face and hit Creep. His head is twisted around, so that he looks over his shoulder at me. His round eyes reflect mirror images of me upside-down. My skin feels like it's going to crawl off of my body and wriggle away.

"He touched me," says Nicole. Her voice is detached, like she's describing an article she read. "And then he made me touch him. And after it was over, he gave me candy." She leans back and folds her arms. "It wasn't just the one time.

He told me I could never tell anyone, because it would tear the family apart."

My head feels like it's hovering over my shoulders. The tears are back and slipping down my cheeks; I wipe my face with my forearm.

"The first chance I got," says Nicole. "I moved as far away from Florida as I could get. I thought I could run away from it, but I didn't know that he was living inside my head. It took me a long time to feel better, and I needed help to do it."

I look at Nicole. Her kind eyes and spiky hair and smile. *She's like me.*

"So," she says. "Is that sort of like your secret?"

Creep clicks his teeth at me. He glares.

My forehead feels filled with concrete. I nod. Once. "But," I say, slowly, quietly, like someone else is saying it. "It's different. We're different. I—" *Love him,* I want to say.

She waits for me to finish.

"… care about him," I say.

"Okay," says Nicole. "First of all, thank you for trusting me. I understand how this feels more than you know. Secondly, I cared about my grandpa, but it still happened. And I still loved him. I know how much of a mindfuck that can be. Thirdly, I've been through years of therapy. And if there's one thing that I've learned, it's this – your story belongs to you, and it's your choice to share it. No one can stop you."

Virgil told me that.

"But he said he would hurt my brother," I tell her. My heart flutters as I say it.

"That's bullshit," says Nicole. "He just wants to keep you scared. His power is in the secret and if you let the secret out, he could go to jail. So he's afraid of what you could do to him."

I imagine Ian cowering. Waking from nightmares. Running from *me*.

"He's afraid?"

"Hell yes, he is," says Nicole. "You need to tell your parents."

Creep hops down from the desk. He squats next to my chair. He reaches up and lays one hand across my arm. It's like ice. A cold dagger of fear slices through my chest.

"What will they think of you?" says Creep. "The things you've done."

"I can't," I whisper. "I really can't."

"I know it's hard," says Nicole. "But you need to. I promise, you need to. I'll be there if you want. I'll hold your hand."

I look at her. My eyes feel swollen.

"Think about it," she says. "Call me if you need help talking to them. Or if you need to talk to me." She scrawls her number on a slip of paper and I stuff it in my pocket. "You're not alone," she says.

As I'm getting out of her car in front of my house, Nicole touches my arm in the same spot that Creep did. "Everything's going to be okay," she tells me. "But you do need to tell them. I'm here, and I'll check on you to make sure you're okay. Just promise me that you'll call if you need help."

"Okay," I tell her. "I promise."

I stand on the porch for a long time. I remember my black secret filling up the house, drowning my family. The door opens silently. I step over the threshold with my breath held.

My mother is asleep on the couch. She looks young. Younger than I feel, when she's sleeping. I pull the throw over her and turn to go back downstairs, but she catches my hand.

"Eleanor," she says, her eyes still closed. Her words are slurred, like when Dad comes home late. "I love you. I'm sorry." She can barely get the words out before she falls back to sleep. I brush her hair back from her forehead. I imagine her as a little girl, afraid to lose her best friend, afraid to be alone with two other children who rely on her, who don't understand her. Just afraid.

I look around the room, expecting to see fear hanging from the corners like cobwebs.

So much fear.

AFTER CHECKING ON JOSHUA — LOKI IS TURNED SIDEWAYS IN the bed, his paws in Joshua's face — I tuck myself into bed.

"You shouldn't have told," says Creep. "Ian keeps his promises."

I don't answer.

"You're playing with fire," says Creep. "Just keep your mouth shut and no one will get burned."

I fall asleep to the thrumming rhythm of Linkin Park's *Breaking The Habit*.

I dream of horses. Virgil's smile. Mia's swirling makeup around my eyes. Her warm hands. Joshua's laugh and the antics of a puppy named Loki. My mother and father are children, holding hands in a meadow. They run through wildflowers. We all swim together in a lake of crystal clear water.

We become mermaids, our legs fusing and coated with the flashing coins of a thousand bright scales. We splash and race and breathe the cleansing liquid deep into our lungs. We push through the water with strong tails. We dance through the ripples.

At sunset we pull ourselves onto the rocks to dry and our legs reform. We watch the sun dip low, the sky burnished with a haze of perfect salmon-colored clouds. My parents are grown again, but different. Content. Whole. They put their arms around me and Joshua as the sun disappears. Stars wink into existence above us and Dad kisses the top of my head.

Time to wake up, I hear him say.

<u>Fears:</u>

Sharks
Tornadoes
Disappearing
Fear itself
That someone will find out

FORTY-TWO

I wake with a headache, but also with the strange lightness of becoming slowly conscious. I don't bolt from my bed in panic. I don't thrash under the covers. I don't jump up with a scream in my throat.

I take a deep breath, becoming aware of my pillow, of the tangled earbud cords, of Joshua talking to himself in his room. Not to himself, to Loki. I blink and yawn. I luxuriate in a stretch, something for which I don't usually take the time. I roll over to look at my horse wall. The pictures are all there, each elegant hoof, lock of mane, majestic turning of the head all the same as when I went to bed, but they look somehow different. Brighter maybe? The colors a little more saturated. I blink at the photos. Creep crawls out from under the bed. He's mumbling to himself.

"What?" I say.

"Nothing." He sits in the corner, chewing on his fingernails. "I was just thinking about Ian. Maybe he could come over this weekend to help Joshua with that tree house."

I sit up and stare at him.

He shrugs, a hideous movement of loose skin and bone. "I think they could be really close. You know, since you've decided to break up with Ian."

"Don't say that," I tell him. The carpet is dense under my feet.

"Maybe I'll put a bug in Mom's ear about calling him for a barbeque."

"You can't do that," I say.

"Oh, Eleanor," says Creep with a smile. "You have no idea what I can do."

I want to argue with him, but I don't want to talk about Ian.

I get dressed slowly, noticing the feel of denim as I pull my jeans on. I run my fingers through my hair and pull it back. It's soft. Ian always loved my hair. He would pet it and pull it and tell me how beautiful it was. *Never cut your hair, gorgeous*, he would say. I imagine chopping it off with my mother's sewing scissors.

Creep follows me upstairs. In the kitchen, Mom is making french toast. Creep climbs up on the counter and leans over to look into the skillet, his face in the steam. The smell of frying butter and egg-coated bread makes me put a hand on my stomach. I'm hungry. I don't remember the last time I was hungry.

Mom smiles at me. "Good morning." She flips a slice of toast. "There's juice in the fridge," she says.

Not sure where we stand after last night, I say, "Morning." I set the orange juice pitcher on the table. "Where's Dad?"

"I dropped him off at the hospital," she says. "He is going to visit some vet friends and then go to treatment. I'll pick him up later. Can you set a place for Joshua too?"

I take two plates from the cupboard as the doorbell rings. Joshua pounds up the stairs and then yells, "Sam's here!"

"Better add three more," she says.

Three more?

Joshua runs into the kitchen carrying Loki, with Sam following behind. And Virgil. And Mia.

"Hi," Virgil says. He raises his cast in a wave. His face is black and purple.

I look at my mom and then back at Virgil.

"I know," says Mia. She's wearing a shirt with a flowery drawing of female reproductive organs that says, *Ask Me About My Uterus*, and thick ragged lashes that look as if she trimmed them with rusty shears. "He's disgusting right? Looks like an episode of *The Walking Dead*."

"What are they doing here?" says Creep.

"Good morning," says Mom. She puts a stack of french toast on the table. "Breakfast is ready. Josh, put the dog in the laundry room. Let's say grace."

Sam, Virgil, and Mia sit. Joshua comes back empty-handed and sits. I am still standing next to the cupboard still holding two plates.

"Eleanor," says mom. "Sit down so we can say grace."

I pull another three plates out and carry them to the table. I sit next to Mia.

"Sam," says Mom. "Do you want to say it?"

"Sure," says Sam. We all bow our heads. I sneak a glance at Virgil. He winks at me.

"Dear God," says Sam. "We are thankful for this food and for the hands that cooked it. We are thankful for Josh's new puppy. His name is Loki and we're thankful you made him so cute. We are thankful for summer vacation. Please let school never start again because it's the worst. In Jesus' name. Amen."

The boys immediately fill their plates. I pour orange juice in my cup.

"Eleanor," says Mom. "Can you help me for a second?" She opens the laundry room door. I follow her in, picking up Loki before he can run out. He squirms in my arms, and then gives up and starts licking my face. The smell of detergent and fabric softener is strong in the small room. Mom leans against the dryer.

"I've been thinking about what you said last night," she says. "About things you're trying to work out. And you're right, you are dealing with a lot. We all are. So I decided that if you are going to be spending a lot of time around Virgil and Mia in the future, I should get to know them better."

Loki's tongue tickles behind my ear. "Okay," I say, not sure how to answer.

"You're still grounded," she says. "Because there was some deception going on, and I know you broke the rules at Bible Camp to sneak off alone, but I want you to know that I appreciate the efforts you have been making. You have been very helpful with Joshua and chores and meals and I want to thank you for that."

"Okay," I say again. Loki breathes out a sigh onto my neck. He leans against my chest.

"So, thank you," she says. "Virgil and Mia will be going home right after breakfast, but we can talk next week about evaluating the grounding, if you can promise to follow it until then."

"Okay," I say.

"And I still don't want you spending time alone with Virgil. I don't think that's appropriate. But the three of you in a group I'm okay with. *After* your grounding expires."

I nod.

"Do you have that phone?" She holds out her hand. I hesitate while she looks at me. "I'd like to look at it please."

I fish in my pocket and then hand it to her. She turns it on, accesses the settings and then hands it back. "Your dad and I talked about it, and we decided that with his treatments, school starting, scheduling, and whatnot, it's a good idea for you to have a phone. So we are going to add this to our phone plan. You can keep it as long as you promise to be responsible and appropriate with this privilege."

My mouth is open in surprise.

She gives me a hug, Loki releasing a little *whump* of air when he's squeezed between us.

"Thank you," I say, too shocked to say anything else.

"I love you, Eleanor," she says. "Maybe you don't believe that, but it's true. I'm not sure where things went wrong with you and me, but I hope we can start to get along better."

She smiles at me and opens the laundry room door. I hold Loki to my face for a moment. He breathes into my hair and then licks my nose.

Mom asks Virgil and Mia about a thousand questions over breakfast. First she asks Virgil about his hand and how he's feeling. The swelling has gone down a lot around his eye, but the bruises are dark and vicious-looking over his brow, across his jaw, and cheek bone. The white of his eye is still stained red but the gash on his lip is knitting shut. He lifts his shirt when Sam mentions his ribs and we see a large purple nebula of bruises where The A-Team kicked him.

"Beautiful," comments Creep.

"The doctor says I was really lucky it wasn't worse," Virgil tells us.

My mother clicks her tongue, calling it outrageous. "Those nice boys from church," she says. "What a disgrace."

"It's always the nice ones," says Creep.

"They're not nice, Mom," says Joshua. "They're jerks."

"Don't call people names, Joshua," she says. "I'm sure they just got caught up in the moment. I'm sure it won't happen again, especially now that the police are involved, right Virgil?"

"We're all on probation," says Virgil. "And I have to do community service, because of my history, and because I started it. Levi didn't deny what happened, he just said it got out of hand. The officer my mom and I talked to said that if we mess up again while we're on probation, the consequences could be serious."

"See?" says Mom to Joshua. "They'll straighten up now."

The five of us kids look at each other across the table.

Mom asks Mia about her uterus, and Mia talks at length about universal health care and reproductive autonomy. The whole time, Mom has a hard set to her mouth and her eyebrows raised. Mom seems relieved to change the subject and asks about Virgil's horses, about his family, about his parents. She asks Mia too, and when Mia explains what her parents do, Mom seems to relax. I can just see her mind putting Mia's radical views into context. I can see a, "Be careful about that Mia girl, she could be a bad influence," lecture in my future. *If only she knew the whole story.*

By the time Mom gets around to favorite classes and aspirations, we've finished eating. Joshua and Sam rinse their plates and get Loki out of the laundry room. Loki scampers under the table, so Josh and Sam follow him, bumping into our legs and laughing.

"Take Loki outside," she tells them.

She gets up to clear the table. "It's been pleasant to talk with you two," she says at the sink. "Eleanor is grounded, so I'm sorry you can't stay. But maybe your families can come over for dinner next week?"

"That sounds great, ma'am," says Virgil.

Mom turns around to smile at them.

"Sure," says Mia. "But my mom doesn't cook. We can bring chips."

Mom blinks. Looks at Mia with the smile she uses at church. "Eleanor," she says. "Why don't you walk them out?"

"Wow," says Creep as we descend the stairs. "She really changed her tune huh?"

"I think she feels bad about our fight," I say.

"You had a fight?" asks Mia.

"Oh," I say. "Yeah."

On the porch, we watch Joshua and Sam. They run around and around the tree trunk with Loki. The puppy chases for a while; his tail whips back and forth, ears flopping. He gives up, falls over, his tawny sides pumping for air. His tongue lolls. The boys tumble down on either side of Loki. Joshua tickles his paws and when he rolls onto his back and kicks at the air, the boys laugh.

Creep somersaults off the porch and stalks across the grass. He swings up into the lowest branches, sitting just above Sam and Joshua. He glares at me through a net of leaves. He bares his teeth and then snaps them together.

"How's your Insta?" asks Mia. "Any photos of oat-milk lattes yet?"

I realize I haven't shown it to her. I open the app. Virgil and Mia, on either side of me, move a little closer to see the screen. I scroll through a gallery of black and white photographs. Images I've taken since Mia gave me the phone.

Sunlight slanting through a horse's stall. Joshua bent over a sheet of paper, tongue at the corner of his mouth, concentrating. Mia smiling into the mirror as she applies mascara. Virgil wiping sweat from his forehead with the back of his hand, cowboy hat pushed back. Clouds caught in high pine branches. Curlicues of makeup around my eye, close up. Mosses at the edge of a stream. My own silhouetted reflection in a puddle. Brother Chad and Sister April offstage, smiling in the middle of a kiss, noses touching. Hope and Grace, heads together, crowned with reflected sunlight. Tree roots snaking through soil. Virgil and Mia, mouths full of laughter at some inside joke. Sam running across the lawn, Loki at his heels. My own fingers tangled in Pancake's mane.

Mia says, "Holy shit, Elle. These are sick."

Virgil is nodding. "Wow," he says. He reaches out to scroll back up to a photo of himself. "You make me look good, Eleanor."

"Oh please, Virge," says Mia. "As if you don't already know you're cute as a damn button."

"I talked to Nicole," I say.

Virgil's jaw drops. He and Mia stare at me. I don't look at them, but I can tell.

"I thought about what you said," I tell them, as I slide my phone back into my pocket. "About how I should talk to someone. About how it would help. Virgil said she was a good listener. Now that I think about it, she did most of the talking." I shove my hands in my pockets.

"Yeah, she talked a lot at first when I started going in there, but when I got more comfortable, she just sat back and let me do all the talking," says Virgil.

"I was shy," I say.

"No. *You?*" Mia says. Virgil laughs. His laugh wants to lift me right out of my shoes. "But you told her? About the thing? The one you didn't want to tell me?"

"Yeah," I say. My chest expands with the word. *Am I getting taller?*

"And how do you feel about it?" Mia asks.

"Different," I say. "Not so heavy."

"Good," Virgil says. "That's great." He steps off the porch into the grass, then turns around. He's grinning. Mia is standing next to me. We look down at him. "I wanna kiss you," he whispers to me. Mia groans. We look at each other. Mia winks. It's the tiniest flutter of her choppy lashes matching a flutter in my chest.

Virgil holds up his fist and we bump knuckles.

Mia sighs, rolling her eyes. "Y'all awkward A-F."

"See you later." He heads across the lawn. Mia follows him. "See you after dinner, Sam," he calls.

Sam waves. "Bye."

Mia turns around to blow a kiss at me. Virgil tells her something and she laughs and shoves him. They move down the sidewalk arguing. Mia's giggle drifts back, lighter than air.

Dear Jesus.

I don't think we're on the same page.

Gonna see how I feel about just figuring
this out on my own.

~~Amen.~~

Bye.

FORTY-THREE

Since Mom's home and I'm grounded, she gives me a lot of chores. I wash windows, clean baseboards, dust the living room, sweep and mop the kitchen floor, scrub both bathrooms, vacuum the entire house, and take out the trash. I do it all with my earbuds in, so Creep loses interest and lies in the corner talking to himself.

I melt onto the family room floor, thinking I'll read for the rest of the day when I hear her calling from upstairs.

"I have to go to a study group." She shoves books into her backpack. "And then I'm picking up your father, so I would really appreciate it if you could help with dinner. Could you do that for me?"

"Sure," I tell her.

"Okay," she says. "It's just lasagna. So if you can get it in the oven at five, we can eat at seven. Make a salad and use that French roll for garlic bread." She searches through her purse for her keys.

"Okay, Mom," I say.

She pauses. "Thank you, Eleanor."

I MAKE MACARONI AND CHEESE FOR THE BOYS FOR LUNCH AND then set them free for the rest of the day. Joshua and Sam are in and out, up and down the stairs. They build a couch-cushion fort for Loki, catalog their armory of toy weapons, organize Joshua's airplane collection, and build an alien moon base out of Legos. I spend the afternoon reading short stories out of a college literary anthology I find in the family room bookcase. I lay on my stomach in the middle of the family room and listen to The Decemberists while I read. I make a list of my favorite stories to share with Virgil and Mia.

At five I pull the lasagna out of the freezer. I unwrap it, bend the foil lid, and put it in the oven. I chop a head of lettuce, two tomatoes, a cucumber, and a long gnarled carrot into a bowl while I sing along to Morrissey's *I Know It's Over*. I add a green apple and put the bowl in the fridge.

I am heading back down the stairs when I meet Joshua and Sam coming up carrying baseball equipment.

"We're going to the park," says Joshua.

"We're going to teach Loki how to field balls for us," says Sam.

"Are you taking your bikes?"

"Yeah," says Joshua. "And look." He turns around to show me his backpack. Loki's head poke's out of the partially done zipper, like a coon hound pup in *Where The Red Fern Grows*.

"Wear your helmets," I say. "Do you have water bottles?"

"Oh no," says Joshua. He sets down his armload and runs up the stairs. Sam carries things out to their waiting bikes. His bike is equipped with a big basket into which he puts the mitts and balls. Joshua runs out with the water bottles. They buckle their helmets into place.

"Do you have your watch?" I ask Joshua. He shows it to me.

"Be home in an hour," I tell him. "Then you'll have time to clean up before Mom and Dad get home."

"Ready?" Joshua asks Sam.

"Yup," he says and they ride across the grass and down the sidewalk, Loki's head bobbing. I wave at the puppy as they turn the corner.

I DECIDE TO SHOWER WHILE I WAIT FOR THE BOYS TO COME back. While the water heats up, Creep watches me undress.

"Why are you always staring at me?" I ask him. I avoid looking in the mirror that runs the length of the bathroom counter. I can see my white form moving in the corner of my eye.

"Does it bother you?" he asks.

"Obviously," I tell him, stepping into the tub, I whisk the shower curtain back into place and press it against the shower wall to block any water escaping.

"I don't know why," he says. I see his hunched black form outside the frosted white of the curtain. "You should love your body, right? Everyone else does. Well, you know. Certain people specifically."

Please don't.

I scrub the sweat of housework off of me. Working quickly, I scrub with the loofah until my skin is red.

Creep is still talking, but I try to block him out. Think of anything, anything but Ian. I remember the stories I read today. A nervous woman held alone in a yellow room until she goes insane . . . no. I probably shouldn't think about the stories I read. Creep yammers on. His words begin to coil around me. A headache forms.

"Stop!" I yell. I wrench the dial toward hot. Water stabs. "Just shut up!"

Creep falls silent. Everything burns. I switch the water off, trembling.

When I walk up the stairs, I see Sam's baseball bat standing in the corner by the door.

"Good luck hitting balls without this," I say aloud.

I put my shoes back on.

"Where are we going?" asks Creep.

"I'm just going to take their bat over," I say.

"What about your grounding?"

I open the door and close it, barely missing Creep as he squeezes through the gap and scoots over the threshold to avoid being hit.

"I don't know why you try so hard to be nice," says Creep. "It's hot out here. Why not just let them come back for it on their own?"

"You don't have to come, you know," I say. "You could just sit in the shade and eat crickets or whatever it is you do."

"I don't mind the heat," says Creep. "But you do. Besides, you're my favorite, Eleanor. Wherever you go, I'm right there."

We turn the corner. We pass houses with cactus in their yards, grass wilted by the heat. My wet hair is already starting to dry. The streets are deserted. All the kids in their houses playing video games.

"You're not *my* favorite," I tell Creep.

"That is just hurtful," says Creep. "You are just a hurtful creature, Eleanor. Who taught you to be so hurtful?"

"Duh," I say, sounding like Joshua. "You."

Creep laughs. "If it's not me, who's your favorite then?"

"None of your business," I say. I see a cactus the same color as Virgil's eyes, it has a flower on it the color of Mia's lipstick.

"Is it Virgiiiil?" says Creep. "It used to be Ian."

I skip once so that I can kick at him. He hops away, giggling.

"Why do you always have to bring him up? Just shut up for once."

But Creep doesn't shut up. We pass more houses and he keeps talking about how much he misses Ian. How we should get back together, like we were dating in a sitcom. How much he cares about me, obvious because of his *so sweet* visit. The heat and his voice combine to make me nauseous. Every cactus we pass, I imagine shoving Creep into the noxious prickles. The thorns pierce his flesh, drawing blood, and holding him there. Every movement tears at him, leaving him in shreds. I allow myself a tight grin. He doesn't notice, the acrid jumble of his words crackling along the sidewalk, making himself laugh. I would try to hit him with the baseball bat if I thought it would work. I swing it over my shoulder, grateful when I see the end of our walk.

There is a break in the houses, an alley, and then the park.

The park is really more of a water reclamation site with a playground tucked in the back. Tall trees scatter around the playing field. A few faded picnic tables and playground equipment. It reminds me of the playground behind the apartments, where I used to dig in the sand.

There's no one here. I look around in confusion until I see their bikes upright next to one of the benches.

"Where are they?" I ask Creep, but he trots away from me to sniff at a trash can.

I hear a voice, very faint, from the other end of the park. I walk along the line of trees toward the back of the field where a corner of the park is obscured from view by the playground equipment. As I get closer I hear more voices, older ones, and Joshua's voice rising above them as he shouts something.

I start to run. "Josh?"

Then I hear him scream. Still carrying the bat, I sprint across the last quarter of the field and hit the playground sand. It slows me down and I stumble once. I call Joshua's name again.

I round the play structure at a skid, spraying sand.

There in the corner blocked from view of the street, shaded by spreading mesquite branches, are three larger figures and two smaller ones.

The A-Team.

I recognize Levi from behind. He moves into a profile view and I can see that he's holding Joshua in front of him. Another boy holds Sam. The third one is carrying a small bundle, holding it up for the little boys to see. They're all laughing. Joshua and Sam are crying.

Joshua screams. He struggles in Levi's grip. Levi jerks backward and Joshua loses his balance. Levi hauls him up.

Joshua is screaming, "Leave him alone!" There's blood on his face.

The boiling animosity I had been feeling toward Creep freezes in an instant. I feel every piece of me go absolutely still. Except for my legs. They keep moving. They've moved this entire time, bringing me every moment one stride closer.

I can see Loki clearly now, he seems fine, ears flopping, held aloft by the one who is dancing back and forth. Joshua screams, "Put him down! He's scared!"

They're all focused on the puppy and the boys. They don't see me coming.

In the moment before I say his name, my brain records every detail of this scene, frozen in a high-speed snapshot. The blond who holds Sam – a crucifix glints on a chain around his neck. The one taunting Loki has brown hair. They laugh like hyenas. And Levi's ears are pink, standing out from his head like car doors. Joshua's scream hangs in the air. Tears sparkle on Sam's face under the late-afternoon sun. A distant cloudbank, the electric feel of an impending storm, and the thick smell of summer.

"Levi," I say.

He turns. They all do. The boy holding Loki drops his hands a little, holding the puppy closer to his chest.

I raise the bat. "Let them go."

Levi laughs. But it's a nervous laugh. "Or what?" He sneers.

"Or I'll bash your face in," I say.

He starts to say something. Then he stops. He looks at the other two boys. Their eyes flick between him and me. He says to me, "No, you won't."

My hands tighten on the bat. I tense my muscles. His eyes widen. I step forward and throw my weight into a hard swing. Levi flinches.

He cries out in a voice pitched high with fear, expecting me to connect with his skull. He drops Joshua. It happens so fast he doesn't even have time to raise his arms. I stop the bat a couple of inches from his face.

He stands there for a second, his little scream hanging in the air, cowering, shoulders hunched. The other two boys start to laugh. Joshua stands up. Levi's shoulders relax as I lower the bat.

"I will," I say. "I'm not afraid of you."

I turn away from him. I stalk toward the boy holding Sam. He still has one arm wrapped around Sam's neck, his mouth hanging open. The one holding Loki gets out of my way.

"Let him go." I point the bat at the blond. He releases Sam. Sam runs to me. I put my arm around his shoulders. I turn to Joshua, who has gone to get Loki. He walks back to me, Loki in his arms.

"Joshua," I say. I have to touch his head. He turns to look at me. One side of his face is bruised. There's a cut on his cheek. Blood runs out of his nose. He wipes at it.

"Eleanor," he says.

"I know," I tell him. "Go home. Now."

"Eleanor," he says again.

"It's okay," I say. "Just go. Leave your bikes. I'll see you at home."

I watch the little boys walk back to the street and turn toward home. They look back over their shoulders and I wave them on.

The A-Team is silent.

I turn back to Levi. I raise the bat again. He flinches.

"If you ever bother me, my family, or my friends again," I tell him, "you'll wish all I had done was bash in your face."

He doesn't answer. I tighten my fingers on the bat, like I'm getting ready to hit an all-star home run. "Fine," he says. The other two snicker.

"That goes for you too," I say to them. "You have nothing better to do than harass puppies and eight-year-olds? Go home, assholes." The words feel foreign in my mouth, but they push me a little more upright, square my shoulders. They look at each other. Back at me. Then they start to move off, without Levi's permission. One of them mutters, "Crazy bitch," under his breath as they pass. Levi follows them out of the park.

THE PARK AND PLAYGROUND ARE EMPTY. THE SUN DIPS LOW IN the sky and shadows are long across the ground. The clouds have loomed closer, a black mounded streak along one edge of the sky, tinted orange. I walk under the trees, looking for any of Sam or Joshua's belongings. In the sand I find their backpacks, mitts and balls. Water bottles spilled under the swings. I put all of the equipment in Sam's backpack and carry it all to their bikes. I find Creep squatting nearby.

"Look who it is," he says. "Ellie, warrior princess."

"Don't," I say. "Just don't."

I walk back around the play structure, making sure I didn't miss anything.

Creep walks beside me, kicking up sand. I stop. Creep crouches in my shadow. He looks up at me.

"Go away," I say.

"Touchy, touchy," says Creep.

"I'm serious," I say. "Go away. Get out of here."

"Eleanor—," he starts, but I interrupt him.

"No," I say. "I'm done with you. You're horrible."

He goes still. His eyes roll back and he clicks his teeth together.

"You don't mean that," he says. "You don't want me to leave. You wouldn't know who you are without me." His fingers flex like claws into the sand at my feet.

I drop the backpacks. I step toward him. "You don't *define* me." The words come out between clenched teeth. "You don't even *know* me." He skitters backward.

"I know everything about you. I'm your best friend," he says. "I was everything. I was the only one you had."

"Not anymore," I tell him. "I'm different now. I don't need you anymore. I don't want you. Go."

"Don't say that," he says. He's quiet, but bristling. If he were a cat, he would arch his back and hiss.

"Leave!" I shout. "Go!"

Creep looks around, his head swings back and forth, like it's loose on the dowel of his neck, about to fall off. "I'll be Joshua's friend," he threatens. "You tell me to leave and I'll see how he likes me."

"No, you won't," I say. "You're a dirty coward and a liar and I'm not listening to you anymore." He crouches lower, flinching, like every word is a blow.

Then his face twists and he presses the heels of his hands into his eyes. His fingers curl up over his scalp. He starts to wail.

"Don't!" he cries. "Don't say that. What will you be without me?"

"I'll be *alone*," I say, loud. "Finally. I *don't need* you anymore."

His face is turning slick as he screams. Oily black tears run out from underneath his hands to drip off his chin and elbows. The sound is intense. I cover my ears. It doesn't block the howling. I move away from him, tripping over one of the backpacks, nearly falling. He reaches one hand out to me, his mouth a grotesque frown, drool and snot sliding over the shards of his teeth.

"No!" he begs. "Do-o-o-n't!" He crawls toward me.

Instead of being frightened by his display, I feel a surge of rage. My fists clench as a thousand days of Creep's grating whisper break over me. The clasping layers begin to slough, and I see the person I could be without him dogging every step. I see myself running toward my brother, baseball bat in hand. I watch myself hit a bully in the face. That bully becomes Ian.

The sun is behind me and Creep kneels in the pool of my shadow, holding up his slimy hands now caked in sand.

"Don't," he says again.

"No!" I shout at him with the force of all the 'No's I've been holding in for years. "No! We're done!"

At first it looks like Creep is getting smaller. Then he begins to scrabble at the ground and I realize that he's sinking. His legs have already disappeared. They melt into the dark place that is my outline shaded. With the sand at his waist, he tries to stop himself by grabbing at me. But I'm not close enough to catch, and handfuls of sand pour between his fingers. His cries mount into a panicked screech. Dropping faster now, he raises one hand in a final desperate appeal. I watch his eyes widen as his upturned face flattens and dissolves into the surrounding shadow, his last resounding shriek vibrating the sand under my feet.

I stand for a moment disbelieving. I look around. *Is he gone?* I want to say.

But for once, there's no one to ask.

I lift my feet from the ground, one at a time, to separate my shadow from my body. I half-expect it to ooze from the soles of my shoes, but it is smooth and dark as usual across the sand, moving in an echo of myself. I turn in a circle. I walk around the play structure, peering into tunnels and under slides, thinking that this has to be a trick.

Nothing.

I stand for a long time, watching the clouds, every moment expecting to hear his voice.

Nothing.

Wind rises. I pick up the two backpacks and sling them on the bikes and walk home.

Alone.

Time to wake up —
it's something my dad said to me once, in a dream.
Dream Dad.
I feel like I've been underwater my whole life.
I'll wake up from a dream and it feels like I'm
still inside one.
Maybe I can have an awakening.
Maybe it's time to wake up.

FORTY-FOUR

With a shovel from the carport, I dig a deep hole near the back wall. My face pours sweat by the time I'm finished. Every shovelful of earth, I feel as if I'm going back in time. I see myself at twelve, at ten, at eight. I see myself in the apartment, at school, at church. Shadowed every moment by Creep. I see back to the little girl who drew the pictures and read stories to Creep. The girl with no friends who just wanted someone to talk to. With the last shovelful, I see the little lonely girl in her bedroom, in the marigold garden, in a climbing tree. Alone. Before her brother was born. Before the babysitter. Before Creep.

She smiles.

I put a box in the hole. In it are things from my childhood. The white church dress. The baby blanket. A worn box of crayons. A crumbling copy of *There's a Monster At the End of This Book*.

I wait for a clever comment from Creep.

Nothing.

Joshua comes out to ask me what I'm doing. He has Loki next to him. The puppy sniffs at the hole and then falls in. It makes both of us laugh. Joshua rescues Loki. I tell Joshua that I'm burying the old me.

"You're weird," he says. "Want to watch Batman later?"

"Yes," I say. And he wanders away.

I start to fill the grave. The little girl stands alone in my mind's eye, and with each shovelful, I watch that girl grow up again. She has a little brother. They play together. She teaches him to read. She is bold and smart. She has lots of friends. She does well in school. She doesn't hide, doesn't fear. She dances and sings and draws and paints. She sleeps long and hard after every day of discoveries, every sleep full of wonderful dreams. She grows tall and wise. She grows out of *she*, and into *they*. When they are fifteen, their family moves to a new house. They meet new people: a boy to whom they give their first kiss. He loves horses, just like they do. And a nice funny girl dressed in black who is honest and kind. They share a kiss with her too. And the kisses are sweet and tender and they carry the kisses inside of them like a bright golden treasure. And when their father becomes sick, they are the strength on which their family draws. Because they are strong.

When the hole is filled and covered, I am out of breath. My muscles ache. But I stand up tall as a storm wind blows over the city. It sweeps my hair back from my face.

I close my eyes.

That girl is inside of me. She always was. I'm something else now. But she got me this far, and she will always be there.

Virgil and his mother come to get Sam. We all talk to the police together when they arrive. They ask specific questions and look at Joshua's face.

"Thanks for bringing this to our attention," says one of the officers. "This kind of thing is a crime, and after what happened with Virgil this past week... These boys are going to face some serious consequences."

When they leave, Sam hugs me.

"Thank you," he says. "You're a hero, Eleanor. You should wear a mask like Catwoman." Virgil's mother puts her arms around me and holds me close for a long time. Her tears wet my hair.

"Thank you," she says. "I don't know what would have happened if you weren't there. Thank you."

Virgil kisses my cheek in front of everyone and no one even cares. "Thank you for saving my brother," he says. He hugs me one-armed and awkward.

After they leave, Mom tucks Joshua into bed. He clutches Loki. The puppy gnaws on Joshua's fingers. She says Loki can sleep with him just this once, but we all know it's a permanent arrangement. She gives him a long hug and sings him to sleep. Both Mom and Dad thank me again. They hug me more than once.

"You're the best sister Joshua could have hoped for," says Mom. "And the best daughter." I don't tell her I'd prefer "offspring." The thought almost makes me laugh. I don't think she's ready for that.

I shower, always looking around me for Creep. The water is scalding. It leaves me raw and breathless. When I step from the tub, my chest is filled with tight expectation. I know I will see his rough-cut angles on the bathroom rug.

Still nothing.

I fall asleep to the sound of a summer storm breaking over the house. Joshua is too tired to wake, so it's the first night storm in years without a thunder fort. Rain beats on the roof and the deck. Thunder rattles the windows. But there is no grating voice in the night.

Right before dawn, I awake from a nightmare of smothering fear. The hallway again. Ian and his heavy hands, stroking me, calling me *beautiful*. Meeting his kisses with a willing mouth. The taste of him a viscous memory. Through shuddering breaths in the dark silence of my room, I realize that Creep is gone. He's not here humming. Asking what I dreamed about. He's gone. But the lead weight of secrets tug heavy at my dreams. I take a swallow of water from the glass at my bedside. I turn toward the horse wall and drift away again listening to the quiet chords of Leonard Cohen's *Hallelujah*, imagining the smells and sounds of the barn.

Joshua sleeps late. Dad's in the driveway tinkering on the car when I get up. I climb the stairs in my pajamas and stand in front of my parents' bedroom. I'm afraid to knock, but then I remember the girl standing tall inside of me and I tap on the door.

"Yeah," calls Mom. "Just a sec." She opens the door. She smiles. "Good morning, Eleanor." She goes back to her makeup table. "How did you sleep?"

I stand in the doorway. "Okay," I say. "What about you?" Soft light falls through the gauzy curtains. The room is airy. It smells of lilacs.

"Surprisingly well," she says. "Considering everything. Did you need something?"

I hesitate at the threshold, then step across into the room. I glance around my feet, looking for Creep.

Mom starts talking about church tomorrow, how she wants to join the choir and thinks I should too. She's applying blush, sucking in to find her cheekbones. I wonder if she started wearing makeup when she was eighteen. I touch the bottles of amber perfume on the dresser. I pick up one of them and unstopper it. It smells like citrus. Another is vanilla. I open the music box. Jewelry mounds under the tinkling notes. I expect rainbows. Angel voices. But it's just bright and peaceful. I touch brooches and necklaces and earrings organized into pairs. I leave the box open. There are wallet-sized photos of Joshua and me in tiny frames next to each other, and another sepia-toned photo of her and Dad, sitting on a boulder in the woods. Dad is kissing her cheek and Mom is laughing.

"Actually, Mom," I interrupt her. "I didn't sleep very well."

"Oh?" she says.

I sit on the edge of her bed. The comforter is silky and blue with embroidered flowers. I think about pressing my face into this bed as a child, waiting for the belt to fall. It's so strange, changing shape and mood, sometimes my mother's, sometimes my father's. But still the same room. Never somewhere I really belonged.

She closes her makeup drawer. "Everything okay?" She sits next to me.

I look down at my hands, and then my eyes shift to hers, clasped in her lap. A little larger, freckled, with short fingernails painted shimmery turquoise. I realize it's the same color I would choose.

"I like your nail polish," I say.

She lifts one of the hands and smooths a lock of my hair. She tucks it behind my shoulder. Morning sun through the window outlines her in light.

"Eleanor," she says. "What is it?"

"It's just Elle now," I tell her.

"Elle," she says, like she's trying it out. "Okay." She pats my knee. She can tell there's something else. She waits. Giving me a second. Giving me space. Listening.

I take a deep breath.

"Mom," I say. "I have something to tell you."

EPILOGUE

It's been two years.

When I started therapy, Brian said one of my homework assignments would be journaling. He said it would help me untangle everything.

"You're a natural writer," he said. "You keep a journal already, even if you don't call it that. You have your sketchbooks and your lists and your observations. Just keep doing what you're doing."

My current journal is the color of Mia's lipstick. I've filled three before this one.

Mia and I have just returned from a civil rights march, happy to leave the sweltering heat outside. I prop our signs next to the bedroom door, drop our masks into the hamper, and collapse on my bed. I pull out the red-bound book and roll onto my stomach. I grab my phone and add a few photos to my account.

Black and white images of children holding up signs. People dancing. A photo of Mia wearing a shirt that says, *Stop killing us*. Masked teenagers talking to riot police. I put my phone away and flip to the next blank page in my journal. Mia comes into the room with two sweating glasses of lemonade and hands me one. Putting hers on the bedside table, she flops down next to me. She scrolls through social as I start to write.

Her phone dings.

"Virgil wants to know if you're still on for the ride tomorrow."

"Tell him yes. I'll be there at five." I grin at her. "You're still invited, you know."

"I'm telling him, and I'll say it again to you: any activity involving being up at sunrise, trail dust, cowboy hats, cactus, and horse sweat doesn't interest me." She drops a kiss on my cheek. "But I still love you."

I'm already writing again. "I love you too," I say absently.

"Hey," she says. When I don't answer, she says, "Hey." I turn my head, chin on shoulder, to look at her. She drops another kiss, this one on my mouth. "What are you writing?"

"New month inventory," I say. "A list of all the things about myself." I say in Brian's voice, "Qualities and aspects of yourself seen objectively. Neither good nor bad." I roll my eyes, but these lists have gotten a little easier.

She watches me write, and then maneuvers to lie on her stomach, her shoulder at my shoulder. I don't mind her watching as I make the list. I don't keep things from Mia anymore. She knows everything.

She gives suggestions. "Terrible at fashion. Questionable taste in music. Mistress of the night."

I look back at her. "Sorry," she says. "*Master* of the night. Survivor," she says. "No, *warrior*."

There's a tap on the door, which is only cracked. Mom pokes her head in. "Guess who I just got off the phone with?"

I shrug, raising my eyebrows.

"Kate," she says. "Apparently Josh and Sam filled the toilet with Diet Coke and Mentos. Something they saw on the Internet."

I snort. Mia asks, "Did it destroy the plumbing?"

"No," says Mom. "Thank goodness. She's having them deep clean the bathroom now. How was the protest?"

"It was a march," I tell her. "It was good."

"Ugh," scoffs Mia. "It was hotter than hell."

Mom laughs. "They do say when the Devil wants to get a tan, he comes to Phoenix."

"I've literally never heard anyone say that," says Mia. "Citation please."

"Do your own research," Mom tells her. Mia laughs.

"How did scans go?" I ask her.

She leans against the door frame. "They went well," she says. "The doctors can't say 'cancer-free,' but they are using the word remission. So… yeah, scans went well."

I smile at her. "That's great, Mom."

She smiles back. I go back to my writing. She steps into the room. "What are you working on?"

"Therapy homework," I tell her, not looking up. "Making a list of my attributes."

She reaches out to straighten my hair, one fingertip pushing it back from my forehead. "You should add something about this."

I look up at her, scrunching my face. "I know you hate the pink."

She says, "I'm getting used to the color, and the length. Just don't forget to put sunscreen on the back of your neck."

Mia elbows me. "Told you," she says.

"Tacos for dinner tonight. And Elle?" Mom waits for me to look up again. "You know the rules. Please leave your bedroom door open when Mia is here."

"Okay," I say. Mom leaves it open and goes upstairs. Mia gets up and closes it.

She pretends to sneak back to the bed, whispering, "To hide your mother's innocent eyes from us abominations."

I laugh. "She's still hoping Virgil and I will get back together."

"A Christian mother's hope springs eternal," Mia says, she sprawls next to me. She has the bubbles.

"One more kiss," I say, "before you taste like soap."

Her lashes brush my cheek. She kisses me. Slow, sweet, and then punctuated by three little pecks at the end. We smile, our noses touching. "Oh my God. Ugh," Mia says. "I just realized something." She lies back and blows the first cloud into the ceiling-fan breeze.

"What?" I say.

Bubbles swirl.

"We're one of those disgusting couples. The ones that make you want to vomit."

<u>Things About Elle:</u>

Rides horses
Keeps a sketchbook
Goes to therapy
Has a girlfriend
New enby hair
Forgets self care
Lots of nightmares
Wants a tattoo
Mia says "brave"
Working on self-esteem
~~Survivor~~ Warrior

ACKNOWLEDGMENTS

This book was first a short story by the same name, penned for a creative writing class while I was going to art school. Eleanor's name was Fynn, but Creep was the same. Parts of that story appear in the dream sequence between chapters 10 and 11. I'd like to thank Alisha Geary — as the first one to read that old version of *The Angel Room* — who realized I had something bigger brewing under these vaguely disturbing short stories written for a freshman-level college class, and instead of grading them, wrote on them in red pen: "Just keep writing." Thank you. After all these years together, I'll say this: I kept just one copy of *Jane Eyre* when I was transitioning from book hoard to small library, and it's the one you gave me.

Thank you to Carol Lynch Williams, who after an intense spontaneous conversation about *Twilight* in 2010, invited me to WIFYR. I became serious about writing there, and thus began my twelve-year journey in bringing this book to print. Thank you to my beloved WIFYR workshop faculty Ann Cannon and Ann Dee Ellis. To Julie Nichols. And to the searing and stupendous Karin Anderson. All of you gave me just what I needed at the time I needed it.

To Dee, loyal friend, fellow artist and human on the strange road of self-discovery — the audiobook wouldn't exist without you. Thank you for your constant support of this project and of me and my tall offspring in general. All those demos on Discord wouldn't have been the same without your tipsy input.

And speaking of the audiobook, thank you times a million to the incredible Skye Alley. Your performance convinced me finally that this book was a real thing, in the real world, and not just in my head. You brought it to life in a way I could never have imagined.

To Courtney, bestie, alpha reader, and purveyor of nine-hour phone conversations — I think you've only read this manuscript 98 times. Ready to red-pen the print version? Thank you for believing in this book when I wanted to throw it out the window. *I'm so hot. Someone has died. The world is ending. Business as usual.* What if Doug had a Creep outfit? Kloveyoubai.

To Karla, my very first writing partner. You sneak into so many of my stories. And no wonder, what with our gumshoe detectives, and Vinnie the Vulture, spontaneous poetry slams, smuggled boxes of thin mints during *Interview with a Vampire*, the Village Inn Llama of Happiness at 2am, wearing cloaks to *Phantom of the Opera* at Gammage… I will forever think of *Bjork* when watching Vader cut off Luke's hand. Who else but us would combine *November Spawned a Monster* and *Star Wars?* Forever my muse, thank you.

Thank you to my Patrons, who get to preview everything and still stick around. Thank you for the memes and the sticker sales and the book mail and the gifts of your authenticity, as well as your uplifting enthusiasm. Drink water, take your meds, and check your laundry. Let's get together for coffee someday, yeah?

Thank you to my family: 1. Thank you to my spouse, Tyler. You've always been generous with your story ideas, and with your endless encouragement. Thanks for reading a draft of this book, even though YA novels aren't really your thing. I know you probably deserve a longer acknowledgment, but really I couldn't do this without you, and that means everything. 2. All my tall offspring, who generously compliment my art and my writing, even when it's weird and esoteric and features jokes from twenty years ago. I'm always apologizing for bringing you into this late-stage capitalist, dystopian hellscape without your permission, but I am overjoyed that you exist. I gestated four whole humans, and they're all rad as hell. 3. Thank you to my sister-in-law, Rachel. You always make me feel seen. 4. To my parents, thank you for encouraging me to pursue my art. Endless stacks of "scratch paper" and a million crayons produced this mess of a human. Whaddya think?

And of course, thanks to Jon, for Skittles and ninjUNO and lemonade and popcorn and a million rentals of the same VHS tape of *The Last Unicorn* and a lifetime of *Dune* quotes and *LOTR* jokes and *Star Trek: TOS* with Shatner's visible panty-line and developing a language of trauma unique to the two of us. How did we make it out? You're the Theo to my Vincent. Someday I'll pay you back, if we don't die in an apocalyptic cataclysm first. I hope you like this book. It's full of love letters — to friends, to family, to myself, to every queer kid holding a secret, even if that secret is just that they're not ready to come out. But the love letter that runs the most deep here is the one to you, my little brother.

ABOUT THE AUTHOR

Lee Call draws things for a living and writes things for fun. They hold a BFA in Illustration, and they dream of getting an MFA in Writing for Children and Young Adults. They were born under a waning crescent moon five days before Christmas, but their favorite holiday is Halloween. Lee can be found painting, drafting in coffee shops, analyzing movies, and suffering from insomnia (it's 2:38AM as they are writing this) in the Sonoran Desert where they live with several rescued animals, 95 houseplants, and a bunch of tall humans. *The Angel Room* is their debut novel. You can find them at CallTheWriter.com.